I0563478

The *Unhinged* Trilogy

NICOLE EDWARDS

Writing as

TIMBERLYN SCOTT

By Nicole Edwards

The Alluring Indulgence Series
Kaleb
Zane
Travis
Holidays with the Walker Brothers
Ethan
Braydon
Sawyer
Brendon

The Austin Arrows Series
Rush
Kaufman

The Bad Boys of Sports Series
Bad Reputation
Bad Business

The Caine Cousins Series
Hard to Hold
Hard to Handle

The Club Destiny Series
Conviction
Temptation
Addicted
Seduction
Infatuation
Captivated
Devotion
Perception
Entrusted
Adored
Distraction

The Coyote Ridge Series
Curtis
Jared

The Dead Heat Ranch Series
Boots Optional
Betting on Grace
Overnight Love

Nicole Edwards Limited
PO Box 806
Hutto, Texas 78634
www.NicoleEdwardsLimited.com

Copyright © Nicole Edwards, 2014
All rights reserved.
This is a self-published title.

Without limiting the rights under copyright reserved above, no part of this publication may be reproduced, stored in or introduced into a retrieval system, or transmitted, in any form, or by any means (electronic, mechanical, photocopying, recording, or otherwise), without the prior written permission of both the copyright owner and the above publisher of this book.

The Unhinged Trilogy is a work of fiction. Names, characters, businesses, places, events and incidents either are the products of the author's imagination or used in a fictitious manner. Any resemblance to actual persons, living or dead, business establishments, events, or locales is entirely coincidental.

Cover Image: © Artem Furman - Fotolia.com
Cover Design: © Nicole Edwards Limited
Editing: Blue Otter Editing | www.BlueOtterEditing.com

UNHINGED:
Copyright © Nicole Edwards, 2014
ISBN (ebook): 978-1-939786-30-2
ISBN (print): 978-1-939786-31-9

UNRAVELING:
Copyright © Nicole Edwards, 2014
ISBN (ebook): 978-1-939786-32-6
ISBN (print): 978-1-939786-33-3

CHAOS:
Copyright © Nicole Edwards, 2014
ISBN (ebook): 978-1-939786-35-7
ISBN (print): 978-1-939786-36-4

THE UNHINGED TRILOGY
ISBN (ebook): 978-1-939786-92-0
ISBN (print): 978-1-939786-91-3

Dear Reader,

I wanted to take a moment to introduce my writing style as Timberlyn Scott. Just so you're aware, if you're expecting the erotic elements that you are familiar with in my other series and standalone novels, you won't find that here. As Timberlyn Scott, I'm exploring a different aspect to my writing, including 1st person POV and a more contemporary/new adult feel. However, you will find a spicy love story. With that said, I hope you enjoy Sebastian and Payton's story.

Love,

Nicole

Dedication

This book is dedicated to my husband, my daughter, and my two boys.

Your unwavering support and pride in what I do humbles me. Because of you, I strive to be better each and every day.

You are my heart. Never forget that.

The Unhinged Trilogy, book 1

Have you ever met that someone who steals your breath with just a look? That someone you can't stop thinking about, no matter how hard you try?

I have.

I met her in a dream. Never would I have expected her to step right into my reality, though.

But she did.

Although I can't explain why, Payton Fowler makes me want things I never imagined I could have. She soothes the chaos in my head. But she doesn't know who I really am, and she doesn't see the darkness that lives inside of me.

She's supposed to be off limits to me. But that's not a problem because I've perfected the art of breaking the rules.

My name is Sebastian Trovato, and this is the story of how I met the woman who unhinges me.

Prologue

I knew I was asleep. I had to be. Even knowing that, I was having a hard time deciphering the dream from reality. There was no way this could be real. Could it?

I didn't want to wake up. I didn't want to lose this moment.

This person, whoever they were, they mesmerized me, drew me in. I couldn't pull my eyes away, couldn't break the spell they had on me. Something in the way they walked, talked, moved.

Breathed.

So familiar, yet not.

I felt like I knew them, like I'd met them before, but for the life of me I don't remember any such encounter. Had we met? Was this my mind conjuring up the image of something from my past? Or was this some sort of vision from the future?

Either way, I didn't want to open my eyes. Didn't want to face reality if they weren't in it. I wanted to get closer, to look into their eyes, to know what they were thinking.

I was unabashedly staring, unable to look away.

Whoever this person was, there was something about them...

Something that unhinged me.

Chapter One

Payton

Monday morning

"MS. FOWLER, I'LL NEVER BE able to stress enough how important this is," the domineering woman who stood just a few feet away, hands on her hips, head cocked to the side, said as she glared down at me. "Mr. Trovato's biggest pet peeve is his calendar."

I tried to pay attention, really. I was doing my best to jot down notes, but I'd recently learned — in the last hour and forty-seven minutes — that Jasmine Masters talked faster than anyone I knew. And based on what this woman told me, Mr. Trovato, the man I was now working for, was quite needy — at least in my humble opinion.

As much as I was trying to like Jasmine, the feat was rather difficult to do with a woman I'd met less than two hours ago. The same one who insisted on narrowing her blue eyes on me as though I was growing mold on the side of my face or something. Even once I got past her condescending tone and belittling stare, I still wasn't sure how she managed to sneak so many words into a single breath.

Maybe talking like punctuation wasn't in existence was one of the requirements of being an administrative assistant to the most-powerful man at Trovato, Inc., and if that were the case, I was beginning to wonder whether or not I was actually qualified for the job.

When a representative of Trovato, Inc. had called a few weeks ago to tell me that I'd passed the first series of aptitude tests and to come in for an interview, I had nearly passed out. I wasn't sure what to expect when I submitted my application, but without any other alternatives, I'd given it a shot. Now, I wasn't so sure I was going to fit in here.

"Every morning, you need to make sure you have his calendar printed and placed on his desk. He will also check and double check it on his phone. He gets here no later than six o'clock, so I suggest you get here at five."

I wondered if Mr. Trovato knew that his admin made him sound like an anal wack job. Who did that? Who studied their calendar like that? I didn't state the question aloud. After all, that wasn't my business. I'm sure I had a few quirks people didn't understand.

"He'll expect coffee and a briefing of what his day entails," Jasmine added before turning and walking away from me.

Where was she going now? I wondered as I took off after her.

"Briefing?" I realized just a second too late that I sounded like an idiot.

"Yes." Jasmine glanced back at me as though I was a third grader who had just screwed up reciting the alphabet. Then again, maybe I had. With so many instructions and rules running through my overloaded brain, I wasn't even sure whether today was still Monday or if we'd already moved on to Tuesday.

"When he arrives, make his coffee, give him ten minutes to get situated and then knock on his door," Jasmine instructed as she retrieved a sheet of paper from the printer before thrusting it in my direction.

I skimmed the page, unable to read the fine print, but I did clearly see the title: HOW TO MAKE COFFEE.

Awesome. I could hardly make coffee for myself and now I had the responsibility of making it for someone else. The day just kept getting better.

"Once he invites you in, you'll go over his meetings for the day," Jasmine continued. "Be sure to tell him who he's meeting with and when, whether or not he'll be taking a call or if he's expected to be somewhere."

Wouldn't he already know this if he studied his calendar three times?

Rather than ask that, I nodded. "Are most of them calls?" I waited for Jasmine to answer while I wondered just how this all worked. Since the extent of my job history was as a billing assistant at a small computer company and the little bit of time I'd worked at my dad's body shop, I just didn't know.

"Not usually, although he'll have plenty of them. Most of the time he'll meet with people in his office."

I would too if I had an office like his. The place was the size of a starter home and that made me wonder just what kind of pompous asshole I was going to be dealing with. I mean seriously. The building wasn't all that big to begin with, but that office… it was roughly the size of the warehouse area downstairs.

"If he has a trip coming up, make sure you remind him every day until the day before," Jasmine continued, evidently oblivious to my internal thoughts. "Getting his itinerary right is crucial. Make sure everything's in order, flight information, car service, hotel, dinner reservations. And if you screw that up, he'll make you come along on future trips so you can suffer right along with him."

Come along? Oh, no. No way. I certainly wasn't signing up to travel that was for sure.

"But that should be easy for you," Jasmine commented snidely.

What should be easy for me? I was lost for a moment, staring back at Jasmine. Was she saying that I wasn't capable of handling this job? Did she doubt me, too? Or was that just me?

I didn't get to ask any questions because Jasmine tacked on, "I'm sure you know what I'm talking about."

No, actually, I was completely lost, thank you very much.

My head was spinning, and I was already convincing myself that I would screw this up. I possibly already had based on the way Jasmine was scowling at me.

"Come on, girl, you can do this, right?" Jasmine pinned me with her sapphire eyes.

I was pretty sure those were contacts, but I wasn't getting close enough to find out, mainly because Jasmine never stopped moving.

Focus, Payton.

"Sure," I lied, trying to sound confident. I'd been an assistant before, so surely I could figure this out. It wasn't rocket science. I mean how freaking hard could it be to manage someone's calendar and to bring him coffee every morning?

I got the distinct impression that those were just two of the millions of things I would have to do as Mr. Trovato's assistant. The only frame of reference I had where the job was concerned was my father's shop. I'd been his assistant for a short period of time, but since he owned a small body shop with roughly ten employees, it really wasn't the same thing. Jasmine had kindly informed me that Trovato, Inc. had somewhere around two hundred employees.

Yep. That's like… one hundred times two.

That might not sound like a lot, but to me, it was.

Jasmine placed her hands on her slender hips and faced off with me once more. Not wanting to appear any more incompetent than I already had, I squared my shoulders and looked up at the woman. She made me feel as though I were two feet tall and that didn't have anything to do with the fact that I was short either.

I fought the urge to squirm in the ill-fitting business suit I was wearing. Although it was supposed to be a power suit, it didn't help me feel at all powerful when I was greeted by Jasmine, who was wearing a pair of designer jeans and a colorful blouse, her auburn hair severely pulled back in a ponytail. I figured the woman was in her mid-thirties, but she looked all of eighteen dressed like that.

Since I hadn't seen anyone other than the gray-haired receptionist who greeted me at the main entrance — and she was sitting behind a desk — I really wasn't sure what the dress code actually was around this place. *Was it different for me because I was new? Or did everyone wear casual wear to the office on Monday?*

As I fought the urge to scratch beneath the itchy polyester blend, I prayed someone would tell me. I wasn't looking forward to dressing up tomorrow, not to mention, I really wasn't sure what else I had to wear. I'd spent a pretty penny on this stupid suit, along with another one that I'd worn to the interview three weeks ago.

"What time did I say he gets here?" Jasmine asked, her snootiness dragging me out of my thoughts, forcing me to forget about what was hanging in my closet in my tiny little apartment.

Refusing to look down at my notes, it took me a second to scan my memory. I had to mentally flip past the few pairs of jeans in my closet before it came to me. "Six," I stated uncertainly.

"Good."

I was tempted to stick my tongue out at her, feeling incredibly childish and a tad rebellious. I wasn't sure what it was about me that made this woman want to look down her narrow nose, but it was really beginning to grate on my nerves.

Jasmine laughed haughtily, at what, I don't know. I don't think I stuck my tongue out, but hell, maybe I did.

"And what time will *you* be here?" she asked, her arms crossing over her chest, as though she figured I surely couldn't answer two questions in a row.

"Five," I stated more affirmatively. Although I sounded somewhat sure, I was already trying to figure out just how I was going to drag my ass out of bed that early in the morning. As it was, getting here at eight that morning had been hard enough. But to be there by five, I was going to have to get up at… three. *Oh, crap.* I fought the urge to hang my head in defeat.

When I had originally applied for the job, I admit that I hadn't paid any attention to where Trovato, Inc. was located. I'd Googled the address for the interview only to find that the company had recently moved. Rather than their previous location near downtown Austin, they had moved to be more centrally located to the Circuit of the Americas. Since the new Formula One race track had been constructed south of the Austin airport that put me, oh, like an hour away. Okay, maybe not that far, but it was at least a forty-minute drive and that was if I took the toll road. The idea of paying for tolls didn't sit well with me, especially when money was tight at the moment. But then again… a few dollars for an extra half hour of sleep. Hmm.

The job was paying well, so maybe I could work that into my budget.

Jasmine leaned over her desk, placing her perfectly manicured hands flat on the top as she stared back at me. When she began to tap one fingernail repeatedly, I realized she was waiting for me to say something.

Oops. I think I'd gotten lost in my own head again.

Rather than answer, I got distracted by the little design on her fingernail.

Note to self: this weekend get a manicure and have highlights touched up.

Yeah, it was safe to say that even wearing this uncomfortable blue suit, by comparison I still probably looked like a slob although I was the one dressed up. Where Jasmine's chestnut hair was pulled back in a ponytail, not a single hair out of place, my waist length brown hair was loose, not to mention frizzy, thanks to the humidity. I hadn't bothered to curl it, something I knew helped me look not quite so young, because I'd been out of time. Thanks to my alarm clock. Well, technically it was the snooze button's fault. If there wasn't a snooze button, I probably wouldn't have hit it five times. As a result, I'd been running late on my first day.

"There's no option for failure here, girl. He'll eat you alive if you don't get it right."

"Don't listen to her," a rumbling voice sounded from behind me.

My heart kicked into high gear, mimicking the way it beat when I attempted to work out at the gym. *Attempted* being the key word there. I was pretty sure I looked like a floundering hog when I struggled to run on the treadmill.

Hoping whoever was behind me didn't realize I was startled, or thinking about floundering hogs, I spun around to face him.

Oh, wow. He was... so not what I expected to see attached to that deep, booming voice.

If I thought Jasmine was tall, well, this man made the other woman look petite by comparison. It didn't help that I barely topped five feet, although my driver's license read five-two, thanks to a little fudging on my part. Aside from towering over me, the man was nicely dressed, clean shaven, with thick eyebrows hovering low over piercing brown eyes.

"And you are?" he asked, his voice reflecting the authority I was pretty sure he brandished.

I glanced down to see his hand — also well-manicured — as he held it out to me, I tried to remember why I was there. Pure instinct had me reaching out to take the proffered hand as I said, "Payton Fowler."

His grip was firm, confident. His skin strangely soft.

Manicure. Right.

"Nice to meet you, Payton Fowler. I'll call you Payton if you don't mind."

I shook my head. "I... uh... No, sir, I don't mind."

"Good. And you can call me Conrad."

I nodded, trying to figure out where I'd heard that name. Conrad... Conrad...

Oh, for heaven's sake, there was no doubt about it. I was screwing it all up.

I was in the process of shaking the hand of the founder and CEO of Trovato, Inc., Conrad Trovato himself.

With a name like Trovato, I had assumed Italian. Don't ask me why. But this guy didn't resemble any Italian guy I knew. Not that I knew many.

If any.

Okay, so that didn't matter.

When he glanced down at our joined hands, I realized I had latched on, and he was in the process of trying to pull away, but I wasn't letting him go. I was too busy staring at him, trying to remember why I'd agreed to take this job. What had made me think I was capable of being an administrative assistant to a self-made billionaire in the first place?

Someone cleared their throat and I wasn't sure whether it was Mr. Trovato or Jasmine. At the moment, their voices sounded eerily the same. But either way, I pulled myself together and released his hand, meeting his formidable gaze.

"I'll be meeting my wife for lunch today. Ensure we have reservations at eleven."

Yeah. Okay. So he was talking to me. I knew I should have uttered something smart, but for the life of me, I couldn't remember what he'd just said. The powerful aura that radiated off the man had paralyzed my brain, making me worthless.

"Yes, Mr. Trovato." Jasmine's throaty chuckle sounded way too fake.

"She'll do fine."

Conrad obviously was *not* talking to me. Thank God.

I wanted to ask him how he knew that. Maybe he'd enlighten me because I definitely didn't feel like I was going to do fine.

"We'll get the reservations taken care of immediately," Jasmine assured him, smiling.

Conrad nodded his head, turned and walked toward the office that spanned the north side of the building, closing his door behind him. Jasmine had given me a fleeting view of that room when I arrived. Other than noting its ridiculous size, a glimpse of the floor to ceiling windows lining the entire north wall, the grand walnut desk that sat in the middle of the room and the row of bookshelves on one side was the extent of my tour. I do remember thinking that that one single space was probably larger than the three-bedroom apartment I shared with my two closest friends.

I stared after Conrad. He was distinguished, some would probably even say handsome. For an old man. Err... Old*er.* I didn't know exactly how old he was, but the crown of perfectly styled gray hair led me to believe he was older.

"You're gonna have to do better than that, girl," Jasmine whispered, her smile falling.

"He's so…" *Do not say old. Do not say old.* "Intimidating." I wasn't even aware I had spoken aloud until Jasmine snorted with laughter. Until then, I was beginning to wonder whether she knew how, and now the rusty sound echoed through the open reception area of the second floor.

My floor.

Technically the floor belonged to Mr. Trovato, but aside from his office, the only other occupied space was an area where my desk was positioned and a small section that contained a fancy leather sofa for clients to wait for Mr. Trovato. There were windows everywhere, providing enough natural light to light up the entire space, and that was without the help of the dangling fluorescent bulbs from above.

A miniscule kitchenette, equipped with a refrigerator, sink, and an industrial coffeemaker was tucked into a nook in one corner; a place Jasmine told me would be essential for me to learn my way around since Mr. Trovato loved his coffee more than he loved his family.

I was pretty sure she'd been joking about that last part.

"That's an understatement, girl. Now, let's continue. I'm only here for two more days and I suggest you pull it together or you're gonna be looking for another job."

No, not that.

At twenty-three, I had spent the last seventeen months looking for a job, coming up empty except for the occasional temp placement. It had been more than a year since I had graduated from college with big dreams and even bigger expectations. As it turned out, there was something like forty percent of people in Austin, Texas who had a bachelor's degree or higher, which meant that businesses could be as particular as they wanted to be in hiring.

That was something that would have been beneficial to learn in college. *Before* I picked a major.

With a degree in English Literature, I wasn't having much luck finding a job in a city that was dominated by tech companies. But three weeks ago, my dad had stumbled upon an ad on the internet for an administrative assistant position at Trovato, Inc. Of course, my father knew everything there was to know about the company that manufactured performance engines because he made it his business to stay up to date on the ins and outs of the automotive industry.

Not exactly the place I saw myself working for my first real job out of college, but now that I was here, I had to admit it wasn't quite as bad as I'd expected.

From the instant I stepped through the main doors, I'd been in awe of the place. Glass and steel constructed the building, and there were actually engines that decorated the space.

Engines. Like the things that went in cars.

The walls were white, the floor slate gray and the décor interesting.

It went without saying that those engines — or the components within them, I wasn't quite sure — had made Mr. Trovato rich.

When I arrived that morning, I hadn't had a lot of time to admire the unusual decorations. As I had attempted to ascend the stairs to the second floor, I was nearly tackled by a big, beefy security guard, who defended the stairs as though they led to heaven and I hadn't yet been permitted to pass the pearly gates.

"Earth to Payton."

I blinked twice, looking up at Jasmine.

"Two days, remember?" Jasmine nodded her head toward the notebook in my hand. "You might want to start writing. It's gonna be a long day for you."

I had a feeling that Jasmine was full of understatements. And her crash course in managing Mr. Trovato's calendar was just beginning.

Chapter Two

Payton

Monday night

BY THE TIME I WALKED to my car in the deserted parking lot, it was after seven, the sun had long since gone down and I was starving. Mr. Trovato was apparently an early riser and he had a penchant for staying at the office late, which didn't do anything to help the fact that I hadn't brought my lunch with me — something I had realized after my stomach started rumbling.

While Jasmine had gone out with some of her friends (in case there was any doubt, *no*, I wasn't invited), I had sat at the desk and pretended to munch on an invisible granola bar although no one was there to talk to me about the nutritional value in the pretend meal.

Didn't help that I had spotted a vending machine on the main floor — *just now* — on my way out the door.

During the two hours it took for Jasmine to celebrate her recent engagement and upcoming relocation to New York, I had fielded at least thirty phone calls. Thirty freaking calls.

I'm pretty sure Jasmine was on the verge of a heart attack when she came back and tried to make sense of the mess that I'd made with that little pink message pad. Luckily, it hadn't taken that long to sort out, but we — translated to *she*, because I don't think she trusted me at that point — spent the better part of the afternoon calling people back and scheduling meetings for Mr. Trovato.

Now, as I approached my car, my feet were hurting, my head was pounding, and my eyes were slowly but surely drifting closed. I was exhausted and part of me was dreading coming back tomorrow.

Forcing the thought of what tomorrow might bring out of my throbbing head, I climbed into my car — a vintage, carbon steel gray, 1965 fastback Mustang that my father insisted I drive — and cursed the idea of having to look at a computer screen or a telephone ever again.

Speaking of telephones…

My cell phone sang *Baby Got Back* just as I turned the key in the ignition, the tune at war with the powerful throb of the engine. I never understood why my father souped-up these cars, or why he insisted that I drove the thing in the first place. I would have been quite content with a little compact car, maybe something with Bluetooth or satellite radio. Or, you know, electric windows. I didn't think that was too much to ask, but my father insisted on me driving an American classic, as he referred to the car, and since it meant no car payment, I couldn't complain too much.

"Hey, Chloe?" I greeted, cutting off the song snippet as it started again.

"Where are you?" she asked, sounding exasperated, which was something I was pretty familiar with. Chloe Tatum, my best friend – *slash* – roommate was nothing if not easily excitable, though you'd never know it by looking at her. I could already picture her lying on the sofa, dark hair fanned out around her head, emerald green eyes staring at the front door as she waited for me to come in.

"I'm leaving work," I explained, leaning my head back on the headrest and closing my eyes.

I wondered if it would be against company policy if I just slept right there in my car.

"At least tell me you're bringing dinner home."

"I can." I peered through one eye to see that the lights were slowly going out inside the two-story building in front of me. It was only seven, but since it was almost November, the days were getting shorter. That should have made me feel a little better, and it would have if I weren't still at work. I loved fall. It was my favorite time of year. Instead, I was imagining crawling into bed and sleeping away the last few days of October. "What did you have in mind?"

"Chinese."

"I'll pick it up on my way. Is Aaron home yet?" I asked, referring to our other roommate.

Aaron, my best friend since junior high school was still a student at the University of Texas, working on his master's degree in business. He and I had shared an apartment since we were sophomores in college, after each spending a year in the dorms. And when I moved farther from campus after I graduated, he had decided to come with me. Unfortunately, he wasn't home much these days, choosing to spend his evenings with his new boyfriend. Unfortunate because I didn't get to see him much, not because he had a boyfriend.

Seeing how incredibly happy Aaron was, I couldn't even find it in me to be bothered by the fact that he wasn't there for me to talk to, or to do his share of chores either. Paying a third of the rent while staying elsewhere ninety percent of the time, I figured the guy deserved a little slack. Since I'd had the pleasure of hearing all about New-Boyfriend-Mark, suffice it to say, I was actually thrilled for Aaron. He'd been looking for love for a long time, and it seemed as though he might have actually found it with Mark. At least according to him. I, personally, didn't know Mark all that well, so the jury was still out as far as I was concerned.

"Nope. He came and went an hour ago. Said he's staying with his love bunny and not to wait up."

"He said that?" I asked, my eyebrows shifting up. "He called Mark his love bunny?"

"No. I did." Chloe chuckled, obviously proud of herself.

"So dinner for two?"

"Unless you're gonna waste more time talking. Then you might as well make it three 'cause I'm starving."

"At least there won't be any traffic," I told Chloe.

"Traffic? At this time of night, you'll be lucky if there're any restaurants open," she said facetiously, following with a giggle.

I couldn't even drum up enough energy to laugh at her lame jokes, so I simply said goodbye and thumbed off the phone, dropping it onto the seat beside me.

An hour and ten freaking minutes later, I was pulling into the parking lot of my apartment complex. Since I'd had so much time to think on the way home, I'd come to one sound conclusion: there was no way I was going to survive that commute every day.

To make a bad day worse, someone had stolen my parking spot in front of my building, so I had to drive around for an extra minute until I found an empty place.

Three buildings down.

Figured.

Dreading the walk in the foot murderers that I called shoes, I was tempted to bust into the food that had been my only companion for the past half hour right there in my car. The heavenly scent of Chinese food taunted me, making my mouth water. I'd made the mistake of stopping at one of my favorite places near downtown Austin, rather than near the apartment, and I'd had to endure the overwhelming urge to eat sweet and sour pork with my fingers most of the way home.

Now, as I lugged all of my stuff toward my building, I worried that I might not be awake long enough to enjoy it at all.

When I walked in my front door a few minutes later, toting my purse on one arm, the computer bag complete with the laptop I was told to keep on me at all times, and the plastic bag holding our dinner, I was panting like I'd been floundering on the treadmill again.

Damn stairs.

"A little help would be nice," I muttered to Chloe, who was lounging on the couch, her Kindle in front of her.

She didn't budge. Not that I had really expected her to. This was Chloe. When she was focused, she made as little movement as possible, which made me hate her for the simple fact that she was so damn skinny, and she never had to work out. She claimed that she kept in shape because she was on her feet all day. Did I mention Chloe was a hairstylist? One of the best, to be exact.

"Fine. I'll just eat your eggroll," I added as I passed her.

"What's *that?*" Chloe's bright green eyes homed in on the computer bag now dangling from my arm, her head turning at an odd angle so that she didn't have to get up.

"Work."

"Why're you bringing it home?" she asked, looking sincerely perplexed.

"No idea." I didn't really care to talk, I preferred to eat, so I made my way to the kitchen, letting the bag and my purse slide to the floor where I left them near my bedroom door. I kicked off my shoes, sending one flying into the wall, the other falling from my aching foot.

After pulling the containers from the bag and gathering utensils, I carried the two cartons of food and two plastic forks — screw the chopsticks, I was just too damn tired to make that happen — into the living room and joined Chloe on the couch.

"So, tell me about him," Chloe stated as she crossed her legs and dropped her Kindle onto the coffee table before reaching for the carton that contained her beef and broccoli.

"Who?" I asked, mirroring her position so I could face her. I feared that if I relaxed too much, I'd fall asleep right there.

"Conrad Trovato." Chloe annunciated his name slowly, dreamily. "He looks so handsome when I've seen him on TV."

I cocked an eyebrow. "Seriously? He's like fifty," I told her, laughing around a mouthful of food.

"That just means he's distinguished," Chloe countered, forking rice into her mouth.

"It also means he's married."

"True. For like the third time if I remember correctly." Chloe kept eating, her full attention on the food in front of her as she continued talking, oblivious to the fact that her mouth was full. "Does he have any kids?"

When she peered up at me, I shrugged.

"You don't *know*? What kind of assistant are you?" Chloe huffed.

"He's got a daughter, I think." I paused, chewing thoroughly, purposely making her wait. "He's got her picture in his office."

"You sure that's his daughter and not his wife?" Chloe asked. "Or his mistress?"

God, I hoped not. The girl was young, and he was... not.

"How old is she?" Chloe inquired before I could even answer.

"She's in college. Aside from that, I didn't bombard him with personal questions on my first day."

"I would have." I totally believed her. "Seriously, Payton. This is Conrad Trovato. He's the mastermind behind those engines that make your girl parts sing."

My eyes nearly bugged out of my head. "Sorry, my girl parts don't sing for engines." Hell, these days, my girl parts didn't sing for anyone.

"Oh, come on. How freaking hot is it when one of those things starts up? I still don't know how you can drive your Mustang and not have an orgasm every damn day. Did you ask him how they make them do that?"

I laughed, nearly choking on my sweet and sour pork. Chloe's mouth did not have a filter; that was for sure. "No, I didn't."

"Well, you should," Chloe said seriously.

No, I shouldn't. I should just do my job and maybe, just maybe, I'd be able to save up a little money to move to a city where I could find a job I actually enjoyed. I didn't share that little tidbit of internal monologue with Chloe.

"Wait!" Chloe exclaimed, snatching up the fortune cookies sitting on the couch between us. She tossed one my way. "Open it," Chloe demanded as she cracked open her cookie and smiled.

Oh, the dreaded fortune cookie. This had become a ritual for us anytime we picked up Chinese to go, which was about once a week these days. The rule was that we had to open the cookie before we ever finished our meal. If there was a particular protocol around reading those things, I was pretty sure we'd mucked that up a long time ago.

Placing the container on my leg, I followed suit, tearing the plastic wrapper and then breaking the cookie. I stared at the message, blinking several times as I did.

"What does yours say?" Chloe asked inquisitively.

Glancing up, I met her eyes. "Uh…" My attention slid back to the paper. "It says 'Get ready for something to shake up your life.'"

Chloe sighed heavily. "Lucky you. Mine says 'You'll take a trip to Asia.' I mean, come on. That's not a fortune. Asia. Right. Like I'll ever be that lucky."

I stared at the paper in my hand, wondering for once if it might come true. I needed something to come along and give my life a little shake.

Not that I wanted to think about that now. Right now, I just wanted to finish my food and pray that my feet would carry me the short distance to my bedroom.

After all, I still had to get up and do it all again tomorrow.

Chapter Three

Payton

I KNEW I WAS ASLEEP. I had to be. Even knowing that, I was having a hard time deciphering the dream from reality. There was no way this could be real. Could it?

I didn't want to wake up. I didn't want to lose this moment.

This guy, whoever he was, he mesmerized me, drew me in. I couldn't pull my eyes away, couldn't break the spell he had on me. Something in the way he walked, talked, moved.

Breathed.

So familiar, yet not.

I felt like I knew him, like I'd met him before, but for the life of me I don't remember any such encounter. Had we met? Was this my mind conjuring up the image of something from my past? Or was this some sort of vision from the future?

Either way, I didn't want to open my eyes. Didn't want to face reality if he wasn't in it. I wanted to get closer, to look into his eyes, to know what he was thinking.

I was unabashedly staring, unable to look away.

Whoever he was, there was something about him...

Something that unhinged me.

My eyes flew opened and I stared at the ceiling. My heart was racing, my skin hot to the touch. The blankets were twisted around my feet, trapping me. I glanced around my bedroom. The dim glow from my computer's screen saver allowed me to see.

There was my desk, my dresser, the few pictures I had hanging on the wall.

And just as I feared, I was alone.

There was no one there. No handsome stranger.

Blinking a few times, I willed the dream to come back. I knew that no matter how hard I tried, I wouldn't be able to close my eyes and bring him back, but I wanted to. Oh, how I wanted to.

Rolling over onto my side, I tugged the blankets from between my feet, pulling them over me. I squeezed my eyes shut again, hoping he would come back.

I had no idea who he was; I just wanted him back.

Chapter Four

Payton

(Just shy of) two weeks later
Thursday

"PAYTON!"

"Damn it," I grumbled under my breath, reaching for a napkin from the stash on my desk.

You'd think that after two weeks of this, I'd be used to Mr. Trovato shouting at me from his office.

Nope. Still not used to it.

He once again startled me, and now I had coffee dripping from my hand and down the front of my favorite off-white V-neck sweater. I knew I should have started drinking my coffee with a straw. Then maybe I wouldn't keep having these mishaps.

"Another one bites the dust," I mumbled as I got to my feet, wiping my hand and blotting the coffee on my chest, knowing that it wasn't going to do any good. The good news, if there was any, was that this sweater didn't have to be dry cleaned.

You'd think I would learn to stop wearing light colored clothing.

One of the perks of the job I found out was that I didn't have to dress up unless Mr. Trovato was expecting a client, or a high-level employee, to show up. Today was one of those days when I was supposed to be ready to greet the sales director, which was why I was wearing one of my favorite skirts and a sweater I'd fallen in love with and picked up on sale last week after I received my first paycheck.

I hadn't wanted to go shopping, but I hadn't had much of a choice. Unfortunately, I'd learned about the casual dress code from Maude, the snarky old receptionist on the main floor, *after* she and Ron, the security guard, spent several days making bets on whether or not I would ask about it. Had Maude not felt guilty for taking Ron's money, she probably would've let me go on looking like a wannabe executive. As it turned out, Ron had no intention of telling me since he found my thrift store wardrobe — his words — rather amusing. Hence, the reason for my shopping trip.

I grabbed my notepad and started toward Mr. Trovato's office, swiping at the brown spot in the center of my chest. Two weeks of this and I was ready to show him how to use the phone's intercom because his yelling was starting to be a problem for my wardrobe.

Not that I would *ever* tell him that.

Holding my pen and paper close to my chest in order to hide the newly forming stain, I approached his office.

"Yes, sir?" I asked as I stood in his open doorway.

Conrad, as always, looked well-put together in his dark suit, crisp white shirt and bright red tie. His face was clean shaven, his reading glasses perched on his long, thin nose, and on his head, not a single gray hair out of place. By noon, I knew he would've lost the jacket, the tie would be dangling from the back of his chair, and his sleeves would've been rolled up to his elbows, so I often wondered why he even bothered with the whole get up each day.

He had actually freaked me out last Friday when he came in wearing jeans and a black polo. Even in his fifties, the guy could rock a pair of distressed jeans. I just hadn't expected it.

"I need you to run to my house," he told me, reaching for the landline phone on his desk.

Umm… what?

"Sir?" I knew, should he actually turn and look at me, that Conrad would see my bewilderment written right across my face. And it wouldn't be the first time either. He was randomly asking me to do odd things, such as go out to his car and get his briefcase, or look up one of his old buddies from college, or once he even had me go down to the mechanic garage and get a wrench.

No, I didn't ask.

But his house?

"I left my cell phone at home and my wife can't bring it to me." Conrad continued as he placed the receiver to his ear. "I need it before my afternoon meeting."

Well, that explained why Mrs. Trovato had called the main number three times that morning and it was only ten.

"Umm…" I wasn't quite sure what to say. Where did he live? Was I just supposed to ask him?

"Just ask, Payton." Mr. Trovato was apparently reading my mind. He was also smiling, which I took as a good sign. I was pretty sure I amused him to no end, but luckily, he'd been patient with me so far.

"I don't have your address," I blurted.

"That wasn't a question," he informed me.

No, it wasn't. I took a deep breath and met his intimidating stare from across the room. "I feel like I should know this."

"Have you had a reason to go to my house?"

"No, sir."

"Then you probably shouldn't know my address. My daughter Aaliyah is home. She'll be there for the next half hour, but then she has class. So you better get going."

I didn't bother asking him why Aaliyah couldn't bring the phone because that really wouldn't have gone over well. I was his assistant and, as I had recently learned, if he yelled, I was supposed to jump.

I was getting good at that.

"Yes, sir," I said by rote, turning around to walk out. Only when I was a few feet away did I realize that I never got his address.

"I'll email it to you, Payton," Mr. Trovato called from behind me, his tone full of amusement.

Swallowing hard, I nodded although I knew he couldn't see me.

As I walked back to my desk, I remembered Jasmine's parting words: *It'll get easier as time goes by.*

I was starting to wonder just how much time it was going to take.

Payton

TWENTY-SEVEN MINUTES LATER, I WAS waiting at the gates to a mansion. Mr. Trovato's mansion to be exact. I had made good time, but only because I had nixed the idea of stopping for coffee on my way over. It had been a tough decision, but I had decided I would do my best not to screw this up too much. After all, Mr. Trovato was expecting me back soon.

I had entered Conrad's address in the navigation app on my cell phone and found that he didn't live too far from the office. I didn't know the area at all, but my trusty phone had gotten me here. It took twenty minutes to get to the sprawling neighborhood, and another seven for me to drive slowly down the streets, up one hill, down another. As I drove, I admired the elaborate, multi-million-dollar houses with their perfectly manicured lawns all while trying to locate the two-story white house — Conrad's exact description — that belonged to my boss.

I had finally resorted to looking at the numbers on the large stone pillars in front of each house until finally I found it. Good thing too because there wasn't a house in sight.

From where I sat in my car, waiting for the security guard to approach, I couldn't see past the narrow road lined with trees in front of me, but the ostentatious wrought iron fence that surrounded the property told me enough.

After manually rolling down the window, — have I mentioned how much I hate that — I peered up at the young man with a military style haircut and forced a smile.

"Can I help you?" the intimidating guard asked, his tone level, his eyes narrowed.

"My name's Payton Fowler. I work for Mr. Trovato. He sent me here to pick up his cell phone."

"License."

Arguing didn't seem appropriate, nor did asking him to say please, so I dug in my purse for my wallet, noticing in my peripheral vision that the guard had put his hand on his gun. What did he think I was going to do? Assault him with a little plastic card so I could raid the property and steal Mr. Trovato's cell phone?

I tossed him a smile over my shoulder as I pulled my license from my wallet before handing it to him.

"Just a minute."

I nodded.

As I waited for the security guard to finish scrutinizing my driver's license, I glanced around the grounds that I could see. Aside from the ornate iron work of the fence, I could see trees. Lots and lots of them. A long row of them flanked the narrow drive that led into the estate. I didn't know much about trees, but they looked a lot like the ones that were in my parents' yard. Pecan maybe. Not that it really mattered, but I didn't have anything else to do except to study the landscape.

On the side of the gate that I was on, there was a small guard station with two windows. It had been painted white, but the door was red, which I found odd. There was a fancy looking golf cart parked beside it. I assumed that was security's way of checking the perimeter. That, or the house was miles away and they needed it to get back and forth.

I glanced at the clock on my phone. Yep, my thirty minutes was up. If this guy didn't hurry, I was going to miss Aaliyah.

"You're good to go," the security guard said when he finally returned, his severe expression hadn't changed. He still looked like someone had shoved his night stick up his butt and left it there.

"Thank you," I replied sweetly, reaching for my license.

When the gate opened, I put my foot on the gas, embarrassed by the way that the engine roared, all throaty and loud. The guard didn't seem to mind. If anything, he was eyeing the car with appreciation.

I got that a lot. Especially from men. They seemed to admire the car. The most awkward moments were when they wanted to talk about it. I think it frustrated them when they found out I actually knew a little bit about what was under the hood — 302 cubic inches of Ford Racing V8 with a Vortech supercharger that turned 444 Dyno-proven horsepower into 423 pounds of stump-pulling torque. Yep, it was safe to say that I'd learned a little from my father when it came to cars.

The car certainly garnered more head turns than I did though. But since I'd spent four years working diligently to get my degree, it wasn't like I'd had any time to date anyway.

Or at least that's what I told myself.

Truth was, I don't think it had much to do with my busy schedule. It was more due to the fact that I was just a little too plain. I wasn't tall or supermodel thin, my legs weren't long, and I had an average face. My nose was a little too pointy in my opinion, and my cheekbones a little too prominent. The only interesting thing about me was the color of my eyes, or so I'd been told. Cat eyes, I had heard the color referred to as. Kind of hazel, though more green than brown, but they were constantly changing and sometimes appeared almost yellow.

My hair was naturally a mousy brown and would still be if it weren't for the magic hands — and a steep discount — of my hair stylist, Chloe. The girl was certainly my savior when it came to looking good.

After following the winding road through the trees, I came upon the two-story white house Conrad had mentioned.

Right.

Like *that* could be considered a house.

I actually hit the brakes as soon as it came into view because I was so taken aback, I forgot where the gas pedal was. And the clutch, which was why the car died. I had to restart the engine before pulling forward.

In the last week, I'd spent a considerable amount of time researching Conrad Trovato. Mostly when I had nothing else to do. I figured it couldn't hurt to know everything there was to know about the guy.

From what I gathered, he'd made his first million roughly twenty years ago. It wasn't until the last decade or so years that he'd hit the Forbe's World's Billionaires list though. Not that a few hundred million was anything to tip your nose at, but Trovato, Inc. had been put on the map when some car manufacturer wanted to use one of their super-charged performance engines for one of their new lines of sports cars, tying the names together — similar to what Carroll Shelby did with Ford back in the 60s. On top of that, the car company had been featured in movies, which had brought a significant amount of exposure to Trovato, Inc.

Based on what I was seeing in front of me, Mr. Trovato and his family weren't hurting.

I'm not sure what I had expected, but it wasn't to be met at the gate by a security guard, or to find two more waving me by when I reached the circular drive in front of the white monstrosity that obviously acted as the Trovato's residence.

31

It looked like the White House. And not just because it was white either.

It was... big.

Oddly, that was the only word that came to mind. As I climbed out of the car, I was too busy taking everything in from the freshly clipped lawn, to the extravagant flowerbeds and towering trees to think about the house. There was even one of those fancy water fountains in the center of the circular drive — just like in the movies.

Someone cleared their throat.

I spun around to see a short, older man standing on the front steps wearing a...

Hmmm.

I was beginning to think maybe I was in a movie.

He looked like he was wearing a butler's uniform. Since I'd only ever seen a butler on the big screen, I'm not even sure if that was an accurate description, but I nodded my head at him anyway. Glancing down into my car, I decided to leave my purse but snatched my cell phone just in case.

When I stood back up, the man/butler was gone, but coming toward me was another guy. This one wasn't sporting a nifty suit and was much, much younger. The sun was shining brightly overhead, making it difficult for me to see him clearly, but the first word that came to mind was... wow.

I pulled my sunglasses off and started walking toward him, trying not to gawk. He was lean and tall, powerfully built with a broad chest and wide shoulders. My breath hitched in my throat as the distance between us slowly disappeared. There was something strangely familiar about him. Like I'd met him before.

When I was close enough to take in his appearance altogether, I noticed he was wearing a white tank top that clung to the hard lines of his chiseled torso and had grease smudged across the front. His arms, from his shoulders to his elbows, were tan, muscular and covered in tattoos. Most of the designs were tribal art as well as some words that I couldn't make out. My gaze continued south, noticing he had on tattered jeans that hung low on his narrow hips, and brown, lace-up work boots.

He was wiping his hands on a thin, red towel as he sauntered toward me.

Yes, the guy sauntered. I mean he had some serious swagger, but it was sexy. Too sexy.

I cleared my throat, trying to rein in my body's strange reaction to him.

Did I know him?

The gap between us slowly diminished and, as I got closer, I tried to make out his face, but the sun was shining from behind him, outlining his body, but making it impossible to make out his facial features.

Maybe he was a mechanic or something. Did rich people have mechanics?

"Can I help you?"

The dark, rough sound of his voice had my gaze traveling north, my eyes darting up to meet his.

I stopped.

Right there, just a few feet away, I just stopped moving, my entire body going on alert.

There was an eerie sense of déjà vu, like I'd met him before.

What happened next could only be described as cataclysmic.

My hand came up to my mouth as I sucked in a breath. He was...

Holy crap.

He was the guy from my dream. The dream I'd had for the last couple of weeks. He was the guy I couldn't look away from, the one I would try to call back just before I would awaken abruptly. That was him. At least I thought it was.

There were still several feet between us, but as I looked up at his face, studying his ruggedly handsome features, I knew it was him.

Every man I'd ever met escaped my mind and the only thing I could think about was this incredibly good-looking guy standing there, his head tilted sideways as though he was studying me. The expression on his face could only be described as confused, almost like he was having a weird moment of déjà vu, too. Similar to the way I was feeling.

I could tell he was much taller than I was. Over six-feet. He looked young. Mid-twenties if I had to guess. Aside from his well-built body, his hair was short and brown, but it wasn't dark, and it wasn't light. Somewhere neatly in between. There were blond streaks in the longer strands on top, as though he spent a lot of time outside and the sun had highlighted various pieces. His jaw was scruffy, as was his chin. I don't think it was meant to be a beard. More like he'd forgotten to shave that morning.

But his eyes...

Oh, heaven help me. The guy had eyes that paralyzed me in place. They were a vibrant, liquid gold. But it wasn't necessarily the color that had me nearly tripping over my own two feet. There was something in those eyes that spoke of sex. And danger. The sexy kind of danger that girls like me ran away from.

I wasn't running, but based on the way my heart rate accelerated, I'm not sure my respiratory system realized that I was still standing in place.

The guy cleared his throat, repeating his question.

"I'm…"

Who the hell am I?

At first, I couldn't break the penetrating stare and when I finally did, I allowed my gaze to rake over his face, admiring the hard angles, the ruggedly handsome features. I would even have to admit that the silver barbell piercing in his left eyebrow was sexy. But I found myself transfixed on his mouth and when his lips parted ever so slightly, I saw that he had a silver ring on his lower lip, right in the center, the metal glinting in the sun.

"Help me out here, Angel. I'm not sure who you're here to see."

Did he just call me angel?

Remembering why I was there, I took the remaining steps to close the gap between us and I held out my hand to him. "I'm Payton Fowler. I came to see Aaliyah."

The guy glanced down at my hand and then back to my face. He left me hanging, so I tried to pretend I wasn't humiliated, switching my cell phone to that hand and clutching it tightly.

"Ahh, one of Aaliyah's little friends. Sorry, you just missed her." Humor danced in his honey-gold eyes as he looked above my head.

I didn't bother to correct his assumption that Aaliyah and I were friends because the sound of an engine caught my attention. I glanced over my shoulder in time to see a Mercedes speeding down the narrow drive. I could only assume that was Aaliyah.

"Well, crap." I realized I spoke my thoughts aloud. Meeting the guy's gaze once more, I followed with, "Do you work here?"

The smile that tipped his full lips had my knees going weak momentarily. I got a glimpse of bright white teeth along with the glint from his lip ring.

"You could say that," he answered.

"And you are?" I asked, needing to snap out of it and get on with the reason I was there. I had a job to do, and Mr. Trovato would be expecting me back in the office before he left for his afternoon meeting with one of the senior vice presidents.

"Name's Sebastian. Don't worry, Angel, I'm sure she'll be back after class."

Crap. Crap. Crap.

That wasn't going to help me now. It wasn't like I could sit around and wait for her to get back just to ask if she had her father's phone.

"Would you know if...," I glanced over at the front door, "if anyone else is home? I'm supposed to pick up Mr. Trovato's cell phone. He told me Aaliyah would be here to give it to me."

"Nope. No one else here," he said confidently as he slung the red rag over his shoulder and thrust his hands into his pockets, the muscles in his thick arms bulging, the black designs that twisted around his arms flexing and moving.

He was breathtaking.

But that wasn't why I was there.

I cocked an eyebrow as I contemplated my next move. I had seen the butler/man standing on the front porch, so I was pretty sure *someone* was home. When Sebastian didn't seem to want to change his answer, I knew I'd hit a brick wall.

Damn. Damn. Damn.

This day wasn't getting any better; that was for damn sure.

When I squinted up at Sebastian one last time, I found his gaze had drifted down to my chest. Feeling incredibly exposed, I immediately covered my breasts by crossing my arms. "Hello-o-o." I made sure he heard my annoyance. "My eyes are up here."

"Sorry," he responded with a smirk, looking not at all sorry. "You've got a stain on your sweater."

As though I didn't know the stain was there, I glanced down at my chest, realizing that by crossing my arms, I'd thrust my boobs up, increasing the amount of cleavage peeking out from the very modest V-neck of my sweater.

"Coffee," I said inanely.

Sebastian met my gaze and grinned before glancing over his shoulder. "I guess I should get back to work."

I nodded, not sure what else I could do. If this guy insisted that no one was home, I couldn't just walk right in even if I suspected otherwise. And I seriously doubted the Trovato's wanted their mechanic traipsing through their house looking for Conrad's cell phone.

Without so much as a goodbye, Sebastian turned and walked away.

That's when I realized that the earth-shattering impact of seeing him for the first time was suddenly overshadowed by the vision of him walking away. Although his jeans were loose, I could still see the shape of his perfect ass behind the soft denim.

On hearing his sexy, gruff chuckle, I immediately looked up and that's when I realized he'd caught me ogling his ass.

At least now I didn't have to worry about Mr. Trovato firing me.

It wasn't going to matter since I was surely going to die of mortification anyway.

Sebastian

HOLY SHIT.

That was her.

That was the girl from my dream.

As I walked back to the garage, I did my best not to turn around and watch her drive away.

I had to give myself a little credit. I think I handled myself pretty damn well considering I'd been shocked as soon as I saw her. She was the girl I had been dreaming about for the last few nights.

Stepping into the shadows of the garage, memories of my dream came back with a vengeance, and I stopped moving as the vision replayed inside my head.

I knew I was asleep. I had to be. Even knowing that, I was having a hard time deciphering the dream from reality. There was no way this could be real. Could it?

I didn't want to wake up. I didn't want to lose this moment.

She, whoever she was, she mesmerized me, drew me in. I couldn't pull my eyes away, couldn't break the spell she had on me. Something in the way she walked, talked, moved.

Breathed.

So familiar, yet not.

I felt like I knew her, like I'd met her before, but for the life of me I don't remember any such encounter. Had we met? Was this my mind conjuring up the image of something from my past? Or was this some sort of vision from the future?

Either way, I didn't want to open my eyes. Didn't want to face reality if she wasn't in it. I wanted to get closer, to look into her eyes, to know what she was thinking.

I was unabashedly staring, unable to look away.

Whoever she was, there was something about her…

Something that unhinged me.

Unfortunately, every time the dream got that far, my eyes would come open, the dream drifting off into nothingness. No matter how hard I tried to call it back, it never worked. Just that morning, I'd lay motionless in my bed, my chest heaving, my heart pounding while the first rays of the early morning sun peeked in my bedroom window. After getting my breathing under control, I had glanced at my alarm clock. Groaning, I then rolled over, refusing to get up at six.

But I was awake now. Completely. Payton Fowler, she was the girl from my dream. And she'd been standing right there in the driveway, looking just as she had in my dream.

Well, save for the outfit. She hadn't been wearing that prissy skirt when I'd dreamed about her. No, she'd had on jeans and a T-shirt, her cute little feet were bare. Her long, dark hair had been pulled back in a ponytail, not hanging loosely over her shoulders. But her smile, the smoothness of her alabaster skin, her pert little nose, those full lips and the way her hazel eyes had lit up when she looked at me… It had all been the same. Every last detail.

"Do I work here, she asked?" I was grumbling to myself as I made my way back to the truck where the stupid ass engine was waiting for me. "Yep, Angel, I work here all right," I mused aloud.

From the moment I laid eyes on her, I'd nearly tripped over my own two feet. It had been surreal, and for a brief moment, I'd wondered if I were asleep again.

I pinched myself, the pain ricocheting up my arm.

Nope, not dreaming. She was real.

And now I was smiling. Even as I resumed my place in the garage where I spent most of my time, — in my world, eight bays, air conditioning and a kickass sound system equaled a garage — the smirk was still plastered on my face.

I thought maybe the muscles were stuck or something. I didn't spend much time smiling these days and certainly not today.

Until I'd heard the guttural purr of the Mustang pulling up, I'd spent the better part of the last three hours fiddling with the damn engine on my cherry red, '63 Chevy truck, yet it was still idling too fucking high. Since the engine was a prototype that I was working on in my spare time, I was used to the minor quirks from the damn thing, but for the life of me, I couldn't get the bugs out of this one.

"Stupid ass engine," I groaned loudly.

After that interruption, I doubted I'd be able to get my mind back in gear. That woman — Payton — had single-handedly knocked me for a loop there for a second. From the moment I saw her walking toward me in those killer fucking heels, I'd had a damn hard time keeping my boner at bay.

I felt like I'd just stepped into a bad porno — the kind where the hot, young executive woman meets the mechanic and things get hot fast.

Yeah, that hadn't happened.

I had reined in my instant primitive reaction to her, but my lust had been quickly replaced with confusion.

At first, I thought I'd met her before, but when I heard the lyrical sound of her voice, I realized there was no way. I would have remembered her. But there had been something niggling in my head. I may not have met her, but I'd certainly seen her before. That was when I remembered the dream.

That chick was fucking hot, even if that outfit didn't do a damn thing for her. The way her glossy brown hair sparkled in the sunlight... It was the first thing I noticed, but certainly not the last.

"Did I work here?" I repeated, grinning.

Thrusting my hands into my hair, I stared at the engine that was hell bent on dissolving my patience.

And still I was smiling.

Conrad's new assistant, huh? Interesting.

My amusement still didn't die off even as I accepted the fact that, by working for Conrad, Ms. Fowler was technically off limits to me.

My grin widened.

Right. Like that had ever stopped me before.

It wasn't until she mentioned her name that I realized who she was, but that hadn't quelled the notion that I'd seen her before. For the last two weeks, Conrad had been going on and on about the new assistant he had, but it wasn't like I'd been introduced to her yet. Needless to say, Conrad didn't make a habit of introducing me to the women in his office. I doubted that was going to change anytime soon either.

While I'd stood there studying her, I tried to convince myself that the only reason she sounded familiar was the fact that Conrad had been talking about her for the last couple of weeks. I think he was still trying to convince himself that she would work out, eventually, but he had plenty of concerns regarding her ability to do the job.

She was an assistant for chrissakes. How fucking hard could that be?

Not that I'd asked him. I didn't really give a fuck, truth be told.

The only time I'd uttered a word had been when he admitted that he missed his old assistant, Jasmine. I, personally, was grateful that the snooty bitch was gone, and I'd told him as much. If anyone could make me feel like a two-bit reject, it had been Jasmine.

Then again, that's what happened when you were in the shadows, pretending you were nothing more than an employee who was paid extra to make house calls. Right. Like I'd willingly work for Conrad if there wasn't something in it for me.

Retrieving the grease rag from my shoulder, I carried it over to the Mercedes-Benz SLR McLaren that I'd been tinkering with the last few days. Some hot shot millionaire that Conrad knew was willing to pay an absurd amount of money to have the damn thing supercharged. As if half a mil wasn't enough to drop on a car already, now he was willing to pay *my* price to make the damn thing go faster — in a way only I knew how.

Like the asshole could handle the speed in the first place.

While I grabbed my tools, I let my mind drift back to my brief encounter with Payton a few minutes before.

Yeah, I know. I should have probably told her who I was, but she seemed to have drawn her own conclusion already. I didn't want to disappoint her.

The mechanic.

That actually made me laugh.

Technically, it was true. But I wasn't the *family's* mechanic. I was the brains behind the stupid Trovato fortune, although Conrad would never willingly admit as much. He took full credit and I pretended that I wasn't bothered by it. Hell, he was the one responsible for convincing the media that I was nothing more than a lowly employee of Trovato, Inc., but I certainly hadn't tried to correct him.

Little did they know.

It would probably blow their fucking minds to know that if it weren't for me, Trovato, Inc. would still be moving along at a snail's pace, trying to come up with a performance engine that all the damn car manufacturers were looking for these days. Then again, there were even bigger secrets that they'd latch onto if they had the chance.

But, I wasn't looking for glory or acknowledgement.

In fact, I preferred to spend my days entangled in an engine or screwing around on the computer away from the cogs of the company. Even if I wanted to, I would never fit in there. Hell, I barely fit in here.

So, Conrad and I had come to an agreement, he would leave me the hell alone, and I would, in turn, make him more money.

As for me, I wasn't hurting.

At twenty-five, I had enough that my grandkids would never have to work. But that was only one of my secrets. You see, I happen to be the heir to the Trovato fortune... Conrad Trovato's illegitimate son. So, yeah, lowly mechanic I wasn't.

"You're a dumbass, Trovato."

Yep, I'd gotten used to talking to myself. Today was no exception.

I could've let Payton in the house because I happened to live here, too. Although I didn't live in the main house. That wouldn't have been pleasant for anyone involved, just ask my stepmother — the woman who despised me probably more than Conrad did — or my half-sister Aaliyah.

No, I chose to live on my father's estate, in the guest house, of course. The guest house was four-thousand square feet, mind you, so I certainly wasn't slumming it. I wasn't there because the prospect of family made me leery to leave either. No, I was there for convenience. Pure and simple.

The chirp of my cell phone across the room had me ducking out from beneath the hood and wiping my hands again. Seeing that it was my father, I was tempted to ignore it. I knew without answering just what he had to say.

"Yo," I greeted after putting the phone on speaker.

My father hated that.

"Where are you?" he asked, the frustration in his tone echoing through the cavernous space.

"Garage. Why?"

"Where's Aaliyah?"

"School." Not that I was her keeper or anything.

"Why the hell did you tell Payton that no one was home?"

"I didn't know her from Eve," I lied. "What was I supposed to do? Let her in to rummage through the house?"

In case I hadn't mentioned it, I lived to torment my father. We had a love/hate relationship that we'd perfected over the last few years — ever since I was introduced to him.

You see, I'm Conrad Trovato's dirty little secret. Or my mother was anyway.

Needless to say, we didn't particularly like each other, although he'd insisted on taking me in when my mother died. I'd been fourteen at the time, and since I didn't have any other family willing to take in a wild kid with a growing juvenile record, I hadn't had much of a choice.

I was still wild, more so now. The only difference was that I didn't get caught anymore.

Conrad didn't appreciate my wild living, and I didn't appreciate how he had treated my mother. Or the way he talked down to me. We'd come to an impasse before I was twenty-one and the years hadn't improved our relationship one fucking bit.

"I need my phone," he groused.

"Come and get it," I snapped.

"Sebastian," Conrad chastised, drawing my name out in way too many syllables.

I didn't say anything.

"You need to grow up, Sebastian," he finally added.

And you need to go to hell, I thought to myself.

"Was there something else?" I asked, pretending my head wasn't about to explode.

"Actually, there is," he stated.

Damn.

I bit my tongue, knowing he would eventually say something.

"We're having a party tomorrow night."

"Great. Have fun."

Unfortunately, Conrad and his wife Lauren had a penchant for throwing parties all the damned time. They claimed they were for charity, but I knew better. My stepmother loved the limelight. She loved to show off her riches and inviting other affluent assholes to their home was the easiest way for her to do that.

"We're announcing the new concept car."

Fucking shit.

"I want you to be there."

"Not a chance in hell," I told him firmly. Rather than argue because I know the next phase, I simply added, "Look, I gotta work." With that, I hung up on him.

I'd hear all about it the next time I saw him, I was sure. The old man lived to bust my balls, which didn't make me want to do him any favors.

Chapter Seven

Payton

"PARTY?" I STARED BACK AT MR. Trovato, praying my mouth wasn't hanging open while I tried to comprehend what he'd just asked me.

I was pretty sure my jaw was on the floor.

I'd been back in the office for all of an hour, eating my turkey sandwich at my desk while Mr. Trovato left to attend his lunch meeting. He'd been gone less time than I figured he would be and when he returned, I had been filing some paperwork that had been signed last week. I had greeted him as soon as he reached the top of the stairs, and on his way to his office he had mumbled something about a party.

Yes, a party.

Maybe I was hearing things because it sure sounded like Conrad had invited me to a party at his house.

He stopped in the doorway, his hand on the frame as he turned back toward me. "Tomorrow night. Seven o'clock. Black tie. My house. I'll make sure you're added to the guest list," Mr. Trovato clarified.

Yep, it was official. I wasn't hearing things.

I nodded, purely because I had no idea what to say.

As much as I liked my job, despite the bizarre encounter I'd had with Mr. Trovato's mechanic, or the peculiar expression I'd been met with when I explained to Conrad before he left for lunch — for the second time — what had happened, I wasn't all that interested in going to a party.

"Mr. Trovato?" I greeted when Conrad answered his office phone after Maude so kindly transferred me to him.

"Yes, Payton?"

It sure sounded like Mr. Trovato had been expecting me to call, but I pretended not to notice. "I wasn't able to get your cell phone, sir. Aaliyah had already left for school and your mechanic said that no one was home."

"My mechanic?"

"Yes, sir."

"Umm… Okay. Just come back to the office, Payton."

"Yes, sir."

I thought I'd heard a hitch in my boss's voice when I called to inform him I wasn't able to get his phone as I was driving back to the office. But the look on his face when I told him in person was… priceless.

In fact, he probably looked a lot like I did right at that moment.

What was I going to do at a party at his house? Certainly, he wasn't expecting me to assist him. Was he?

Oh, crap. Now I was even more worried.

Between that and trying to figure out what to wear…

It was bad enough that I didn't have anything to wear to work. Now I had to figure out what to wear to a party. Black tie? That meant I had to wear something fancy, right?

Shit.

"Will you be able to make it, Payton?" Conrad asked, pulling me from my wayward thoughts.

"Yes, sir." The words had come out before I thought better of it.

Crap.

"Great. I'll let my wife know to add you. I'll be back in two hours," Mr. Trovato stated as he headed toward the stairs.

Again, I nodded.

Lowering myself into my chair, I dropped my head into my hands and tried to put the errant thoughts running through my mind into some sort of order.

Sexy mechanic. Didn't need to think about.

What to wear to a party. Top priority.

Who would go with me? Good question.

Sexy mechanic.

Ugghhh!

It wasn't working.

Despite the fact that I had more important things to focus on, I was still attempting to replay the conversation I'd had with Sebastian and how it was possible that I'd had a dream about a guy I'd never met. It still didn't make sense. On top of that, I was trying to figure out why I couldn't stop thinking about him *period.* He had called me angel. Angel. Seriously. If that wasn't some sort of patronizing assholishness (yes, I just made that word up), I don't know what was.

Not that I had time to think about Sebastian, or our strange encounter, or whether or not he was really the mechanic. After my conversation with Conrad, I wasn't so sure that was the case. But either way, Conrad didn't seem at all concerned, so I wasn't sure why I was.

Dress.

I had to find a dress.

Yanking my cell phone out of my desk drawer, I quickly dialed Chloe's number. If anyone could help me, she could.

"I've got a problem," I said in a rush as soon as she answered.

"You've got many, but now probably isn't the time for me to point those out. What's up?"

"Thanks. I feel so much better," I retorted, gripping the phone hard enough to nearly crack the plastic. "I need a dress."

"For?"

"And a date," I continued, ignoring Chloe's question. "I need a dress and a date. Shit. Not necessarily in that order."

"Hold up, woman." Chloe laughed. "I'm sure I've got a dress you can borrow."

"Have you seen me?" I asked her, incredulity dripping from every word. "You're like three sizes smaller than I am."

"Whatever. When do you need it by?"

"Tomorrow."

"Seriously? You couldn't give me a little more notice?" she asked, teasing me as always.

"I just found out. Conrad invited me to a party. At his house."

"Girl, should I be worried that he invited you to his house?"

"Shut up." I immediately wondered what she was going to say when she found out I'd already gone to his house. "Can you help me or not?"

"With the dress, yes. If you're asking me to be your date, well, I'm afraid to tell you that you're just not my type."

I laughed, releasing the breath I'd been holding.

"What time will you be home?" Chloe asked. "And yes, I've got something that'll work, you just have to trust me."

"I won't leave here until six or so."

"Well, grab dinner on your way home and I'll work my magic."

"What do I do about a date?" I asked. It was one thing to find a dress, something else entirely to conjure up a date on such short notice.

"What about Aaron?"

Hmm… That wasn't a bad idea actually. He was my best friend, and I hadn't asked him for any favors lately. "I'll call him."

"Text me and tell me what he says. I'll see you at home tonight."

I hung up without saying goodbye, my stomach suddenly churning with nerves. I wasn't worried that Aaron would tell me no if I asked him to accompany me. The worry came from the fact that he was so busy lately and I didn't know what his plans were for tomorrow night.

But, I wasn't going to know until I tried.

Pulling up the contact list on my phone, I scrolled until I found Aaron's number and hit *dial*.

"What's up, Buttercup?" Aaron greeted on the second ring, a smile in his always cheerful voice.

"I need a date," I blurted. I followed my little outburst with a nervous giggle. I could feel my face heat. Thank goodness he wasn't there to see me. He'd laugh.

"What? Like to prom?" he asked deadpan, and just like that all of my tension drained.

Resting my forehead on my palm, my elbow on my desk, I held the phone to my ear and took a deep breath.

"Yes, to prom," I said sweetly. "I need a date to prom."

"Awesome. Count me in. When and where?"

"I'm being serious, Aaron."

"I know, doll. If you weren't serious, you wouldn't've called me."

"That's not true and you know it," I answered defensively.

Aaron responded with a snort.

He was truly my best friend. He understood me in ways even Chloe couldn't. We had a long history together and it started back when I met him in seventh grade. He was a new kid at my school. A *hot* new kid at my school. I remember noticing him for the first time. He'd been standing outside the principal's office and I had been going there for who knows what. As I passed, he tossed me a smirk and a muttered hello. Needless to say, Aaron was the first boy I ever *noticed*. Tall and gorgeous, I'd been in love at the first hello.

Me and the rest of the seventh-grade female population.

It wasn't until high school when Aaron came out of the closet that I realized we'd been destined to be friends. He admitted that he'd known that all along, but he hadn't wanted to hurt my feelings. Being rejected by a guy was mortifying, especially in high school, and Aaron had made sure never to do that to me. So, when he told me he was gay, I can't say that I was shocked. Relieved, maybe. Although I had reprimanded him for not telling me sooner. I had spent the better part of junior high thinking there was something wrong with me.

And from that moment on, my attraction to him fizzled and turned into a love that I'd never known for another person who was not my mother or father. Aaron was my best friend, I loved him like a brother and I would do anything for him. I considered myself lucky, because I knew he'd do the same for me.

"What shall I wear?" he asked.

"A tux."

"Seriously, Payton? You can't just invite me to a cool party, can you? Always makin' me dress up and shit."

"I know. I'm sorry." The last time we'd gone out had been our senior prom, so he wasn't joking.

"No worries. It's about time I donned a tux again. Mark won't know what hit him when he sees me."

There was so much truth in that statement. Aaron was an attractive guy, there was no doubt about that. But when he dressed up... he was irresistible.

But again, not the point. "You don't even know when the party is," I told him.

"Doesn't matter."

"It's tomorrow night." I held my breath, waiting for him to tell me that it was too short of notice and that he had other plans.

"Good deal. What time do I pick you up?" he asked.

"Can you really get a tux that quickly?" I blurted.

"Doll, I can do things mere mortals can't."

My breath escaped me in a rush. This had been far too easy for a last-minute invite. I now had a date, and possibly a dress for a party that I didn't really want to go to in the first place. Things didn't generally work out that well for me.

Which left me wondering... just what was going to be the hiccup?

Chapter Eight

Payton

"HONEY, I'M HOME!" I SHOUTED to Chloe when I came through the front door around seven-thirty that night.

I'm not sure what had gotten into me, but ever since I hung up the phone with Aaron earlier in the day, I'd felt much better. Better than even before I had a party to worry about. We had shared texts for much of the afternoon, which had effectively distracted me from thoughts of the sexy mechanic. Aaron had sent me numerous selfies while he was out and about trying on tuxes. And yes, the man was right, he could do things mere mortals couldn't. He found a tuxedo, convinced the guy at the shop to give him a discount and was now set and ready to go.

I had been conversing with Chloe as well, mainly because Aaron and I were trying to work on what color cummerbund he should get — something he insisted on. Chloe suggested silver and that had me curious as to what she had found in her closet for me. Silver? If she put me in a silver dress, I was going to look like a glittery blow up doll, I was sure.

"What did you get for dinner?" Chloe hollered from her bedroom.

"Tacos." I resisted the urge to storm her room and see what she'd picked out; instead, I made a beeline for the table, setting the paper bag down before depositing my purse and my computer bag in my bedroom and kicking off my heels.

"You're an angel, you know that?" Chloe exclaimed when she joined me in the kitchen, throwing her arms around me from behind and hugging me.

I stilled instantly. Angel.

"You okay?" Chloe asked, making her way around me to the table.

"Fine. Is Aaron home yet?" I asked, her statement still ping-ponging around in my head. Angel. That was what Sebastian had called me.

Strange.

Shaking off the recurring sense of déjà vu, I blinked twice and forced my feet to move.

"Aaron's in his room with Mark," Chloe announced loudly in a singsong voice.

The door to Aaron's room flew open and there stood Mark in all of his handsome glory. Blond hair, blue eyes, built like a swimmer — which he was, so it kind of made sense.

"Hey, pretty girl," Mark greeted me as he made his way down the short hall. When he reached me, he pulled me into his arms and hugged me tightly.

"Hey. I hope you like tacos."

"Girl, I like anything you bring me. But I hope you brought enough."

Did I mention that Mark ate a lot? He said it had to do with all the swimming. He must swim an awful lot because he ate like a horse and never gained an ounce.

"Come on, pokey, dinner's here!" Mark called to Aaron down the hall.

"What do y'all want to drink?" I asked Chloe and Mark as I leaned into the refrigerator and rummaged around for a diet drink. We didn't usually keep them in the house, mainly because Chloe and I would devour them within a day, but I knew I'd hidden a couple in the back. Before anyone could answer, I retrieved the two cans and then held them up so she could see.

Chloe squealed.

Easily excitable, like I said.

"We'll take water." Aaron sounded snubbed as he came over to me and hugged me from behind.

"Don't act like you're upset. You don't drink sodas."

He hadn't had a soft drink in at least five years. I envied his will-power, I did. But I wasn't giving up my Diet Dr. Pepper for anyone.

Aaron retrieved two bottles of water from the refrigerator and then returned to the small breakfast nook where Mark was pulling out the chairs, waiting for Chloe and me to take our seats.

"Thank you." I smiled at Mark as I slipped into my chair, then glanced over at Chloe and added, "Please tell me you found a dress."

She'd already snatched the bag of tacos and was pouring the contents out onto the table.

"Why do you doubt me?" she asked, pretending to be offended.

"I don't. I'm just—"

Chloe interrupted me, her green eyes twinkling. "You're just eating. And then we'll try on the dress."

"Maybe we should try it on *before* I eat. I don't want to be bloated," I told her seriously, my eyes watching for her reaction. "The dress may not fit."

Mark and Aaron laughed while Chloe erupted in a fit of giggles. I sat there staring at the three of them, trying to keep a straight face. "What is so funny?"

"Just eat and tell us about your day," Chloe replied when she stopped laughing.

"Mine was boring," Aaron offered when no one spoke. "You?" He turned to Mark.

"Yep, just as boring."

All eyes turned to me.

"I went to Mr. Trovato's house today," I blurted before thinking.

I kept my attention on my taco, avoiding eye contact with the other three people at the table, but I could feel their gazes boring into me.

When no one said anything, I slipped my eyes up to Chloe's face.

Her eyebrow was cocked, and she had stopped chewing. "I knew I should be worried."

It was my turn to laugh. "It wasn't like that."

"Spill," Mark said as he finished off his first taco. "He's rich, right? Nice house?"

"I don't know. I just saw the outside."

"And?"

"It's a house." I tried to sound indifferent. I seriously doubted Conrad Trovato's home could be classified as a mere house, but that wasn't the point of my story. "Anyway. He left his cell phone at home and his wife couldn't bring it to him. He told me to go. I went. No cell phone."

"What?" Aaron looked thoroughly confused. "Where was it?"

I laughed, realizing how Aaron had taken my statement. "I didn't get it." Without hesitating, I spewed the rest of the story, including the part about meeting the sexy as sin mechanic, never stopping to breathe.

"A mechanic? Are you serious?" Chloe asked, her eyes locked with mine.

I nodded, sipping my Diet Dr. Pepper.

"How hot are we talking? Lukewarm? Or like scorch-your-fingertips-if-you-touch-him hot?" Mark asked.

"The second one," I answered, studying my taco.

I knew I shouldn't have said anything. Chloe would constantly remind me of the mechanic from here on out and Aaron would be worried about me. It was a known fact that I didn't date much. And it wasn't because men didn't ask me out. They did. But I was a firm believer in the physiological reaction that I knew existed, even if I'd never felt it before. Until I found that, I wasn't interested in wasting any more time with guys who just didn't do it for me.

My hand stilled halfway to my mouth.

I'd felt that reaction to Sebastian, hadn't I?

Shaking off the unruly thought, I forced the taco to my mouth, taking a bite and ignoring the sensations that stirred in my belly when I thought about him.

I shouldn't have even brought him up. I didn't want to think about Sebastian, much less have someone ask me questions about him. I doubted I'd ever see him again and that… that kind of bugged me.

I managed to deflect the rest of their questions until finally we were finished eating. Before I could grab the taco wrappers to toss them in the trash, Chloe sprang up from her chair and grabbed my arm, dragging me into her bedroom before I realized we were on the move.

"We'll just… clean the kitchen," Aaron called, laughing.

"Thank you!" I hollered back, stumbling behind Chloe.

There on her bed was the sexiest dress I'd ever seen.

And the good news was that it wasn't silver. It was black.

"What do you think?" she asked, her hand pressed firmly to my back as she urged me closer to the dress.

"It's… It's… Wow. It's beautiful." That was an understatement. "It's also nearly nonexistent, Chloe."

"Not true. Try it on."

Yeah, it was safe to say that *little* was the most-prominent adjective in that little black dress. I grabbed the hanger and held it up in front of me.

"Try. It. On," Chloe commanded.

I could tell she was losing her patience, so I did as she asked. I carried the dress to my bedroom, slipped off my sweater and my skirt and then pulled the slinky, form-fitting dress on.

"This bra's not gonna work!" I shouted from my bedroom as I stood staring at the woman in the mirror.

The dress… Wow. It really was incredible. The kind of incredible that acted as camouflage, hiding all of those little things I hated about my body.

"Holy shit." Chloe whistled when she walked into the room, stopping to stand beside me as I continued to stare at myself in the mirror. "Yep, that'll work."

I reached for the hem of the skirt and tried to modestly pull it down to cover more of my thighs.

"Quit that," Chloe snapped as she slapped at my hand. "It's perfect just like that."

I met her gaze in the mirror and then glanced at the bra strap that was showing.

"Okay, maybe not perfect. But the bra we can fix. Worst case, go without one."

"Chloe!" I exclaimed. "You can't be serious." She *couldn't* be serious.

"You don't need a bra," she told me, reaching out and cupping my breast.

I slapped her hand away and laughed. "I do, too." I might not be well endowed, but I still needed a bra.

"Are you decent?" Aaron called from the living room.

"As decent as we'll ever be," Chloe bellowed.

The next thing I knew, Aaron and Mark were standing side by side in my doorway staring at me.

"Holy shit," Aaron said softly while Mark whistled.

"What?" I asked. "What's wrong?"

"Girl, that dress is fucking hot."

"I think it's the girl *in* the dress that's hot," Chloe corrected.

"That, too."

Aaron's eyes continued to rake over me. I waited for him to meet my gaze.

"What shoes are you gonna wear?" Mark asked. I glanced over to see his eyes trailing down to my bare feet.

Crap. Shoes.

"This we got," Chloe assured me. "We do wear the same size shoes." She practically skipped out of my bedroom, her ponytail bobbing merrily behind her.

I waited not so patiently, perusing my figure in the mirror while Chloe disappeared. Aaron flopped onto my bed and watched me while Mark continued to stand in the doorway.

"What's the party for?" Aaron asked, his hands behind his head, his long, lean body draped across my bed. He really was a good-looking man. Blond hair, blue eyes, tall and trim, not bulky, but definitely well-built.

"Don't know. Mr. Trovato just invited me. I didn't ask what it was for."

"Maybe the mechanic will be there," Chloe said when she returned a second later, a pair of silver closed-toe heels dangling from her fingertips.

I snatched the shoes and glared at her. "He won't be there."

"How do you know?" Aaron asked, his blond eyebrows launching into his hairline.

"Because he's the mechanic," I offered, sounding not so sure of myself.

"Well, I'll cross my fingers for you." Chloe winked at me and then dropped onto the bed beside Aaron while I slipped the shoes on.

I continued to primp in the mirror while my best friends laughed and joked behind me. I lifted my hair up, let it drop down, wondering just how I should wear it. The entire time, I was thinking about Sebastian.

What if he was there? What would I say to him?

A renewed sense of nervousness overcame me. Could this be the shakeup that my life needed?

Or was I just getting my hopes up for nothing?

Chapter Nine

Sebastian

DINNER WAS A NIGHTMARE, JUST as I expected.

I should've gone out, or possibly nuked a frozen dinner at my house. If I had, I wouldn't have had to endure Conrad's wrath in front of my sister and my stepmother. Not that they weren't already familiar with our unique blend of dinner conversation.

Conrad was still harping on the fact that I'd sent Payton on her way without helping her to retrieve his cell phone. I found it amusing: both sending her on her way *and* listening to my father bitch about it.

Mighty fucking funny.

But, the fact that I wasn't taking him seriously had led to a conversation involving plenty of other transgressions that he wanted to call out until I could no longer taste the food I was eating.

Same story, different day.

I was a glutton for punishment. That was the only logical reason for why I put up with his shit. Sometimes I just didn't get it.

Ever since my mother died, I'd been going through the motions. Eleven years was a long damn time to muddle your way through life without having any particular reason for doing what you do. But that's where I was at in my head — lost. Completely and totally at the mercy of all the people around me.

Not that I wanted anyone to feel sorry for me. I'd made my own bed so to speak. By the time I was thirteen, I'd done time in juvie, and since then I'd talked my way out of a shitload of trouble, as well. My motto was that rules were meant to be broken, and I had always aimed to be the best I could be, so that's what I'd done. Ignoring the rules had become my benchmark for success. The more rules I could bend or break, the more successful I was.

Growing up, I didn't have much. My mother and I lived in a one-bedroom apartment, which was sparsely furnished with mostly hand me downs from her older sister. My mother busted her ass to take care of me, even though she was incredibly young — only seventeen when she had me — and barely able to take care of herself. Her parents kicked her out when she told them she was pregnant, and they didn't offer to help even when we needed it most. We lived paycheck to paycheck and the worst part about it all, I had never been old enough to get a job and help out before she died. I'd tried though, working in a couple of mechanic shops for cash, but I never brought home enough money to make a difference.

Child support was nonexistent. In order to get child support, your mother had to do something to make that happen. Rachelle didn't want to have anything to do with Conrad Trovato. The most she'd taken from him was his last name when she put it on my birth certificate. And she'd regretted that every day after.

And as a way of saying thank you for not fucking up his entire life, Conrad pretended I didn't exist. He pretended my mother didn't exist.

Good ol' Conrad Trovato. My mother had been head over heels for him, and the bastard had turned his back on her. Then again, he'd been married to his first wife, Judy something or other, at that time and he was already making a name for himself. It wouldn't have gone over well if he admitted to having an illegitimate child with an underage girl.

Yep. Conrad had been twenty-six and married when he impregnated my seventeen-year-old mother. Needless to say, the two of them hadn't been all that concerned with morals and values when they decided to get together. Or protection, obviously.

Not only had Conrad built a company that afforded him the luxuries he had today, but he also came from old money. Money on top of money. I would never understand it.

But when Conrad attempted to pay my mother for her silence, Rachelle told him to go to hell and kept his secret for free.

That's where she and I differed. I would have taken the asshole's money and exploited him. Break the rules; that was the name of the game.

Every damn time I looked at him, I wanted to break his nose.

Tonight, after putting up with his tirade for a couple of minutes, I had hurried through the meal, excusing myself without his permission and hiding out in the garage attached to the guesthouse. This one was mine, the one place I spent hours and hours alone. It gave me time to think, which wasn't necessarily a good thing sometimes.

As though they knew I didn't need to be left to my own devices, ten minutes after I'd started tinkering with my Camaro, Leif and Toby showed up. My two closest friends tried to convince me to go out to the sports bar that we generally went to on Thursday nights, but I declined. I had too much shit to do — which translated to: *I didn't want to be around people.*

They were my closest friends and it was true, when I wasn't working, I was usually hanging with them. That's what friends did.

After I had refused to go out, Leif and Toby decided to stick around, snatching two beers from the refrigerator and planting their asses on the tailgate of my truck. We were talking about the new big block engine I was working on when my father made an appearance.

Standing to my full height, I put my hand on the edge of the Camaro's open hood and stared at him.

"I wanted to make sure you were planning to be at the party tomorrow night," Conrad stated in that authoritative tone that he generally used on his employees.

He almost made it sound as though I had a choice. I knew better.

"Busy. But y'all should have a grand ol' time," I replied sarcastically, glancing back at the engine.

"You will be there."

That's more like it. I knew it hadn't been a request.

"Why? Why the hell would you even want me there?" I turned my full attention on him then, noticing out of the corner of my eye that Leif and Toby were watching us intently.

"I want to unveil the new concept car."

"It's not ready," I informed him, as though he didn't already know that.

"But it will be."

"Not by tomorrow it won't," I argued.

"Maybe not. But it will be soon. I want to announce it, see if we have any potential buyers."

I should have been used to this shit. It wasn't the first time Conrad pushed a deadline on me. In return, he should have realized by now that the harder he pushed, the harder I pushed back.

"I'm busy."

"You'll be there," he repeated more sternly.

I could see the discomfort on Leif's and Toby's faces and I knew that I needed to chill. My father and I were notorious for going to blows whenever we engaged in conversation and more than once, my friends had been caught in the crossfire. I knew how uncomfortable it was. Hell, I lived this life. No one knew it better than me.

"Fine," I snapped, dropping the hood on the Camaro as a punctuation mark on my temper.

"Black tie. Seven o'clock."

I nodded, keeping my mouth shut for fear of what I might say. I didn't want to go to one of his stupid fucking parties. I didn't want to be anywhere near the assholes that he called friends. A few people knew who I was, but the rest of them had no clue. How Conrad had managed to do that all these years, I still didn't know. I didn't want to know.

If I had to guess, he had paid them off the same way he paid me off. At fourteen, when they were laying your mother in the ground and throwing dirt over her casket, you did what you had to do to survive. You see, my mother died in a car accident. She was T-boned by a drunk driver, or so the story went. Since the driver had fled the scene, no one really knew that to be true. She died on impact, and after losing her, I hadn't been right in the head.

Still wasn't.

I survived the overwhelming grief of losing the only person who loved me by blackmailing Conrad Trovato.

A paternity test proved that he was my father, although part of me had always hoped my mother had been wrong. Considering he was the only man she'd been with before I was born, it was a little difficult for her to make that shit up.

I'd been backed into a corner with only two options. The state would take me, or my father would. I chose option B, which at the time seemed like the lesser of two evils. I still questioned my decision sometimes.

Conrad hadn't been happy with the threat, but he eventually saw the light. That didn't mean that he didn't hate me. I was pretty sure he did.

I didn't fucking care.

"Awesome. You get to put on the penguin suit." Toby's roaring laughter yanked me away from my negative thoughts.

I darted my eyes toward the door, but my father was gone.

"Fuck off. Shut your face or I'll make you come with me."

"Bullshit." Toby recoiled as though I'd hit him with a cattle prod. "You ain't gonna get me anywhere near those people. What if that shit's contagious?"

"What shit?" Leif asked, sipping his beer and peering over at Toby.

"That hoity-toity shit. Man, I don't wanna walk around like I've got somethin' stuck up my ass, thank you very much."

"Too late for that," Leif offered, amused.

I laughed. I couldn't help myself.

Toby was a country boy to the core. He didn't have an issue speaking his mind. He was polite as hell around most people, but when it was just the three of us, he didn't hold back.

"Will his assistant be there?"

I snapped my head over to look at Leif. "What are you talking about?"

"I saw her on television, man. She's pretty fucking hot if you ask me," Leif replied.

"No one asked you," I snarled, remembering that my father had mentioned a spur of the moment press conference he'd held earlier that afternoon. That had to be what Leif was referring to.

"Defensive much?" Toby asked with a bellowing laugh.

"Fuck off."

"Man, you need to get laid. You keep making offers, but ain't no one here taking you up on them."

I flipped Leif off as I headed to the refrigerator and grabbed a beer. Dropping onto the couch in the corner, I crossed my legs at the ankle and reclined against the armrest.

As I closed my eyes, my mind drifted back to Payton, thanks to Leif's comment. I wondered whether she would be at the party. That snotty bitch Jasmine had always been invited to the parties my father threw. Didn't mean Payton would be there, but hell, it gave me something to look forward to.

"Why's your old man releasing the car now?" Leif asked, his voice coming closer to where I was sitting. I forced my eyes open, watching as he made his way to the sofa across from me. Toby wasn't far behind.

"Shit if I know," I answered. "He's been harping on me for a while now. I think he's hoping for seven figures on this one."

"Holy fuck," Toby exhaled sharply. "Seriously, man?"

"Yep. The last one went for just shy of a mil." Personally, I thought it could have gone for more, but my father caved at the last minute, accepting the highest of three offers.

I had to admit, the guy was pretty damn smart when it came to business, but his bargaining abilities needed some work.

"Did he let you take the car out?" Leif questioned, resting his big, beefy arm along the top of the other couch after planting his ass down on the leather.

"Nope." I had been willing to show them just what that car could do, but Conrad had refused, just as he always did.

No one knew that I took the car out anyway. Topped that motherfucker off at two-oh-nine on the track. Too bad no one had been there to see it. Not even Toby or Leif. As much as I wanted to brag about it, I never did. That was my thing, and if someone found out that I raced every car I worked on, I was pretty damn sure Conrad would put a tracking device on me just to keep tabs.

So I kept my mouth shut.

"Speakin' of racin'," Toby said in his good ol' boy drawl, leaning forward and resting his elbows on his knees as he pinned me with bright blue eyes.

"No one said anything about racing," I mumbled, smirking around my beer bottle.

"We're always talkin' about racin', man. Get with the program," Toby retorted. "There's a race. Two weeks from Saturday. Two large to get in, winner takes all."

"How many?" I inquired.

"Three so far. They're waitin' to see if you're game."

"You in?" Leif asked, as though he didn't already know the answer.

"I'm in," I assured him.

"Hot damn!" Toby yelled, grabbing his cell phone from his back pocket and shooting off a text.

It had been almost two months since the last race I was in. So far, over the course of the last two years, I'd gone unbeaten. To be fair to the other drivers, I used the Camaro mostly although I had a couple of other options. I'd dropped a fucking fortune in that car as it was and so far, she hadn't let me down.

I took a long swallow of beer as I stared at the ceiling. I hadn't told Leif or Toby about the dream I'd had. The one that ended with the Camaro in a fireball with me trapped inside. I didn't think that was a subject anyone would want to talk about, so I'd kept it to myself.

Did it freak me out that I might die in one of the street races where there were no rules?

Sure.

Did I care?

No, not really.

I'd never had a reason to.

Chapter Ten

Payton

"GIRL, WE BETTER GET A move on," Aaron yelled from the living room.

I was standing in front of the full-length mirror in my bedroom, my eyes glued to the woman staring back at me. I recognized my dark hair, my dimpled chin, and my high cheekbones, but that was about it.

I looked... different.

Good different, but still different.

It was hard to believe that was me staring back from the glass, but the longer I stood there, the more I convinced myself that it was.

My hair was piled into some intricate design on top of my head thanks to Chloe and her wondrous abilities. A few pieces hung down, framing my face, which had been painted. I wasn't one to wear much makeup, so when Chloe offered to "do me up" as she put it, I'd been leery.

Surprisingly, she hadn't overdone it. My eyes had a smoky shadow on the lid, a thin black line along my lashes and black mascara on them, and a clear gloss on my lips to top it off. Nothing outrageous and I actually liked what I saw. I looked older, or at least I thought I did.

Silver hoops dangled from my ears while a silver chain hung around my neck, coming right above the swell of my breasts — made to appear bigger thanks to the push-up bra that I'd dug out of my drawer. I had forgotten all about that trip to the mall so long ago. I don't even remember what had prompted it, but I do remember spending an obscene amount of money in a lingerie store. Not that I'd ever had anyone to wear lingerie for, but at the time, I think I'd needed the boost of knowing I had something pretty on beneath my clothes.

It was certainly working now.

The sheer black thigh highs had been Chloe's suggestion. Personally, I thought they were an elegant touch, but I feared that if I sat down, the tops would be visible beneath the hem of the short black dress I was wearing. Chloe informed me that wasn't an issue. Whether she meant that they wouldn't show or that they would, I didn't know.

The closed-toe pumps were a nice touch, much classier than anything I owned.

"Here," Chloe said as she walked into my room holding out a small black clutch.

"Thanks. I'm not sure what I'd do without you," I told her, grabbing my cell phone and my lip gloss from my dresser and tossing them inside.

"Well, tonight you'd be going to a party naked."

True. I laughed, sparing myself one last look in the mirror.

"Here goes nothing."

I walked into the living room to find Aaron leaning against the wall and Mark fiddling with Aaron's bowtie. I stopped, momentarily stunned by how handsome he looked in his tuxedo. Sure, he'd been hot in high school, and had actually caused plenty of women to have heart palpitations at our senior prom, but this Aaron — older and wiser — was devastatingly handsome.

"Wow." The single word barely coming out.

"That's exactly what I said," Mark added. "Doesn't he look fucking hot?"

"I'll say."

Aaron offered me a sideways smirk before wrapping his hands around Mark's wrists and pulling him closer. I looked away when the two men kissed, not wanting to invade their privacy.

"Come on, you two. You can play kissy face later," Chloe told Mark and Aaron. "You kids are gonna be late," Chloe declared, urging me farther into the room. "I suggest you get going."

I glanced at the clock on the wall. It was already seven and we still had a forty-five-minute drive ahead of us. That would put us at the party at the perfect time to be fashionably late. That is if I didn't stall any longer.

"Don't keep him out too late," Mark whispered to me as he offered a brief hug. "I'm going to take him home with me tonight and ravish him until dawn."

I blushed. I couldn't help it. It wasn't that I was a prude, but I could totally picture the two of them in my head and … well … I knew I shouldn't have been thinking about that.

Chloe handed me a silky black wrap and I slid it over my shoulders. It wouldn't do much against the chill in the November night air, but she had insisted it would look good.

Vain. That was obviously what I was going for tonight, I had told her, laughing.

"My car or yours?" I asked Aaron as I passed him on my way to the front door.

"Mine," he answered easily, reaching around me and opening the door.

Aaron was the best date ever. Probably because there weren't any expectations. We were friends and we could talk about anything and everything, which we did. From the moment we got into the car, until we pulled up to the guard station at Mr. Trovato's estate, there was never a lull in the conversation.

That changed when we pulled into the circular drive in front of Mr. Trovato's house.

"Holy shit," Aaron whispered as he peered through the windshield of his fancy little Honda with Bluetooth and satellite radio.

"Yep, that's what I thought the first time I saw it," I told him.

Granted, the place looked even more extravagant at night. Lights were hidden in the landscape, strategically placed to show off all of the details of the mansion. There was a line of expensive cars along one side of the driveway and several men scattering in all directions, probably moving the cars to a safer place.

A valet came over and opened my door for me, helping me out with a firm hand. I could have sworn he eyed me up and down a couple of times, but I pretended not to notice, although the sideways glance did wonders for my ego.

Aaron was instantly by my side offering me his arm and walking me toward the steps that led to the front door. A man in a suit — wielding a gun on his hip and an earpiece in his ear — greeted us before opening the front door and stepping back so we could enter.

I tried my best not to gape at what I saw next, but that was rather difficult to do.

Mr. Trovato's house was impressive on the outside, but on the inside, it was ... I wasn't even sure how to explain it. It looked like something straight out of the Roman Empire. Or so it did to me. Not that I'd seen any Roman empires, but if I had, this was what I imagined they would look like.

There were thick white columns that went at least twenty feet in the air on both sides, framing the circular entryway, three on each side. The floor looked like marble. It was a beautiful, gleaming white swirled with darker tones. An enormous sculpture of a semi-nude woman stood in the center of the entry, flanked by two grand staircases that circled up to the second floor. Somehow, I managed not to whistle the way Chloe always did, but I had to say I was impressed.

"May I take your coat, madam?"

I turned to see another man in a suit, this one significantly older than anyone else I'd met so far. He looked like the same man I'd seen on the front steps the other day. I nodded, and he assisted in pulling the wrap from my shoulders before disappearing.

Another man, who looked a lot like Gun Guy by the front door, made his way over to us. "Right this way."

I glanced up at Aaron, lifting my eyebrows in a silent "Can you believe this?" He smirked back at me, looking regal and handsome and totally at ease. As though he actually belonged in a place like this.

I, however, did not feel like I belonged. I was suddenly self-conscious, wondering what other people thought when they looked at me. Was my skirt too high? Could they see the tops of my stockings when I walked? Did I look like a prostitute?

I didn't have time to ponder those questions for long though because we were on the move again, Aaron leading me as we followed behind the man in a dark suit. He took us deeper into the house, through what appeared to be a formal living room decked out with modern, white furniture that looked like it had never been used, and then down a hallway. At the end of the hall, we went up a different staircase, this one just as grand as the ones near the front door with its intricate iron railing, to the second floor and then down another long, wide hallway. By the time we arrived at our destination, I was thoroughly lost. When we came upon a set of double doors, he stopped, opened one of the doors and gestured us inside.

Holy. Smokes.

I didn't stumble, and I'm not sure how I managed that. Aaron and I walked into an enormous ballroom filled with people. A waiter was standing near the door holding a tray of champagne flutes. Because social protocol demanded that I do so, I took one of the flutes, as did Aaron before we made our way inside.

Social protocol probably didn't demand that I down the champagne in two swallows, but I did that anyway.

"How much money does this guy have? And why the hell didn't he hire a better decorator?" Aaron asked, his voice a mere breath against my ear.

Laughing and gently elbowing him in the ribs, I answered with, "A lot."

I didn't know what that number was, but obviously it was enough, and Aaron did have a point. Although nice, the place felt a little stuffy to me. A little too upper crust.

The walls donned a fancy gold and red wallpaper with thick white trim framing it. The floor was dark hardwood, with plush red carpet outlining the room. There were large gilded plaques of various designs hanging above the doors and heavy gold drapes covering the floor to ceiling windows.

Suffice it to say, it did suit Mr. Trovato.

I spent the next few minutes taking everything in. From the sophisticated décor to the fancy gowns on the women and the expensive tuxes on the men. As I figured, most of the people I encountered were older, and just as I thought, everyone seemed to look right past me. If it hadn't been for a man who had bumped into me and politely apologized, I would have believed that I was invisible.

"Hey," a chipper female voice sounded from behind me and I turned, coming face to face with… "You must be Payton. I'm Aaliyah. Welcome to my humble abode."

Aaron snorted.

"I like you already," Aaliyah said to Aaron. "And you are?"

"Aaron." He offered Aaliyah his traffic stopping smile. "Payton's gay best friend who was wrangled into attending."

Aaliyah's grin was radiant, as was the rest of her. She stood just a few inches taller than me, her long, blond hair curled and hanging down her back. The dress she wore probably cost more than I made in a year and it fit her like a glove, the turquoise color setting off her bright blue eyes and olive complexion perfectly.

"I definitely like him," she whispered to me. "Don't worry. It's not as bad as it looks."

"Really?" Aaron asked skeptically making a production out of looking around, earning him another laugh from Aaliyah.

"Okay, it's as bad as it looks. But stick around, things usually get exciting later on."

"Exciting? As in the old people get naked and dance on the tables?" Aaron questioned.

Aaliyah gave my arm a gentle squeeze and laughed. "God, I hope not."

"It's very nice to meet you," I told Aaliyah, grinning at Aaron's joke.

"You, too. I'm sorry I wasn't here yesterday. I had an early class and if I'm late anymore, I'm gonna get in serious trouble."

"No worries," I assured her. I didn't bother to mention to her my interaction with Sebastian, although I wanted to ask her who he really was.

"You two have fun. I'll catch up to you later." Aaliyah gave my arm another friendly squeeze and then walked a few feet away, greeting one of the older couples.

"Mr. Trovato's daughter," I explained to Aaron.

"I figured as much."

"How so?"

"She's probably the youngest person in the place, and though I think your boss probably has a mistress or two, I didn't figure her to be that young."

"He does *not* have a mistress." I slapped Aaron lightly on the arm. I sure hoped Conrad didn't have a mistress.

"Don't be so sure of that." The deep, rumbling voice came from behind me.

I spun around so fast, I nearly dropped my empty champagne flute, but Sebastian retrieved it and set it on a passing waiter's tray like he did that sort of thing every day.

I merely stared at him, a strange tingle igniting deep in my core as I came face to face with the man I'd met just yesterday. The guy from my dream. The mechanic. He looked significantly different than the last time I saw him though. Tonight he wasn't sporting tattered jeans. No, tonight he was wearing a tuxedo and likely garnering the attention of every woman in the place.

The guy made a pair of worn, tattered jeans look incredible, but he wore a tuxedo better than any man I'd ever met.

As we stood there, motionless, neither of us said anything for a few heartbeats. My pulse was racing and if it hadn't been for Aaron's warm hand on my back, I probably would have forgotten where I was.

Sebastian peered over my shoulder at Aaron and I thought I saw a flash of anger glitter in his beautiful golden eyes, but it was gone as fast as it had come, leaving me to think I was imagining things.

"Enjoy the party, Angel," Sebastian whispered, nodding his head at me, our eyes locking briefly.

He didn't linger. He continued walking right past me without looking back.

"Who was that?" Aaron turned at the same time I did, so that he could follow Sebastian with his eyes.

"No one," I murmured.

Mechanic, my ass.

Chapter Eleven

Payton

TWO HOURS INTO THE PARTY, and I was wondering when the fun was going to start. I'd managed to drink six flutes of champagne and was starting to feel the effects of the alcohol, although that hadn't helped to alleviate the nerves that were attacking my insides. Aaron had forced me to eat some of the hors d'oeuvres, which was probably the only reason I wasn't flat on my face at this point.

My head was beginning to hurt from looking around the room, trying to locate Sebastian at every turn. Ever since our brief run-in, I hadn't seen him again, but I could feel his presence. I knew he was there somewhere.

"Care to dance?" Aaron stopped me from taking another flute from a passing waiter.

I glared at him in warning. That earned me a smile.

"No, I do not want to dance," I slurred, but he just took me in his arms and led me to the center of the room.

"You're drunk."

"I am not," I argued, knowing full well that I was. I wasn't much of a drinker, aside from a beer or two every now and again. I didn't even like champagne, yet tonight I'd been drinking it like water.

"Whatever you say, doll," Aaron replied, pressing his hand to the back of my head and forcing my face to rest against his chest. He was holding one of my hands and I slid my other hand beneath his jacket, clutching his back. It probably looked intimate, but I was trying to keep from sliding to the floor and letting sleep take over. That, and being with Aaron made me feel safe.

He pressed his lips against the top of my head as we danced around the room, the music soft and slow. The lights had dimmed a short while ago and most of the couples had migrated to the dance floor, too. As we moved, I closed my eyes, willing my brain to stop spinning.

Aaron must have realized the effect the dancing was having on my inebriated state because he slowed even more, our feet barely moving.

"Who was the guy from earlier?" Aaron asked, his voice low, soothing.

"I told you. No one."

"Right. And I didn't believe you. That's why I asked again. Who is he?"

"The mechanic," I informed him, hating the fact that the alcohol was making my lips flap when they shouldn't.

"Ahh. That explains it."

"I don't think he's the mechanic," I admitted.

I could hear Aaron's gruff chuckle against my ear. I amused him. I knew I did.

I amused a lot of people these days.

"Who do you think he is?"

"No idea," I told him, digging my fingernails into his back. I really didn't want to talk.

Aaron apparently took the hint because we spent the next few minutes slow dancing until the music disappeared. At first, I thought I'd fallen asleep standing up, but then a voice came over the sound system and the lights went out, pitching the room into complete darkness.

An automated voice started talking and several strobe lights began alternating to the bass that kicked in. What happened next was straight out of a movie. Seriously, I was pretty sure I'd seen it before in a movie. I don't remember which one though.

I stayed close to Aaron while the robotic voice rambled on about engines and cars and speed while a series of lights drew designs along one of the walls. There were gasps and clapping and then the lights came up to reveal a car sitting in the middle of the room.

"Impressive," Aaron stated dryly. "I'm pretty sure that's been done before."

Another waiter approached and while Aaron's attention was snagged by the fancy sports car, I grabbed another flute and downed it in one gulp.

I really didn't like champagne; tonight's sampling only solidified that for me.

"You better slow down," Aaron stated firmly when he turned to look at me.

I didn't argue. There was no point. I just wanted to go home. I'd already been there for more than two hours and Mr. Trovato hadn't even greeted me, although I'd seen him at least three times and I was pretty sure he'd seen me as well.

I don't know if he was purposely ignoring me or if it was just my imagination, but I was beginning to get frustrated. As it was, the only person who'd spoken to me all night, besides Aaron, was Aaliyah.

Sebastian didn't count.

"We need to get you some water."

Water was good.

Aaron was escorting me away from the crowd when a wave of nausea hit me. "I... I need to use the restroom," I told him hurriedly.

"I'll take you," he replied softly, taking my arm.

"No," I insisted, pulling back from him. "I'll... I'll be right back."

I needed some air and I didn't want Aaron following me in the event that I did get sick. I met his gaze and waited until he nodded. His eyes met mine briefly, but then I took off for the door. Out in the hall, the sound of my heels on the marble floor made my ears ring, but then blessedly I was on the carpet. When I stumbled once, sliding my hand along the wall to keep myself upright, I knew I'd had too much to drink. As the stairs came into view, I suddenly wondered just how I was going to safely make it down without falling on my face and rolling my way to the first floor.

I stopped at the top and peered down, taking a deep breath and trying to clear the fuzziness from my head. I'd walked down plenty of stairs in my life. Surely, I could handle a few more.

A strong but gentle hand gripped my arm and I looked up, expecting to see Aaron standing behind me. My mouth fell open as I stared up into those glistening gold eyes that had haunted my every thought since meeting him yesterday.

Sebastian didn't say anything, but he didn't look away either. I could tell he was thinking about something, and I suddenly hoped he wasn't thinking about giving me a gentle nudge down the stairs. But then he grinned and every thought in my brain leaked right out.

Without saying a word, he urged me closer to the stairs, his hand sliding down around my waist as he held me close to him. With his reassuring grip on me, I managed to make it down the stairs without an ungraceful face plant and the next thing I knew, he was leading me out through a door at the back of the house, right onto a dimly lit veranda.

I was pretty sure just the patio area was bigger than my parents' entire backyard.

I kept my thoughts to myself as we continued to walk to a shadowy corner, away from a few people who were milling about.

"Thank you," I mumbled, unable to look at him when we stopped walking. I took deep, steadying breaths, willing myself under control. I was no longer queasy, but I was hot. The cool breeze did little to ease the heat that coursed just beneath my skin, but I shivered anyway.

"What are you thanking me for?" Sebastian chuckled, the deep baritone of his voice sending a chill dancing down my spine.

"For not letting me fall to my death down the stairs."

I placed my hands on the concrete railing that wrapped around the veranda, breathing slowly as I stared out into the darkness. The moon was out, casting a white glow on the trees, the moonbeam bouncing off a pond in the distance. My head was spinning, but I think it had more to do with the incredible scent of Sebastian's cologne than the alcohol.

Just as I had earlier, I felt his presence more than I saw him. He was standing just to my right, a step behind me which offered me a small measure of comfort. If he got too close, I feared what I might do. My body had taken on a mind of its own, ignoring all logical instruction from my brain. Being alone with Sebastian wasn't a good thing, at least not where my common sense was concerned.

I don't know how long we stood there, but I didn't move, didn't look at him. For some reason, I was scared to make a sound, not wanting him to leave. I knew he was still there beside me because I could smell him, hear his steady breathing.

I shivered when a gust of wind whipped behind the house, wrapping my arms around myself. But even if I froze to death, I didn't want to walk away. I don't know what it was about Sebastian, but I was drawn to him. Ever since we met yesterday, I'd thought about him endlessly. And now he was standing here, the silence between us surprisingly comforting, but at the same time unnerving.

He shifted, and I thought for a second that he was going to walk away, but then his jacket was resting on my shoulders, my senses overwhelmed by him. I closed my eyes as I inhaled, letting the rich, musky scent of his cologne seep into me while the residual warmth from his body heat enveloped me. I suddenly wished his arms were around me.

But I knew that was crazy talking.

Several minutes passed. I could hear a few people talking, a woman laughing. The music was muted outside, but I could still make out the slow, jazzy tune.

"Feeling better yet?" Sebastian's arm brushed against me as he moved closer to the rail, setting his empty beer bottle on the top.

"Much," I said a little too quickly, turning to face him.

Whether it was the alcohol or my own desire, I wanted to question him, to find out what that niggling was in the back of my mind. "Are you really a mechanic?" I asked bluntly, gripping his jacket closer to my body.

Sebastian took one step toward me. I took one step back, but my butt hit the concrete railing, effectively halting my getaway.

"I'm a mechanic," he stated, his voice low, seductive. He was looking into my eyes as though he could see right through me, as if he knew what I was thinking.

If he knew, I'd be mortified because right at that moment, I was thinking about kissing him. Wondering what his lips would feel like against mine, and if I would be able to taste beer on his tongue.

Sebastian's finger came up and traced a line down my cheek. I leaned into his touch, unable to resist. "What is it about you, Angel?" Sebastian asked, but I sensed that the question was rhetorical, so I didn't answer.

I allowed my gaze to drop to his lips, willing him to move just an inch closer.

He did, and our lips grazed one another's, his breath warm against my mouth. My eyes closed, and I prayed he would kiss me, that he would do something to suppress the ache that had taken up residence between my thighs.

I'd never wanted a man the way I wanted Sebastian.

Never.

"Your boyfriend's probably looking for you." His voice was much lower than before, darker. I could practically sense the hunger in his tone.

I opened my eyes, drawing away from him slightly so I could see his face. My pulse was pounding furiously, my breath coming in rapid gasps. I wanted to say something, but the words didn't come.

So as I stood there memorizing the swell of his bottom lip and the ring that decorated it, the slight crook of his nose, the dark, thick lashes that framed his incredibly beautiful eyes, I didn't tell him that he was wrong. Aaron wasn't my boyfriend. I wasn't even the right gender for Aaron, but for some reason, I didn't want to correct Sebastian's assumption. I didn't know anything about him, other than he wasn't who he said he was. Sure, maybe he was a mechanic, but the fact that he was at a party, dressed to the nines in what I could only assume *wasn't* a rented tuxedo, looking every bit like a man who had money and wasn't put off by it, told me he hadn't been entirely truthful.

I didn't need that in my life. For whatever reason, Sebastian had felt the need to lead me on, to make me believe otherwise and although my body was set to slow boil when he was around, it wasn't in my best interest to acknowledge it. He was a bad boy. One I should run away from, not run toward.

And I was smarter than that.

Sebastian broke away, peering over his shoulder and I turned to see Aaron coming toward us.

"There you are," Aaron said softly, his eyes pinning Sebastian in place.

Aaron rarely looked angry, but as he glared at Sebastian, I could feel his ire. Why was he so pissed?

Without saying anything, Aaron worked his jacket off, pulled Sebastian's from my shoulders and handed it back to him before wrapping me in his warmth. He didn't say a word to Sebastian though and that was what made the moment so awkward.

"Let me take you home," Aaron suggested, putting his arm around me and pulling me against his side. I was tempted to push him away, to ask him what his problem was, but I was too shaken to do so.

"Good to see you, Payton." Sebastian's voice was still soft and seductive, almost as though he was keeping a secret from Aaron. "I look forward to seeing you again."

Oh, hell.

This was one of those testosterone contests. Who had the bigger balls and all that nonsense. I didn't respond, just nodded and leaned into Aaron a little.

When Aaron led me away from Sebastian, I was tempted to look back at him, wanting to know what he was thinking.

"Don't do it," Aaron muttered under his breath, his arm wrapping tightly around me.

"Do what?" I tilted my head back so that I could look up at him.

He just smiled as we walked inside.

We had just made it to the front door when Mr. Trovato came down the stairs.

"Payton," he called, causing me to turn toward him. "Leaving already?"

"Yes, sir," I said, just as Aaron said, "She's not feeling well."

"Well, thank you for coming. I hope you had a good time."

"I did," I lied. "Thank you for inviting me."

I felt a set of eyes watching me from across the room, and I looked past Mr. Trovato to see Sebastian leaning against the wall, his legs crossed at the ankles as he stared at me.

I quickly turned my attention back to my boss, but not before both Aaron and Conrad were looking over at Sebastian.

Conrad met my gaze again and I saw his irritation in the brown depths, but then it was masked quickly. "Take good care of her, son," he said to Aaron, sparing him a brief glance, then looking at me and adding, "And I'll see you on Monday."

Unable to speak through the desert that had taken up residence in my throat, I nodded my head and after receiving my wrap from the butler/man, I allowed Aaron to lead me outside. I managed, I still don't know how, not to look at Sebastian again.

The valet brought Aaron's car around quickly and I kept my mouth shut until we were safely inside before I punched Aaron in the arm. "Why did you do that?" I exclaimed.

Aaron laughed and rubbed his arm. "What did *I* do?"

"Why did you make Sebastian think we were together?"

Sure, I had allowed Sebastian to believe Aaron was my boyfriend, but it was something else entirely for Aaron to act so possessively.

"You've got a lot to learn, kiddo."

"Don't call me that," I shouted unnecessarily. "I'm older than you."

"By a minute." Aaron chuckled as the gates opened allowing us to leave the estate.

"By a month," I corrected him as I closed my eyes and rested my head against the back of the seat, snuggling into Aaron's jacket. "You still didn't answer me."

"Doll, you've got a lot to learn about men."

"Tell me about it." I was referring to the testosterone overload I'd been in the middle of just a few minutes ago. "In the meantime, why don't you enlighten me?"

"It's all in how you play the game," Aaron stated.

"I don't *want* to play the game," I retorted.

"We all play the game, doll."

"But thanks to you, Sebastian's gonna think I really do have a boyfriend."

"Maybe. But that's what you want."

I turned my head toward him and peered at him through one eye. "Why's that?"

"Because men want what they can't have. And, sweetheart, I just set the dominos in motion. Sebastian isn't gonna be able to stop thinking about you."

"Wait." I studied him briefly. "How do you know his name's Sebastian?"

Aaron chuckled, sparing me a sideways glance. "Because you just said it was."

"Oh." Closing my eyes, I returned to my original position, my head facing forward, eyes closed. "It doesn't matter anyway. It's not like I'm gonna see him again."

"Oh, honey, you'll see him again. Probably sooner rather than later."

The gentle hum of the tires on asphalt lulled me to sleep. As I drifted off, I didn't bother telling Aaron that I hoped he was right.

Chapter Twelve

Sebastian

I SHOULD HAVE SNUCK BACK to the guest house when I'd had the chance. If I had, I wouldn't have just spent the last few minutes staring out into the darkness with a woman I knew I needed to stay away from. But the silence had been comforting, her presence even more so. I could've stood there all night, listening to her soft breaths, letting the spicy sweet scent of her perfume tease me.

She had all but dared me to kiss her. How I refrained, I still don't know. It had taken everything in me not to pull her against my body and crush my mouth to hers just to see if she tasted as sweet as I suspected she did. As it was, when my lips brushed hers, I'd nearly come like a fucking teenage boy.

I should've kissed her.

And then her boyfriend had shown up and ruined the moment. The chaos in my head returned the instant he stepped outside, as though whatever filter Payton provided had been interrupted. I don't know what it was, or whether I was just conjuring up crazy bullshit in my head, but I'd felt an overwhelming peace when I was near Payton tonight.

She calmed me, even when she wound me up at the same time.

I'd spent the last couple of hours watching her from the shadows of the ballroom, not wanting her to know I was there. It had been hell on earth watching her laugh, talk and dance with the tall guy who'd arrived with her. At one point, I had envisioned shooting out his kneecaps just because he was with her and I wasn't.

My sister had come over briefly to talk, only to give me a hard time when she caught me watching Payton. Aaliyah had a huge grin on her face when I asked her about the guy Payton was with, having seen the three of them talking shortly after Payton arrived. She informed me that his name was Aaron, and she went on and on about how funny he was and how cute the two of them were together.

I knew her well enough to see through her. She'd been trying to get a rise out of me, but it hadn't worked.

Little witch.

But now Payton was leaving with the blond guy and my night had officially gone to shit.

"Sebastian."

I rolled my eyes at the sound of Conrad's voice. I could hear the click of his Italian loafers on the marble floor as he approached. Slowly, I transferred my gaze from the front door over to Conrad's face.

"Stay away from her," he commanded, his voice rough, his eyes beady.

"What?" I twisted to face him as I stood to my full height. We were nose to nose and I was tempted to punch him in his fucking mouth. I hated when he treated me like a goddamn child.

"You heard me," he growled quietly. "Stay the fuck away from her."

"Or what?" I taunted.

"Don't push me, Sebastian. She's off limits to you. Do you understand? I'm not gonna sit by and let you ruin her."

Ruin her?

What the fuck.

I laughed, but there wasn't an ounce of humor in it. "Right. 'Cause that's what I do. I ruin women." I took a step closer, our noses nearly touching as I narrowed my eyes on him. "I'm not you. I don't use them and throw them away. That's your M.O. Not mine. And if you know what's good for you, you'll take your threats elsewhere, old man."

Conrad didn't back down, but I saw a glimmer of fear in his brown eyes. He knew not to push me. I had a fragile grasp on my temper most of the time as it was. He knew that.

Realizing we'd gained an audience, Conrad took a step back just as I turned to walk away. When he put his hand on my arm, it took every ounce of willpower I possessed not to turn around and nail him between the eyes with my fist. I glanced down at where he was gripping my arm tightly, then back up to his face.

"I'm serious, Sebastian."

I shrugged his hand off. "So am I."

With that, I turned and walked away. I noticed Aaliyah was watching me from across the room, her eyes wide. She'd seen Conrad and I go toe to toe before, but just as I did, she knew that one of these days I was going to lose it.

That, or I was going to implode.

Half an hour later I was in my workout room, *Holler Til You Pass Out* by 3OH!3 blaring from the speakers, sweat pouring from my face as I pummeled the heavy bag hanging from the ceiling. The bass reverberating off the walls matched the pounding in my skull and the throbbing in my knuckles.

While I threw one punch after another, gasping for air as I exhausted my muscles, I pictured Conrad's face on the bag.

This was my stress reliever, something I relied on to keep me sane. That and racing. Those were the only two things that helped to quiet the voices in my head, to calm the fury that pounded in my blood.

I stopped moving, my chest heaving as I wrapped my arms around the bag, trying to keep from falling to the floor.

My thoughts immediately drifted to Payton.

She had calmed me in a way I'd never known before. In a way that no amount of punching a faceless enemy or redlining a powerful engine to its breaking point ever could.

For as long as I could remember, I'd battled the fury that was a living, breathing thing inside me. Chaos was how I referred to it. A constant state of chaos that had a stranglehold on me.

Stay away from her.

My father's words invaded my thoughts, a red haze clouding my vision momentarily.

In all the time that I'd known the man, after all the warnings he had dished out, all of the threats he made, never had I wanted to defy him so badly.

But for the first time, it wasn't to get back at him.

It had nothing to do with him period.

I wanted Payton. I wanted her with a passion I'd never experienced before. I wanted to hold her in my arms, to lay her out beneath me and bury myself so deep inside her that she no longer thought about any other man. I wanted to own her, to possess her.

It was crazy.

I was crazy.

Pushing away from the heavy bag, I retrieved the bottle of water sitting on the window sill. Staring out into the night, I could see my reflection on the window glass. The crazed look in my eyes was something I'd gotten familiar with. I knew what was inside of me. A beast that needed to get out.

No amount of adrenaline had ever extricated the turmoil though, and Lord knows I had tried. Too many times.

I downed the rest of the water and tossed the bottle into the small recycle container in the corner. Placing my hands on the wall above the window, I leaned forward, trying to see past the reflection into the night and that's when it came back to me.

Payton.

The dreams.

It was her I'd seen, even before I met her.

She was the one I'd been drawn to, the reason I hadn't wanted to wake up. Closing my eyes, I tried to conjure up the image of the woman who infiltrated my dreams, the way she looked then. She was just out of reach.

Just like Payton.

Stay away from her.

As Conrad's words bounced around in my head and images of Payton's face continued to drift through my mind, I knew what the right thing to do was.

For her sake, I needed to stay away. I needed to pretend we never met, ignore the fact that I was obsessed with her.

There was only one problem.

She unhinged me.

And I wasn't strong enough to resist her.

Chapter Thirteen

Sebastian

One week later
Thursday

WIPING THE SWEAT FROM MY face with the edge of my T-shirt, I allowed the wrench to fall from my hand and land with a shrill clatter on the concrete floor. The sound was surprisingly reminiscent of the noise that was clanging inside my head. Even with the music blasting, I couldn't block out the frenzied thoughts bouncing around inside my skull.

The garage door was open, the chilly November wind whipping through the open space, but it did little to cool me down. My skin felt hot, my blood was racing through my veins. Although I could usually get myself under control by working, that wasn't even helping today.

"Fuck," I growled, thrusting my hands through my hair, then sliding them down to the back of my neck.

I paced the floor just like that, my eyes on the ground, my hands gripping my neck, the muscles pinched tight.

I'd been strung tight as a bow since last Friday. Six days ago.

The last time I saw Payton.

I could still feel her breath on my lips. I was kicking myself in the ass for not kissing her, for not taking her into my arms and holding her, touching her. I just wanted to know what she would feel like against me. If I could have done anything differently about that night, that would have been it. It was the only damn thing I could think about.

And it was slowly killing me.

It didn't help that Conrad was watching me like a hawk. If I didn't know better, I would have thought he was tracking me. Maybe he was. I actually wouldn't be at all surprised.

If it weren't for my sister requesting that I have dinner with them every night, avoiding him would have been a hell of a lot easier. But it was hard for me to say no to Aaliyah. So, every night, I had to endure my father's scowl at the table. He would purposely bring up Payton's name and every damn time his eyes would be on me. So far, not since the night of the party, he hadn't warned me to stay away from her, at least not verbally, but I knew he was thinking it. I could tell by that tell-tale gleam in his eyes that he was just waiting for me to defy him.

Just so we're entirely clear, I fully intended to defy him, but it had nothing to do with getting back at him. Not this time.

From the moment Payton walked out the front door with that blond guy, the noose had continued to tighten around my neck and it wasn't easing up. The longer I waited before seeing her again, the more frustrated I was becoming.

I had dreamed about her again. The night of the party. I don't know if it was because I'd been thinking about her, or trying to decipher the original dream, but she'd appeared out of thin air. Waking up had been brutal. Reality could be a cold bitch sometimes.

Reaching down, I grabbed the wrench I'd discarded and as I was standing up, the music cut off suddenly and I heard someone clear their throat. I knew without looking who it was.

"Yes?" I asked my father, not bothering to look at him.

"I need an estimate on when you'll have that finished."

Yep. Just as I thought. He was there to ride my ass about the project, wanting me to be finished already. I'd told him a hundred times, I didn't know. He obviously wasn't accepting that answer.

"When I'm done," I told him honestly, tossing the wrench onto the toolbox, letting it clank against the other tools. Grabbing the grease rag, I wiped my hands as I turned to look at Conrad.

"Not good enough," he barked.

Holding my hands up in mock surrender, I smirked at him. "Have at it, old man. You wanna take a shot at making it work, do your worst. Or wait, better yet, why don't you get your guys over here, see what they can do with it."

He'd tried that before. Not that the guys he had working for him weren't good at what they did. They were. I was just better. It required a good ear to listen to a car, a steady hand to fine tune it, and I'd proven time and time again that no one could solve an issue better than I could.

I didn't bother to tell him that I was stalling on purpose. That wouldn't have gone over very well.

"Sebastian."

"Yes?" I feigned innocence. I was so fucking tired of this dance we were doing. Conrad could give two shits about when I had this prototype complete. I was pretty sure, after the spectacle he'd made at the party that someone was ready to throw a ton of fucking cash at him and he was just greedy.

As far as I was concerned, they could wait. And so could he.

"This is absurd." Conrad moved closer. He didn't get too close, probably worried he'd get grease on that pretty fucking shirt of his.

"You're tellin' me," I agreed. If he would stop breathing down my neck, we wouldn't have to go through this every damn day.

"You've got three days," he finally said, surprising the shit out of me.

I spun around to face him directly, trying to rein in my temper. "Excuse me?"

"You heard me. Three days. I want that damn thing finished by Monday. If it means you work through the weekend, so be it."

I could hear my teeth grinding together, feel the muscle in my jaw flexing.

"And if I don't agree?"

Conrad took a deep breath. "Then we'll have to have a discussion regarding our little arrangement."

"Good idea," I taunted as I took a step closer. He took one step back. "Why don't we do that, *Dad*? Why don't we just sit down and hash it out? Maybe call a press conference. I think the media would be thrilled to learn more about the man behind the fake fucking smiles and the fancy ass suits."

"Goddammit, Sebastian!" Conrad yelled, storming across the room and stopping abruptly, his back to me. "Why the fuck do you have to keep doing this? I've given you everything you could possibly want. Every goddamn thing and this is the thanks I get?"

I swallowed hard. "I'm sorry," I said facetiously when Conrad spun around. "I forgot about all the things you gave me. I was too busy remembering," I walked toward him, my voice lowering, "all the shit you took away from me."

Conrad glared, but he remained silent.

We were through here. There was nothing left to say. This was how it usually ended between us. A stalemate. He thought he could threaten me, but what he didn't realize was that I wasn't some dumbass fourteen-year-old kid anymore. I'd long outgrown my initial fear of being accepted by him. I didn't want his approval. I didn't need it.

"I've got to go back to the office," Conrad stated, as though that was the reason for the end of our conversation.

"Oh, one more thing." I waited until he turned to face me again. He cocked an eyebrow in question. "How's Payton?"

With that, Conrad spun on his expensive fucking heel and waltzed right out the door, leaving me standing there. All alone.

Just as I always was.

Chapter Fourteen

Sebastian

I ENDED UP HAVING DINNER out that night, choosing not to face my father's wrath. I'd pushed him too far and I didn't want to deal with the repercussions. Not to mention, I didn't want to put Aaliyah through that either.

That and my curiosity was going to get the best of me if I had to listen to Conrad talk about Payton over dinner one more time. He would do it too, just to irritate me.

One of these days, I was going to lose my shit and it wasn't going to matter who ended up as collateral damage. Where Payton was concerned, I was a ticking time bomb. It was as though I needed my next fix. I was a junkie, an addict. I wanted a woman I knew very little about and no matter how hard I tried, I couldn't understand what the fuck it was about her that had me so obsessed.

I was slowly going crazy.

I wanted to know more about her. No, scratch that, I wanted to know *everything* about her. Where was she from? How old was she? What did she look like naked?

I was definitely interested in the last part.

So, instead of risking a slip of the tongue in front of my father, I was sitting at a sports bar, watching hockey and drinking beer with my two closest friends, Leif Connelly and Toby Brindle.

"Man, are you picturing some chick naked?" Leif questioned, lifting his beer bottle in my direction.

"I was thinkin' the same thing," Toby added in that slow, southern drawl that drew women like a magnet.

"Shut up, assholes," I mumbled, hating how well they knew me.

Okay, so yes, I was picturing Payton naked. Didn't mean I had to share my thoughts with anyone, let alone the two people who would harass me until I wanted to punch them in the face simultaneously.

"Who is she?" Leif asked.

"No one," I barked.

"Right. 'Cause *'no one'* makes you drool when you picture her naked," Toby inserted, smiling around the lip of his beer bottle.

"Did I mention you could... fuck off," I bit out, unable to keep from smiling.

It wasn't a secret that I didn't spend my time with many women. Oh, there'd been a few, sure. After all, I wasn't a saint. But nothing serious.

Not that I didn't find women fascinating, nor was it due to the fact that I didn't have my fair share of female attention. But I'd learned early on, thanks to who my family was, that women tended to see dollar signs when they found out where I lived. I didn't make a habit of bringing women to the estate, but there had been a handful. Needless to say, the caliber of female that I usually attracted were more interested in what they could get *from* me rather than what they could do *with* me. If that wasn't a turnoff, I don't know what was.

"So now you've got imaginary girlfriends? What the hell is this world coming to?" Leif razzed good-naturedly.

"Who the hell are you tryin' to kid?" Toby snorted. "He's always had imaginary girlfriends."

I knew Leif and Toby would give me a hard time. They always did. Didn't matter that Leif usually got the waterfall of women that I left in my wake or that Toby had his hands full on nearly a nightly basis. We were usually together, which meant when one girl arrived, there were normally two more not far behind. Sometimes more than that. Chicks loved Leif and Toby, which, according to them, were their reasons behind their playboy statuses.

I'd known Leif since I was fourteen, since my first day in a new school when I was pissed off and hated the world. Leif had been my saving grace, I guess you could say. He hadn't taken any of my shit when I wanted to do nothing more than fight with anyone who crossed my path. His ability to ignore my bullshit was the main reason we'd become friends. That and he was as much of an adrenaline junkie as I was. The only point of contention between the two of us was that he had the hots for my sister, something I wasn't particularly fond of. So far, I'd managed to keep the two of them apart, although it was getting harder and harder these days.

But I didn't want to think about Leif and Aaliyah. Not now. Not ever.

As for Toby, we met our freshman year of high school. I'd smoked him in a street race, but rather than threaten to kick my ass like a lot of assholes did, Toby shook my hand. We'd been friends ever since.

"She's not imaginary," I grumbled, sipping my beer. I rested my forearms on the table and picked at the label on my bottle, trying to keep my head down.

Leif twisted in his chair to face me directly. "So there *is* a girl?"

"Of course, there's a girl," Toby declared, looking not at all shocked.

"No," I lied. "Ain't no damn girl." No reason to get Leif all worked up. He was always giving me shit about dating. I tended not to do it by design.

"So, I saw your father on TV again today." Leif looked at me and then glancing over at Toby, mischief gleaming in his dark brown eyes.

I leaned back in my chair, tipping it onto two legs. While I watched Leif and Toby, I tilted my beer bottle to my lips, contemplating whether or not I wanted to know where this was going. Instead of answering, I cocked an eyebrow at him.

"I have to rescind my original statement about Conrad's new assistant. She's not just hot. She's *fucking* hot."

Toby laughed. "And the difference is…?"

Dropping my chair back onto all four legs, I stared at Leif. Okay, he'd effectively gotten my attention. I purposely ignored Toby.

"Let's just say… I'd do her."

I growled. It wasn't something I could have controlled. I didn't even realize the deep rumble had come from me until Leif's eyes widened.

"Chill, man. I'm kidding. But she is hot," Leif tacked on, smirking as he sipped his beer.

"Good for her." My tone was snide, and I realized it was too late to pretend I wasn't interested in Conrad's new assistant. If anyone saw through me, it was Leif.

"Just think, if you do her, you'll piss your father off for good," Toby blurted, evidently oblivious to the tension radiating from me.

I scowled at Toby, my anger nearly getting the best of me. As it was, I hadn't been able to stop thinking about Payton for a fucking week, but the idea of using her to piss off my old man didn't sit well with me. Not at all.

Leif laughed, tipping his own beer bottle to his lips as he studied me. "He's kidding, man."

The hell he was. "Comedy isn't your strong suit," I snapped, downing what was left of my beer.

When Toby didn't say anything more, I squeezed my beer bottle between my hands, turning my attention to Leif. He knew I wanted to know what the fuck he was talking about. Not just about Payton, but the press conference that clearly went on without me knowing. Again.

So I waited none too patiently.

"Your father was making a statement about a donation to the children's hospital. She was there with him. Not that he introduced her, but the media made a big deal out of it."

A donation. Right.

As for the media making a big deal out of Conrad's new assistant, I could understand why. I had the pleasure of meeting her, I knew what the draw was. But they made a big deal about every damn thing when it came to my father. Especially the local news. My father did a lot for the Austin area, I'd give him that. He made generous donations to various charities and he'd even sponsored a new children's hospital. All in the name of charity.

Right.

Because Conrad Trovato was so fucking charitable.

But I doubted that was the reason the media had grabbed the story. They were always looking to dig up dirt on my father. One of these days, they were going to dig just deep enough, and Conrad's world was going to crumble around him.

I hoped I was there to see it.

"Have you met her yet?" Toby asked.

"Who?" I pretended not to know what they were talking about.

Thankfully our waitress arrived before either of them could continue. She delivered the wings Leif had ordered, then slid a plate of nachos in front of Toby, and I asked for another beer. After Leif had hit on her, she walked off, hopefully remembering my beer.

"I take that as a no," Leif said, staring at me.

"No," I lied.

I knew better than to tell them that yes, I'd met her. That I'd led her to believe that I was a mechanic who worked for Conrad. Or that I'd almost kissed her. They didn't need to know that.

Payton had no idea who I really was and probably never would. Just because she worked for my father, the chances of ever actually seeing her again were slim to none. Especially when it seemed Conrad was planning to stand in my way.

Not wanting to dwell on that depressing thought, I turned my attention back to the hockey game, ignoring that knowing smirk on Leif's face and the way Toby chuckled under his breath.

Assholes.

Payton

"WHY DO YOU INSIST ON dragging me here every Thursday night?" I questioned Chloe as she, quite literally, dragged me toward the door of *Instant Replay*, the downtown Austin sports bar that she had turned into our Thursday night hangout.

"How many times do I have to tell you? There are hot guys who come here on Thursday night."

"I'm sure they come here every night. Hot guys, that is," I argued as I pretended to resist.

In truth, I welcomed a night of beer and hockey. After the week that I'd had, I was ready for a cold one. Or three.

Mr. Trovato had been in rare form ever since I walked through the door on Monday morning. Although I had arrived at five a.m., I found him already in his office, a cup of coffee on his desk. I think he had expected me to apologize for not being able to read his mind and show up an hour earlier than I normally did. A little rattled, I had gone on with my day, business as usual. More than once I had caught him staring at me, but it wasn't one of those creepy old guy stares. It was more like he was trying to figure me out.

If that wasn't bad enough, Conrad had taken to asking me questions. Not too personal, but definitely more so than I expected. When did I graduate? Did I enjoy school? Did my parents live close by? Did I see them often? Was I dating the guy I came to the party with? Was it serious?

Those were the questions he'd plied me with throughout the week and then some. It wasn't that I minded talking to him, but I definitely noticed a change in his demeanor. He was treating me differently. I had wondered if it had something to do with Sebastian, although, for the life of me, I couldn't figure out how. I just remembered the look on Mr. Trovato's face when I left his party with Aaron in tow. I hadn't imagined it, I knew that much.

It wasn't like I had seen Sebastian again since then. I hadn't had any reason to go to the Trovato estate and though I had dreamed about him showing up at the office, I didn't see any reason for him to do that either.

Aaron had done his best to keep me preoccupied through the week, showing up at the apartment with dinner each night, sometimes with Mark. He even stayed long enough to watch TV with Chloe and me. I knew that Chloe was curious, but I had managed to blow her off, giving her just enough details to curb her curiosity without revealing what had really happened.

Aaron, bless him, hadn't blabbed either.

Since the day after the party, we hadn't talked about Sebastian. No one. Not me. Not Aaron. Not Chloe. I think Aaron was worried about me, but I could have assured him that he had no reason to. I'd moved on. I don't know what had transpired between the two of us out on the veranda that night, but it was over and done. Thinking about Sebastian wasn't doing me any good.

I shook off the thought of him as I reached for the restaurant's front door when Chloe held it open.

Chloe and I walked inside the sports bar and one of the waitresses immediately greeted us by name, reaching for two menus before walking us to a table in the far corner. I glanced around as I walked, realizing the place was busier than usual. My gaze traveled up to one of the televisions on the wall as I walked.

Ahh... That explained it.

The Dallas Stars were playing the Nashville Predators. Always a good game to watch. I, myself, was a huge hockey fan, something I'd taken to because of my father. When I was younger, we always went to games, mostly to Dallas to see the Stars play because my dad was a diehard fan.

I bumped into Chloe when she stopped, my attention still on the television. Smiling and shrugging, I then waited for her to pick a seat — the woman was anal when it came to which chair she would take at the table. Just one of her many quirks. This time it only took her five seconds to figure it out, which was probably a record for her. I quickly hung my purse on the chair between us, choosing to sit across from her. I retrieved my cell phone before sitting down and facing my friend. Chloe was already perusing the menu, spouting off things that sounded good to her.

No way could I eat that and not gain ten pounds, but my friend, she could eat anything and not gain an ounce. Have I mentioned that I hated her for that?

"What do you think?"

"About?"

"Food, Payton. *Food.* Why do you think we came here?" Chloe asked, her eyes boring holes into me.

"I thought it was for the hot guys." I pretended to be confused.

"Well, there is that." Her gaze migrated slowly around the room.

I didn't bother to look around. I knew what I'd see. The place was a hangout for the younger crowd. Being that Austin was a college town, you didn't have to walk very far before you bumped into at least one college student. Or ten.

The waitress returned with a huge smile on her face. Chloe rattled off her order in rapid succession and I waited my turn. When she was finally finished, I smiled up at the waitress and said, "I'll have a Corona Light with lime and I'll pick off her plate."

Chloe grumbled from across the table.

"Don't worry, I'll pay for half."

"I'm not worried about that," Chloe said softly. "I'm worried about you eating half my food. I'm starving."

"You're always starving."

Chloe grinned, and I knew what she was about to ask before the words even tumbled out of her mouth. The gleam in her green eyes told me everything.

"When are you gonna tell me more about that mechanic you met last week? Was he at the party?"

Yep. That was the question I was hoping to avoid.

I should have known that her silence on the subject matter had been too good to be true. As hush-hush as I'd wanted to be where Sebastian was concerned, I had been drunk when I came home on Friday night. When Aaron brought me inside, I'd resorted to thinking aloud, bitching and moaning about The Mechanic as I liked to refer to him. Chloe had been there. I think she suspected that something had happened the night of the party, but for whatever reason, she had let it go.

Obviously not completely though.

She had brought it up tonight when I got home, but because she had been ready to go out by then, I had used the fact that I needed to change as an excuse. I had again dodged her in the car, encouraging Chloe to tell me about her day and I'd hoped she wouldn't bring it back up. After all, it had been a brief lapse on my part. I should have never mentioned him to her in the first place.

But I should have known that Chloe wouldn't let it go.

"He was hot, and he was a mechanic," I told her, letting her believe that the only time I'd seen him was the first day I met him. I definitely didn't want to tell her about our interaction at the party. "What more is there to say?"

"Uhh… Plenty. You can start by telling me why you don't want to talk about him," she stated, thanking the waitress when she placed the beers on the table.

Ah. So she noticed.

"Nothing to talk about. It's not like I go around talking about people's mechanics."

"Conrad Trovato really has a mechanic that works at his house? How much freaking money does this guy have?" she asked.

I could tell she was humoring me.

"Too much," I answered, going right along with her. If she could fake it, so could I.

But that statement took me back to that day. The day I met the man who had plagued my dreams before I ever met him. The same guy who had haunted my dreams for nights on end ever since. I had thought it strange, when I'd finally given it any thought at all, that Mr. Trovato had a personal mechanic that worked at his house. Even more so when I saw him at the party. He wasn't just a mechanic. I knew that much.

"What did he look like?"

"Hot." I wished she would just let it go.

As it was, I could still picture him in my head, all tall and sexy with the tats and the piercings. Then the image of him in that tux would flutter through my head. All of the tats had been covered that night, but the piercings had been visible. I even found myself daydreaming about what he looked like without his shirt on, something I hadn't had the opportunity to see.

Unfortunately.

Did he have tattoos everywhere?

"I got that part," Chloe said, interrupting my thoughts. "But what did he *look* like?"

"Tall, brown hair, brown eyes," I explained, pretending it was nothing. It was something all right because his eyes still mesmerized me, from my damn dreams. Realizing I was grinning from ear to ear, I added, "But his piercings..."

Don't ask me why I was going along with this. I was getting caught up in the moment and I didn't want to admit that talking about him made me feel better.

"In his face? Oh, God, that's hot."

Yes, it was. "Eyebrow and lip," I told her.

"What about his tongue? Was his tongue pierced?"

"How would I know?" I asked, exasperated. "I didn't get near his mouth."

Not close enough to find out if he had his tongue pierced anyway. I kept that little tidbit of info to myself.

"But you wanted to, huh?" She nudged me in the arm.

Sometimes I thought Chloe acted more like a guy than a girl. Especially when it came to talking about the opposite sex. It could have been the fact that Chloe had four brothers, all of which were just like her. Or maybe she was just like them. I didn't know.

"He was hot. Can we just leave it at that?"

"Do you think you'll go back to Mr. Trovato's house?"

"Why in the world would I do that?"

"Oh, I don't know. Maybe because you need your car serviced?"

"If that's some kind of sexual innuendo, you suck at them."

Chloe was grinning.

The two of us sat there for a moment, our eyes glued to the television. Three minutes into the third period and the Stars were up by two. I didn't really care who won. I wasn't partial to either team like my dad was. It wasn't until the waitress brought our food out that I turned my attention back to Chloe.

It was then that my night took a very interesting turn.

Chapter Sixteen

Payton

"CAN I GET ANOTHER BEER?"

The gruff voice came from behind me. At first, I thought nothing of it considering we were in a sports bar full of men. A lot of men had deep, booming voices.

"Yeah, thanks," the man said.

I immediately stilled, my heart triple timing it in my chest.

That voice.

That raspy tone. It sounded familiar.

That deep baritone… it was…

No freaking way.

An elbow gently bumped my shoulder from behind. I twisted in my chair to see a man sitting directly behind me. The place was packed, and we were crammed into the place like sardines, so it wasn't unusual for someone to bump me.

"Sorry about that." The brief apology caused me to turn around fully, only to come face to face with…

"Sebastian," I whispered at the same time he said, "Angel."

"I'll be damned, Trovato. Did you conjure her up from your thoughts? You're gonna have to teach me how to do that shit."

I was staring into liquid gold eyes, hardly registering what his friend was saying. But then… it clicked.

"*Trovato?*" My stomach rapidly plummeted to my feet. Sebastian *Trovato?*

Oh.

My.

God.

I had to give him credit, he looked a little embarrassed.

"You're not a mechanic," I accused, rage dripping into my blood stream. I knew my face was red, but I couldn't help it.

The devious grin he shot me didn't help.

"Oh, my God! *You're* the hot mechanic?" Chloe exclaimed, leaning over to see around me.

"Not helping, Chloe," I warned, my eyes still locked with Sebastian's.

Although I was angry, I knew the rapid beat of my heart didn't have anything to do with that. No, what had caused my heart rate to accelerate and my blood to fizz in my veins was my visceral reaction to this man. Just as he had every time I saw him — in my dream, the first time we met, at Conrad's party — Sebastian *Trovato* had captivated me.

And damn it all to hell, sitting this close to him wasn't helping.

Trovato.

Damn it.

"Why didn't you tell me who you were?" I probed, still not quite sure who he was. Conrad's nephew, maybe? With the last name of Trovato, he had to be related in some way.

"I did tell you who I was." His voice was rough, belying the amused grin on his perfect lips.

Dang it. He had a tongue ring.

Not that I was fascinated by it or anything. It's just that we were less than a foot apart and it was hard to miss when he spoke.

"You told me you were a mechanic," I stated firmly, my voice softer than before. I hated that we had an audience when I wanted to rage at him for lying to me.

"No, you *assumed* I was a mechanic."

I did not. Okay, maybe I did. Whatever.

"You didn't correct me."

"You didn't care."

No, he was right. It had never *really* mattered to me who he was. When I was in his presence, I was more worried about trying to get my libido in check.

"So did you lie to me? Are you really a mechanic?" I repeated softly, realizing he hadn't answered me moments ago.

"Mechanic." One of the guys sitting at Sebastian's table smirked, laughing as he sipped his beer.

Sebastian glanced over his shoulder at his friends before returning his gaze to mine.

"Leif, Toby, meet Angel. Angel, meet Leif and Toby."

"My name's not Angel," I snapped. I glanced over Sebastian's shoulder and forced a smile. "My name's Payton."

"Nice to meet you, Payton," the two guys said at exactly the same time, the humor dancing in their eyes was a little off-putting, mainly because I wasn't sure what the inside joke was. They were enjoying this.

Too bad I wasn't.

I met Sebastian's gaze for a long second.

"Sorry to interrupt your dinner." I broke the eye contact with Sebastian and looked past him. "Nice to meet you both."

"Feel free to interrupt anytime, Angel." Sebastian's smooth, deep voice flowed over me like silk and damn it if my body didn't light up like someone had doused me in gasoline and lit a match.

I forced my traitorous body to turn back around only to see Chloe staring at the men behind me. In truth, I'd never seen Chloe speechless. I'm not sure if I liked it or not.

"If you're gonna sit there with your mouth open, at least put something in it," I scolded Chloe, pushing the plate of nachos in her direction.

Her eyes met mine and the mischief I saw there made the hair on the back of my neck stand on end. "No. Don't you dare," I whispered, trying to keep my voice calm. "Don't you dare interfere, Chloe. Keep in mind, I need my job."

"What does he have to do with your job?" Chloe leaned in conspiratorially.

"He's obviously related to Mr. Trovato. Which means I can't get involved."

"Says who?" she inquired.

"Says me. Hurry up and eat so we can get out of here." I'd lost my appetite, and the beer suddenly tasted like dirt. I just wanted to get out of there, so I didn't have to think about the fact that the hottest guy I'd ever met was sitting directly behind me, probably laughing about the fact that he'd pulled one over on me. Twice.

"Oh, God," I groaned when I remembered what I'd told Mr. Trovato upon my return to the office that day. No wonder he had looked at me like I'd lost my mind. And again, at the party… When I'd been leaving, Mr. Trovato had caught me looking at Sebastian. I'd seen frustration in his eyes. Did he think…?

"What?" Chloe asked, interrupting my thoughts, her gaze roaming my face. "Spill it."

"Last week, when I went to his house to get his cell phone, I told Mr. Trovato that I hadn't seen his daughter, but I had talked to his mechanic briefly. He must think I'm a nutcase."

"Doubtful," came a voice from behind me.

I fought the urge to turn around and look at him, hoping he didn't notice the way my shoulders tensed when he spoke. His voice was a strange mixture of rough velvet and smooth silk, it pulled me in and I knew... I knew that was the last thing I needed to be worried about.

"So, how're you related to Mr. Trovato?" Chloe asked, speaking loud enough for Sebastian to hear.

I wanted to strangle her.

I felt rather than saw when Sebastian turned in his chair. He was so close, I could feel the warmth of his arm against my back although he wasn't touching me. I did my best not to move away, not wanting to let him know just how affected I was.

How freaking crazy was this? Here I was, twenty-three years old and I was acting like a teenager with a crush.

"Let's just leave it at *related*." Sebastian's grumbling voice sent chills down my spine.

"Are you done yet?" I asked Chloe, doing my best to ignore the man behind me.

Chloe's lips twitched, telling me her answer without words. She was enjoying my suffering, and this was one of those times when I wished I'd brought my own car. Instead, I had let Chloe drive.

For the next fifteen or so minutes, Chloe actually paid attention to her food. Well, sort of. Her eyes kept drifting over my other shoulder and I assumed she was looking at the mammoth of a man that was sitting at Sebastian's table. Leif or Toby. I didn't know who was who.

I wasn't hungry, so I alternated between peeling the label off my beer and staring up at the television. The game was almost over, and I knew when it was, the place would clear out fast.

I wanted to be gone before that happened. I wanted to be far away from here when Sebastian decided to take his leave.

The waitress returned to check on us, and to my relief, Chloe requested the bill. I dug in my purse for cash, wanting to pitch in, but Chloe put her hand on mine. "My treat. It was totally worth it."

I glared at my roommate. "I hate you," I whispered, trying to keep my expression stern.

"Of course you do."

Chapter Seventeen

Payton

BY THE TIME WE WERE walking to Chloe's car, I was geared up to run a marathon. I just wanted to get out of there, fearful that if I didn't do something fast, I would turn right around and march back inside just to see Sebastian's handsomely smug face one last time.

I was infuriated with him. He had lied to me, convinced me that he was Mr. Trovato's mechanic.

Kind of.

The ass had told me he was a mechanic, which I guess didn't necessarily mean he worked for Conrad. But still. He had even confirmed it at the party. But what really burned me was the simple fact that his last name was Trovato, regardless of the relation to my boss, which meant he could have easily gone inside that ginormous mansion and retrieved Conrad's cell phone. But noooo… I had to go back to the office and look like an idiot when I explained that I'd had a conversation with the mechanic because Aaliyah had already left.

And then at the party… What had happened between us outside, the way my body responded to him, desperate to get closer…

But he was off limits! Off freaking limits because he was related to my boss.

Ugghh!

I wasn't sure whether I was more upset that he had lied to me or that he was off limits.

And that only pissed me off more.

"Hey, princess!" someone yelled from across the parking lot.

Don't ask me why I turned and looked. I was certainly not a princess, nor was I an angel.

It had been that damn smoky voice that had me searching the shadows for Sebastian. I caught sight of him coming toward us, while Leif and Toby (I still didn't know who was who) headed in the opposite direction.

"Hold up!" Sebastian called out as I opened the passenger side door of Chloe's car.

To my absolute horror, Sebastian walked right up to Chloe and asked to speak to her for a minute. I was seething, a red haze disrupting my vision as I watched Sebastian talk to my roommate, both of them smiling and even laughing.

What the hell? Why would he pick *her*?

I stomped my foot, unable to control myself.

Sure, Chloe was pretty. If you liked teeny tiny, green eyed, leggy brunettes. Yes, if that was your preference, she was pretty.

But I wasn't a slouch, thank you very much.

The thought had me glancing down at my outfit.

Well…

I kind of was a slouch right then.

After wearing heels for most of the day, I'd stripped right out of the skirt and, yes, another coffee-stained shirt and changed into jeans and a long sleeved, black T-shirt. It was clean. Wrinkled a little, maybe, but still clean.

I touched my hair.

It was still pulled back in a ponytail, which meant I probably looked like I was in high school. The sports bar we'd just left was perhaps the only establishment that didn't card me and that was only because I'd been coming in every week for the last few months.

But still…

"You're a doll," Sebastian told Chloe and I was ready to scream.

But then, my voice was stuck in my throat when Sebastian made his way around the car and strolled right up to me, his eyes serious. Where had all of his amusement gone?

"Let me take you home," he said softly.

"What?" I exclaimed. "No way. I don't even know you."

He merely cocked an eyebrow — the pierced one — and I got the feeling that he was used to women just giving it up to him for his crooked smile.

Not me.

No way.

"You know me well enough," he whispered.

I glanced over at Chloe and that jealousy I was feeling a moment before returned. If I didn't let him drive me home, would he offer to drive Chloe home? Would she accept?

Son of a…

"Come on, Payton. What d'ya say? We'll stop and get ice cream."

"Ice cream?" Was he serious? Ice cream. Did people really do that?

"You got something against ice cream?" Sebastian asked.

"No. I do *not* have anything against ice cream." I turned toward him, studying his face for probably longer than was appropriate. But it was the only thing I could do when I was practically sandwiched between him and the car door at my back. "What I have a problem with is leaving with you. I don't *know* you."

I knew he understood what I was telling him. He had lied to me. Whether it was by omission or not, he had let me believe something that wasn't entirely accurate.

Sebastian stared at me. He looked like he was waging a war inside his head. Did he want to tell me something?

No. He probably just wanted to blow me off, figuring I wasn't going to be a sure thing.

I was *not* going to be a sure thing.

Little did he know but I hadn't had sex in like two years, and before that, it had only been with one person. With my college boyfriend, Paul. Even then, I'm not sure that could be considered sex. Paul seemed just as inadequate as I had been for the six months that we dated.

I certainly didn't consider myself experienced in that department.

At this point, I'm not even sure that I knew how it was supposed to work. Sex, that is.

"I promise." His hand came up, the backs of his fingers brushed my arm. "I just wanna talk."

Talk.

I didn't mind talking. Maybe then he could explain just who the heck he was.

I considered it for a moment before looking back at Chloe one last time. She nodded and grinned.

"Fine," I said decisively. "We can talk."

His smile widened, and I was momentarily fascinated by his lip ring.

"But only if you tell me who you are and why you lied to me."

Sebastian laughed, the sound even sexier than when he spoke. He nodded his head to Chloe. "I'll have her home in an hour. Promise."

"Okay. I'll be waiting for her," Chloe answered, looking somber for a moment.

Sebastian surprised the crap out of me when he took my hand and linked his fingers with mine. I nearly stumbled over my own feet as I stared down at our joined hands.

I hadn't held anyone's hand in … well, probably not since high school. If even then.

But the feel of Sebastian's work-roughened fingers against mine wasn't the only surprise of the night. I nearly swallowed my tongue when he stopped at the black-as-night sports car that I'd seen in the parking lot earlier.

"Is that a…?" For the life of me, I couldn't even think of the name of the car.

"A Camaro. Yeah." Sebastian chuckled as he opened the passenger side door and waited for me to climb in.

Right. A Camaro.

Oh, crap. New car smell.

After he climbed in and started the engine, I peered over at him and asked, "Is this yours?"

"Maybe." That slow smirk tilted his lips and I wanted to reach over and touch his mouth.

With mine.

Shaking off the thought, I turned and looked out the windshield. "You mentioned ice cream," I said blandly, hoping he couldn't see the lust that was likely causing smoke to seep out of my ears.

"Yes, ma'am." With that, Sebastian put the car in gear.

At that point, I held on for dear life.

Chapter Eighteen

Payton

IT WAS A GOOD THING Sebastian chose an ice cream shop just a few miles away. If I'd had to spend any more time in that car with him, I might have had a nervous breakdown.

I was pretty sure he didn't even know that speed limits existed.

The only positive was that he handled the car like a professional. It was both disturbing and strangely exciting. Watching him shift gears, admiring his big hands ... Yeah, needless to say, I needed a cold shower more than I needed ice cream.

Luckily, Sebastian came around to open my door because, for the life of me, I couldn't figure out how to open it on my own after fumbling in the dark for a moment. From that point on, I didn't say anything until the cute girl behind the counter asked what ice cream we wanted. I was surprised that she heard me, considering she was batting her eyelashes and ogling Sebastian the entire time she was working.

Sebastian hovered close behind me while she prepared our ice cream. When she was finished, he paid and then took my hand again. I was still trying to get used to the idea of holding his hand. It was oddly settling. I felt almost ... cherished. Protected.

"Let's eat outside," he said, carrying both paper bowls of ice cream.

I glanced around the inside, noticing there were three perfectly good tables available, but there was also a family sitting at one table with two little kids playing tag around a chair. Did he not like kids?

I didn't ask him because we were on the move once again and I was simply trying to remember how to walk, much less talk and walk at the same time.

"I take it you're close to Toby and Leif," I commented once we were seated at a small metal table in front of the little shop. A worn red umbrella hovering over the table flapped in the cool night breeze.

"I've known Leif since I was fourteen. Met Toby in high school."

"Do they live with you?" I didn't even know where Sebastian lived, so it was a logical question.

"Nope. At least not yet. Leif's looking for a place. We've talked about him renting a room from me."

"Do you live in a house or apartment?" I didn't mean to ply him with so many questions, but I couldn't help myself. I wanted to know everything there was to know about him. It probably would have been awkward if I'd just sat there and stared at him, too.

"House," Sebastian answered, his tone changing. I wondered if that was a sore subject. Seemed strange that he wouldn't want to talk about where he lived, but I took the hint.

"What about you? House or apartment?"

"Apartment. I live with Chloe." For some reason, I didn't want to mention that I lived with Aaron as well, which I knew wasn't completely honest. Aaron was my roommate, my best friend, but he was still a guy. Gay or not, I wasn't sure how Sebastian would take the fact that I did live with a guy, so I kept my mouth shut.

A couple of families made their way into the ice cream shop and I busied myself by watching the little kids run around in circles. Sebastian seemed to be intently studying me, and I fought the urge to squirm under his penetrating gaze.

"Why'd you let me believe you were Mr. Trovato's mechanic?" I asked bluntly, when it was clear Sebastian wasn't going to restart the conversation.

"Why'd you assume I was?"

I stared blankly at him, my spoon halfway to my mouth. "Because you were covered in grease?"

"If I'd been covered in flour would you've thought I was the cook?"

"No." My answer came just a little too quickly.

Damn it. He was right. I'd made the assumption all on my own.

"See my point yet?" Sebastian's glowing eyes locked with mine.

"Fine." I shoved the little pink plastic spoon in my mouth, accepting that he was right. The rich chocolate flavor burst on my tongue, but the only thing I could think about was how much better it would be if I could cover Sebastian in it and then lick it off.

"Quit picturing me naked," he said smoothly, arrogantly.

I narrowed my eyes at him. "In your dreams."

"That's what I'm worried about," he mumbled almost too softly to hear before spooning vanilla ice cream into his mouth.

His ice cream caught my eye and I glanced back and forth between his and mine. Chocolate and vanilla. Total opposites. Why did I have the feeling that our choice in ice cream probably wasn't the only thing different between us?

I didn't know him. Other than the way he looked, that he lived in a house not an apartment, and that he went out tonight with two guys he'd known for a long time anyway. I knew he worked for Conrad Trovato. In what capacity, I wasn't sure. I knew his last name was Trovato, which could only mean he was related to Conrad in some way. I mean seriously, Trovato wasn't a common name, so what were the odds?

I scraped my ice cream with my spoon as I met his gaze again. "Do you work for Mr. Trovato?"

"You could say that," he mumbled.

"What do you do for him?" I asked, curious.

"A little of this, a little of that."

My anger reignited, and I stabbed my ice cream with my spoon. "Would you mind taking me home?" I was suddenly too frustrated to sit there with him. He'd been relatively forthcoming with my questions earlier, but they'd been significantly less personal. Seemed that when I wanted to dig deeper, he just wanted to close himself off.

I didn't want to play that game with him.

His eyes widened, the golden orbs drawing me in yet again. "Why?"

"I clearly misunderstood your reason for wanting to get ice cream. I thought we were here to talk, yet you won't give me a straight answer to any of my questions."

"Not true," he countered. "I answered you."

"Yeah," I huffed. "You told me that you live in a house. You didn't elaborate, didn't share anything more than that. And now that I want to know something more personal, you just clam up."

Sebastian didn't say anything, he turned his attention back to his ice cream, avoiding looking at me altogether.

I sighed.

"Since I'm not interested in anything else from you, aside from maybe some friendly conversation, I think it's safe to say we're done here."

I got to my feet, looking down at him.

He slowly rose from his seat and I kept my eyes locked with his until I had to look up at him.

"Look." Sebastian took my hand, watching me as though he thought I was going to run.

What was it with this guy and holding my hand? It wasn't that it didn't feel good, I was quite fond of the way he touched me, the spark that sizzled along my skin from the connection, but it disarmed me at the same time. And I had a feeling that I needed as much armor as possible when it came to Sebastian Trovato.

His thumb brushed over my knuckles a couple of times before he spoke. The sweet touch made my knees *and* my anger weaken.

"You're right," he finally said, closing his eyes briefly. "I'll take you home."

Leaving the ice cream to melt on the table, Sebastian motioned toward the car and then followed me without saying another word.

The most awkward car ride ensued, the only words spoken between us were when I had to give him directions on how to get to my apartment.

I was trying to figure out what to say, if anything, when Sebastian stopped in front of my building. I peeked over at him to find him staring down at his hand on the gear shift.

"Uhh…" I knew I at least needed to say thank you. That was the polite thing to do, right?

"Where's your boyfriend?" His words were spoken so softly, they were hard to make out.

"What?" I was confused.

He looked up, meeting my gaze in the darkness. "The guy you were with at the party. Your boyfriend. Why aren't you with him tonight?"

Oh, crap. I'd let him believe that Aaron was my boyfriend.

I looked away quickly, choosing to stare out the windshield while I tried to gather my thoughts.

"He's not your boyfriend, is he?" Sebastian questioned.

"No," I admitted, hating the fact that he'd caught me in a lie. Aaron had been my excuse, the only logical excuse I had to stay far, far away from Sebastian.

"Then who is he?"

I closed my eyes, trying to come up with an answer that wouldn't make me sound like I had lied to him or led him to believe something that wasn't true. The way he had done to me.

Before I could get the words out, Sebastian surprised me by reaching over and sliding his hand behind my neck, pulling me to him. One minute he was sitting still, the next he was pulling me toward him, his mouth meeting mine. He wasn't rough, but he wasn't gentle either. And when our lips touched, all of my air escaped in a pathetic little sigh.

His tongue slid over my bottom lip before coaxing its way into my mouth. I reached for him, unable to resist the opportunity to touch him. His shoulders were hard, the muscles tense beneath the navy T-shirt he wore. The short hair on the back of his head sensually scraped against my palm as my tongue slid against his. To my utter embarrassment, I moaned. And that only spurred Sebastian on. He pulled me closer, our lips crushed together as he devoured me. That was the only description for what was happening between us.

And holy crap! It was a good thing I was sitting down because my legs had turned to jelly, my entire body quaking from the intensity of his kiss.

I slid my hands higher, pulling his hair gently, sinking my fingers into the longer locks on the top. Oh, God. What was I doing?

I knew absolutely nothing about this man other than he was a shitty conversationalist and the world's greatest kisser and though my brain was screaming for me to pull away, to jump out of the car and run far and fast, I couldn't do it. I was scared if he kept kissing me, I was going to figure out a way to climb his body and that would be a devastation that I'd never survive.

But then he was pulling away, nibbling at my lips briefly before his eyes met mine. His hand was still cupping my nape, his thumb rasping over my cheek. We were both breathless, and I still wasn't trying to get away from him.

"So, no boyfriend?"

I shook my head.

"Then we're even."

I knew what he was referring to. He had led me to believe he was Conrad's mechanic, and I had led him to believe Aaron was my boyfriend. So, yes, we were even.

"Let me see you again, Angel," Sebastian whispered, resting his forehead against mine. "I…" He paused, his eyes still peering into mine. "I just need to see you again."

"Why?" I asked, wanting to know.

It was clear he didn't want to tell me anything about himself, and I'd been honest when I said that was what I wanted from him. I was quite capable of controlling my own hormones, although you might not be able to tell it by the way I'd kissed him as though my life depended on it.

"I can't explain it."

I couldn't either. And none of it made sense.

I'd met guys like Sebastian. They were the bad boys that good girls like me stayed away from, the ones that were looking for fast and dirty sex — something I was pretty sure I couldn't even offer, thank you very much.

With every intention of telling him that we'd be better off just moving along, I was shocked to the roots of my hair when I whispered, "Why don't I give you my phone number and we'll see how it goes?"

Sebastian pulled away and I immediately missed the warmth of his hand on my neck. "Let me see your phone," he stated gently, his eyes never leaving mine.

I grabbed my phone from my purse and handed it to him as though there wasn't anything weird about giving it to a complete stranger.

He's not too much of a stranger, you know what his lips feel like.

I ignored that little voice in my head while I watched him dial a number. A second later, his cell phone rang. He hung up and then did the opposite, calling my phone from his number.

"Done."

Yes, I guess we were. "Okay, then." I twisted in my seat, ready to reach for the door handle.

Once again, Sebastian caught me off guard when he reached for me. This time his lips brushed mine ever so gently and I breathed him in. He smelled good. Something spicy and rich and I wanted to inhale him until the scent was embedded in my brain.

"I need to see you again," he whispered against my lips, and this time, I heard the desperation in his tone. Or was that just lust?

It was strange. It didn't sound like he was trying to push me to invite him in, but that he truly wanted to see me again in the future. And as upset as I was at him for duping me earlier in the day, I couldn't lie and say that I didn't want the same thing.

Rather than drag it out any longer, I leaned in and pressed my mouth to his, feeling the metal of his lip ring against my bottom lip. Unable to resist, I slid my tongue over the cool metal, but I didn't linger past that. I nodded my head and then reached for the door handle, finding it instantly although I hadn't even seen it earlier.

Without another word, I climbed out and closed the door, glancing back one more time as I made my way up the stairs. Sebastian's car remained in the parking lot until I entered my apartment.

Once inside, I quickly closed and locked the door behind me. As I listened until the throaty rumble of the car's engine disappeared into the night, I closed my eyes and leaned against the front door, wondering just what I was supposed to do now.

Chapter Nineteen

Payton

BY NOON THE FOLLOWING DAY, I was counting down the seconds until I could go home. Conrad had taken the day off, but I still had to remain in the office to field his phone calls and work on the logistics for an upcoming trip he was taking to Las Vegas. Apparently the SEMA show was as big a deal for Trovato, Inc. as it was for my father and his little body shop. Then again, they were both in the automotive industry, so it made sense. With the trip coming up next week, I had to finalize the details. Thankfully, Jasmine had scheduled everything months ago, so I was just confirming that it was all still in order.

I was pretty sure the universe was out to get me because, from the time I arrived at eight, coming in later because Mr. Trovato wasn't going to be in the office, the phone rang all of seven times. Two of those had been solicitors that I had politely asked not to call back. I had learned already that when Mr. Trovato was out of the office, no one generally came to see him, which was no different today. I was sitting on the second floor by myself, willing the phone to ring so I'd at least have someone to talk to for a few minutes.

The rest of the time I was thinking about Sebastian and the kiss we'd shared the night before. I couldn't stop replaying his words over and over in my head. *I need to see you again.* It hadn't slipped past me that he'd used the word *need* rather than *want.* And when he said it, that was exactly how it made me feel. As though it was critical that we didn't let this end before it ever got started.

The universe must have heard me moaning and groaning because the phone on my desk rang. I eagerly reached for it, answering with "Trovato, Inc. Conrad Trovato's office. How may I help you?"

"Payton."

I instantly sat up straight when I heard my boss's voice on the phone. I hadn't expected him to call, and a million things ran through my mind. Was he upset? Did I do something wrong? Was he going to fire me on the phone?

Don't ask me why I got so antsy, I just did.

"Yes, sir?" I replied, holding my breath.

"You're working on the trip to Vegas next week, right?"

"Yes, sir."

"Good. I need you to plan to go with me."

Oh, no. Please no. I did not want to travel. It just wasn't my thing.

Not that I could tell Conrad that. My job was to assist him and, technically, if he needed me to go along on a business trip with him, I wasn't supposed to argue. "Okay," I answered hesitantly.

"My wife and daughter will be coming along. Book yourself a hotel room. Make sure you're in the same hotel that we are."

"Yes, sir." It seemed those were the only two words that still existed in my vocabulary.

"Thanks, Payton. I'll see you Monday morning."

"Yes, sir."

There was a click, signaling that Conrad had hung up, so I dropped the receiver in the cradle and stared at my computer screen.

Las Vegas.

I'd never been to Las Vegas.

I wasn't sure I wanted to go to Las Vegas.

Knowing that fretting about it wasn't going to get me anywhere, I typed in the web address for the hotel where Mr. Trovato was staying. After attempting to locate a room using their online tool, I came up empty. No rooms were available for that time frame. I figured it had to do with the show.

Maybe that was how I could get out of it. If they didn't have a room, I wouldn't have to go.

Knowing that Conrad would expect me to call them directly, I grabbed the receiver and dialed the number that Jasmine had noted with the reservation.

Twenty minutes later I wasn't feeling any better. The kind woman on the other end of the phone had only been too happy to help me, instantly getting an additional room for Mr. Trovato. Apparently, he was a VIP and the lady had been quite enamored when I mentioned his name.

Crap.

So much for lucking out on that one.

Once that was done, I took care of the flight, encountering another very helpful employee at the airline who ensured me they had an additional seat in first class, on the same flight Mr. Trovato and his family would be on.

Great.

I had just finished taking care of everything, printing out my itinerary for the trip and urging my stomach to stop churning. I knew that being an administrative assistant wasn't just going to consist of me sitting in the office and answering Conrad's phones, but I had truly hoped that I wouldn't have to travel with the man. Sure, it helped that Aaliyah was going. I liked her. I figured we'd get along well, but still.

My cell phone chirped from inside my desk drawer while I was still staring blankly at the computer screen.

Without a second of hesitation, I snatched it, hitting the button to bring the screen to life. The words I saw there made all of my previous worries disappear instantly.

Dinner with me tonight.

That's all the text said, but I knew who the number belonged to because last night, after I'd managed to get my heart rate back under control, I had added Sebastian's number to my contact list, not wanting to accidentally delete it.

Who is this?

I sent a text back, smiling as I did.

Your mechanic

Now, if I said my heart didn't skip a beat, I'd be lying.

Mine. He was *mine?*

My fingers were shaking, my nerves in an uproar as I typed a message back.

I'm not sure I need my car serviced at the moment but thank you anyway.

The response didn't come quickly, and I was starting to think Sebastian had taken me seriously. I was still staring at my phone a minute later when the next message finally came in.

That's good cuz I wanted to take you to dinner, not service your ... um ... car

I felt the heat rise to my face. He'd effectively embarrassed me, and I was grateful that he couldn't see me right then. Caving, I shot a quick message back. *When?*

"Right now."

I fell out of my chair.

Yep, without an ounce of grace, I fell right out. Of. My. Chair.

I would have been embarrassed, except the shock to my heart was so powerful, I was gasping for breath and holding my hand against my chest, trying to keep the damn organ from jumping up through my throat.

"You scared me," I declared, pushing to my feet before Sebastian could help me. He was faster than I was, his strong hands gripping my arms when I stood. "How'd you get up here?" I peeked around him, fully expecting Ron to come up the stairs ready to shoot to kill.

"I'm persuasive like that," Sebastian answered. "Are you okay?"

Okay? Was I okay? No, I was not. I was embarrassed and happy to see him all at the same time. "I'm fine. Just call me grace," I mumbled, looking down at the floor.

The silence was stifling until Sebastian used his finger to tip my chin up, forcing me to look at him. "Are you ready?"

No, I wasn't sure I'd ever be ready for anything this man had to offer me.

I didn't tell him that though. I simply nodded before I could think better of it.

It took me a minute to shut down my laptop and place it in the bag, but once I did, Sebastian retrieved it from my desk and put it on his arm. His big, bulging, muscular arm. The one decorated with tattoos.

I still wanted to know how he'd slipped past the security guard.

Maybe it was his last name.

"Time's wasting." His silky voice sent a shiver racing through me.

I nodded, not sure what else to do. Tossing my cell phone in my purse, I hauled it onto my shoulder and glanced back at my desk one last time.

It was only four, and I had no idea whether or not Mr. Trovato would be angry that I left early, but my boredom was going to have me running out the door screaming if I didn't go now anyway.

There was no hand holding as I followed Sebastian out of the building. I looked around to see if I could find the Camaro he'd been driving the day before. I saw a multitude of cars, but none of them was his sleek black car.

"Where'd you park?" he asked as he stepped off the curb in front of the building.

"Me?" Wow, that sounded stupid. "I thought you were taking *me* out."

"I am."

"Then why are we taking my car?"

"Who said we were?"

I glared at Sebastian. The man was infuriating and way too cryptic.

That's when he took my hand and his simple touch jolted me instantly. He could have said we were walking and I wouldn't have argued with him at that point.

Chapter Twenty

Sebastian

I KNEW I WAS TAKING a chance when I showed up at my father's office to see Payton unannounced. After last night, anything I did where Payton was concerned was a risk, but I couldn't help myself. The minute I learned that Conrad and his wife had gone out of town, I knew what I had to do.

Waiting until four o'clock had been the kicker. I'd spent the day screwing with my truck until finally I got the damn thing running the way it should. How I managed that, I still had no idea. My thoughts had been on Payton since I pulled out of her apartment complex the night before. Even then, I knew that staying away from her was going to be impossible, but I hadn't wanted to look too desperate.

Whatever it was about her, I needed more. And need was a strong word, but I was drawn to her in a way I'd never been drawn to anyone the way I was to Payton, let alone a woman. Since I didn't know her all that well, I wasn't quite sure what the allure was, but I'd be damned if I wasn't going to try and find out.

When we reached her Mustang, I waited for her to unlock the door. I slipped her computer bag inside and then put my hands on her hips before she could disappear inside the car, too. "What are you hungry for?" I asked, trying to keep from touching her too much.

I didn't know Payton well enough to be touching her period, but I felt a connection to her. Maybe it sounded fucked up, but it was as though she and I had been destined to meet. Despite my ability to frustrate her to no end with my lack of conversational skills, I wanted her to like me. I wanted her to want me.

I wanted her to *need* me.

After spending just a few minutes in her presence, the woman unhinged me. Even as fucked up as I was, it didn't matter. I swore to do whatever it took to make her want me.

"Pizza," she said quickly, her eyes roaming my face.

I smiled down at her, admiring the intriguing color of her eyes. Last night I noticed they were an unusual shade of yellow-green. Today they were just green. It probably had a lot to do with the emerald green sweater she wore, the one that outlined every luscious curve.

Pulling my eyes away from said curves, I met her gaze. "Pizza?" I was a little surprised by her selection.

"You got something against pizza?" She used the same phrase I'd used on her the night before, her smile radiant as she rested her palms on my chest. Seeing her look so happy made me want to do whatever was necessary to ensure that smile stayed in place.

"Pizza works." Hell, I'd eat dirt if it meant I got to have dinner with her. "I'll meet you at your apartment."

"Do I have time to change?"

"If you want. I happen to think you look good enough to eat," I told her, glancing back down at her breasts before slowly sliding my gaze up to hers once again.

The pink that infused her cheeks made me feel invincible, like I could conquer the world. The idea of her feeling a little off-kilter was empowering, something I hadn't felt before.

"Okay." Her eyes darted away from mine quickly. "But you'll have to let me go if you expect me to drive home."

I didn't want to let her go, I wanted to feel the warmth of her skin beneath my palms, but I knew she was right. I nodded, releasing my grip on her hips and taking a step back. Her hands fell from my chest and I wanted to grab hold of them and plant them there again just so she didn't stop touching me.

Moving out of the way, I stood by patiently until she climbed into her car and closed the door. Resting my hand on the roof, I waited until she started the engine before backing up. And it wasn't until her car pulled out of the parking lot that I started walking to my truck.

I glanced up at the building, wondering just what my father was going to say when he found out I was dating his assistant. He had already warned me to stay away from her. Not that I ever intended to listen.

I had a sneaking suspicion that I was pushing too hard this time. But I didn't give a shit.

Conrad and I didn't see eye to eye on many things. He hated my piercings, cringed when he caught a glimpse of my tattoos, and he detested my choice in music. But Conrad Trovato loved money more than he loved anything, so he managed to overlook much of what I did, only because I was the one who'd put his fucking company on the map.

Performance engines were my specialty. I had taken a personal interest in Trovato, Inc. as soon as I found out that my father owned it. I made it my mission to show him that he wasn't all that. I'd proven myself by doing what his best engineers couldn't do. And I didn't have to sit behind a desk every day to do it. That was the best part.

I pulled out onto the street when there was a break in traffic and I slammed my foot on the gas, the truck took off, the engine growling. I smiled to myself at the thought of all those people in that building who still had no idea who I was. There were only a handful of people who knew that I was Conrad Trovato's son. A very limited few. And I wouldn't be surprised if those people had been threatened within an inch of their lives if they disclosed what they knew.

I certainly wasn't going to be the one to break the news to anyone.

Well, except for Payton.

I knew I had to tell her. If I expected this to go anywhere at all, I had to tell her all about myself.

I only hoped she didn't freak. That was one of the reasons I was trying to hold off until I could make an impression on her... a good impression. I wanted her to think about me the way I had thought about her for the last week. And then I'd tell her all of the tragic details of my life.

Pulling up in front of her apartment building, I didn't bother pulling into a parking space. I probably should have done the gentlemanly thing and gone to her door, but I couldn't. I feared that if she let me in, ordering pizza would be the extent of dinner because if we had just a little privacy, I wasn't going to be able to keep my hands off her.

And that wasn't going to go over well with Payton. Not on a first date, for sure.

My attention was drawn to the stairs when I noticed her coming toward me. She'd changed into a pair of faded jeans and a T-shirt, just a little more casual than what she'd worn to work.

I decided right then and there that those jeans were now my favorite. Even from this distance, I could see that there was a hole in the thigh and I got a glimpse of golden skin beneath. I would have preferred she put on a skirt, so I could get an eyeful of her incredible legs, but this would work, too.

"Nice truck," she complimented when she climbed in. "What year is it?"

"'63."

"Did you restore it yourself?"

"I did."

Just like the Camaro, I'd dumped a lot of money into the truck. New interior, new cherry-red paint job. It cost a pretty penny. But what was under the hood said it all.

"Nice job," she said approvingly.

"Thanks. So pizza, huh?"

After searching the seat around her, Payton peered up at me from the other side of the cab, her eyebrows raised in question.

"What?"

"Seatbelts?"

I chuckled. "Sorry, this one didn't come with seatbelts. But you don't need 'em if you come sit by me."

"I don't need one? I do remember how you drove last night, you know."

"I'd been showing off then," I lied. I hadn't been showing off. That was how I drove. Speed was the name of the game. I was an adrenaline junkie, there was no doubt about it, which was why the license plate on the Camaro read *BLUR* and the main reason I had roll bars installed in it. The truck, however, did not have roll bars. "I'll be more careful this time."

I patted the seat and watched her.

I noticed the instant she decided to give in. She scooted toward me and I kept my hand on the shifter on the steering column. Three on the tree in the middle of downtown Austin meant my hand would be otherwise occupied, unfortunately, but having her beside me was enough.

Thirty minutes later, I pulled into a small pizza place downtown. Traffic was a bitch, especially since they were preparing to close Sixth Street off to through traffic for the night, but I managed to make my way to a parking garage close by.

"You don't mind walking, do you?" I asked, after we had parked.

"If I said I did?" Payton retorted, a glowing grin on her face.

I couldn't resist the urge to kiss her. It was overwhelming with its intensity, so I leaned over and pressed my mouth to hers. The soft purr that escaped her had my body hardening instantly.

Shit.

Starting the night off with a hard-on wasn't going to go over well, but that's just what happened. My body responded to her, the taste of her lips, the light floral fragrance of her hair... I couldn't get enough.

Pulling back before I took things too far, I placed both hands on the steering wheel and stared out the windshield, taking deep breaths.

"You okay?" I could hear the amusement in her tone.

"Never better," I whispered, rather impressed that my voice worked at all. Inhaling sharply, I gripped the door handle before glancing over at her. "Come on. Let's eat."

The walk to the pizza joint took us fifteen minutes, but Payton spent most of the time talking about the bars, tattoo parlors, and stores that lined the main drag. I'd taken her hand as soon as she climbed out of the truck and hadn't let go. I didn't intend to let go. Not until I needed to use that hand to eat, and I was even debating that.

When we reached the pizza place, I pulled open the door and a bell rang overhead, announcing our presence. The short, heavy set man with thick black hair and a wide grin glanced up and smiled from behind the register.

"Trovato!" he greeted, making his way out from behind the register. "How the hell ya been?"

Payton was staring at me like I had two heads coming off my shoulders, but I just clutched her hand as Rocco approached. I didn't let her go even when Rocco insisted on throwing his burly arms around me and squeezing, jarring my teeth with numerous slaps on my back.

"Rocco, this is Payton. Payton, this is Rocco. He's an old friend."

Payton smiled and held out her hand, but just as I expected, Rocco reached for her, thankfully not slapping her on the back but hugging her hard enough for her to let out a startled squeak.

"Be easy, Rocco," I warned playfully.

"No, it's fine," Payton said, sounding a little breathless.

"What can I get you kids?" Rocco asked as he turned back toward the counter.

We fell into step behind him and I looked at Payton for suggestions.

"Pepperoni."

"My kinda girl," I teased, turning my attention to Rocco.

A few minutes later we were seated at one of the booths with the red and white checkered table cloths. Rocco brought two beers in clear plastic cups before disappearing into the back.

The restaurant was surprisingly empty, but I knew that would change. It was Friday night and the college campus wasn't far. Pretty soon, the place would be full of people laughing and joking, grabbing a bite to eat before a night on the town.

"How do you know him?" Payton asked when we were alone.

"He was friends with my mom," I told her, realizing instantly what I'd just said.

"*Was?*"

I stared at Payton for a moment. Honest to God, I wanted to tell this girl anything she wanted to know, but I didn't want to start the date off like that. But I couldn't leave her hanging. "How about this," I started, reaching for her hand quickly. I brushed my thumb over her knuckles. "I'll tell you all the personal details you want to know, but... Wait, let me finish."

Payton huffed, making me smile.

"I'll bare my soul to you, but let's wait until the second date. Tonight's about having fun. Deal?"

Payton didn't look at all good with the suggestion, but she finally agreed. "Fine." Her frown turned into a mischievous grin and I knew I wasn't going to like what came next. "Under one condition."

"Hit me."

"No more kissing until you answer my questions."

The woman drove a hard bargain, I'd give her that. "No promises, Angel," I told her, keeping my voice low. "As much as I'd like to say I was good with that, I'd be lying through my teeth."

Payton looked a little shocked by my honesty. She was also momentarily speechless, but just as I expected, that didn't last long.

"So what's a safe subject?" she asked just as Rocco was bringing the pizza out to the table. He handed us paper plates and napkins before leaving us alone again.

"You," I suggested. "Tell me about you."

"What do you want to know?" she asked, reaching for a slice of pizza.

I loved the fact that she didn't pretend to be a bird, didn't act as though one bite of pizza would require her to spend two months at the gym. No, not Payton. She grabbed a slice and took a bite before I could even come up with a question.

"What are you smiling at?" Payton was studying me as she reached for a napkin and then wiped the sauce from her lips.

"You," I admitted truthfully.

"Well, quit."

Not a chance in hell. There hadn't been a damn thing in my life to smile at for as long as I could remember, but now, with Payton, I wasn't sure I would ever stop smiling.

"Are you from Austin?" I asked after snatching a slice of pizza.

"Yep. Born and raised," she admitted. "My parents are from here, too."

"They still married?"

"Yeah. My dad owns a body shop and my mother's a CPA."

"Brothers or sisters?" I asked between bites.

"Nope. Only child."

"Did your dad restore your Mustang?"

"He helped. He owns a body shop, so it was a project they all undertook for a while. It was a gift for my eighteenth birthday."

"Not a fan of the Mustang?"

"It's fine. I just wish it was a little more ... modern."

"But it's a classic."

"That it is. And by classic, I think you mean old."

"Not quite what I meant, but okay, I get your point." Laughing, I consumed my pizza, watching Payton do the same. Was it strange that I found the way she ate pizza incredibly sexy?

While Payton stopped at one slice, I had four. By the time we finished, the place was filled to capacity. I had to wrap my arm around her — certainly not a hardship — just so we could make it to the door.

Once outside, the scent of gasoline and fall assaulted me.

"Where to now?" Payton asked as we strolled down Sixth Street once again.

"It's your night. You tell me."

"Why is it my night?" She peered up at me as she spoke.

I just wanted to push her against the building and ravage her mouth until neither of us knew what day it was.

But I didn't.

I was trying to control myself. That's what you did on a first date, right? Especially if you wanted the first date to lead to another. And then another.

"Because it is," I told her. "Want to stop in one of the bars?"

"Sure. You pick though. I'm not good at that."

"Picking bars?"

"Picking anything." Payton's smile was beautiful. So damn beautiful.

As we walked down the street, I pointed to one of the tattoo shops. "That's where I got most of my work done."

"Really?" Payton stopped suddenly, looking up at me. "How much art do you have?"

"Not much more than what you see," I told her. My arms and my shoulders were the main areas I'd focused on. I had a cross on my back, between my shoulder blades.

"Do they have meaning behind them?" she asked, still not moving.

"Some do. Some don't. There for a while, I just did it to piss off..." I stopped myself immediately, realizing that I was headed down a conversational dead end.

"Off limits tonight, huh?" She obviously understood why I stopped.

"Just tonight," I explained, squeezing her hand.

"Okay." Payton's eyes slid down to my mouth.

I could feel the heat in her gaze and I desperately wanted to kiss her. It didn't matter that we were standing in the middle of a crowded sidewalk on one of the busiest streets in downtown Austin for a Friday night. I couldn't promise her that I wouldn't kiss her for the rest of the night, but I did remember her stipulation. For now, I was going to do my damnedest to give her what she asked for.

"Come on. Let's see how much trouble we can get in." I forced a smile, my brain working overtime on how I was supposed to not kiss her. The temptation was just too great.

After all, the night was still young.

Chapter Twenty-One

Payton

THE FOLLOWING MORNING, I FOUND myself lying in my bed, unable to get up.

Although it was November, and the temperature at night hovered somewhere in the low fifties, it still managed to get cold in the apartment thanks to the crappy insulation. No one seemed to have a problem with the colder temperatures except me. Chloe liked the cold and Aaron hadn't been home enough for it to matter to him. And since Chloe was anal when it came to controlling the thermostat, the heater obviously wasn't on, which was why I was snuggled beneath the down comforter on my bed, staring around my room. I was freezing.

Chloe was the reason I was awake. She was the reason I was usually up early every Saturday morning, in fact. The woman was up with the sun, another one of her many quirks. And on Saturday mornings, she always got up and made blueberry pancakes while singing in the kitchen.

It sounded worse than it was.

The woman could sing. I mean she could belt out a tune like nobody's business. It was incredible and there were certainly worse ways to wake up.

But now that my eyes were open, the sun peeking in through the curtains on my window, I thought back to last night.

First date.

Yep, that had been a first date to top all first dates.

After Sebastian and I had left the pizza place, we stopped to watch a guy paint mind-blowing pictures using just spray paint and little cardboard cutouts. I hadn't been in any hurry to move on, especially when Sebastian wrapped his arms around me, allowing me to lean against his chest. We probably stood there for a solid half hour and during that time, the guy with the spray paint completed three pictures. They were incredible.

By two o'clock, Sebastian and I had decided to call it a night. We'd spent several hours people watching, laughing and joking about random things and keeping our conversation light and impersonal.

At first, I'd been disappointed that Sebastian didn't want to open up to me, but when I recognized the storm clouds in his brilliant gold gaze, I knew whatever he was holding back was hard for him. That didn't mean I didn't want to know, but I also didn't want for our date to go to crap right off. So, we'd had a couple of beers early on at one of the popular bars on Sixth Street and then closed the place down at two. We'd stopped drinking early, so it hadn't been the alcohol talking when I had wanted to take him back to my apartment and ravish him until dawn.

Just like the personal conversation, that hadn't happened either, and now I was wondering when I'd get to see him again.

There was a light tap on my bedroom door before it flew open and in strolled Chloe. She was wearing an oversized T-shirt that read "My imaginary friend thinks you have serious mental problems." That was one of her favorites, although she had a drawer full of different ones.

"Mornin' sunshine!" Chloe exclaimed moments before she flung herself onto my bed and cuddled up beside me. "Whatcha doin'?"

"Just laying here," I told her, pulling the blanket up to my nose. I don't know how the girl could stand it to be so cold in the apartment, but she was the culprit who continued to turn down the temperature until ice was practically forming on the air vents. I would admit that it probably wasn't quite cool enough outside to turn on the heater, but I was pretty sure we could have gone without the air conditioner for a couple of weeks.

"How'd your date go?" she asked, flopping onto her back and staring at the ceiling along with me.

"Amazing," I told her, unable to stop the grin from forming on my face.

"Yeah?" Chloe turned her head to the side and looked at me. "So, the mechanic can fix more than just cars, can he?"

"Shut up," I scolded her, laughing. "It was nice."

"Nice. I'm sure that sexy bad boy would love to know you called him nice."

"I didn't call him nice. I said the date was nice."

"I'm sure that's what he was going for," Chloe said with a laugh. "What time did you get home?"

"It was after two. Where were you anyway?" I turned my head to look at her.

Chloe wasn't home when I arrived, so I hadn't had anyone to share the details of my date with. Which was probably a good thing because, at the time, I'd been floating on a cloud and I would have sounded pathetic.

"Out."

"That's it. That's all you're gonna tell me?" I asked, turning my head and looking at the ceiling again.

"Yup!" she squealed and jumped to her feet. "Breakfast's ready. Come eat with me."

The only reason I agreed was because my stomach grumbled loudly, reminding me that I'd only had one slice of pizza for dinner last night and that had been early. If I had been out with Chloe or Aaron, I would have had at least two, but with Sebastian, I didn't want to look like a pig, so I'd cut myself off.

The scent of sweet blueberries drifted from the kitchen, seemingly calling out to my stomach. Snatching my white, fluffy robe from the small chair beside my bed, I wrapped it around myself and followed Chloe to the kitchen.

I nearly tripped over my own two feet when I stepped into the small breakfast area.

There, sitting in one of the kitchen chairs was…

"Payton, you remember Toby."

"I … uh …" Yeah, I remembered him. Although I hadn't been positive what his name was, but I certainly remembered him.

I patted my hair, wondering just how bad I looked and then decided to slip into the bathroom. Although, *run to the bathroom* was a more apt description.

Sebastian's friend Toby was in our kitchen.

Our kitchen.

Toby.

And Chloe was still in her pajamas.

I stared at myself in the mirror above the sink, trying to remember what Toby had been wearing. Jeans and a T-shirt, maybe? Did he have on shoes? The powers of deductive reasoning were telling me that Toby had spent the night. But I was hoping that I was missing something.

Why didn't Chloe mention this to me before? Why would she let me stumble out of my bedroom looking like death warmed over just to find a strange man in my kitchen?

After brushing my teeth, I splashed cold water on my face and massaged the skin beneath my eyes, willing myself to look more awake. I took a brush to my hair but then decided to pull it back in a ponytail. Without makeup, I really did look like a teenager, but at the moment, it beat the alternative: looking like a zombie apocalypse had started and they'd taken me first.

Shit.

A gentle knock on the door had me spinning around and clutching my hand to my chest.

"You okay in there?" Chloe called from the other side of the door.

No. I wasn't. But that's not what I said. "Yep. Be out in a sec." I hoped my voice sounded more chipper than I felt.

"You can do this," I told the woman in the mirror. "Just walk out there and have a civil conversation with Sebastian's friend. It doesn't matter why he's here. It doesn't even matter that he might've stayed the night."

Like hell.

Another splash of cold water on my face and I was scrubbing it off with a hand towel before tightening the belt on my robe and reaching for the door knob.

Part of me expected to see Chloe standing in the hallway, ready to tell me just what the hell was going on, but the only thing that met me was the lingering scent of pancakes and syrup.

Taking a deep breath, I pasted a smile on my face and walked into the living room.

"Oh, my God!" I squealed like an idiot, spun on my heel and darted into my bedroom before slamming the door behind me.

Sebastian was in my kitchen.

Oh crap. Oh crap. Oh crap.

I buried my face in my hands and started laughing uncontrollably.

Chapter Twenty-Two

Payton

I HAD NO IDEA HOW long I stood there like that, but then there was a knock on my door. "Come in." I could hardly speak through my laughter, but I figured Chloe was back to check on me, so I forced the words out.

"Hey."

I was pretty sure I had a minor heart attack. Grateful that my bed was close by, I dropped to my butt and stared at the sexy man standing in my bedroom doorway.

"You okay?" he asked, that mischievous gleam in his eyes disarming me.

"Nope. Not okay," I mumbled loudly. "Not sure I'll be okay ever again."

That only seemed to intensify his amusement, and Sebastian moved into the room and closed the door behind him.

Shit.

Not good.

"What…" I closed my mouth, cleared my throat and tried again. "What…?" *are you doing here?* I couldn't seem to get the last part of the sentence out of my mouth, but I knew I was gaping at Sebastian.

"Cat got your tongue, Angel?" Sebastian stalked closer to me.

That was the only way to explain the predatory gleam in his beautiful eyes. I felt like a mouse who'd been cornered by a cat, and I didn't know quite what to do about it.

The next thing I knew, I was on my back with my feet resting on the floor, and Sebastian was above me. His hands were planted firmly on the bed as he held himself up. I was in desperate need of air because being this close to him was…

"Good morning," he whispered in that raspy tone that I'd come to want more of.

I was suddenly grateful that I had brushed my teeth.

"Morning." Oh, Lord. Was that my voice? Did I just croak?

The smirk that tilted the corner of Sebastian's mouth sent my hormones into overdrive. I could feel the warmth of his body through my robe although he wasn't touching me.

I cleared my throat, intent on not looking like a love-struck fool as I lay beneath him, staring up at his handsome face. "What are you doing here?"

"Toby mentioned breakfast."

"Why is Toby here?" I felt a little better now that I'd found my voice again. The fact that Sebastian was still hovering above me was doing strange things to my insides, but at least I sounded like I was unaffected.

Maybe.

"Chloe invited him."

"So he didn't stay the night?" I attempted to sit up only to find that Sebastian wasn't going to move.

"Not my business," Sebastian murmured, his eyes drifting down to my mouth.

No, it wasn't. Nor was it my business, but I had to admit, I wasn't used to waking up to find strange men in our apartment. I'd lived with Chloe for the last year after I'd decided that in order to save money, I needed to take on an additional roommate. Aaron and I had been in a two-bedroom apartment until I met Chloe when I decided to try a new hair stylist closer to where we'd moved. From the moment we started talking, we'd been instant friends and a few short months later, Aaron and I moved to a three-bedroom apartment following the logic that with three people splitting the rent we'd save more money.

It had worked, and until now, especially with Aaron always gone, things had been rather boring at home.

Finding strange men in my kitchen first thing in the morning took boring and shattered it into a million pieces.

"What are you thinking about?"

Sebastian's question pulled me from my thoughts. "Nothing. What are *you* thinking about?" I realized he was still looking at my mouth.

"Kissing you. It's the only thing I *can* think about."

Okay, so that one sentence sent a torrent of tingles through my insides. I was tempted to rub up against him like a cat, wanting to press my body to his, to feel every hard plane of his body against me. Thankfully my legs were shut, but I couldn't move because Sebastian was practically straddling me, his feet still planted firmly on the floor, legs spread wide, his knees trapping my thighs between them.

"Well, you know the rules," I whispered, wishing the rules would take a flying leap right out the window. I wanted him to kiss me. I'd wanted that since I made the stupid rule in the first place.

Sebastian had thrown me for a loop last night. After we had left the pizza place, aside from holding my hand and putting his arms around me while we'd watched the painter, we hadn't touched at all. No kissing, no making out in the parking lot. Nothing.

And even when he had walked me to my door at two-thirty in the morning, he didn't even offer a good night kiss. It had left me desperately wanting him.

I was pretty sure that was his plan.

"I do know the rules," he said softly. "But you know what I think about rules?"

"Hmm?" I asked, unable to tear my gaze from his lips. When he talked, I could see the silver barbell through his tongue.

Sebastian didn't answer my question with words. He simply leaned down and pressed his lips to mine.

It was like an explosion occurred inside me. Unable to resist, I threw my arms around his neck and kissed him back. I was the aggressor, forcing my tongue into his mouth until we were crushed together. The growl that erupted from him made my body ignite and I feared that I was going to go up in a puff of smoke any minute now.

"Angel," he growled against my lips, his hand sliding behind my head.

The next thing I knew, Sebastian was flat on the bed and I was lying on top of him, straddling his hips. I could feel his erection pressing against me and holy smokes, I wanted more of him.

But he didn't touch me, and I didn't touch him, other than where our bodies were resting against one another. His tongue dueled with mine and his hands were cupping my head, but he wasn't trying to cop a feel.

God, I wanted him to cop a feel.

Shit.

Now I was acting like a horny teenager.

Someone pounded on the door and I drew my mouth from Sebastian's, staring down at him.

"Come on, kids. Time to eat," Toby called through the door.

I giggled when Sebastian rolled his eyes.

"You heard him," Sebastian said, his voice raspy and breathless. At least he was feeling the same thing I was.

"Yes, I did," I told him. "I'm not hungry."

"I am," Sebastian replied, his eyes sliding to my mouth again. "But not for food."

"I hope you're dressed, 'cause I'm comin' in," Toby announced from the door, and I jumped off Sebastian, getting to my feet and nearly falling over.

"He's kidding." Sebastian sounded sure of himself, but I realized he'd gotten to his feet too, and he had planted his hands on my shoulders, keeping me from falling into the small desk in the corner. "Come on. Let's eat."

I nodded. I had no choice.

Once again, my voice had disappeared into thin air.

As we walked into the living room, I checked to ensure that my robe was closed while hiding behind Sebastian. Not that I was worried about anyone seeing the shorts and tank top that I was sporting, but I felt a little exposed. That was the reason I used the fluffy cotton robe to cover myself because I certainly wasn't cold anymore.

Sebastian stepped out of the way and allowed me to take a seat before he did the same. No one said a word, but I heard Toby and Chloe snicker a time or two. I was halfway through one of my pancakes when I asked, "So what the hell's going on here? Did you stay the night?"

Toby's eyes widened, and his smirk disappeared immediately. I guess he hadn't expected me to call him to the carpet.

I shot a sideways glance at Sebastian and smiled. At least, for the moment, we were out of the hot seat. After all, it wasn't like we were sneaking around. He hadn't stayed the night with me. But I wasn't so sure that Toby and Chloe hadn't done the horizontal mambo last night.

"No, he didn't stay the night," Chloe said, annoyed.

"No? Then why is he here?"

"Because he likes pancakes."

"Is that right?" This time Sebastian spoke, eyeing Toby across the table. "Since when?"

"Since right now," Toby answered quickly, his eyes trained on his pancakes.

"You sure?" Sebastian inquired.

He was waiting for Toby to look at him, but it was clear the man wasn't going to.

"I take it the two of you are seeing each other?" I asked Chloe when no one said anything else. She seemed just as interested in studying her pancakes as Toby.

"I'd say that's a yes." Sebastian looked at me, then lowered his voice and leaned closer. "He hates pancakes."

"I do not! These are fucking perfect," Toby growled.

Sebastian and I laughed, Chloe's face turned beet red, and Toby just watched the three of us.

Then the table erupted in laughter.

"Fine, I hate pancakes."

"You do?" Chloe asked, her eyes wide.

"Yeah."

"Then why are you eating them?" she asked.

"Because I don't think I can say no to you."

All laughter ceased immediately. My gaze bounced back and forth between Chloe and Toby. Yeah, there was something going on there for sure. I just didn't know what it was. I wanted to ask her, but I knew now wasn't the time.

Toby pushed his pancakes away and Sebastian laughed. "Told you."

Chloe reached over and smacked Toby on the arm. It wasn't hard, more like a love tap which had me joining Sebastian as we chuckled.

I'm not sure when I'd had that much fun. At least not in a long time.

"So, what's the plan for the day?" Toby asked, not talking to anyone in particular.

"I've got to go see my dad," I announced.

"You gonna take your boyfriend to meet him?" Toby joked.

"He's not my boyfriend," I blurted, although there wasn't any heat behind it. Who said boyfriend these days?

"Based on that look, I'd say you're wrong," Chloe commented.

"Whatever." I didn't look at Sebastian, but I could feel him looking at me.

Whatever was happening between us … it was hopeful. I could admit that much. The chemistry was off the charts, something I hadn't experienced with anyone in a long time. But the fact of the matter was, I worked for Mr. Trovato. I needed my job, and I didn't think it would go over well if he found out I was dating Sebastian. I still didn't know how they were related, but I knew they were. Too many coincidences and all.

"What about you? What're your plans for the day?" Toby asked Sebastian directly.

"I've got a couple of errands to run. Then … who knows."

I watched Sebastian speak, but I barely heard the words. He was so incredibly handsome. There was that bad boy vibe that I got, but it belied the way he treated me, which was surprising. I'd always thought that bad boys had a God complex, but Sebastian wasn't like that. There was an air about him. He had a quick smile, although I could see something raging in his eyes. But he certainly wasn't the cocky, arrogant type. Not all the time anyway. He had a magnetic pull on me. And likely plenty of other women, but when I was with him, I saw something else. Something deeper.

Wow. And now I was acting like I actually knew him. We still hadn't hashed out any of our personal histories and I'd only met him a week ago, yet here I was acting as though this might actually go somewhere.

I really needed to get a grip. I had too much going on at the moment and getting involved with someone who clearly could make me lose focus wasn't a good thing.

Since I wasn't the type of girl to sleep with a guy just because my hormones thought it was a good idea, I wasn't even sure whether this would continue anyway. When Sebastian looked at me, I saw heat in his gaze. And it was burning me alive. But I knew I couldn't give in to it. Not yet.

Maybe not ever.

"Okay, well…" I pushed my plate away, trying to play it cool. "I've got to take a shower. I've got things to do."

With that, I pushed to my feet and looked at the three of them.

I was just about to walk away, proud of myself for putting a little distance between me and Sebastian when he looked up and smirked. "Need help with that?"

Yes. No. Damn it. The answer was no.

"No. Thanks for the offer though," I answered, my voice choppy.

Yep, it was safe to say that I was in no way equipped to deal with a guy like Sebastian. It didn't even matter how much I tried to talk myself out of it, I knew if he continued to work his way into my life, I was going to give in.

And that was the last thing we all needed.

Chapter Twenty-Three

Payton

"HEY, KIDDO!" MY FATHER GREETED when I walked into Fowler Body and Frame an hour later. Several heads turned to look my way, a couple of waves followed.

"Good morning, Amy." I smiled at my father's receptionist who was sitting at a small desk near the front door.

"Mornin,' Payton," Amy replied, not looking up from her computer screen. "How's the new job?"

"Great." I didn't bother to stop and address her directly. Truth was, Amy didn't like me all that much. I knew her pleasantries were for my father's sake. Not that there was any love lost on my part. I didn't particularly care for Amy either. I thought she was a manipulative, vindictive bitch. And an attention whore.

"Hi, Daddy." My smile intensified as I approached my father.

"What're you doing here?" he asked, his surprise to see me written across his handsome, aging face.

My father was in his late fifties but working in the body shop industry had aged him. He looked quite a bit older than that. He kept his dark hair clipped short, mainly because he was balding, and he had plenty of laugh lines around his eyes and mouth. But no matter what, he was still one of the most handsome men I'd ever know.

So I might have fibbed a little earlier when I told Sebastian that I had to go see my father. It had been the first thing that I thought of, but I knew I needed to have a plan for the day. The last thing I needed was for Sebastian to think I had been planning to sit around my apartment and hope he would call. Yeah, so, coming to see Harold Fowler wasn't really a scheduled thing, but I figured since I had told Sebastian that I had to stop in and see him, I probably should. That or my spur of the moment comment would have been a lie.

When my father wrapped his arms around me, I hugged him back. "Just wanted to stop by."

Sitting around waiting for a guy didn't really work for me. I was supposed to pretend to be only partially interested in Sebastian. Anything else would make me look desperate.

I was a little desperate.

Especially when I thought about the way he kissed me, the hard planes and angles of his body beneath my hands. I wanted to throw caution to the wind and jump him.

I was thankful for the little bit of common sense I had left.

I knew that until Sebastian opened up and told me some things about himself, I wasn't going to give in. So his inability to share about himself was my only saving grace.

"Want something to drink?" my dad offered after he released me, rubbing the top of my head like I was five.

"Sure," I replied, trying to smooth my hair back into place.

I followed my father into the small break room at the back of the building, passing two other employees who merely offered a brief wave before burying their noses in their computer screens once again.

I didn't go to my father's body shop often. Fowler Body and Frame was one of those places that made me feel out of place. The people were nice, but I knew what they saw when they looked at me. After all, even though my father had wanted me to, I never gave in to working there full time. It wasn't for me.

I enjoyed the time I spent with my parents, namely my father who had toted me around to hockey or baseball games and car shows as a kid. There was no doubt about it, I was definitely a daddy's girl. But even though I loved spending time with him, I didn't want to work for him. Aside from the few times I had filled in when Amy needed to take time off, or my stint as my father's assistant during my senior year of high school, I didn't spend a lot of time there.

Sure, I knew about cars. More so than I cared to, really. I could change my oil, fix a flat tire, and even identify certain engines based on the set up under the hood. But other than that, being at the body shop wasn't high on my list of favorite things to do.

"How're you, kiddo?" Harold, better known as Hal, asked after retrieving two cans of soda from the small, secondhand refrigerator that stood in one corner of the break room next to the sink and a long counter complete with a used microwave. On the other end of the room was a flat screen television mounted on the wall and one of those water jug machines.

"Good," I answered, pulling out one of the metal chairs and sliding down into it while I glanced around the room. "Did you paint in here?" I asked, noticing something was different.

My father surveyed the room briefly before meeting my eyes again. "Yeah." He pointed to a spot in the ceiling. "We had a water leak, ended up having to paint the whole room after they fixed it."

"I like it," I told him, unable to think of anything else to say.

"Did you watch the Stars beat the Predators the other night?" He grinned widely.

"I did. Good game."

"It was. One of these days we'll have to go see the Stars play again."

We hadn't been to a hockey game in at least two years. Mainly because of my father's busy schedule. "I'd like that."

"So, how's work? Did you meet Mr. Trovato?"

I smiled, leaning back in my chair and wrapping my fingers around the cold soda can. "It's good."

My father cocked an eyebrow, obviously waiting for me to answer the other question.

"And, yes, I met him." I laughed. "I'm his assistant."

He nodded as though he was contemplating my answer. "Have you met a lot of people?"

"Not really, no. I'm kinda isolated at the moment. I did have to go to Mr. Trovato's house last week though."

My father's eyes narrowed on me.

Oops. That probably didn't sound right, especially when I blurted it out.

"He left his cell phone at home and his wife couldn't bring it to him."

"That's a strange thing for a receptionist to be doing," he said simply.

"I'm not a receptionist, Dad. I'm an administrative assistant."

"Same thing."

I smiled. No, they weren't the same. At least not in a company the size of Trovato, Inc., but I wasn't going to argue with my dad.

"How're you?" I asked, not really wanting to talk about me.

"Good. Busy."

"Yeah?" I was a little surprised by his hurried response. There hadn't been any cars in the parking lot when I arrived. Since it was Saturday, I kind of expected them to be busier.

I also knew that things had slowed down quite a bit for my father in recent months. My mother had mentioned it one day, and I'd heard something in her tone that I hadn't heard before. Concern.

"Is there anything I can do to help?" I offered, sipping my soda.

My dad chuckled. "We're good. You should be enjoying your day off, kiddo."

I knew I should. But that meant sitting around my apartment thinking about Sebastian and that was something I wasn't comfortable with. It was bad enough that I'd woken up that morning and the first thing that had crossed my mind had been him. I didn't want to be that girl. I was twenty-three, not seventeen. I had things to do and places to go.

Liar.

Okay, so I had nothing to do on a Saturday. Shopping was out of the question because I was trying to save money. Hanging out with Chloe wasn't an option because, shortly after I mentioned needing to go see my father, I found out she had planned to spend the day with Toby. I still intended to bombard her with questions where they were concerned, but I couldn't do that until she was home. Alone.

"How's Aaron? And Chloe?" my father asked, his gaze darting out the door.

I twisted to see someone standing there, clearly waiting to talk to my dad.

"I'll be there in a minute," he told the guy before turning his attention back to me.

"They're good," I told him. "Aaron's spending most of his time with his new boyfriend. And Chloe's busy with work."

"Boyfriend, huh? I assume he's a good guy?"

My parents loved Aaron, always had. Considering we'd spent so much time together, he was practically a member of the family. In fact, my parents had helped Aaron when he had concerns over talking to his own parents about being gay.

"He's nice," I told my father honestly. "I kinda think they're spending too much time together, but I'm not a relationship expert, so what do I know."

"Have they been together long?"

"A few months."

My father nodded and, as I was looking at him, a question flitted through my head and before I knew it, I was speaking it aloud. "Do you know if Mr. Trovato has any kids?"

My dad's brows turned down and I could see that I'd taken him off guard with the question.

Explaining my reasons for wanting to know the answer to something like that would have probably been a good thing, but I kept my mouth closed. Well, actually, I pretended to take a drink of my soda until he finally answered.

"He's got a daughter, I know," my father explained hesitantly. "There'd been a rumor a while back that he had a son as well, but that had died quickly. I think he's got a nephew that lives with him."

My soda nearly came out of my nose. A son? Was Sebastian Conrad's son? It made sense. They did kind of look alike. But...

Nooo. No way was Sebastian Conrad's son. He couldn't be.

I thought back to the pictures in Conrad's office. There were several of Aaliyah growing up, including several of her in recent years. He had pictures of his wife, Lauren, on the bookshelves that lined the far wall. But other than that, he didn't have any other pictures. Certainly, none of Sebastian.

Why would Conrad keep that a secret?

He wouldn't, that's all there was to it.

"Nephew, huh?" I asked when my coughing fit settled.

"Why do you ask?"

"No reason." I shrugged, placing my can on the table. "Look, I know you're busy and I've got ... something to do."

My father stood when I did, concern etched on the hard lines of his face.

"Tell Mom I said hi," I told him as I hugged him quickly and then turned toward the door.

"Payton."

Ahh, crap.

I stopped walking and turned to face my father.

"Is something going on?" he asked quietly, his voice low.

"Nope. Not a thing. I just have to run. Talk to you later, Dad."

I couldn't wait around for him to dig deeper. I wouldn't be able to keep my thoughts to myself.

And until I heard the words from Sebastian's mouth, I didn't want to jump to conclusions.

Although, I was pretty sure I already had.

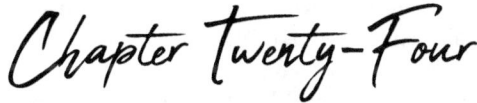

Payton

TWO HOURS LATER I WAS pacing the floor in my living room, staring at my cell phone on the coffee table. I was disappointed that Sebastian hadn't texted or called. Granted, he thought I was busy with my father. It still bothered me that I hadn't heard from him at all.

Should I text him? Should I leave him alone? Should I pretend he doesn't exist?

Wow. The last question drew me up short.

My thoughts deviated to the conversation I'd had with my father earlier. Was it really possible that Conrad Trovato was Sebastian's father? If it were true, why didn't Sebastian just say so? And why didn't Conrad have any pictures of Sebastian in his office?

"What the hell? Who could do that to their kid?" I spoke aloud although no one was home to hear me.

The guttural roar of an engine jump-started my heart. I darted to the window, scanning the parking lot below for the car and there it was.

Sebastian's sleek black Camaro was parked next to my Mustang, and I found I couldn't move as I watched him climb out. He was so damn hot. The way he moved, the way he carried himself. All masculine grace and power. Watching him took my breath away.

Yeah, I was pretty sure he was a god sent to this planet to make women forget their own names. He was ... beautiful.

Tall, with narrow hips and a broad chest. His hair always looked like he'd been running his hands through it. Today he was wearing a black leather jacket and I felt the saliva pool in my mouth.

I hadn't realized that I'd been standing there staring at him until there was a knock on my front door. I closed the distance in two steps and flung the door open, coming face to — well, not face because he was so much taller than me — chest with Sebastian.

"Hey," he greeted in that dark, sexy tone.

"Hey back. What're you doing here?" I asked stupidly. I hadn't expected to see him, especially since we hadn't made any plans that morning. I had wanted to, just hadn't expected to.

His eyebrow darted up slightly and he stared at me, his eyes narrowing. "We need to talk."

Oh, crap. I didn't like the sound of that.

Sure, we needed to talk, but did we need to *talk*?

The way he said it sounded bad.

"Come in." I stepped out of the way and motioned for him to come inside. My stomach had plummeted to my feet, and I felt a little lightheaded as I stared after him.

He was wearing jeans — no surprise there — and a body-hugging black T-shirt beneath the leather jacket and a pair of black work boots. He looked like a fallen angel with his golden-brown hair, the top just a little long, and his brilliant gold eyes. The five o'clock shadow darkening his jaw made him appear rugged and even sexier than when he was clean shaven.

"Can I get you something to drink?" I asked, wanting to be the polite hostess. More importantly, I didn't want to stand there and stare at him. Only because the idea of getting caught was a little embarrassing.

"I'm good," Sebastian said, not making eye contact with me.

That bothered me.

That had been one of the first things I noticed about him. He always made eye contact. And not the simple kind where he just spared you a look. No, Sebastian's eyes practically dug into your soul. He left me feeling exposed in every way. And now he wasn't looking at me at all.

"Want to sit down?" I asked, motioning for the couch.

Sebastian nodded his head, but he didn't move.

Unsure what to do, I moved closer to him, standing directly in front of him and looking up. He didn't meet my gaze.

"Is something wrong?"

His eyes slowly slid up until they were locked with mine. I'd say something was wrong. Where I'd previously seen mischief and excitement, at the moment I saw … fear?

No. That couldn't be it.

How could this strong, brave man be afraid of anything?

"Sit down," I whispered, reaching for his hand and tugging him toward the couch.

Before he could answer, my front door flew open and in walked Chloe.

"Hey, y'all. Don't mind me. I'm just here to shower and change. I'm gonna grab some clothes and go out for…"

Chloe's string of words died on impact as she came to a stop in the middle of the living room.

"What's wrong?" I was confused by the way she was looking at Sebastian.

"You okay?" she asked Sebastian directly, not answering my question. "You look pissed."

Sebastian's head lifted, and he forced a smile. "Peachy. Just here to talk to Payton," he mumbled, his voice gruff. Chloe merely nodded and then spared me a glance before she started toward her bedroom. Before she got there, she turned back to look at me. I thought she was trying to tell me something, but I pretended not to notice. I wasn't sure what just transpired in my living room, but I didn't want to talk to her. I wanted to talk to Sebastian.

"Come on," I told Sebastian, taking his hand and leading him into my bedroom before closing the door behind us. With Chloe in the apartment, there was no way we would have any privacy sitting in the living room.

Without thinking, I climbed on the bed and sat cross-legged as I watched him.

"Sit," I instructed as I patted the comforter, feeling awkward that he was still standing.

He looked at me then at the bed before shaking his head. "Not a good idea."

Oh.

O-o-oh.

Okay.

"Then pull up a chair," I stated, clearing my throat. I hadn't thought about what it would look like if I flopped onto my bed and invited him to join me.

Sebastian shook his head again and walked back and forth in the few scant feet that were allotted him. He pulled off his leather jacket, hung it on the back of the chair, but that was the only time he stopped moving. He resumed his pacing, his eyes glued to the floor.

My apartment was small. The bedrooms were big enough to hold a queen-sized bed, dresser and a small desk. Nothing more than that. And I had more than that in mine, so that left even less space to maneuver around. Considering I only used the room to sleep, it had never bothered me. With Sebastian standing there, my bedroom felt even smaller.

"You want to talk?" I felt like I was poking a stick at a scared animal. Any second now, I thought he was going to turn and run.

"Yeah." He still wasn't looking at me.

Okay, so this was getting weird fast.

"Please sit. You make me nervous when you pace the floor."

Sebastian dropped onto the edge of the bed and I couldn't believe my eyes. A minute ago, he hadn't wanted to sit there for whatever reason and now ... well, there he was less than a foot away.

"Is something wrong?" I asked when he didn't speak. The silence was unbearable. I was focused on the way he was breathing. Shallow and choppy.

I knew the answer to his question before he said it.

"Yeah," he muttered. "Something's wrong."

"Oh."

Well? I wanted to shake him, force him to spill it, but I thought better of it. Touching him probably wasn't a good thing right now. I could see the strain in the muscles of his neck.

Sebastian shrugged out of his jacket, setting it on the back of the chair near the bed.

That's when I saw the muscles of his arms, his bulging biceps decorated with black ink, the corded lines of his forearms, a clean slate for whatever tattoo he might want in the future.

"What is it?" I finally asked when the silence stole the oxygen from the room.

Sebastian twisted until he was looking directly at me. The heat in his eyes was potent, hot enough to scorch the surface of the sun.

"I want you, Payton."

Uh...

I wasn't sure what to say to that.

"And I shouldn't."

"Why?" Hmm ... I was starting to think I sounded a little needy. If that one word hadn't come out quite so breathless and anxious, I wouldn't be worried, but I knew how it sounded.

"You work for..."

I waited. This was the moment of truth. He was going to tell me who he was. Truthfully, I knew we couldn't even attempt to go any further until he did, so I held my breath.

"Who?" I wanted him to tell me, to open up and let me in.

Sebastian was instantly on his feet, pacing the floor again. At this rate, the cheap carpet was going to have a hole in it before he was finished.

Moving closer to the edge of the bed, I reached for him when he made another pass by me. He stopped instantly, staring down at where my hand touched his.

Then slowly — ever so slowly — his eyes moved up my arm, my neck, my mouth until we were staring at one another.

"Payton, I can't explain it—"

I didn't give him a chance, I tugged on his arm and he moved closer until he was kneeling on the bed in front of me. I continued to pull him, trying to bring him closer. For a second, I thought he was going to resist but then he was hovering above me and I was pulling him even closer. Close enough that our lips touched.

The room could have exploded right then, and I wouldn't have cared. The only thing that mattered was the warmth of his body above me, the feel of his rough fingers as they gripped my chin almost forcefully. Our tongues were battling, and I was trying to suck air in through my nose, but it was difficult. All of my senses were aware of him. His unique, musky scent, the way the short hairs on his head tickled my palm, the hard plane of his chest pressed against my breast.

It was safe to say that I'd never wanted anyone the way I wanted him.

Never.

And it didn't even matter that I didn't know much about him other than his name and that he was related to my boss.

Sebastian pulled back, the muscles in his arms flexing as he held himself above me. "Payton. Angel," Sebastian breathed against my lips before coming down over me and delving into my mouth once again.

If you've ever had an out of body experience, then you know what I was feeling in that moment. The stars had aligned, the planets gearing up to collide, the earth had started a backward orbit around the sun...

And I didn't care because I was meant to be right there. I was meant to be with this man. There was a little voice in my head that assured me this was what was supposed to happen.

Chapter Twenty-Five

Sebastian

MY HEART WAS RACING, MY skin electrically charged, and I wanted more of her.

I needed more.

This woman soothed the chaos in my head. Just being near her muffled the noise that was constantly screaming through my brain.

But I couldn't have her.

Or at least I knew I shouldn't.

Somehow, I managed to break the kiss, pushing myself up, holding my body above Payton's. The feel of her breasts crushed to my chest, the warmth between her thighs against my leg … it was too much.

And I didn't trust myself.

I don't know why I came. I'd been driving around for the last half hour, trying to convince myself that it was a bad idea.

I should have called Toby or Leif, asked them to get a beer or even head down to the track. But I did none of that. Then I was there, in front of Payton's apartment building, pulling my car into a parking space next to hers and I just wanted to see her.

I'd had a fight with my father.

A knock down drag out that ended badly.

"I wanted to let you know that we won't be needing you in Vegas this year," Conrad informed me when he walked into the garage where I'd been working on the McLaren, trying to pass some time before I called Payton.

"What?" I asked, standing up straight.

He was standing in the doorway between the house and the garage. He was wearing a polo and jeans, his usual weekend attire.

"You heard me," he said as he stepped into the garage and closed the door to the house. "You've got to finish the concept car, and I don't think it's a good idea for you to go this year."

"We've had this planned for months." For the last five years, I had attended the SEMA show in Vegas. Truth was, I enjoyed that trip, actually looked forward to it each year. Aaliyah had just turned twenty-one and we'd made plans to go out and celebrate. I'd invited Leif and we were going to enjoy the nightlife. It was the only time I actually looked forward to spending time with my father. For whatever reason, during the show, we didn't argue. We managed to get along for the few days we were there, even if life went right back to normal the instant we returned, I still looked forward to the show each year.

"Not going to happen this year, Sebastian. I don't think you deserve to go out there."

"Deserve?" I growled, wondering if I'd actually heard him correctly. *"You don't think I deserve it? How fucking old do you think I am? Five? Oh, wait, you weren't there when I was five, so that can't be it."*

"This is exactly my point," Conrad countered, his tone frustratingly calm. *"You're out of control and I can't deal with your unprofessional attitude."*

I wanted to tell him to fuck off, but I bit my tongue.

"Anyway, I've asked Payton to go. I need her there. She can keep Aaliyah company and help with the show."

I swallowed hard as realization dawned. He wasn't insisting that I stay home because he thought I was unprofessional, he didn't want me around Payton. Rather than just accepting his decision and doing what I wanted anyway, which was to go to Vegas with or without his approval, I lost my shit.

"Fuck you, Conrad. I'm not a fucking kid anymore and in case you hadn't noticed, I'm the only fucking reason your company's still making money hand over fist. I'm twenty-five years old, I make my own decisions. You don't want me there, fine. But don't expect me to work on anything for you."

"You don't have a choice," Conrad yelled. *"I fucking own you, Sebastian. You're my son. You will do what I tell you to do or you'll be out on your fucking ass."*

"Is that right?" I marched right up to him and got in his face.

"That's right. And if you don't like it, I'll take every fucking penny you've got."

The laugh that escaped me was filled with anger and disbelief. *"You think so? You think you call the shots? Well, I've got news for you. I've got a few secrets of my own and if you want to have a pissing match, we'll just see who wins. Try me."*

Conrad's eyes widened, but he wasn't finished. "There was a reason I tried to pay your mother off, Sebastian. I didn't need the headache. I didn't need the shit that would come with it. And I was right. I should've let the state take you. I should have just turned my back on you like everyone else."

I felt like I'd been punched in the solar plexus. I stumbled backward. Conrad had said some pretty shitty things in my life. He'd done my mother wrong and I'd heard him and his wife actually talking about her on occasion, but never had he said anything that nasty to me.

I nodded, unable to get any words to form.

"You won't be going to Vegas, Sebastian. I've already told you, I don't want you anywhere near Payton. And if you don't want to find yourself out on your ass, you'll do what you're told."

It had taken everything in my power to walk away without ripping Conrad's head from his body. Somehow I managed, and I made it back to the guest house, grabbing the keys to the Camaro from the bar along with my wallet before storming out. I had needed someone to talk to, someone who would listen and not judge me. The only person I could think of was Payton, although I had no idea whether she'd be the one who wouldn't pass judgment.

I suspected she wouldn't, which was why I was there.

When Payton's cool fingers scraped the skin on my sides, I realized she was reaching for the hem of my shirt, lifting it higher, her fingers sending chills down my spine as they grazed my overheated skin.

I should have stopped her. It would have been the right thing to do, but I didn't. And when she lifted the T-shirt over my head, I held my breath, staring down into her mesmerizing hazel eyes.

She was looking at me, touching me. It wasn't easy to control myself. While she studied the black ink that decorated my arms, the tip of her finger traced over the designs.

"No tattoos on your chest," she mumbled, her hands coming to rest on my pecs.

My chest was heaving, as though I'd run a mile just to get here, my abs were tight, every muscle in my body coiled as I fought the urge to devour her. She slowly slid her fingers over my skin again, her fingernails grazing my nipples, her eyes slowly sliding up to meet mine. My breath hitched.

My cock was rigid, a painful throb between my legs that was impossible to ignore. "You're making me crazy, Angel," I whispered.

"I know."

She sounded so sure of herself. As though she knew that she was tempting the beast. There wasn't an ounce of fear in her beautiful eyes.

If she only knew, she would be terrified. If she knew the demons that lurked inside of me, she wouldn't be lying beneath me. She would be barring the door, keeping me on the other side at all times.

I was a rubber band, pulled tight, ready to snap. I wanted to touch her, to taste every delicious inch of her. And I didn't want to stop until she was screaming my name.

For a moment, I thought I could do this. I thought I could give in and take her the way I'd dreamed about. I had imagined slowly stripping her clothes from her, kissing a trail up her body, teasing, tormenting until she was begging, pleading for more. I wanted her more than my next breath. I wanted to lose myself in her for hours. "Are you sure about this?" I asked softly.

"I'm not sure about anything, Sebastian," she admitted softly.

God, she felt good. Soft against hard. She calmed me. I'd never known anything like this. For as long as I could remember, I'd had the noise in my head. The fear and the anger, it was a living, breathing thing inside of me. All of my suspicions, they took control of my thoughts until I was blinded by the rage.

I didn't know how this would end, but right then it didn't matter. I would fight through hell to have her, to keep her.

But moving too fast was a surefire way of ending this before it ever got started.

And that was the last thing I wanted.

I leaned forward, burying my face in Payton's neck, inhaling her sweet scent.

"Quit thinking so hard."

Her words pulled me from my thoughts. "I can't help it. This isn't why I came. I didn't plan for this." My words were muffled against the blanket beneath us. "God, Payton, I'm not sure I can keep my hands off you."

I didn't want to, I knew that much. I wanted to touch her.

Everywhere.

But I couldn't. Not yet.

Not after what happened earlier. Not after the falling out I'd had with Conrad, the horrible things he'd said, the things I'd said.

If I made love to Payton the way I wanted, Conrad would turn it around on me, and he would make her believe that I had done it just to defy him.

That's the way the bastard worked.

And I damn sure wasn't going to let him come between me and Payton.

I wasn't going to let anyone come between us.

So, my conscience got the best of me and I rolled off Payton, flipping onto my back next to her. Without hesitating, I pulled her to me, her head resting on my chest, her palm planted over my heart.

I slid my hand under the soft cotton of her T-shirt, finding warm, smooth skin beneath. I settled for touching her, feeling her breath against my skin.

"We need to talk." I tried to regulate my heartbeat.

Payton didn't say anything.

Part of me was surprised she allowed me to stay in her room. After all, I was the spawn of Satan. Then again, she still didn't know, because I hadn't told her. I had chickened out, which was probably the only reason she hadn't thrown me out.

But that wasn't the only secret I had.

It was just one of many.

And I needed to tell her everything. I needed to open up and share, or the chaos was going to break me. I was going to implode.

"So, talk," Payton encouraged, her fingers trailing down to my navel. I sucked in a harsh breath, willing my body under control.

I couldn't get the words out although she'd given me the perfect opening.

"I want to know everything there is to know about you," Payton said softly, her body coming closer, pressing against my side.

"I'm not sure you do."

Payton lifted her head, her beautiful green-brown eyes peering into mine. "I do."

I could almost believe her.

Almost.

But I knew the instant that she learned my story she was going to run for the hills and never look back.

I looked away, staring blankly across the room. "Conrad Trovato is my…"

I swallowed hard, trying to get the words out, but they wouldn't come.

Payton leaned in, pressing her lips gently to mine. "You can tell me anything, Sebastian."

She was saying that now. In a few minutes, I wasn't so sure she'd feel the same.

"Conrad Trovato is my father." I exhaled deeply and turned my head, meeting her gaze head on. "Conrad Trovato is also…" I swallowed again, nearly choking on the words that hung on my tongue.

"Tell me," Payton demanded softly, her eyes wide.

"I'm pretty sure he's the man responsible for—"

Before I could get the words out, the front door opened and then slammed closed, rattling the window above Payton's bed and knocking a small vase from a shelf on the wall.

Payton flew off the bed, running to the door and pulling it open.

"Aaron!" Payton yelled. "What's wrong?"

Shouting ensued and I was on my feet in two seconds flat, pulling my T-shirt on over my head before following her into the living room. I had no idea what was going on with Aaron, but I was almost tempted to thank him for the interruption.

His abrupt appearance had just stopped me from telling Payton something that I wasn't sure she was ready to hear.

Something that I wasn't sure she'd ever be ready to hear.

Unraveling

The Unhinged Trilogy, book 2

Secrets and lies… No good ever comes of them. My life is proof.

For eleven years, I've suffered from a suspicion that has waged a war inside my head, filled me with rage. Left me feeling helpless.

But then she came along.

The darkness continues to consume me, but when I'm with her, I can ignore it, push it away. Even if only for a little while.

Payton calms me. She manages to quiet the noise in my head. But the secret is still there, still continuing to plague me day after day. Yet I still can't bring myself to tell her even though she deserves to know. She needs to know.

I love her. And I'll do anything to protect her.

Although I've found some peace, my life continues to unravel, no matter how hard I try to stop it.

\My name is Sebastian Trovato, and this is the continuation of my story.

Chapter One

Sebastian

Saturday night

I'LL BE THE FIRST TO admit that I wasn't sure how things went south so quickly, but one minute Payton was lying in my arms and I was mustering up the strength to tell her who I was. And then bam! In walked Aaron, slamming shit around in the other room, and Payton was gone.

As much as I wanted to say I was disappointed, the truth was … I wasn't.

My nerves were shot, there was no doubt about that, but the guy's timing couldn't have been better, to be honest. There could've been plenty of other times when Aaron's volatile arrival would've put a damper on things that might have been going on between Payton and me in her bedroom, but not today.

Didn't matter that I had no idea why Aaron was there in the first place.

Regardless, he had actually just saved the day as far as I was concerned. I had almost spilled my guts to a woman I was hoping to hang on to for longer than a fucking minute. Damn near spewed the thoughts that I had never spoken to anyone before. Not Leif, not Toby. No one. The secret that I've kept locked up inside me was one that would change the life of many, and not in a good way, either. So Aaron's interruption was welcome.

As it was, I had informed Payton that I was related to her boss, although I had done so without giving her the disturbing details. Telling her that I was Conrad Trovato's son hadn't freaked her out, which I was a tad surprised by, but I also considered that a good thing. But the earth-shattering revelation that had nearly followed likely would have. Okay, there really was no "likely" about it, she would have freaked.

But I hadn't shared my deepest, darkest secret, and here I was, following Payton into the small living room of her apartment while she yelled at her friend Aaron and he yelled back.

"What the hell is going on?" Chloe shouted when she joined the rest of us in the living room dressed in some sort of form-fitting pink yoga pants and a black T-shirt, her hair wet and dripping down her back.

And now there were three.

I laughed. I couldn't help myself. Everyone was yelling, but the only thing they seemed to be saying was "Why is everyone yelling?"

Counterproductive if you asked me.

But no one did because ... well, because they were too busy shouting at one another.

I glanced over at the tall blond guy who'd accompanied Payton to Conrad's party last week to see him standing in the kitchen, his head hanging down, palms planted firmly on the counter. His muscles were tense, the skin on his face pulled tautly, and if I wasn't mistaken, he was shaking.

He looked pissed, but then again, that could have been his happy face.

I didn't know the guy.

"What's wrong?" Payton asked Aaron again, her voice significantly lower.

"Mark."

That was the only word that Aaron said, yet Chloe and Payton both nearly crumbled as they ran to Aaron's side, throwing their arms around him.

I fought the growl that rumbled deep in my chest. Watching Payton put her arms around another man wasn't something I would ever enjoy seeing, I realized right then. Clearly, she cared for this guy, but to watch her hugging him went miles past my comfort zone. Instead of interrupting, I leaned against the doorjamb and continued to observe quietly.

"What did he do, honey?" Chloe asked Aaron, her wide green eyes intently focused on him.

"The bastard cheated on me," Aaron grumbled.

Ahh. So it went like that, did it?

Hug away, Payton. Hug away.

Could I say that I was happy that this Aaron guy was pissed off? It wasn't all that enjoyable to watch, so no. However, finding out the guy was gay pretty much made my whole fucking day. And at this point, after the fight I'd had with my father earlier, I'd had a pretty shitty day.

Aaron was gay.

You're probably asking how I know his sexual preference based on his reaction. Well, it all made sense now, and it really didn't have anything to do with his outburst. First off, any guy would have to be gay not to look at Payton with lust in his eyes, and aside from a severe possessive expression when he'd approached us on the veranda the night of Conrad's party, Aaron hadn't looked at her like he was ready to toss her on the bed and have his wicked way with her. That had been one of the first things I'd noticed that night. And hell, even my two best friends had shared their desire to "do her," although I'd been ready to string them up by the balls at the time. Second, the guy's hair was too fucking perfect, as were his clothes. I mean, seriously, he had an emblem on his navy-blue polo. Dude had to be gay.

Sure, I guess it was possible that this "Mark" person was really Markanne or Markella, but I highly doubted it. After all, the guy was a bastard, according to Aaron.

"I'll go over there and punch him in the nose," Payton offered Aaron, her tone sympathetic.

Damn. And now she was threatening physical violence. My dick was instantly hard again. Fan-fucking-tastic. Such a sweet face, so innocent and pure, was threatening to punch some asshole in the face. I think I fell in love with her right then.

Aaron turned his head slightly to the left to look at Payton. From where I stood, I could see a small smile tilting his lips.

"You wanna talk about it?" Payton asked him, and that was the moment Aaron must have noticed I was standing there, because he looked up, his tired blue eyes meeting mine.

He wasn't smiling anymore.

"What the hell are you doing here?" he asked me directly.

I smirked. I had no idea what the hell to say to that.

Payton smacked him in the arm. "Don't be rude."

"Sorry," Aaron replied, but I knew he wasn't apologizing to me. The guy was protective of Payton. That was obvious.

Again, I couldn't say that his brotherly response to Payton bothered me.

Although I didn't need help in the protective department, it didn't hurt that someone had her best interest in mind. As long as he and I could get along, we'd do fine.

"Fuck him," I stated firmly. "This Mark guy, that is," I explained as I continued. "You don't need that cheating bastard."

All eyes turned to me, a little dazed and a lot confused. I fought the urge to laugh again. These three amused me.

"What?" I pushed off the wall and took two steps into the small living room.

A knock on the front door pulled me up short. We all glanced over, but no one made a move to answer. I turned back to Payton and cocked an eyebrow. She nodded, and I made my way to the door, gripping the knob and pulling it open.

"Hey, dude. What's up?" Toby greeted me with a cheesy-ass grin.

With a smile of my own, I closed the door in his face and turned back to the others.

Aaron laughed, Payton smirked, and Chloe glared at me.

What did she expect?

"Let him in," Chloe instructed, her hands on her hips, head tilted to the side as if she couldn't figure me out.

No one could. I liked to think that was part of my charm. "He's a big boy. He knows how to open a door," I told her before dropping onto the couch to watch the show.

And just like I'd predicted, Toby turned the knob and walked into the apartment, still grinning from ear to ear.

A couple of good things about Toby: he didn't get his feelings hurt easily and he rarely ever held a grudge. Hell, it wasn't often that I even saw the guy in a bad mood.

"No one mentioned there was a party," Toby said, looking from one person to another, his gaze stopping on me.

"No party. We're consoling the gay guy," I offered, propping my ankle on my knee and leaning back on the couch. Nodding in Aaron's direction, I added, "His douche of a boyfriend cheated."

"No way," Toby said, pretending to be serious. "Dude, you don't need that shit. I say fuck that loser."

"Not a good idea," I said in a mock whisper, looking directly at Toby. "The fucker's already got that covered."

"Oh. Right," Toby stated, his fist resting beneath his chin, his index finger tapping on his lips as though he was thinking. "String him up by his balls. It's the only way to fix it."

I glanced over at the three still in the kitchen, waiting to see what they'd say to Toby's words of wisdom.

And just like that, everyone was laughing.

That was what I loved about Toby. He didn't take anything seriously. Well, most things, anyway. There was a time and place for everything, and Toby was mature enough to know that, but for the most part, he was a laid-back, good ol' boy with a wicked sense of humor. And since I wasn't all that fond of confrontation thanks to the constant battles I had with my father, I tended to try to lighten the situation when it got too deep, and Toby usually played along.

Looked like it'd worked.

"Are you really okay?" Payton asked Aaron softly when he stood up straight.

"I will be. Don't worry about me, doll."

Yeah, the guy was young, he'd be fine. But I knew that sitting around on a Saturday night stewing about shit like that was never a good idea, which was why I said, "Why don't we get out of here for a while?"

"I really shouldn't leave him," Payton told me, clearly assuming I was only talking to her.

"All of us, Payton. I know a place we can go."

"He knows a place," Toby smarted off. "I've heard that before."

Apparently, Chloe was satisfied with Aaron's reassuring statement, because she joined Toby in the living room. She surprised the shit out of us all when she walked right up to him and put her arms around his neck, pulling him close and kissing the shit out of him.

"Get a room," Aaron grumbled, smirking.

Toby wrapped his arms around Chloe, sliding his big hands down to her thighs, then easily lifted her off her feet and turned her toward her bedroom. With her legs wrapped around Toby's hips, Chloe released his lips, slapping his shoulder and laughing.

"But he said... No?" Toby asked, grinning. "Fine. If we don't go in there, we go with him."

Chloe looked down at me. Her green eyes narrowed, her lips quirking slightly as though she was considering the implications of doing just that. And then she smiled. "Fine. I'm game. How bad could it be?"

"You might wanna save that question for later, babe," Toby told her, giving her a quick kiss on the lips before lowering her back to her feet and then smacking her ass.

"Let me change," Chloe said, giggling before darting to her bedroom.

I stood, watching Payton. I could tell she was torn between staying with Aaron and going with us. I wasn't leaving without her, so I said, "Grab a jacket. It'll be cold."

Aaron started down the hall, and I figured he was planning to sneak off to avoid me, so I stopped him with my next statement. "That means you, too, Blondie. Where's your jacket? We've got things to do tonight and whining like a little fucking girl ain't gonna work."

Aaron spun around and faced me, frowning. The guy really was too fucking pretty. We were probably ten feet apart, and I could see the annoyance in his eyes, but even I could see that he wasn't really pissed at me. He probably wanted to be, but he wasn't. He knew I was joking, even if he didn't know me that well. Because if I hadn't been joking, he wouldn't still be standing there.

"Fine," he groused before turning away again.

"It's settled then. Five minutes," I called after Aaron. "Then we're out."

I glanced at Toby, and he nodded before dropping onto the couch.

When Payton came to my side, I pretended Toby wasn't still there watching us. I pulled her against me and pressed my lips to hers— I couldn't help it. The woman had the most kissable lips. If it were up to me, I'd kiss her all damn night.

I backed my way into her bedroom, fully intending to grab my jacket and something to keep her warm, but I didn't release her lips. I didn't want to.

Stopping just inside her room, I cupped her face with my hands and drew back a little so I could look in her eyes. Her skin was so soft, her eyes reflecting her innocence. Just looking at her unhinged me, made me feel things I'd never thought possible. Rather than a constant state of chaos, the woman filled me with peace. I didn't know how that was possible, but since I'd never experienced it before, I knew it was something about her. Just her.

Remembering our conversation from earlier and the fact that we'd let it drop when Aaron had stormed into Payton's apartment unannounced, I figured now would be the time to make sure she wasn't ready to toss my ass out. Probably good to know before I went any further.

"You okay with what I told you earlier?" I asked, keeping my voice low so Toby couldn't hear.

Payton briefly closed her eyes and sighed. "Conrad's your father."

Her eyes slid open, and she met my gaze, obviously waiting for a reply. I nodded.

"Why is it such a big secret?" she asked, her hazel eyes narrowing on my face.

I really didn't want to get into the details yet. My story wasn't one you'd tell if you were expecting to have a pleasant evening. I was willing to tell her whatever she wanted to know, but I wasn't sure now was the time to go into more detail. Especially not when there were people waiting on us.

"That part's not so easy to explain," I told her, sliding my knuckles along her cheek. Damn, I loved touching her. When Payton started to say something, I put my fingers to her lips and continued, "But I will if you want me to."

I could hear Chloe's voice coming from the other room. She was laughing at something Toby said. Payton glanced over her shoulder and then back at me. "Promise we'll pick up where we left off earlier?"

"I promise." There was plenty more we needed to talk about where Conrad was concerned, especially since Payton worked for him, but now wasn't the right time. "Does that mean we can put kissing back on the table?"

"Maybe." She touched my face with her hands, and I pressed my forehead to hers, relishing the smoothness of her skin against mine, the way her fingers left tingles in their wake.

"Good. 'Cause I plan to do a lot of that tonight."

"That's what I was hoping you'd say."

I pressed a kiss to her nose and reluctantly released her to retrieve my jacket from the chair where I'd left it earlier. If we kept this up, I would forget all other plans in lieu of spending the night alone with her.

Shrugging into my jacket, I turned to face her. She was still watching me.

"What's wrong?"

"Nothing," she replied, looking sad. "It's just… About Conrad, I don't—"

Two steps forward and I stopped her midsentence, placing my fingers on her lips again. "I know you've got questions. And I've got plenty of answers. But maybe we can table them for a bit. Let's get out of here. Have some fun tonight." I moved my fingers and kissed her gently before cupping her face and tilting her head so she looked at me. "I'll tell you anything, Angel. Anything you wanna know. And if you want to close that door and bombard me with question after question, I'll even answer them now. But I can tell you, it won't be a fun conversation. For either of us. So, what do you say we go out with them" — I tipped my chin toward the other room — "and we'll pick up where we left off later."

"Promise?"

"Swear," I assured her.

Payton nodded, and I took the opportunity to steal one more kiss, unable to keep my hands off her. I cupped her ass and pulled her against me, showing her just what she did to me. When I pulled back, we were both breathless and her face was flushed.

It took everything in my power to walk out of that room. I would have preferred to shut the door and toss her on the bed.

But that would have to come later.

That, I could definitely promise.

Chapter Two

Sebastian

TWENTY MINUTES LATER, AFTER AARON grabbed his jacket from his little girly car and Chloe and Payton argued with him in the darkened apartment complex parking lot about who he would ride with, the three of them finally decided that Aaron would go with us.

Watching him cram his tall, lanky body into the backseat of my Camaro had me holding back a laugh. Not that Toby's car would've provided more leg room. Toby had arrived in his '69 Camaro SS, and when I quietly informed him where I intended to go, his face had lit up like a kid on Christmas morning. Without a word, he had dragged Chloe to his car and helped her in, his eyes continuing to dart back to me. He was excited, there was no doubt about that.

The mood in my car was somber, thanks to Aaron and his pissy attitude. Payton wasn't talking much, either, so I didn't have to tell either of them where we were going. No one had questioned the fact that we were taking two cars, either. Then again, it wasn't like we could have taken one car in the first place. No one had one big enough to hold five people comfortably, so taking two made sense, and I wanted to keep our destination a secret for a little while longer.

When everyone was safely inside their respective vehicle, I made my way out of the parking lot, took a left toward the toll road. Hitting the entrance ramp at eighty, I headed south, back toward my house, but I had no intention of going home. I wanted to show Payton something, and this was the perfect opportunity. The fact that Toby was there was only an added bonus.

I was just about to turn up the radio to fill some of the deafening silence in the car when Payton rotated in her seat and looked back at Aaron. I darted a glance her way, then checked on Aaron in the rearview mirror.

Oh, crap.

I didn't know every one of Payton's expressions just yet, but I did know women. That look meant she wasn't at all ready to drop the discussion from earlier. She was clearly curious, and she was ready to ask questions.

I kind of felt sorry for Aaron.

Kind of.

"So, what happened?" Payton's question was as loaded as they came, which I found comical. Glancing in the rearview mirror again, I saw Aaron roll his eyes, but he wasn't smiling. He clearly wasn't much on talking about the event that had caused his earlier tirade, but I got the feeling Payton was persistent, which was the main reason he looked like he was ready to give in.

"Mark's a bastard."

"Well, that's a given," Payton agreed. "But that doesn't tell me what he did."

A heavy sigh sounded from the backseat. I grinned at Aaron's obvious discomfort, but I kept my eyes on the road, trying to keep my speed to a reasonable level. That was often difficult for me to do, especially when we hit the toll road. With a speed limit of eighty, going over one hundred was relatively easy for me. But, for Payton's sake, I kept it closer to ninety. As it was, we hadn't been in the car long, and she'd kept her hand firmly on the *oh shit* handle until just now.

"We were supposed to go out tonight," Aaron explained sadly. "Or so I thought. We made plans last weekend, when I stayed the night after the party."

My thoughts drifted back to that party and the way Aaron had hauled Payton out of there after practically throwing my jacket that she'd been wearing in my face. I grinned to myself. He had purposely made me believe they were together. Sly bastard. As understanding dawned, I realized he'd been playing me then. Keeping Payton away from me made her all the more desirable — or so he'd probably thought at the time. Little did he know, but I'd already set out with the intention of making her mine. His interference hadn't been necessary, but it proved he did care about her.

"When I called him earlier in the week," Aaron continued, "he kinda blew me off, but I thought it was because he was busy. He told me work was kicking his ass, so I tried to ease off."

"Man, tell me you didn't just go over there unannounced?" I asked, figuring it was my car so, by default, I was part of the conversation.

"I did," Aaron admitted, glaring at me in the rearview mirror.

"Dumbass," I said teasingly.

As I watched in the mirror, Aaron flipped me off from the backseat.

"Was he…?" Payton asked, her hand coming up to cover her mouth when Aaron didn't elaborate.

"Yep. Right there in his bed."

"What did he say when you caught him?" Payton asked, twisting in her seat so she could see him better.

Aaron didn't answer right away, and I glanced in the mirror again, waiting. I was just as interested in hearing the answer. If it'd been me and I'd walked in on some chick I was dating to find her in bed with another guy, I would have beaten the shit out of him.

Not that I thought Aaron was the type of guy to speak with his fists. Pretty boys didn't usually do that shit. Not to mention, Aaron looked considerably more reasonable than I was.

"He said he was sorry. A little difficult to believe when he was wrapped around another guy."

Payton laughed, but the sound was strangled. I could tell she was pissed for her friend. Hell, I was pissed for him and I didn't even know the guy.

"Did he at least try to stop you?" she asked.

"Yeah. I told him to get fucked," Aaron said, chuckling, obviously acknowledging the double entendre.

"Seriously, man. That's bullshit." Again, I joined in the conversation just because I could.

I didn't know Aaron all that well, but it was evident that he and Payton were close. I figured if I had any chance with her, it wouldn't hurt to get on her friend's good side.

"So I stormed out. And that's when I came home."

I nearly drove off the road. "Wait. What?" I jerked my head over to look at Payton. "Home?"

When she shrugged, I glanced in the rearview mirror to see Aaron looking back at me, smiling. His grin lit up his entire face. "She didn't tell you? I live with her."

Great.

Payton turned toward me. "We've been roommates since our sophomore year of college."

Double great.

"I've known her since junior high. And no, I'm not her boyfriend now, and I never was in the past, either," Aaron confirmed, laughing.

"I kinda got that part." And it was only because the dude was gay that I didn't pull off the road and drop his ass on the side of the highway.

We were halfway to our destination when my cell phone rang. I knew who it was without looking. Toby had a big fucking mouth, and I knew he wouldn't be able to resist. I figured he'd probably waited three minutes before calling Leif, but that would've been the longest. Toby was the last person you would ever want to share a secret with. He wouldn't last five minutes before sharing the news with anyone who would listen.

I dug for my phone in my jacket pocket and glanced at the screen. Yep. I was right.

Toby had a big fucking mouth.

Knowing Leif would kick my ass if I didn't answer, I hit the talk button and put the phone to my ear. Less than a minute later, I was tossing the phone on the seat.

"Who was that?" Payton asked, turning in her seat to face me.

"Leif."

"What did he want?"

Enjoying Payton's nosiness, I cast a look in her direction and smiled. "He doesn't want to be left out."

"Of?"

"You'll see."

Clearly, she had no idea what I was talking about, but surprisingly she didn't ask any more questions. At least not of me. As for Aaron, he got pummeled with questions, most of them having to do with Mark.

Fifteen minutes later, I exited the highway with Toby less than a car length behind me.

"Where are we?" Payton asked when we turned off on a back road.

I nodded toward the south. "Your office is about five miles that way."

"So why are we here?" she asked after glancing out the window into the dark.

"One of my buddies has a track. He lets me use it whenever I want. He hasn't had a race there for a couple of years."

I'd considered buying the place when Stu Strickland had stopped holding races but had talked myself out of it due to the location. Part of me was grateful for my fear of commitment, because I'd recently located an even better location farther north. In fact, I'd shot off a text earlier in the day to a real estate buddy of mine to put in an offer. I wasn't usually one to make big decisions when I was pissed, but after fighting with Conrad, I'd come to one final conclusion: I was done with the bullshit.

And now, if things worked out the way I hoped they would, I'd be gearing up to build something bigger and better than the deserted track we were about to embark upon. Although the place was abandoned, the track was still in great shape.

"Race? As in cars?" Aaron asked from the backseat.

"Yep," I confirmed.

"Thank God," Aaron said on a deep exhale. "I was praying you weren't taking us to some redneck bar."

"Not into that sort of thing?" I countered, trying to imagine Aaron in a redneck bar.

"Not usually, no."

"Then we'll get along just fine. I don't care for them, either. But don't tell Toby that. He's a redneck. Those types of places are like his second home."

"Is that...?" Payton's question trailed off as we pulled into the eroded parking lot a minute later.

"Leif? Yeah." I wasn't surprised to see him there already. He'd been at his mother's house, where he still lived, which wasn't far from the track. My guess was that he'd broken the sound barrier in an attempt to get there before we did. The guy was as competitive as I was.

I drove across the potholed parking lot to where Leif was waiting in his fancy-ass Mustang. Pulling up beside him, I told Payton and Aaron to stay put while I unlocked the gates. After pushing the eight-foot-tall, chain link fence open, I made my way back to the car while Toby and Leif pulled through first. I wasn't far behind.

A few more minutes passed while I pulled in and locked the gates behind us, then ventured to a small building where the control panels were. After flipping on the track lights, I returned to the car to find Payton and Aaron waiting patiently. Then, finally, I was driving down the narrow concrete path to the track.

"You aren't gonna race right now, are you?" Payton asked, her hazel eyes wide as she stared over at me. The blue glow from the dashboard cast her face in shadows, but I could see the curiosity there.

"Not yet," I told her truthfully, smiling to myself.

I fully intended to race — after all, why waste a perfectly good opportunity — but even I wasn't crazy enough to do that with her in the car. For now, I was content just being with her. This place was isolated, quiet, which meant it was the perfect spot to just chill. It was one of the few spots I came to hang out these days. Most of the time I came alone, though, so this was a nice change of pace.

When we reached the overgrown grassy area that surrounded the track, I pulled off. Leif and Toby parked their cars relatively close to mine, everyone piling out. I glanced back at Leif's '06 Mustang in time to see him and his brother getting out. I wanted to laugh, but I knew no one else would have any clue why I was, so I kept my amusement to myself. After all, no one could have planned it better.

Coincidences like this just didn't happen every day.

"Took you long enough," Leif smirked as he strode toward me when I opened Payton's door to help her out. "Was your grandma drivin'?"

"Fuck off," I muttered, grinning. "You better enjoy the feeling while you can. It's the only time you'll beat me."

Leif laughed, and his brother slapped him on the back when he joined us. Toby and Chloe weren't far behind, and when everyone gathered around my car, I made the necessary introductions. "Payton, remember Leif? And this is his brother, Garth."

"Man, fuck you. My name ain't Garth," Garrett retorted without heat, his distinct Texas drawl making me smile. "Name's Garrett. Don't listen to this asshole."

Payton laughed as she eased against my side, reaching out to take Garrett's proffered hand. I wrapped my arm around her shoulder and pulled her against me. The sweet scent of her hair instantly soothed the riot that was still clamoring in my brain.

I wanted her more than I wanted air, and it was killing me to hold back. I wasn't used to dating a girl prior to sleeping with her. In fact, I didn't usually date, period. But with Payton, taking her to bed wasn't the first thing that came to mind when I thought about her. Although, it was a close second.

"Nice to meet you," Payton said shyly, shaking Garrett's hand. "These are my roommates, Chloe and Aaron."

I watched with voyeuristic fascination as Garrett shook Chloe's hand and then Aaron's, his eyes slowly trailing from Chloe to Aaron. Yep, just like I suspected, instant chemistry.

Garrett Connelly, who I liked to call Garth, was the kind of guy who women flocked to like flies to honey. He was one of those people who caused crowds to part when he walked through. Big guy. Six four. He would've been lanky if it weren't for the muscle that lined his lean frame. He looked a lot like Leif, just a few inches taller and wider.

Just like all four of the Connelly brothers, Leif and Garrett sported the same dark hair and dark brown eyes. Neither of them regularly shaved, so they were always sporting a scruffy jaw. Garth was a couple of years older than Leif, who was the youngest Connelly and the same age as me. At twenty-seven, Garrett was the only one of Leif's brothers who hadn't ventured into the automotive industry. Garrett was a drummer. One of the best I'd ever heard. I called him Garth because back when he was in high school, he had aspired to be a country music singer. A phase, he called it.

"Didn't know you were in town," I said to Garrett as I watched him watch Aaron.

Oh, did I mention Garrett was gay? Well, bisexual was probably a better term for it, but it seemed Garrett preferred the same sex, for the most part, although he'd been known to bag some of the groupies, too.

Like I said, coincidence.

"For a few days," Garrett answered, finally looking back at me. "Then we're back on the road."

Toby walked over and slapped Garrett on the back. "What's up, Garth?"

Garrett elbowed Toby in the gut, making him grunt as he bent over. "Nice to see you, too, dude."

"So, what is this place?" Chloe asked, walking over to stand by Payton, her eyes roaming the darkness that surrounded the track.

"Racetrack," Aaron informed her.

"I got that part, Einstein. Why are we here?"

"To race," Toby said quickly, grinning at her as though he hadn't just stated the obvious, as well.

"No shit?" Aaron asked, glancing around at everyone, his bright blue eyes landing on Garrett. And staying there.

"I'm here to race," I informed them. "Y'all are here to lose. But not yet. Come on."

I took Payton's hand and led everyone down to the track, Toby mumbling something that sounded a lot like, "There's a first time for everything."

I grinned.

For now, I'd show them around. And a little later, I'd show them how it was done.

Chapter Three

Payton

IF I SAID THAT I would've ever thought I'd be standing in the middle of a deserted racetrack at night with Sebastian close by, I'd be lying. Heck, standing on a deserted racetrack at all was so far out of my element I was having a hard time keeping up.

But Sebastian *was* there with me, his arm wrapped tightly around my shoulders as we walked from the grassy knoll down to the track. The way he kept me close, insisting on touching me at all times, was incredibly comforting. And strangely erotic. If it hadn't been for everyone else being there, it would've been romantic.

When we'd left the apartment a short time ago, I wasn't sure what I had expected. A sports bar, maybe. Pizza place, possibly. I certainly hadn't anticipated this.

It was something out of a movie, and if Sebastian hadn't unlocked the gates in front of me, I would've thought we were trespassing. Except he looked as though he was used to being there. And that settled some of my nerves.

But Sebastian was right. It might not be a place that saw many people these days, but it seemed in relatively good shape. The grass surrounding and through the middle of the track hadn't been cut in a while, but that was about the only clue that no one spent time there.

As we walked down the steep embankment to the asphalt, I was trying to take it all in. Sebastian's nearness, our friends talking and joking, the overhead lights brightening the area as though it were daytime. I felt almost like I was intoxicated, but I hadn't had a drop of alcohol, so I knew that wasn't the case. Part of me kept waiting to wake up to find that this was some sort of crazy dream. I mean, I was still reeling from Sebastian showing up at my apartment, and then the odd conversation we'd been having when Aaron interrupted.

If it hadn't been for the others moving about, laughing — mainly at Toby and his antics — I would've considered pinching myself to see if I woke up. Then again, if this was a dream, I wasn't sure I wanted to.

Even with everyone causing a pleasant distraction, I was still having a hard time keeping myself from staring at Sebastian. He might not know it, but he was the center of the attraction — and not just for me. It seemed that everyone enjoyed being around him. Leif and Toby were constantly getting his attention, pulling him into the conversation. I noticed they were especially attentive when Sebastian grew quiet. It was as though they didn't want him to get lost in his own head, even for a little while.

He wasn't an easy person to ignore. Not that I'd tried.

He just seemed larger than life, so enigmatic and intense. And I was drawn to him. When he was anywhere in the vicinity, it was as though I forgot about everything and everyone else. Aaron was just lucky that I loved him as much as I did, because deserting Sebastian to check on him earlier hadn't been an easy thing for me to do. I wanted to spend every minute with Sebastian.

Sebastian's unexpected arrival at my apartment had started a chain of unexpected events, which had led to me standing on a racetrack with the uber sexy guy who'd plagued my every thought since the day I'd met him. It wasn't easy to pretend not to be affected by him, either. When he put his arm around my shoulders, pulling me close, I could smell the delicious scent of his cologne mixed with the wonderful smell of leather. He was overwhelming my senses. The way he was constantly touching me made my skin tingle. I could feel the heat of his body everywhere. And the simple fact that he kept me close to him made me feel as though I'd known him all my life when, really, we hardly knew one another.

He made my body burn, and I was already contemplating whether or not I was going to ask him to stay the night tonight. I didn't know if he would consider it too early in our relationship for what I had in mind, but I wasn't sure how much longer I could wait, either. That was one of the first signs that I was in over my head with him, because I certainly wasn't the type of girl who was generally ruled by my hormones, but there was something about Sebastian. My head was filled with crazy ideas whenever I thought about him. Even more so when I was near him.

For whatever reason, whether because he was a gentleman or possibly something else, Sebastian seemed to be refraining from going too far with me, which had me questioning my own desires.

And to see this side of him... It was more than I could handle.

Although we'd been having a serious conversation and he'd dropped the father bomb on me earlier, he had been a good sport when Aaron had come barreling into the apartment ready to tear it to shreds because he'd caught his boyfriend cheating.

As soon as Aaron had mentioned Mark's name, it had been a no-brainer that I had to spend the evening with Aaron. After all, he was my best friend and he needed me. I just hadn't expected Sebastian to want to hang out, as well. But somehow, he'd managed to lighten the mood and then turn it around completely.

Knowing Aaron, he would've preferred to sit at home and wallow in his hurt, but Sebastian hadn't given him much of a choice. Actually, Sebastian hadn't given him a choice at all.

Which was why we were standing on a racetrack, listening to Leif and Toby argue over the official terminology for everything. They were bantering back and forth like children, Toby interrupting to correct Leif whenever he could. Everyone was laughing. Everyone except Sebastian, who was constantly looking around, aware of everything around him, not just his friends.

Although the track intrigued me, I was more interested in watching Sebastian. The way he moved, the way he spoke. He was a dichotomy. I knew there was something dark and dangerous lurking inside him, because I'd seen a glimpse of it, but here, tonight, with his friends and mine, it wasn't as noticeable.

When Sebastian had arrived at my apartment earlier, he'd been upset. Actually, angry was a better way to describe his demeanor when he'd arrived unexpectedly. The little make-out session we'd had in my bedroom had helped ease some of the tension, but this certainly wasn't the direction I'd seen the night going. Sebastian had done a complete turnaround just because Aaron had needed someone to cheer him up. And for that reason, among other things, I had a sneaking suspicion that I was quickly falling for him.

Okay, that wasn't entirely true. I don't think there was any suspicion. I was falling for Sebastian Trovato. Fast and hard. And surprisingly, that didn't bother me in the least. Being with Sebastian felt right.

While everyone laughed and joked, Sebastian remained close to my side, one arm wrapped around my shoulders, the other crossing over in front of me, the fingers of his right hand linked with my left. With my head resting against his chest, his mouth frequently brushed my hair as he spoke. It was intimate, and so natural. I felt safe in his arms.

I paid attention to the way he interacted with Toby and Leif. It was apparent that they had a close friendship. They teased in a way that only good friends could do, and from what I'd seen so far, they were always having a good time when they were together, even though Sebastian's intensity hadn't lessened any.

"Are you cold?" Sebastian asked, turning his attention to me while Toby and Leif continued to rib one another good-naturedly.

"No." I wasn't cold. In fact, I was rather warm, and it had nothing to do with the jacket Sebastian had insisted that I bring, either. "Thanks for doing this, by the way."

"Happy to. I'm just glad you're here with me," Sebastian said, his voice soft and low.

"Me, too." He would never know how happy I was about that. If I had my way, I'd never be apart from him. And I knew that we hadn't known each other long enough for me to feel that way, but time didn't even seem to be relevant when we were together. I felt like I'd known him for a lot longer than just a little more than a week.

"So, Garrett, you said you were only in town for a couple of days?" Chloe's question had me engaging in the conversation, curious as to what had brought it on. "What is it that you do?"

Garrett glanced over at Leif, then to Sebastian, but Toby was the one who answered. "He's in a band."

"Which one?" Chloe asked, her eyes widening.

As though he felt the need to stake his claim, Toby made his way to Chloe's side, gently pulling her against him.

"Heat Seekers," Garrett replied.

"Are you freaking serious?" Chloe exclaimed. "Oh, my God!"

The girl's excitement meter had just redlined. I had no idea who the Heat Seekers were, but apparently, she did. That or she was just strangely excited by the name.

"I saw y'all play at Stubb's last year. Wow. Small world. Great show, by the way."

"Thanks." Garrett looked a little bashful, which surprised me. Then again, his appearance surprised me, too. He looked so ... normal. Aside from the tattoos coloring his forearms — the only part of his body I could see besides his neck and head — he didn't look like a rock star. He was very clean-cut with his short dark hair and lack of piercings. Even the scruffy jaw looked more preppy than rugged.

I noticed Aaron was watching Garrett as though the guy had just announced he was on the cover of *People* magazine and had just been named sexiest man alive.

"So, are we gonna get our race on or what?" Leif interrupted.

"Dude, quit bein' a baby," Toby interjected. "Just 'cause my girl's droolin' over your brother doesn't mean you gotta speak up. We like you better when you're quiet."

Leif elbowed Toby this time, making him grunt. "Y'all are gonna have to stop doin' that shit."

"I was thinking that Toby should be the one worried," Aaron said. "Chloe's got that wild look in her eyes."

Chloe merely smiled at Aaron. I could tell she was a little star struck by Garrett, but that look was nothing compared to the look she gave Toby every chance she could.

"Seriously," Leif stated. "We gonna do this?"

"In a minute," Sebastian answered, smiling down at me as though he were waiting for me to tell him that it was okay.

"I wanna watch you race," I whispered, the adrenaline from everyone's enthusiasm coursing through me. I had to admit, the idea of watching Sebastian race was sexy as hell.

"You heard the lady," Toby called out. "She wants to watch."

Chapter Four

Payton

A FEW MINUTES LATER, SEBASTIAN released me from the circle of his arms, but he kept his fingers linked with mine as we made our way up into the stands, the others following close behind. When we reached the top of the stairs, he let me take the lead, still holding my hands behind me and directing me with ease.

When we reached the section of the stands in front of the starting line, Sebastian stopped.

"Kiss for good luck," he demanded, turning me around to face him as he cupped my face in his big, warm hands.

I definitely had no intention of arguing. Going up on my toes, I met his lips with mine, loving the way the metal from his lip ring slid across my lower lip. The hunger returned, and I wrapped my arms around his neck, not caring where we were or who was watching. I wanted this man with a passion I didn't understand. When he slipped his tongue in my mouth, I raked mine over his, the barbell through his tongue making me even crazier with lust. He was so damn sexy.

"Get a room!" Aaron shouted from somewhere behind me.

Sebastian smiled against my mouth and pulled back, leaving me feeling a little dazed. My heart was racing, and it wasn't just because of Sebastian's kisses. Although that was a huge part of it.

Sebastian steered me to a bench and ordered me to sit, so I did. "Don't move."

"Yes, sir," I retorted, saluting him.

He then leaned down and pressed his lips to mine one more time. He didn't linger, and part of me was disappointed. I could've kissed him all night, but I knew it was going to eventually lead to something more. I was ready. Too ready, so I admired Sebastian's self-control. He had managed to pull us back from the brink when I was ready to jump in with both feet.

Did that make me a bad person? I'd only known him for a week, yet I felt like I'd known him my entire life and getting naked with the sexiest man on the planet had suddenly become one of my only goals in life. That should've freaked me out, but as I watched Sebastian walk away, I couldn't bring myself to care. The guy was absolutely gorgeous.

Chloe joined me on the bench, scooting close to my side, linking her arm with mine and snuggling against me. Aaron and Garrett were deep in conversation, leaning against the rails in front of us.

"Is this hot or what?" Chloe asked, her excitement palpable.

"Pretty hot." Anything that had to do with Sebastian was hot, though. At least in my opinion.

"I'm gonna ask Toby to stay the night," Chloe mentioned, her voice low enough that only I could hear.

I jerked my head to the side to look at her. "You mean he hasn't already?"

Chloe shook her head. "Not yet."

Thinking about what that meant, I narrowed my eyes at her. "Are you ... sure?"

I had known from the night we'd seen Sebastian at the sports bar that Chloe was captivated by Toby. And then when I'd found him sitting in my kitchen just that morning, I'd known she was serious about him. They were cute together, I'd give them that. I hadn't been around them much, but they did seem to enjoy one another's company. I just didn't want to see my friend jump in too fast. Chloe was impulsive, but usually not when it came to men. Then again, I was contemplating doing the same thing, and we were very much alike in that regard. In my defense, I'd known Sebastian a little longer. Granted, I had only seen him once during the first week of knowing him, but it was still technically longer.

"I really like him," Chloe answered. "I mean *really* like him, Payton."

I turned back to watch the guys getting into their cars, resting my head against Chloe's. "Just be careful. And I'm not just talking about safe sex," I clarified.

"I'll do my best."

Chloe was a lot like me in the sense that she didn't date often. Admiring guys from afar was what we usually did, both of us too busy to deal with relationships. But during the time I'd known Chloe, she had been in two serious relationships, both of them ending badly. I hated to see my friend hurt, but more selfishly, if things didn't work out for her and Toby … that could potentially have negative implications on my relationship with Sebastian.

The rev of Sebastian's engine as he slowly drove down to the track wrenched me from my thoughts. Sebastian's glossy black Camaro was followed by Leif's fire-engine-red Mustang and Toby's matte black, older-model Camaro pulled up the rear as they made their way back onto the pavement. All three cars would have blended with the night if it weren't for the sports lights that lit up the area like it was daytime.

From where I sat in the bleachers, I was looking down at the track. Admittedly, I wasn't much of a racing fan. I didn't follow NASCAR, nor did I watch Formula One, although Austin had recently built a track for the latter. If there was a regulation size, I didn't know, but this track didn't look like anything I'd seen on television other than it was oval-shaped with four banked corners. Just a few minutes ago, we had been down there, so I knew firsthand just how steep those corners were. My gut twisted as my anticipation mixed with a tiny amount of nervousness.

I held my breath as the three cars started down the track. They weren't going fast, and from what I knew of racing, which was very, very little, I figured they were warming up their tires first. That was something my father always warned me about, considering it had been his bright idea to put Pirellis on my Mustang. For what purpose, I would never know. But I knew firsthand that when they were cold, they were slick on the pavement.

And that's exactly what the three cars did for a few laps, weaving back and forth across the track, keeping their speed to a minimum. I watched, admiring the American muscle. All three cars were impressive. I happened to be partial to Sebastian's, but that was because it was Sebastian's. I still remembered the first time I'd seen it. I'd been so nervous; the name of the car hadn't come to me.

When they pulled to a stop at the starting line, I held my breath.

Chloe squeezed my arm, her legs bouncing, her feet tapping the concrete beneath us.

"My money's on Sebastian," Garrett said, his deep voice carrying on the chilly night air.

"Why's that?" Aaron asked.

"The guy's never lost."

Really?

That made my heart swell with pride. Why, I had no idea.

As I watched, eagerly waiting for them to start, I realized I was still smiling. By the time the night was out, I was sure my cheeks were going to hurt.

And then they were off. I had no idea how they determined when to go, but all three engines revved, and then they peeled off the starting line, the front ends surging forward, all that horsepower flooding the night with a sexy rumble.

Chloe squealed, squeezing my arm tightly. My body buzzed and hummed, the intensity of the moment sending a flurry of butterflies through my tummy.

Once they got going, I only had eyes for Sebastian's Camaro. He steadily gained speed until he was flying around the track, going up the banked corners and then back down the straightaways, the other two cars close behind him. The faster he went, the tighter my hands clenched, until the circulation in my fingers was cut off. I was gritting my teeth, and I could feel the adrenaline coursing through me although I wasn't the one in the car.

"How fast are they going?" Chloe shouted to Garrett and Aaron.

"I'd say ... about one thirty. Maybe one forty," Garrett replied.

"Holy shit."

Yep, holy shit was right.

I was so enthralled by the action I had no idea how much time had passed before Sebastian slowed after crossing the finish line one last time. He'd won, just as Garrett had said.

"That was fucking awesome!" Chloe screeched, jumping to her feet and making her way down to where Aaron and Garrett were standing. I didn't get up, mostly because I wasn't sure I could. I was still reeling from watching Sebastian.

Toby, Leif, and Sebastian razzed each other as they made their way back to the stands, all three of them laughing. Toby took Sebastian in a headlock and rubbed his knuckles over Sebastian's head. Yeah, it didn't seem to matter to the three of them who had won. It was the thrill of the race that apparently got them off.

To each his own.

I couldn't take my eyes off Sebastian. Right there, at that moment, he looked like my wildest fantasy come to life. His hair was mussed, his smile wide. He must have ditched his jacket in the car, because I could see his tattoos peeking out beneath the sleeves of his T-shirt, his biceps pulling the fabric tight. He was breathing heavy, as though he'd just run a mile. I figured that had to do with the adrenaline.

When he met my gaze as he came toward me, I saw the exhilaration there. It was potent. So much so that my body warmed instantly; the chill in the crisp November evening was overshadowed by that heat.

"So?" Sebastian asked when he made his way back to me, stopping a row down and standing in front of me.

"So *what?*" I asked, my voice shaking from my excitement, but I was trying to play it cool.

"What'd you think?"

"Eh," I teased, pretending indifference.

Sebastian leaned back against the rail that ran the length of the bleachers, his foot propped on the lower rung, his elbows resting on the top.

Lord, have mercy, the man made my heart race.

"Oh yeah?" he asked, chuckling. "That good, huh?"

"It was kinda … hot," I admitted, laughing, trying to keep from blushing.

"Wanna try it?" he asked.

"Nope," I said as confidently as I could. I didn't mind watching, actually enjoyed it, but I definitely wasn't a race car type of girl.

"Ready to get out of here?"

I nodded and got to my feet. Sebastian waited for me to go down the stairs first and then followed close, everyone else somewhere behind us. I hoped he didn't see that my hands were shaking. Watching him drive had been incredibly stimulating but nerve-racking all the same.

When we reached his car, he came to the passenger side, but before opening the door, he turned me to face him and backed me against it. Again, without thinking about where we were or who was with us, I wrapped my arms around his waist, sliding my hands beneath his T-shirt so I could feel his heated skin against my palms.

"What did you really think?" he asked softly, peering down at me.

"It was incredible," I admitted breathlessly, pushing up on my toes and pressing my lips to his. I flicked his lip ring gently. "I've never seen anything sexier. Well, besides you."

Sebastian watched me for long seconds, not saying anything. His hands were planted on the roof of the car, one on each side of my head, his rock-solid body pressed into me. I could see his jaw flexing, as though he wanted to say something but thought better of it.

"I hope we're gonna get food after this," Toby said. Who he was talking to, I had no idea. Nor did I care.

"About earlier," Sebastian said on a sigh, those mysterious storm clouds gathering in his golden eyes once again. "About Conrad…"

His statement took me by surprise after all the laughter and joking that had been going on for the last hour. I put my finger against his lips, my eyes locked with his. "We need to talk more. I know that. But you needed this." I don't know how I knew that, but I did. I knew that whatever he had going on in his head, he needed this. He used racing as a release; he'd pretty much told me so.

"I need *you*, Angel," he said, his warm breath fluttering over my lips. "That's all I really need."

My heart beat faster, so fast that I nearly lost my breath. The meaning behind those few words was so much deeper than what I'd expected.

Could it be possible that this was meant to be? That Sebastian and I had been destined to meet? I thought back to the dream I'd had about him before I ever met him, and it was then that I realized that yes, whatever this was, it had been in the cards all along.

"I need you, too," I whispered.

Sebastian rested his forehead against mine briefly.

"Come on, y'all. Let's go eat," Leif called out.

"You hungry?" Sebastian asked, his voice low.

Unable to resist, I answered with something he'd said to me before. "Yeah. But not for food."

"Angel, you're gonna be the death of me." Sebastian chuckled and then pressed his lips to mine quickly before pulling back and opening my door. "Come on, let's go eat."

I nodded my head. I wanted to tell him that I'd much rather take him back to my apartment and feast on him for a little while. But part of me worried that it was too soon. As much as I wanted to go somewhere private and spend the night in his arms, I knew that was something we would have to work up to.

Unraveling

I just secretly hoped it would be sooner rather than later.

Chapter Five

Payton

DINNER CONSISTED OF EGGS, BACON, and pancakes. Well, for everyone except Toby. He opted for hash browns instead of pancakes, which I found highly entertaining, especially when Sebastian told the story about Toby's first breakfast with Chloe. The decision to go to IHOP had been unanimous, mainly because it was the first restaurant that we'd come to after leaving the track. That was where all seven of us spent the next two hours, crammed into an oversized, semi-circle booth, eating, laughing, and having a good time.

I wasn't sure I'd ever been as happy as I was right then.

Watching the interaction between everyone at the table was amusing. Chloe and Toby were giving one another bedroom eyes, and I was kind of surprised they hadn't opted to forego dinner in lieu of sneaking back to our apartment. Garrett and Aaron were … well, I wasn't sure what they were doing, but if I had to guess, Aaron wasn't thinking about Mark anymore at all.

The two men seemed to have a lot in common: they were both obsessed with Sons of Anarchy, both avoided redneck bars (as Aaron referred to them) if at all possible, and they detested wine. Oh, and they were clearly attracted to one another. Which, by the way, had come as a little bit of a surprise to me.

I didn't claim to have any super sense, or *gaydar*, as some people referred to it, but I had not received any sort of vibe from Garrett that suggested he was gay. It wasn't until we were back in the car on the way to the restaurant that Sebastian had told me. Granted, Sebastian's exact word was bisexual, which had left me both curious and a little concerned for Aaron.

I was happy for Aaron, but also worried. He was my best friend; not to mention, he was incredibly vulnerable right now. Hell, he'd just found his boyfriend in bed with another man. But as much as I wanted to see him happy, I didn't want him to do something he would regret later. I tried to remind myself that he was a grown man; he could make his own decisions.

I just had to keep telling myself that.

After Chloe and I finished our coffee, the check was split three ways, Sebastian picking up the tab for Aaron and me. I thanked him, making sure he knew he didn't have to do that. He insisted, and the look in his eyes said I shouldn't argue with him. So I didn't.

"We're gonna get out of here," Chloe said as she leaned over to me, resting her chin on my shoulder.

"Okay." I wasn't sure what I was supposed to say to that. I knew where they were going; it was evident. Either our apartment or wherever Toby lived.

"See you at home later?" she asked.

Looked like our apartment won the coin toss there.

"Yep."

After saying their good-byes, Chloe and Toby left hand in hand.

Sebastian must've realized I was worried about her because he leaned over and pressed his lips against my ear. "He's a good guy. I swear to that."

"I just don't want to see her get hurt," I told him softly.

"Not to say she'll hurt him," Sebastian said, his breath warm against my ear, "but there's a better chance of him getting hurt first."

I didn't want to see that, either, but I didn't tell Sebastian as much because Leif interrupted our private conversation.

"We're gonna head out and get a beer. Wanna join us?"

Sebastian glanced at me and I shook my head. I was tired. It had been a long day, and I wasn't up for being out all night. It was already midnight and crawling into bed was starting to sound better and better.

Preferably with Sebastian, but I didn't tell him that.

"No, thanks," Sebastian answered for us. "I'm gonna take her home and then head home myself."

"You coming with us?" I asked Aaron.

"I'm gonna go with them," Aaron informed me, nodding his head toward Garrett.

As much as I wanted to tell him to be careful, too, I bit my tongue and kept my comment to myself. I needed to take my own advice, not dish it out to everyone else.

"We'll bring him home in a coupla hours," Leif added as the three of them stood and offered more good-byes before they headed out the door.

And then we were the only two left at the table.

"You ready to go?" Sebastian asked, his arm sliding around my shoulders.

"As ready as I'll ever be."

Truth was, I was ready to leave the restaurant, but I wasn't ready to leave Sebastian.

Now I just had to figure out how to tell him that.

Half an hour later, Sebastian was pulling into my apartment complex. I was a little sad to see it hadn't taken long to get home. Even though conversation had been minimal for most of the drive, Sebastian had insisted on holding my hand. Oddly, his mere touch had been all that I needed. Words hadn't been necessary, and the silence that ensued was comforting. But now I didn't want to let him go.

He pulled into an empty spot close to my building and shut off the engine. Neither of us moved for what felt like an eternity, and then Sebastian turned to me. I watched him nervously, wishing I could tell him what was on my mind. When his eyes darted down to my lips, I knew what was coming next.

Rather than wait for him to kiss me, I leaned over, sliding my hand behind his neck and pulling him to me. His arms instantly wrapped around me, our lips sliding together. The kiss started out sweet and gentle, yet there was a hum of hunger vibrating just beneath the surface. I didn't have to take the lead that time, because Sebastian thrust his tongue into my mouth and I moaned, giving in to him.

The air in the car warmed several degrees, my body likely the main contributor. When Sebastian's hands slid beneath my T-shirt, his warmth caressing my back, I knew what I had to do. I didn't want to leave him, didn't want to spend the night without him.

But then he was pulling back, his hands disappearing from my body and returning to the steering wheel as he peered out through the slightly fogged windshield.

"Thank you for tonight," he said quietly.

I knew I should've been the one thanking him, but I couldn't get my voice to work. I wanted to invite him upstairs, to take him to my bedroom and pick up where we'd just left off, but I didn't tell him that.

The next thing I knew, Sebastian was exiting the car and walking around to open my door. Feeling slightly dejected, I accepted his hand and allowed him to help me from the car. I was surprised to see that he was going to walk me to my door. Surprised, but not disappointed.

Once we were up the stairs, Sebastian waited while I slid the key in the lock, but he stopped me before I opened the front door. Without hesitation, he spun me around and pressed me against the door, his lips finding mine while his big, callused hands cupped my face. The hunger returned with a vengeance, our lips crashing together, tongues colliding. I melted into him, wrapping my arms around his waist, sliding my hands beneath his T-shirt, where I found the hard muscles underneath. Digging my nails into his skin, I pulled him closer, desperate for more of him. He smelled so good — the rich scent of his cologne mixed with the sultry scent of his leather jacket. It was a heady mixture.

At that moment, I didn't think I would ever get enough, and the thought of him leaving, even for a little while, wasn't making me feel better.

When he pulled back, my lungs were starved for oxygen and my heart was pounding like a drum, loud enough that I was sure he heard it, too.

"I want to invite you in," I whispered nervously.

Sebastian's thumb grazed my cheek as he watched me, his eyes locked with mine. "I *want* you to invite me in."

Did that mean I was supposed to ask? Or was it assumed now that I'd mentioned it? It almost sounded like there was a *but* in there somewhere, so I waited for Sebastian to say something.

It never came, and I swallowed hard, trying to spit the words out. But then words weren't necessary because someone else took care of that for us. From inside my apartment, I heard Chloe moan, followed by, "Damn, baby. Oh, Chloe."

Needless to say, my face turned scarlet.

Sebastian exhaled on a gruff laugh.

And when Chloe screamed Toby's name, I couldn't help but laugh, as well.

Sebastian reached behind me and relocked the door before pulling the keys from the lock and taking my hand. "Come on."

Following him down the stairs once again, I continued to laugh. It was that or cry, but not because I was sad. My best friend was inside my apartment getting it on with Sebastian's friend, and here I was trying to figure out how to convince Sebastian to stay the night with me.

"Where're we going?" I asked when he joined me inside the car.

"My place."

My breath caught in my throat, and I couldn't look away from him.

"Payton, if you don't want to go, say so now."

I could barely make out his face in the darkness, but I studied him anyway. "I want to go," I said, my throat tight with anticipation.

"Are you sure?"

I didn't even hesitate before I replied. "I've never been more sure about anything in my life."

I could see the heat flare in Sebastian's golden eyes, and I knew that we were about to take this to an entirely different level.

And I hadn't been lying when I'd told him that I wanted it.

In fact, I wanted it more than anything.

Chapter Six

Sebastian

BY THE TIME I PULLED into my garage forty minutes later, I had damn near broken every speed limit, my palms were sweating, and I'd probably lost two pounds just from how hard my heart was thumping in my chest. Honestly, I was surprised my entire body wasn't sweating since it felt as though I'd done a major cardio workout during the drive back to my house. I didn't think it was possible for something to make my adrenaline pump as fast as it did when I was racing, but this pretty much blew that shit out of the water.

I had never once, not even my very first time, been nervous about taking a woman to bed. But Payton wasn't just any woman.

She was everything.

And here I was, taking her back to my place knowing that I should have just left her at her apartment. It would've been the gentlemanly thing to do. She would've probably locked herself in her bedroom and turned on her stereo, effectively drowning out Chloe and Toby, but I couldn't leave her there.

Okay, so *couldn't* was probably a little strong of a word. I didn't want to. That was more accurate. Anything to keep Payton with me.

So, during the painfully long drive back to my house, I had fought every single thought that filled my head, every one of them revolving around all the things I wanted to do to her when I got her naked.

If I got her naked.

I was beginning to second-guess my decision to bring Payton back to my house, recalling the argument I'd had with my father earlier. It wouldn't bode well for me if Conrad decided to interfere with my relationship with Payton. And I damn sure didn't want him trying to use what might happen between us against me.

"Nice," Payton said when the garage door closed behind us, pulling me from my negative train of thought. I mean, seriously ... I had Payton there with me. Thoughts of my father — negative or otherwise — weren't conducive to my current frame of mind.

"What? The house? Or the cars?" I asked, trying to focus on the present.

"Both. Do you live out here?"

I glanced through the windshield, trying to see the garage as she did for the first time. There were couches and chairs sitting in one corner, a refrigerator and sink on the far wall. The rest of the space was filled with either my vehicles or my tools. Yeah, I guess it kind of did look like I lived out there. "I spend a lot of time out here," I told her.

"I can tell," she said, smiling. "What is that?"

I looked over to see her staring out the passenger window at the white car parked next to us.

"Ferrari 458 Spider."

"Wow. Do you drive it?" Payton cast me a sideways glance while she waited for me to answer.

"On occasion." I chuckled, pushing open my door and climbing out, taking a deep breath as I walked around to her side. Opening her door, I inhaled sharply again.

This was actually happening. Payton was at my house.

My house.

Well, technically, the place I called home wasn't mine. It belonged to my father, but I'd lived there since the day I'd turned eighteen. I would've left altogether, except Conrad had insisted that I stay in the guesthouse, probably his way of keeping me under his thumb a little while longer. His excuse had been that I needed to be close if I expected to be able to work from the house. It was that or he was going to insist that I go to the shop, which was something I refused to do.

I briefly thought about the house that I was in the process of buying and wished like hell that I was taking Payton there, rather than here. Unfortunately, this place would have to do for now.

We were alone and there wasn't a chance for anyone to interrupt us. Well, unless my asshole of a father decided to invade the guesthouse. Since he hadn't done so up to this point, I held out hope that he would stay away tonight.

Pretty soon I wouldn't have to worry about him invading my space. That was another reason I was moving. Well, that and clearly it was time that I took control of my own life. As much as I liked the convenience of living and working on the Trovato estate, it was time for me to make a stand. For the last few months, my relationship with my father had started deteriorating beyond repair, and it was only getting worse with every day that passed.

Brushing off the thoughts of Conrad, I took Payton's hand and led her through the crowded garage. She was gazing around, checking everything out. I opened the door to the house and stepped back so she could go in before me.

Once inside, I felt a little more at ease. After all, there were no expectations. I just wanted Payton there with me. Even if it meant we spent the rest of the night watching movies on the couch.

When I walked inside, the noise in my head grew a little louder. It was the house. The fact that I hated being there was making me crazy. Again, another good reason that I was finally going to do something about it. Unfortunately, these things took time. I'd been eyeing a particular house for a while, which was the only reason the paperwork was now underway. That decision was the only logical one I'd made all day, with the exception of showing up unannounced at Payton's.

And bringing her back there with me.

She had single-handedly calmed the riot in my head that afternoon when I had shown up at her apartment. It had been a little iffy there for a while, my anger had been a firestorm burning out of control, but just as I'd suspected, the moment I'd looked at her, I had calmed down. Didn't mean I had completely forgotten about the argument I'd had with Conrad, but it went a long way toward keeping me from stewing about it, letting it fester into something that would ultimately tear me apart from the inside out.

I slid off my leather jacket and tossed it on the back of a chair and then helped Payton remove hers, leaving it beside mine.

She was looking up at the twenty-foot-high ceilings that spanned most of the downstairs and then over at the wall of windows that made up the outside of the house when she finally said, "This is … beautiful, Sebastian."

I figured she was referring to the house based on the way she was looking around, but I pretended to misunderstand. "Yes, you are." I eased up behind her, sliding my hands into the front pockets of her jeans and pulling her against me.

The instant we touched, my body reacted to her nearness, the chaos dwindling, immediately replaced with something equally distracting: a desperate, aching need for this woman. It was impossible to control my reaction to her. Just her simple touch made me hard, made me eager to have her in every possible way imaginable. And I knew I wouldn't be able to hide it from her for long, if at all. I could hardly control myself around this woman. Each time I saw her, my craving for her only intensified until it was a conflagration threatening to get out of control.

Not that I wanted her to know that.

Yet.

"Want a tour?" I asked, pressing my lips to the soft skin of her neck.

"Yeah," she said, sounding a little breathless.

Reluctantly, I released her so I could show her around. It wasn't that I wanted to give her a grand tour of the house I would be moving out of in the near future, but it was that or toss her over my shoulder and carry her to my bedroom. I wasn't a patient man, but with Payton, I knew I had to make a concession. The last thing I wanted to do was scare her off.

So, we made our way to the kitchen. I didn't use the area often, mainly because I wasn't much of a cook, and living alone, it just wasn't a place I spent a lot of time. The stainless-steel appliances were state-of-the-art and picked out by my stepmother. They looked good with the modern white cabinets and black granite countertops, also designed by Lauren. The decorations that sat on the tops of the counters weren't my idea, either, but since the housekeeper dusted and cleaned once a week, I didn't bother to toss them into a cabinet. Like I said, this was the room I probably spent the least amount of time in.

"What's in your refrigerator?" Payton asked, grinning at me before releasing my hand.

"Are you hungry?" I asked, confused by her question.

"Nope. But what's in the refrigerator tells a lot about a person."

"That right?" I'd never heard that before.

And I wasn't sure the few things in my refrigerator were going to say a lot about me. Especially since I didn't do my own grocery shopping, either.

"Orange juice, yogurt, milk, cheese … water." Payton glanced back at me, her waist-length dark hair sliding over her shoulder and falling down her back. Her smile was radiant, and I knew right then that I wanted to see her in my kitchen more often. Not so that she could cook for me or any sexist bullshit like that, just because she made the space that much more welcoming.

"What does that say about me?" I asked, hopping up onto the counter and watching her.

"It says you're boring, Sebastian."

I chuckled, continuing to watch her rummage through the contents. "Boring, huh?"

"No beer?"

"I don't drink that much. Usually only when I go out." I hadn't bothered to mention to Payton that I had a highly addictive personality, which was the reason I avoided certain things. I didn't drink much, rarely at home; I didn't smoke, although I'd stupidly done so to be cool when I was younger. I'd never tried drugs, either. My drug of choice was adrenaline, which was why I raced. I released the pent-up anger by beating the shit out of the heavy bag in my weight room, knowing that if I didn't, the undercurrent would eventually invade my life and turn me into someone I didn't want to look at in the mirror each day.

"Interesting."

I wanted to know just what was going through her head, but I didn't get to ask because she was on a roll.

"Do you eat cereal?" Payton closed the refrigerator door and opened the freezer.

"Sometimes. Would that make me less boring?"

"Maybe. At least you've got ice cream."

"I do?" I really had no idea.

"Vanilla," she said, grinning widely. "Imagine that."

"I'll have to remember to add chocolate to the grocery list," I told her, remembering the first time I'd taken her out for ice cream.

"You do that. Get chocolate syrup while you're at it."

Yep, my ass hopped right down off that counter so damn fast it was a wonder I didn't face plant on the gray travertine floor. "Alrighty, then. Time to see another room." I grabbed her hand and tugged her into the formal living room, shifting uncomfortably as my jeans became just a little too tight.

And then there we were, in another room I didn't spend much time in. After all, there wasn't a television, which meant I had limited interest in the space.

"I'm sensing a theme here, Sebastian."

"Yeah? What's that?"

"Did your decorator only see things in black and white?"

She sounded serious, but I was pretty sure she was joking.

"My stepmother deserves all the credit for the decorating. Even before she was married to Conrad, she…" I tried to think of a nicer way to say what was on my mind. "Let's just say Lauren's always been a part of Conrad's life. At least for as long as I can remember."

Lauren Trovato was a woman who went after what she wanted. And just like the saying went, nothing would stand in her way. Not even Conrad's previous wives.

But yeah, I got where Payton was coming from on the décor. It was right there in … well … in black and white. The two sofas were black leather, the side chair was white leather, and they were wrapped around a chrome-and-glass table that sat atop a plush black-and-white rug. The centerpiece for the room was the fireplace, which was shared between two rooms, fixed in a wall constructed of jagged natural quartz tiles stacked from floor to ceiling that separated the area from the formal dining room.

"It needs color, huh?"

"It needs something."

I pulled Payton to me until her breasts rubbed against my chest. I took both of her hands, linked our fingers together, and then pulled her arms behind her, holding them at the small of her back. The position left her fully at my mercy. "Right now, it's got everything I could possibly need."

Her cheeks turned a lovely shade of pink, and she licked her lips, making my dick throb. God, this woman was unraveling me.

"Well, what do you say we add this room to the list?" Payton's raspy tone held a seductive note that wasn't doing anything to quench the lust surging through my veins.

"What list?" I dared to ask.

"The list of rooms we christen later."

Oh, hell. A loud rumble came from my chest as I leaned down and pressed my mouth to hers, pulling her more tightly against me, trying to refrain from laying her out right there on the couch. "Angel, you're tempting a very hungry man right now."

Payton's answer to that was a smile that sent a shockwave through me, similar to a direct hit from a lightning strike.

"Next room," I mumbled against her lips, not wanting to release her just yet.

Unable to resist, I thrust my tongue into her mouth, licking her tongue, tasting her sweetness. When I did pull away, her face was flushed and her chest was rising and falling rapidly, similar to mine. To see her reaction to me, it was as much of an aphrodisiac as kissing her.

Knowing we were playing with fire, I led her to the next room.

"Do you actually eat in here?" Payton asked, pulling me to a stop when I would have just kept going. I'd been wrong earlier when I'd said I spent the least amount of time in the kitchen. Truth was, I rarely stepped foot in the dining room, and I knew for a fact, in the seven years that I'd lived in that house, not once had I eaten at that table.

"Not once," I answered and kept moving.

I led her down a narrow hallway to two guest rooms with elaborate baths attached. Prior to my impromptu plan to move, I had intended for Leif to move into one of the guest rooms while the other would continue to go untouched. Truth was, I had used those rooms on occasion, but only when I brought a woman back to my place. I'd never taken a woman to my bedroom, preferring something a little less personal. Needless to say, I wouldn't be using either of those rooms tonight. If Payton was going to be in bed with me, we were going to be in my bed.

"Want to see the room I spend the most time in?" I asked her, purposely lowering my voice.

She blushed and nodded.

I knew what she was thinking, but I didn't bother to tell her that she was wrong. The room she was thinking about was actually upstairs, which I did spend a fair amount of time in, if sleeping counted. She trailed behind me, still holding both of my hands, which I had behind my back. We had to detour back through the dining room, then the living room, and once again the kitchen before heading down a wide hallway.

I took her through a set of industrial glass doors and outside onto the patio surrounding the massive pool.

"This isn't a room," Payton told me, squeezing my hand.

"Nope, it's a pool."

"And this is where you spend most of your time?"

"Nope," I answered honestly. "That would be where I spend most of my time." I nodded toward a separate structure that housed my workout room. It was technically a guesthouse — I know … a guesthouse at the guesthouse. A little pretentious, but what did you expect from Conrad?

"What is it?" Payton asked.

"Workout room." I led her to the far end of the pool, punched in a key code, and slid open the glass door so she could see inside. The open space was relatively empty except for a heavy bag hanging from the ceiling, a treadmill in one corner, and a wall of free weights sitting in perfect, obsessive-compulsive order on one side. I nodded my head to the opposite end of the room. "There's a kitchen on that side, and a bathroom, complete with sauna, on the other end."

"I can see why you're in here so much. If it were my place, I'd probably sleep out here."

"The floor's a little hard, but likely doable," I told her as I stepped up behind her and licked the outer shell of her ear.

Payton shuddered, and my body tensed yet again.

By the end of the night — or morning, considering it was already closing in on two o'clock — I would likely need to dunk myself in that pool regardless of how fucking cold it was.

Because I had been right earlier … I was definitely playing with fire.

Unraveling

Chapter Seven

Payton

I KNEW THAT CONRAD TROVATO was loaded. After all, I worked for the man, I saw the way he dressed, the car that he drove. Hell, I'd even been to his house.

So, it was only logical that I'd considered the fact that Sebastian might be wealthy, as well. He had informed me that Conrad was his father, which made the assumption relative.

However, after seeing his house, I was starting to wonder just what kind of money these people really had.

The guesthouse had a guesthouse. I mean, really. Come on now.

But rather than trying to determine Sebastian's net worth, I was really interested in the first question I'd had when we'd driven through the main gates of Conrad's estate a short while ago. Why did Sebastian live on his father's estate?

My initial surprise had come when we'd passed the well-lit main house before heading down a winding road that led to this secondary house. It was then that I realized where we were. It just didn't make sense to me that Sebastian would live so close. Especially considering their volatile relationship. As much as I wanted to know why that was, that wasn't something I was going to ask him at the moment. The last thing I had on my agenda for the night was to bring up Conrad. I preferred to enjoy my time with Sebastian, not cast a black cloud over it by bringing up a sore subject.

Up to this point, I'd just been enjoying our time together, watching him, listening to his voice. My entire focus had been on him.

Well, that was until I started feeling a little uneasy about where he lived. Not that I cared about the money. In fact, I was having the opposite reaction, I think. I was a little intimidated, not at all comfortable around this kind of wealth.

I was more of a pizza-and-beer type of girl. I certainly wasn't a fan of champagne and caviar. Not that Sebastian seemed the type, either, but I knew very little about the lifestyle of the rich and famous. My thoughts drifted back to the party I'd attended last weekend, the overdressed socialites who'd been present, the long list of people who worked for Mr. Trovato, including the butler. It was awkward to be around that.

My parents weren't loaded. My father owned his own business, and they made a good living, but they were frugal with their money, and they'd passed that trait on to me. I certainly didn't make the sort of money to keep up with someone like Mr. Trovato — it'd probably take me a lifetime to make what Conrad brought home in a week.

And until seeing this place that Sebastian called home, I hadn't seen anything that would lead me to believe Sebastian was following in his father's footsteps in the finance department. But Sebastian's house looked like it came right out of a magazine, right down to the gleaming surfaces of everything in the place. What was worse was that it didn't look like anyone actually lived there and that ... well, it kind of bothered me.

Truth was, I felt a little out of place. No, make that a lot out of place.

The only thing that helped to settle my anxiety was the fact that Sebastian didn't act like he had money. Or like he lived in a house that was probably the size of my entire apartment building.

Realizing that I was getting lost in my own thoughts again, I turned around to face Sebastian. "You gonna show me the rest?"

The heat in his golden gaze sent another tremor through my insides. I was so out of my element with this guy but being with him just felt so right. It didn't matter if we were at my apartment, the racetrack, at IHOP sharing pancakes, or even here, in this ostentatiously decorated, cold place that Sebastian called home.

None of that mattered when he was with me.

"Not a lot left to see," he replied, his voice rougher than before. His eyes were raking over my face, briefly pausing on my mouth, and I could feel my breaths coming in more rapidly.

"You have to sleep somewhere," I whispered.

"Upstairs. Bedroom. Not much to see there," he said in a rush.

This was what we'd been dancing around since we'd arrived. The whole reason we'd spent the last half hour taking a tour of his house. Sebastian was avoiding the inevitable, and I knew he was giving me an out. As much as I loved him for that, I didn't want an out. I was burning alive, eager to be with this man. I wanted to spend the night in his arms, curled up against his body. But first, I wanted to feel him. To feel his naked body pressed against mine while he slid deep inside me.

Another shudder racked my body, and I knew it had nothing to do with the relatively chilly night air blowing in through the open glass door.

Knowing he wasn't going to say anything more, I slid my hands up Sebastian's hard chest, feeling the flex of his muscles beneath my palms, observing the heavy rise and fall as his breathing quickened, watching his face as his eyes studied me. "Show me your bedroom, Sebastian."

I was astounded by my own forwardness but not enough to care. Having spent the last few hours with him, the subtle teases, the mind-blowing kisses, they'd turned me into an inferno of desire, and I wasn't sure I was going to last much longer.

Sebastian's eyes locked with mine, and I didn't break the contact, willing him to read my mind, to know just what I was thinking.

I was ready for this.

More than ready.

As though he heard the unspoken words, Sebastian nodded, sliding his hands down my back and cupping my butt firmly before pulling me flush against him. His erection pressed into my belly, and I was suddenly anxious to see him naked, to admire all of him. "I want this, Sebastian," I assured him.

Another nod and then I was following him back into the house. He flipped off the lights as we made our way through each of the downstairs rooms. He paused once more when we ended up at the bottom of a beautiful half-spiral staircase that led to the second floor.

For a brief second, I thought I was going to have to take the lead, but then we were moving again. Sebastian's fingers tightened on mine as we took each step. When we reached the second floor, I realized instantly that this was where he spent most of his time. At least when he wasn't working out.

The space was open and airy with high vaulted ceilings, two oversized ceiling fans dangling above, and a wall of solid windows on the far end. I couldn't tell what was beyond the glass because there was nothing but darkness on the other side. I hadn't noticed when we were downstairs, but a half wall offered a view of the main living area below. There was a giant flat-screen television mounted on one wall above a sophisticated, modern fireplace.

Aside from two oversized leather recliners, there was a black sofa that lined the half wall and faced the television. A black-and-white rug with giant circular patterns covered a large portion of the hardwood floor.

"Well, at least now I know," I said, trying to fight my nerves.

"Know what?" Sebastian asked, placing his hand on the small of my back as we walked through the room.

"That the color wasn't hiding up here."

Sebastian's sexy chuckle eased me somewhat.

And then my body stiffened when he placed his hand on the doorknob that led to the only other room upstairs.

When he pushed the door open, I went inside first and smiled.

"This is more like it," I said, not meaning to say the words aloud.

His bed was unmade, the bright white comforter haphazardly twisted as though he had just climbed out of bed. There was a bottle of water on the nightstand, and the television remote was lying on the rumpled sheets. "At least I'm not the only one who doesn't make my bed every day."

Although I was trying to lighten the mood, the tension was thick because we both knew exactly why we were there.

The door clicked when Sebastian closed it behind him, and my heart skipped a beat. I was nervous, but it wasn't a bad nervous. I wasn't having second thoughts or doubts of any kind. I was just…

I didn't have time to complete that thought because Sebastian was stalking toward me, his gaze intense and incredibly sexy. And just like that, the world disappeared, and the only thing in my universe was Sebastian Trovato.

His strong hands gripped my hips as his mouth brushed against mine. Not wanting to waste another second, I reached for the hem of his T-shirt, slowly lifting it up until I'd revealed the delicious golden skin beneath. His hand disappeared from my hip, but not for long. He reached behind his head and grabbed a handful of cotton, then easily pulled his shirt over his head and tossed it onto a nearby chair.

I took a moment to drink him in, my eyes sliding along the intricate lines of his tattoos, the hard ridges of muscle that made up his chest, the rippling edges of his abs. When he put his hand back on my hip, I saw his biceps flex as he gripped me tighter.

"Angel."

His voice was rough, sexy. As though he was just as affected by this as I was.

Placing my palms flat against his skin, I slid them up to his collarbone, then higher, over the thick muscles of his shoulders. I continued to touch him, memorizing every glorious inch of him until my fingernails were gently scraping the back of his head, letting his short hair tease my fingers.

To my relief, Sebastian's hands moved upward, beneath my T-shirt, warming my back. And the next thing I knew, my shirt was being discarded with his.

"Fuck," he breathed out. "You're … so damn beautiful." His words were raspy and rough, the admiration in his tone sending chills snaking down my spine.

This was seduction, pure and simple. There was no rush as we both took the time to enjoy what we saw. The way Sebastian's eyes flared when he looked at me gave me a strange sense of feminine power. No man had ever looked at me like that. Never had anyone taken the time to seduce me thoroughly, and I was pretty sure that no other moment in my life would live up to this one.

Sebastian walked me backward until my legs hit the edge of the bed. One of his hands slid behind me, bracing my back as he lowered me down, his other hand on the mattress so that he didn't come down on top of me. As I lay there, looking up at him, I knew that when I eventually went back to my normal life, I was not going to be the same person I was right then.

I'd already fallen a little bit in love with him, and I was sure that, by the time the sun came up over the horizon, I was going to be in deep. Deeper than I'd ever imagined possible.

"Payton." The way he said my name had my insides quivering. The way he looked at me, as though I were the only important thing in the world, had another wave of desire crashing through me.

I reached for him then, catching him off guard and pulling him down on top of me. His knee slid between my legs, grinding against my sex, making me crazy with lust, wishing like hell that we didn't have the rest of our clothes between us.

When his mouth met mine, I gave in to his kiss, meeting his tongue, sliding against it slowly. Although the tension was ratcheting up several notches, he was still going slowly. I wanted to beg him to hurry because I wasn't sure I could stand much more. I needed to feel him against me, the rough pads of his fingers on my skin, the gentle scrape of his scruffy jaw against my...

"Oh, God." The words slipped out as Sebastian's mouth traveled down to my breast; the delicious rasp of his tongue against my oversensitive flesh had my body bowing into him.

A flutter of sensation erupted in my core when he slid my bra out of the way and took my nipple into his mouth. Warmth flooded me, causing my eyes to close, my body to tingle. The sensual torture continued for long seconds, and then he was trailing back up to my mouth.

His kiss turned hungry, desperate, and I met him with a fury of my own. Feeling bold, I slid my hands down between our bodies, the tips of my fingers sliding into the waistband of his jeans before I deftly unhooked the button and lowered the zipper.

Sebastian's lips brutally assaulted mine, making me moan into his mouth as I slid my hands into his jeans and boxers, finding his steel-hard length and stroking him slowly. The growl that erupted from his chest spurred me on. I maintained a slow, steady pace, eager but not wanting to rush this. I wanted to touch him, to taste him.

"Payton." Sebastian's breath was heaving in and out of his lungs as he pulled back, staring down at me. His eyes were a little wild, and I imagined I looked much the same. "Angel. Oh, damn, that feels good."

The guttural sound of his voice only intensified the ache that had started between my thighs. I was grinding myself against his leg, trying to ease the desperate need but failing.

"Your hands are so fucking soft," he mumbled, his mouth hovering over mine but not touching. His forehead rested against mine, as though he didn't have the strength to hold himself up. I didn't stop, enjoying the smooth, velvety length of him in my hands. His hips thrust forward a few times, followed by more growls.

And I knew then that I might not survive the night, but heaven help me, it was going to be so worth it.

Chapter Eight

Sebastian

PAYTON'S HANDS WERE LIKE SILK. She was so tentative with her touch I was surprised I could breathe. The woman was going to kill me little by little, and I couldn't think of a better way to go.

I was trying to be gentle, unhurried, not wanting to overwhelm her, but I wanted to lick my way up her body. Slowly. So that I could drive her as crazy as I was. And yet she was the one holding the reins, controlling everything from my respiration to my thoughts.

"Payton," I rasped, hardly able to get her name out of my mouth. As it was, I was resting my forehead against hers as the pleasure overwhelmed me. I never wanted her to stop stroking me, but if I didn't do something, I was going to be the only one at the finish line, and I wasn't ready for the race to be over just yet.

Somehow — don't ask me how — I managed to get my brain to function, to send instructions to my hands to get them moving. Gripping her wrists, I succeeded in halting her mind-blowing movements. She didn't release my cock, though, causing me to gasp for air as she teased the tip with her thumb and making me sweat as she did.

"If you only knew how good that felt," I told her, inhaling deeply. "But unless you want me to finish now, you're gonna have to release me."

Her smile lit up her face, her bright yellow-green eyes glowing in the dim light cast by the bedside lamp. God, the woman was so fucking beautiful when she smiled. She was beautiful anyway, but when she smiled, she was otherworldly.

Finding a minimal amount of strength within me, I managed to push myself up off the bed, sliding my hand down the center of her body as I got to my feet. Down her neck, her chest, between her luscious breasts, and then down her flat belly, I stopped at the button of her jeans. Watching her face, I slowly unhooked the button. The only sounds I heard were my own heartbeat pounding in my ears and the combined rasp of our rapid breaths. Her chest expanded as I lowered the zipper, the metal teeth releasing one at a time. Leaning forward, I pressed my lips to her stomach, sliding my tongue into her navel as I pushed the denim down over her hips, revealing a pair of silky black panties that matched the bra she was still wearing.

As I pushed her jeans down her trim thighs, she moved, slipping her shoes off and letting them land with a gentle thud on the hardwood.

"So fucking beautiful," I muttered, the words but a mere whisper as I stared at her in awe. Her skin was so smooth, so soft, and I couldn't resist touching her, not wanting to stop.

Ever.

Once her jeans were discarded, I hurried out of my own, keeping my eyes on her the entire time. I couldn't turn away, even if I had wanted to. Which I damn sure didn't.

Not wanting to rush, I left my boxers on, but before I could join her on the bed, Payton surprised me yet again by sitting up, her legs dangling over the side.

I thought for a moment that I was going to swallow my fucking tongue.

She was sitting on the edge of the bed, her legs spread while I stood inches from her. Her lips pressed against my stomach, her tongue gliding against my skin. I slid my hands into her hair, holding her. I told myself it was so I could stop her, to keep her from doing something that would blow my world to pieces, but I knew better.

I wasn't strong enough to resist her.

Her hand slid up my thigh, beneath my boxers, and when she cupped me, I damn near came right then and there. Her touch was so gentle, almost reverent, and I swear, in all my life, I'd never felt anything as good as Payton's hands on me.

And when she lowered my boxers, freeing me completely, the grip I had on her hair tightened.

Her sharp inhale had me looking down as she wrapped her fingers around my length. She was looking up at me, still smiling, a sexy, mischievous gleam in her eyes that had my body throbbing. Every ounce of blood I had made an immediate detour to my cock.

"Payton." I knew what she was going to do. She was going to make me lose it, but I was powerless to stop her. When her eyes left mine, her soft hand stroked me once, twice, and then her mouth was on me. "Oh, fuck. Payton. Baby. Angel. Oh, God, yes."

Yes, I knew I was rambling, but my brain cells were obliterated when she wrapped her lips around me. She was so gentle I wanted to beg her to take me deeper, to suck me harder, but I was scared I would freak her out. Her tentativeness, her hesitancy, spoke of inexperience. Part of me was thrilled with the idea that Payton might not have been with another man before, the other part wasn't sure she could handle me.

The beast that lived and breathed inside of me was clawing to get out. I wanted to climb on top of her and drive myself deep inside her body, pounding into her until she was screaming my name, her body gripping mine. It was all I'd thought about for the last few days, and here we were. By the grace of God, I was managing to hold back.

Barely.

I gripped her hair tightly and pulled her head back. I couldn't handle much more. She was going to send me over the edge far too soon if she kept doing that. When she looked up at me, I noticed her eyes were glazed, her pretty pink lips swollen.

Someone was testing me. That was all there was to it.

"My turn," I told her as I released her hair, sliding my hand down her back and deftly unhooking her bra before pulling it from her body and tossing it with the rest of our clothes. "Lie back," I instructed, and when she did, I slipped her panties down her legs.

And nearly had a heart attack.

She waxed.

Yep, there was no doubt about it, someone was testing me.

I was pretty sure I was going to fail the test, but I really didn't give a shit at that point.

While I locked my gaze with hers, I kicked off my boxers, then lowered myself to my knees on the floor beside the bed, my shoulders forcing her legs wider, opening her to me.

"Sebastian." My name on her lips sounded very much like a warning, but I didn't heed it. I leaned forward and took her in my mouth, kissing her tenderly, softly, using my fingers to separate the soft, slick folds of her sex. Similar to the way she'd handled me. And when she was writhing on the bed, her hands clutching the comforter beneath her, I continued to torment her with gentle licks, firm flicks of my tongue, until she shattered.

I knew I wasn't going to last much longer. Not this first time. As much as I wanted to spend the rest of the night getting her off with my mouth, I knew I wasn't going to last.

I made it to my feet, admiring the way she looked, a soft sheen on her skin, her eyes hooded as she peered up at me. I gave her a moment while I retrieved a condom from the nightstand drawer and rolled it on. When I looked up, I saw that she was watching me, and I knew it was time. I had to have her. I couldn't wait any longer. I crawled over her, forcing her to move farther up on the bed until her head rested on my pillow, her dark hair fanning out around her beautiful, flushed face.

"I've wanted this since the very first time I laid eyes on you," I told her, nuzzling her neck, sliding my tongue over her skin. "I've wanted to bury myself inside you, feel you gripping me…"

When her arms wrapped around me, her nails digging into my back ever so slightly, my body hardened even more than I thought possible. I trailed kisses along her jaw, then met her mouth with mine, plunging my tongue inside, letting her taste herself on my lips. She moaned, the sound so fucking perfect I wanted to make her do it again and again.

Easing between her legs, I rested on my forearm, reaching between us and guiding myself to her entrance. Her breath hitched when I slid into her, her head pressing into the pillow.

I paused, not daring to go any deeper. "I don't want to hurt you, Angel."

Payton opened her eyes and met my stare. "You won't hurt me," she said, and she sounded so sure of herself I slid forward slowly, sinking into her.

"Angel." I could barely speak, my lungs seizing up from the sheer ecstasy of her body contracting, pulling me deeper.

"Sebastian."

I stilled, watching her. The emotions that fluttered over her face had my heart pounding harder. Thank God I wasn't the only one feeling this. Whatever it was, it was stronger than anything I'd ever felt. And I damn sure wasn't the type to confuse sex with love. But this wasn't just sex. The only way I knew that was because this felt unlike anything I'd ever known before.

I kept myself propped on one forearm, sliding my other hand down her body and cupping her thigh, pulling her leg up and opening her more as I slid deeper. Impossibly deep.

Our eyes met, locked, held. I didn't look away. As the overwhelming pleasure accosted me, I peered into Payton's eyes and she into mine. I was baring my soul to this woman, and I was pretty sure she realized that. Her hands gripped my back, her fingernails scraping my skin. It was a sensual torture that had chills racing down my body.

"I don't know how long I can do this," I told her.

"Do what?" she asked, breathless, a small smile tipping the very corners of her mouth.

"Go slow. It's … killing me. You're… Oh, damn, Payton. You unhinge me." I smiled, despite the pleasure-pain that was building to a crescendo as I continued to penetrate her, easing in deep, withdrawing slowly.

"I don't want slow," she said, her smile luminous.

When she slid her hands down my back and grabbed my ass, pulling me to her, the last of my restraint dissolved.

And as I made love to Payton, driving into her, faster, harder, until she was crying out my name, begging me to make her come, I knew that I would go to the ends of the earth for this woman.

She owned me.

And no one … absolutely no one would ever keep her from me.

Chapter Nine

Payton

Sunday morning

SEBASTIAN'S BEDROOM WAS DARK, THE heavy shades pulled over the window blocking out the early-morning sun. As I lay there, my head resting on Sebastian's chest, his fingers trailing softly up and down my spine, I knew I should have given in to my exhaustion but going to sleep seemed like a waste of the moment. Even there in his arms, with his warmth wrapped around me, I had no desire to leave him, even just to sleep.

"What're you thinking about?" he whispered, kissing my forehead, the stubble along his jaw gently scraping my skin, reminding me of what we'd just done.

"You," I admitted truthfully. Fact was, I was always thinking about him.

His body tensed slightly, and I ran my palm over his abs, feeling the muscles tighten. There was so much I knew about him, mostly how his body felt inside me, how his breaths rushed hard and fast when he came, how he growled out my name when his climax overtook him, and the incredible scent of his skin. But there was still so much I didn't know. So much I wanted to know. Realizing that the timing might never be right to ask the difficult questions, I went with my gut, deciding to go for it.

"Why do you keep it a secret that you're Conrad's son?" I asked, keeping my tone soft, even.

"It's not a secret I keep," he informed me, his voice carrying an edge of frustration.

"Why does Conrad keep it a secret?" My mind drifted back to the mental images I had of Conrad's office. There weren't any pictures of Sebastian in there. Only ones of Aaliyah growing up, a few of Conrad's wife, but none of Sebastian. My heart clenched painfully in my chest.

"I didn't know who my father was until I was fourteen years old," he explained, his tone sounding far away. "The year my mother died."

My stomach ached from his admission, and I suddenly regretted my decision to bring it up. He sounded so lost. While my mind tried to piece together just what that meant, my heart hurt for a little boy who'd lost his mother and been thrust into a world he wasn't familiar with. He hadn't known his father? I didn't say anything, just curled up tightly against Sebastian, hoping he would continue.

"I had two choices when she died. Go live with a man I didn't know or take my chances in foster care."

"There wasn't anyone else? What about your mother's parents?"

"I didn't know my grandparents. They disowned my mother before I was born. She was a senior in high school when she got pregnant with me. When she refused to get an abortion, they threw her out of their house."

Oh, my God.

"From what she told me, from the stories my aunt shared, they were God-fearing people. A bastard child was unacceptable in their world, something that would be frowned upon by those they knew. They weren't willing to endure the wrath of God for my mother's sins."

I bit my tongue, not wanting to interrupt Sebastian's story, but I was suddenly worried I wouldn't be able to handle the horror of what it had been like for him growing up. I had two parents who had doted on me. My grandparents, both paternal and maternal, had been wonderful, loving people who never judged anyone. My grandmother on my father's side was the only one still alive, the others having passed through the years from old age and natural causes. I still visited my grandmother although she didn't really know who I was anymore. The benefit was that I still got to see her. And above all else, I still had so many incredible memories of my childhood.

"The only person who helped my mother was my mother's only sister, Tina. But even she couldn't do much. And when my mother died, Tina had been in and out of drug rehab for several years, and according to the courts, she wasn't equipped to handle a rebellious teenager. I took my chances with Conrad."

"How did your mother die?" I asked, swallowing hard as I waited for his answer.

Again, Sebastian's body tightened, his breath hitching in his chest. I clung to him, hoping he would continue, worried he wouldn't.

Several minutes passed before Sebastian spoke again. "My mother died in a car accident. She was T-boned on her way home from work one night. She'd recently started a second job, waitressing at a different restaurant, working the late shift. That night, she never came home."

Doing the math in my head, I knew that Aaliyah had to be relatively close to Sebastian in age, and that meant... I couldn't bring myself to ask the question that hovered on the tip of my tongue. I wasn't sure I wanted to know whether his stepmother had been there for Sebastian, taking him in and trying to fill the hole that would have been left within him when his mother died. Instead, I said, "Tell me about your mom."

Sebastian sighed, his arm tightening around me. "She was fun. We didn't have much, but she always made sure that what we lacked in material possessions, she made up for in the time we spent together. It was always just the two of us.

"When I was born, Conrad tried to pay her off, refusing to be part of my life. He was married at the time." Sebastian paused, his chest rising with his deep inhale. "Twenty-six years old and married to his first wife. My mother was seventeen when she had me."

I tried not to show my shock, but when Sebastian's lips brushed the top of my head, I knew I had failed.

"He tried to buy her silence. At first he tried to pay her to have an abortion. She refused him the same way she refused her parents. And when I was born, he tried to pay her off to keep her quiet." Sebastian paused again. "My mother loved him. She loved him, and I don't think she ever stopped. Maybe she should've taken the money..."

"It sounds like she was a strong woman. She did what she thought was best for you."

"She was great. She was my best friend. But I wasn't the best kid. As I got older, I started hanging with the wrong crowd. By the time I was thirteen, I'd been arrested several times. Most of the time for stupid shit. Petty theft, street racing. I hated going home because, as the years passed, the light in her eyes continued to dim.

"I remember her mentioning to me that she was gonna try to get in touch with my father. We were flat broke, and I'd started working for cash at a local mechanic shop to help out. She hated that I had to work to try to help out. She was working two jobs, waitressing at two different places. But it wasn't enough."

"Did she get in touch with him?" I asked, knowing the answer before he responded.

"If she did, she didn't tell me. She tried to shelter me from that shit. I remember her always pretending that we had more than we did, but I knew. I knew when I looked in the refrigerator that the only thing I would find was a jug of water, sometimes milk. I knew that when I woke up to go to school, she'd be dead on her feet in the kitchen, pouring what little milk we had into a bowl or pulling bread out of the toaster for my breakfast. And I knew when I finally decided to come home after school, she'd be going to her second job."

"But Conrad took you in when she died?" I asked, hating how that sounded.

"Not willingly," Sebastian said, his tone reflecting the anger I'd sensed in him yesterday when he'd showed up at my apartment.

I lifted my head, peering at him in the darkness, waiting for him to explain.

"I'm not a saint, Payton," he whispered. "You should know that now."

I was surprised by his admission, but I didn't know what it meant. What he said next was not what I expected to hear.

He moved, effectively coming over me as I rolled to my back.

"But I swear to you, Angel," he whispered, his voice dark and dangerous, "I'll never hurt you. I'll never let anyone hurt you."

His words sounded like a warning, like he was telling me something, but I just didn't know what. I could hardly make out his features in the dark, but I could see enough that I knew the anger was back. I wanted that anger to go away, to disappear entirely. Placing my hands on his face, I forced a smile I didn't feel. "I believe you, Sebastian."

His eyes flared briefly and then his lips were on mine. I knew the conversation was over. At least for now. And when he positioned himself over me, reaching for a condom on the bedside table, I didn't try to stop him. And when he finally slid inside me, I wrapped my arms around him, nuzzled my face in his neck, and held him as close as I could.

This man … he wasn't the only one unhinged. I sensed the darkness and the danger that lurked inside him, but it didn't scare me. In fact, I felt just the opposite. I was drawn to him. So much so that I knew my life was irrevocably changed from that moment forward.

After all … I loved him.

Two hours later, I awoke alone in Sebastian's bed, tangled in the expensive sheets. A quick glance around his still-darkened bedroom told me he wasn't there. Forcing myself out of his bed, I ignored the sweet ache between my thighs that reminded me of the last few hours. I grabbed his black T-shirt from the chair and pulled it on over my head. I didn't even bother to try and find a mirror, knowing that I was a mess.

Something told me that I needed to find Sebastian.

When I walked out of his bedroom, the bright light of day filled the house, momentarily blinding me with its intensity. There weren't any window coverings to block out the natural light that filled the space. I waited a moment for my eyes to adjust, and then I went in search of Sebastian. When I didn't find him downstairs, I headed outside, my feet carrying me to the separate building. That was where he'd said he spent most of his time, so it seemed like the logical place to look.

I found him in his workout room. The sliding glass door was open, and he was whaling away on the heavy bag hanging from the ceiling, music blaring loudly. I recognized the song — "Not Falling" by Mudvayne — which made me smile. We had similar taste in music.

He didn't seem to notice me at first, and I didn't announce myself, content to watch him as I leaned against the doorframe. The way his muscles flexed and bunched as he moved. He was pure masculine grace.

He was wearing jeans but nothing else. I took him in from his bare feet, up over his thick legs, his washboard abs contracting with every jab… I was just getting to his chest when he moved, turning completely away from me.

The air in my lungs escaped as if I were the one punching that bag.

The tattoo…

Holy crap.

The tattoo that covered his back left me momentarily speechless. He had mentioned that he had a cross on his back, but that… Yeah, that was so much more than a cross. What caught my eye was the angel wings that spanned the entire width of his back, surrounding the cross. It was … breathtaking.

I didn't move, didn't breathe as I watched his body shift with so much precision it made my mouth dry. The tattoo shifted over his muscles, the wings seeming to move as he did.

I don't know if he knew I was there or if he was just stopping because he was tired, but all of a sudden, he wasn't moving, his hands gripping the heavy bag, the muscles in his shoulders tense. When he turned to face me, I realized he had to have known I was there. How, I don't know. It wasn't like he could have heard me over the sound of the music pulsing through the room.

His chest glistened with sweat, his hair disheveled, his eyes wide as he looked back at me. Without thinking, I moved to him, unable to stay away. He took three steps, closing the gap between us. The next thing I knew, Sebastian had lifted me, my legs wrapping around his hips as he moved to the wall, using the hard surface to support my weight as he crushed his mouth to mine. I twined my fingers in his hair, pulling. I don't know what came over me, but whatever it was, I was powerless to resist even if I had wanted to.

Which I didn't.

The song changed, but the tempo did not. The music was fast, almost angry, the bass thumping to match the sound of my pounding heart. I didn't release him, my hands sliding down his back, digging into his flesh as he pressed me into the wall.

He was breathing hard, the kiss stealing what was left of the oxygen in the room.

His arm moved, sliding down between us, and that was when I realized he was unfastening his jeans. He pulled back, our eyes meeting, and the unsaid question hung between us. Unless he had a condom in his pocket, we were without protection, but still I wanted him. Maybe more now than ever.

"I'm on the pill," I said in a rush. I let the silence linger between us briefly, waiting for him to speak.

"Payton—"

I cut him off by slamming my mouth to his. I trusted him. I trusted him implicitly, and I didn't need to hear anymore.

"Now, Sebastian," I urged, nipping his lower lip beside his lip ring. "I need you inside me now."

What came next could be described as nothing more than pure, unadulterated fucking. It was extreme, and although we were using one another as a release, there was so much more to it. So much more that bubbled just beneath the surface.

Sebastian shifted, and then he was slamming inside me, my breath lodged in my throat with the first gloriously brutal thrust of his hips.

"Angel," he breathed against my ear. "I need you."

"I'm here." I would always be there. I didn't tell him as much, but there was something between us. A connection, a bond that was stronger than anything I'd ever felt, and words weren't necessary.

"Harder," I pleaded, my fingernails digging into his skin.

Sebastian didn't hold back. He was pounding into me, driving me higher and higher until there was no holding back. The friction ... the wonderful feeling of him inside me was too much. My orgasm crested, and I shattered right there in his arms, pressed up against the wall. The roar that followed signaled Sebastian's release, and the grip he had on me intensified until I wasn't sure I could breathe from how tight he was holding me. It didn't stop me from pulling him closer, crushing him to me.

It was then that I knew... Whatever this was between us, it was so powerful, so potent, there was no way that either of us would survive it intact.

Chapter Ten

Payton

Sunday evening

"WELL, IT'S ABOUT TIME, KIDDO," my father greeted me when I walked in the front door of my parents' house at five thirty. Harold Fowler, better known as Hal, got to his feet and came toward me, pulling me into a bear hug before Aaron even managed to close the door behind us.

"Women," Aaron muttered with a grin as he passed me, making his way to my father and reaching out to shake his hand. "It takes 'em forever to get ready."

Considering I'd come right home from Sebastian's, hopped in the shower, and pulled my wet hair up in a clip, I knew Aaron was talking out his ass. And likely trying to cover for me. Which I loved him for, by the way. I had threatened him within an inch of his life if he even mentioned to my parents that I was seeing someone. Although he had pestered me relentlessly, promising that was the first thing he was going to tell my father, I knew he wouldn't.

"Sometimes I think you might have the right idea, Aaron," Hal teased, and I nearly choked as I pulled off my jacket and tossed it on the back of the long sofa where my father had been sitting when we came in.

"Trust me, Dad," I said as I moved through the room, glaring at Aaron, "gay guys are incredibly high maintenance. Don't let him fool you."

Aaron's laugh was the last thing I heard as I slipped down the hall toward the kitchen.

"Mom?" I called as I stepped into the kitchen to find it deserted, despite the heavenly aroma that drifted through the open, airy room.

My parents still lived in the same house where I'd grown up. The décor had changed over the years, and they'd done quite a few upgrades here and there, but other than that, it still felt like home to me. A place I knew I could come whenever I needed comfort. Or food.

I needed food, but I probably would've just stayed at the apartment and snacked on popcorn if it hadn't been for the dinner invitation my father had issued on my voice mail. When he'd invited Aaron as well, I couldn't tell him no, so here we were.

"In here," my mother hollered back.

I turned to see her in the separate dining room, setting plates and silverware out on the table.

Susan Fowler was an incredibly beautiful woman, even when she was wearing a Dallas Stars sweatshirt, old ratty jeans, and an apron. Her short blond bob framed her face and made her appear years younger than she was. Not that she was old. But at forty-six, people often mistook her for my sister. My father insisted that I got my good looks from her, but in reality, I looked more like him. I had inherited his dark hair and hazel eyes, while I had gotten my height — or lack thereof — from my mother's side.

"It smells fantastic," I told my mother when she returned to the kitchen, pulling me to her for a quick hug. "What're we having?"

"Homemade chili," she replied with a giant grin. "And sweet cornbread."

My mother was an extraordinary cook, and she was always trying new things, which meant that there was probably some twist to this homemade chili, but I didn't doubt that it would be fabulous. If nothing else, I could probably survive off her sweet cornbread — she knew it was my favorite.

"I'm starving," I told her, pulling out a barstool and hopping onto it while I watched her move efficiently through the kitchen.

"Good. And I hope you brought Aaron, because I made enough to feed a small army."

"The army's here," Aaron said as he joined us. He made a beeline for my mother, hugging her tightly before sitting beside me at the breakfast bar.

"How's school?" Susan asked Aaron as she washed her hands in the sink in front of us.

"Oh, you know … boring," Aaron answered easily, gifting her with his infectious smile.

"Of course it is," she agreed before turning her attention to me. "How's work?"

She turned to the stove, reaching for a spoon to stir the pot as she glanced back over her shoulder at me.

"Great," I said. I didn't know what else I was supposed to say. "Oh, I'm going to Vegas on Tuesday."

My mother dropped the spoon onto the stovetop, jumping back to avoid the splatter from the chili. She reached for a hand towel while she stared at me. "What do you mean you're going to Vegas? With who?"

"My boss and his wife," I informed her, glancing over at Aaron, who looked just as surprised by my news. The gleam in his eyes promised retribution later. Apparently we hadn't talked much since I'd started seeing Sebastian, but in my defense, he had been pretty wrapped up in Mark until recently.

"For how long?" my mother asked, but before I could answer, she yelled at my father, telling him to join us in the kitchen.

I sighed. I knew I should have waited until dinner was over and I was getting ready to leave before I gave her the news.

"I'll be back sometime on Friday."

"What is this trip for?" My mother had stopped what she was doing to give me her full attention.

"The SEMA show," I told her as my father made an appearance around the wall.

"The SEMA show?" he asked, looking at me and then to my mother. "What about it?"

"It looks like your daughter will be going," she said, sounding not at all pleased by the news.

"With who?" he asked, his eyes narrowing on me.

"Mr. Trovato and his wife. I think their daughter may go with them."

"Where will you be staying?"

"Caesar's Palace."

"What will you be doing?"

My father's questions were rapid-fired at me, and I suddenly felt like I had when I had asked if I could go on a senior trip to Galveston. Glancing at Aaron, I smiled. "Does this sound at all familiar?"

"Little bit," he offered with a grin.

He had been on the receiving end of those questions back then, too, so at least he understood some of my pain.

Not that he tried to help run interference. He seemed quite content watching me squirm under their heated stares.

"I'm Conrad's assistant, Dad. I'll probably be taking notes, getting him coffee, making sure he knows where he's supposed to be." Truth was, I really didn't know what I would be doing while I was there. I'd been just as shocked as my parents were now when Conrad had insisted that I attend.

"The SEMA show is a trade show, Payton. Giant rooms full of people showing their skills and trades. It's all about cars and trucks. I'm just not sure I understand why you need to be there."

I sighed.

"Let's take this to the dinner table," my mother instructed, placing oven mitts over her slender hands and carrying the pot of chili to the dining room table.

I hopped off the barstool and resigned myself to having to deal with getting the third degree from my parents for the next half hour. I knew I should have just kept my mouth shut.

Half an hour turned into an hour and a half. By the time Aaron and I climbed into his Honda to make the short drive back to our apartment, I had been officially grilled and then grilled some more.

"They took that well," Aaron said facetiously, his chuckle reverberating through the car.

I sighed and pressed my head against the seat, staring out the window into the night. I already missed Sebastian. I hadn't been away from him for long, but I couldn't stop thinking about him. We had spent the entire day together, and I'd been reluctant to go home but hadn't wanted to overstay my welcome, either. When it'd become clear that he wasn't going to ask me to leave, I had found the courage to request it myself. Not because I had wanted to but because it was necessary.

"They'll be fine," I told Aaron. "I guess it's a good thing I didn't mention I was dating Conrad's son."

Aaron's head snapped toward me as if his neck were made of rubber. "His son?"

Well, apparently there was something else I hadn't told my best friend. "Yeah. His son."

"And you didn't know this?"

"Nope." I tried to sound casual, but it really was a big deal. Even I realized that. After all, I worked for Conrad. He signed my paychecks, and clearly he didn't have a good relationship with his son if they managed to keep the fact that they were related out of the press. It still stunned me how they had managed to do that, considering how high-profile Conrad was in our area. Even my father, someone who kept up with everything that had to do with the automotive industry, didn't know that Conrad had a son. He had mentioned a rumor that he'd heard, but even he had dismissed the notion.

"Holy crap, Payton. That's... Wow. I don't even know what that is. What does Conrad think about you dating Sebastian?"

I turned my head to look at Aaron and raised my eyebrows. "He doesn't know."

"How would he not know that his assistant is dating his son?"

That was the question of the hour. One I couldn't answer, either.

I must've stunned Aaron with my revelation, because he was quiet for the remainder of the drive, and it wasn't until we walked into the house to find Toby and Chloe sitting on the couch watching a movie that he said something.

"Payton's dating Conrad Trovato's son."

Chloe's eyes widened, and she clicked the mute button on the television. Toby looked like he'd just stepped into the twilight zone. Of course, being that he was Sebastian's friend, he would already know this.

"Sebastian is your boss's son?" she asked, sounding almost hysterical.

Sure, I thought it was a big deal, but not *that* big of a deal. I shrugged, said a quick hello to Toby, and then escaped to my bedroom.

I should have known that Chloe would follow me. Less than a minute later, she was flopping onto my bed and staring at me as I began rummaging through my closet, trying to figure out what I would wear to the office tomorrow.

"His son?" she asked, her voice low. "Was that a secret or something? How could you think he was just a mechanic and he turns out to be Conrad's son?"

"No idea," I told her truthfully. "But I really don't wanna talk about it." I didn't want to talk *period*. I couldn't get my mind off Sebastian as it was. I was missing him fiercely, and we'd only been apart for a few hours. Ever since I'd brought up Vegas to my mother, I had been trying to figure out just how I was going to make it through the next five days without seeing him.

"Well, if he's related, does that mean he's going to Vegas?"

"He hasn't mentioned it," I replied, pulling out a black skirt and a black sweater and laying them on my desk for tomorrow. I would have to go with red shoes to add a little color, I thought to myself. And that thought led me back to Sebastian as well, remembering how much his house lacked color.

I sighed.

"Did you ask him?" Chloe's curiosity was apparently getting the best of her.

"Why would I do that?" I asked, turning to face her and propping my hands on my hips. "I don't talk about work with him."

"What do you talk about?" she retorted, a glimmer of frustration in her green eyes.

"I don't know," I answered.

"Hey, Chloe!" Aaron yelled from the other room. "I think your boyfriend's getting bored in here."

Chloe's face lit up, her smile dazzling as she mouthed the word boyfriend.

And just like that, I was off the hook.

I smiled back, unable not to. I loved seeing her so happy.

When she left my room, Chloe closed the door behind her, leaving me to my thoughts. I was still smiling at how happy she was when my cell phone chimed, signaling an incoming text. I figured it was my mother, still wanting to talk about my upcoming trip.

I was tempted to ignore it, but the thought of it possibly being Sebastian had me lunging for my purse. When I pulled up my text app and saw the message, I slid to the floor, my smile weighing me down.

It was Sebastian.

And the text: *I miss you.*

Needless to say, I spent the rest of the evening thinking about him even more.

Unraveling

Chapter Eleven

Payton

Tuesday morning

THE ANXIETY THAT I'D STORED up about getting on an airplane was exacerbated by the fact that I was now on an airplane with Conrad, his wife, Lauren, and their daughter, Aaliyah. It didn't even matter that we were sitting in first class, being served champagne by a very attentive flight attendant who continued to smile at Aaliyah as though she'd hung the moon.

The champagne wasn't doing much for me, although I had downed it like water, spurred on by the minor panic attack I was currently having. Seeing that the man who was greeting each passenger with a huge smile and a pleasant good morning was more interested in Aaliyah wasn't helping to distract me nearly enough, either.

In her defense, I don't think Aaliyah even noticed that the young man serving us was practically drooling over her. And it wasn't because she was ignoring him or being in any way snooty. The woman seemed seriously oblivious to the number of heads she turned when she walked into a room — or on a plane, as was the case now.

The only positive in the whole screwed-up situation was that I was sitting in the first-class section, beside Aaliyah on the back row, and her parents were sitting in the front row of seats, which put at least six people in between us. If I'd had to be any closer than that, I probably would've needed one of those oxygen masks to drop down from the ceiling.

"Relax," Aaliyah said kindly, patting the top of my hand where I was clutching the armrest as though the damn thing might just fly off my seat if I let go.

"Easier said than done," I told her, gritting my teeth as I spoke.

"It's gonna be fine," she assured me, but it didn't make me feel any better.

The captain had just informed us that we would be taking off soon and instructed the flight attendants to ready the cabin.

Closing my eyes, I pictured Sebastian, pulling up all of the images I could from the day we'd shared on Sunday. I hadn't seen him yesterday, not even after work, which had bothered me more than I was willing to admit. Although we had talked on the phone last night when I'd gotten home, not seeing him had been the wrinkle in my entire day.

Not that I had let him know that. I had tried to play it cool, not wanting to overwhelm him by asking that he come over. I was pretty sure that he would have, but I had stayed my ground and refused to make the request.

After spending the entire day with him on Sunday, swimming in his pool — which was heated, by the way — lounging in his Jacuzzi, and sharing three meals with him, I figured he might need a little time to recoup. I sure did, but that didn't mean that I wouldn't prefer to spend that time with him anyway.

When I'd informed him that I was going to Vegas with Conrad, he hadn't acted surprised. The brief "Be careful while you're there" that he'd offered wasn't much of a response, either.

"So, you're dating my brother, huh?" Aaliyah asked casually as she continued to flip through a magazine.

I turned my head to the side and peered over at her through one eye.

"What makes you say that?" I asked. I wasn't going to lie to her, but I did intend to feel her out a little before I divulged all of my secrets. Although I liked her immensely, I didn't know her all that well. Yet.

"That."

I had no idea what "that" meant, but I continued to focus my attention on her. She looked cool and collected, just as she always did. Her long blond hair was pulled back in a fancy up-do, her makeup was perfect, and her outfit reflected her immense wealth.

We were polar opposites. While I was short, Aaliyah was tall and willowy. She made me feel clumsy just sitting beside her. But she was so down-to-earth it was easy to overlook her beauty and class. Sort of. The fact that she was wearing a short turquoise dress that clung to every perfect curve had me wanting to hate her.

As for me, I was wearing jeans and an emerald-green sweater. Not dressy but not too casual. I had gone with heels rather than flats to add a little oomph to my outfit, but in no way did I resemble the blue-eyed debutante who had turned damn near every eye in the airport.

"What does 'that' mean?"

"The way your face turns just a little pink when he is mentioned. *He* being my brother."

I forced my gaze forward, feeling the warmth in my cheeks. "It does not," I countered without heat.

"It so does." Her laugh turned a few heads in the small section of the plane, including the attendant who gifted her with a wide grin.

The plane began its journey down the runway, gaining speed, and I clutched the armrests a little tighter. If I gripped them much harder, my fingers were going to break. I didn't open my eyes or release my death grip on the seat for a solid ten minutes and only then because Aaliyah nudged my shoulder. When I opened my eyes, it was to see a very helpful man was handing us a towel.

I glanced at Aaliyah, then at the passengers in front of us. What the hell was the towel for? Not wanting to look stupid, I reached for it and followed Aaliyah's lead, wiping my hands. Damn, that was hot. I tossed it between my hands, trying to force it to cool down a little, hoping no one noticed.

"He likes you, you know."

"Who?" I asked, glancing up at the attendant who was now walking away.

"Sebastian."

I jerked my attention back to her. "How do you know that?" I felt like a girl in high school, trying to find out if the boy I liked really liked me back. Although I wasn't the one who'd brought up the subject, I knew my eagerness for an answer was written all over my face.

"He's very protective of you."

I wasn't quite sure what Aaliyah was referring to, so I humored her. "How so?"

"When my father talks about you, Sebastian's ready to pounce."

The first part of that statement was what caught my attention. "Why does your father talk about me?"

"Oh, you know, normal dinner conversation."

Being the topic of Trovato dinner conversation didn't make me feel all that comfortable. I mean, sure, I got it ... I worked for Conrad, but for him to discuss me over dinner... What the hell was there to talk about?

"If you wanna know the truth," Aaliyah said as she leaned closer to me, "I think he does it to piss Sebastian off."

That didn't sound all that fun. Why would Conrad do that?

I thought about the weekend I'd just spent with Sebastian ... the things we'd done, the conversation we'd had. I knew if my mind drifted too far, my face would be beet-red. In order to avoid that, I turned back to Aaliyah. Letting my curiosity get the best of me, I changed the subject.

"How did your parents meet?" I knew the question was overly personal, especially to ask a woman I barely knew, but I wasn't interested in talking about Sebastian. I missed him already and knowing that I was going to be away from him for the next few days was killing me.

"My mother used to work for him," Aaliyah said, closing her magazine and sliding it into the seat pocket in front of her. She pulled out the tray from the armrest of her seat, lowering it slowly in front of her and resting her clasped hands on the top.

She was so graceful, so sophisticated, it made me feel like a klutz. I pretended not to notice the vast differences between us.

When I had arrived at the airport, after making my way through security and locating my gate, I'd been a jumble of nerves and not just because I was about to get on a plane. But the moment Aaliyah had seen me, she had eased my nerves somewhat. She had approached quickly, giving me a brief hug and telling me to breathe. So, it had been obvious to her that I was starving my lungs for oxygen, too.

That was when I'd noticed the significant differences between Sebastian and Aaliyah. Considering they were half siblings, it was interesting to see that they didn't look much alike at all. In fact, aside from a few similar facial features like their nose and their cheekbones, the two of them looked nothing alike. Sebastian was tall, dark, and dangerous, while Aaliyah appeared sweet and innocent with her light hair and bright eyes.

"My mother was Conrad's assistant back in the very beginning."

"The beginning of what?" I asked, confused. Sebastian had told me that Lauren had been around for a long time, but I wanted more details.

"Back when he first started Trovato, Inc. She was his first assistant, and she remained with him for years. In fact, she worked for him up until he proposed."

I knew from my research and the minimal details Sebastian had offered that Lauren was Conrad's third wife. Which meant... "So, they've known each other for a long time," I said, unsure just how to voice what was really on my mind.

"Definitely," Aaliyah said confidently. "My mother was there when Conrad's first and second wives left him."

I wondered why they'd left. Did it have anything to do with Lauren? Or because Conrad was clearly unfaithful? Had he been unfaithful with Lauren, too? After all, he had been married to his first wife when he'd gotten Sebastian's mother pregnant.

Not that I was going to ask those questions — it seemed a little presumptuous to think that Lauren might've been the very reason Conrad's previous marriages hadn't worked out. I had no idea how old Lauren was, but if I had to guess, based on her looks, she was several years younger than Conrad. That or she had an incredible plastic surgeon.

Truth was, I didn't think Lauren liked me all that much. I had only spoken to her on the phone until that morning when I had met them at the airport. But when Conrad introduced us that morning — something I thought he would've done long before today, like at the party he'd invited me to — she'd held out her limp hand for me to shake, and though her words were kind, the glimmer in her blue eyes was not. Surely she didn't see me as some sort of threat, did she? Conrad was old enough to be my father.

Having done the math, after pulling up more information on Conrad last night when I sat at home alone, I knew that Conrad had married his first wife when he was twenty-three, divorced four years later. During that time, he had obviously been with Sebastian's mother, because that was when she'd gotten pregnant. He'd then married his second wife when he was twenty-eight, divorced her when he was thirty. He was fifty-one now, and Aaliyah was twenty-one, which meant … Conrad had gotten Lauren pregnant when he had still been married to his second wife.

"Does she get along with Sebastian?" I inquired, fearing I might've overstepped with that question, but I wanted to know. I wanted to know what would've possessed Conrad to abandon his child. Married or not, he should have taken responsibility for his actions.

"Sebastian doesn't really get along with anyone," Aaliyah said with a traffic-stopping grin. "Except for me."

I was happy to hear that their relationship was good. Sebastian needed someone in his corner, and unfortunately, it didn't look like he had his father backing him up.

"I thought he'd be going to Vegas," I said softly.

Aaliyah looked at me and her smile fell. "He was supposed to. I don't know what happened, but it sounds like my father told him to stay home."

My eyebrows shot into my hairline. Was she serious? Why would he do that? "Was it before or after he asked me to come along?"

The question was out before I could stop myself. I watched Aaliyah, waiting for her to brush me off or scold me for being too nosey. She didn't. She only sighed and said, "I honestly don't know. I was just as surprised as you to find out he wasn't going. I was looking forward to it."

"Have you been to Vegas before?"

"Yes. But not since I turned twenty-one. Sebastian promised to take me out to celebrate when we got there. That was his birthday present to me."

My stomach plummeted to my feet. Sebastian had promised to take his sister to Vegas, and yet he wasn't there with her. That didn't sit well with me. Sebastian didn't seem like the kind of guy who would let his sister down. He'd been let down so many times in his life, I just couldn't picture him doing that to someone.

The attendant delivered breakfast to us on trays, and our conversation dwindled down to mere pleasantries. If I had to guess, Aaliyah was thinking about the fact that her brother wasn't there with us. Truth was, I was thinking about it, too.

I missed him.

Although we'd only been together a short time, every minute we were apart felt like an eternity. In such a short time, we had established a connection, something stronger than even I had anticipated. Having spent the night with him, his arms wrapped around me, his body heat warming me ... being without him was almost painful.

I knew I probably shouldn't be getting too attached to him. As much as I wanted to believe in happy ever after, I had to wonder whether there were alternate forces working against Sebastian and me. After all, I did work for his father — a man who had kept Sebastian a secret for all these years. I could understand Conrad being concerned about what people would say. He had impregnated an underage girl, and he'd been married at the time. But to think that his reputation could have caused him to abandon his own child... That made me want to throw something at him.

After I had picked at my food for a few minutes, I gave up. I wasn't hungry. My nerves were shot to hell, and I knew I had to spend the next four days with Conrad and his family. Well, *part* of his family. Working would likely be the only thing that could keep my mind occupied, and even then, I feared I wasn't going to be able to stop thinking about Sebastian.

Unraveling

I wasn't sure I would ever stop thinking about him. No matter what was going on.

Chapter Twelve

Sebastian

Tuesday
In Vegas

MY PLANE LANDED TEN MINUTES earlier than anticipated, which meant I had to wait a little longer than I wanted to, but I was okay with that. Really. It beat the alternative of being late, which would have been just my luck.

Early was good.

Well, I was trying to be okay with being ahead of schedule, but Leif wouldn't shut the hell up, and he was irritating the shit out of me with his incessant rambling. He was raring to go, ready to toss quarters into the slot machines that lined the center aisles through the terminal. I had already told him to go for it, but then he got distracted when we passed a Cinnabon. Apparently, he was hungry.

I was hungry. But not for food.

Leaving Leif in line at the restaurant, I checked the monitors to confirm the gate I was supposed to be going to. Seeing that the plane was on time, I made my way past the many shops and restaurants, dodging passengers who seemed to be in a hurry.

When I reached my destination, I glanced around, noticing that the travelers waiting for the next flight were all sitting, which meant the plane that had arrived hadn't released the passengers yet. As I propped myself against the wall, I stared out the huge panes of glass, willing the people to get off the damn plane that sat just outside the window. It had only been sitting at the gate for a minute, maybe two, and I was ready to storm the damn thing.

But I didn't. Probably not a wise idea in an airport.

So, I stood there, leaning against a pillar while I waited, pretending to be casual. I wasn't even worried whether or not someone snagged my luggage, which was probably spinning around a carousel all alone at this point, because the only place I wanted to be was right there.

I glanced over my shoulder to see if Leif had returned, and when I turned back, there she was.

My heart stuttered in my chest.

I get it, I was acting like a fucking pansy, but shit, I couldn't help it. When it came to Payton, I found myself feeling and doing a lot of crazy shit. She was, by far, the most beautiful woman in the entire world with her long dark hair, her big hazel eyes, flawless skin, and her kissable lips.

And just like the first time I'd seen her, my heart skipped a beat and my hands began to sweat.

Payton was smiling and offering a thank-you to the airline personnel who stood near the door she was currently walking through. I don't think she noticed me, and that was all right. I just wanted to look at her for another minute without interruption. I'd done it the other night when she'd spent the night. Lying in my bed with Payton in my arms, I had watched her sleep until I couldn't take it anymore. Not wanting to wake her, I had snuck down to the workout room. What had happened when she'd joined me had been unexpected but something I would never forget.

And now, here she was.

"Payton." I watched her look around, and the instant our eyes met, the smile she bestowed me with had my heart thudding painfully in my chest, the air rushing from my lungs.

"Sebastian." My name was but a whisper on her lips, but I heard it as though someone had shoved a fucking megaphone in my ear. I smiled, watching her eyes light up in surprise.

Before I could move, before I could reach for her, there was my father. His glare should have incinerated me right there on the spot. I watched him look around briefly before he started my way. Rather than deal with him, I took matters into my own hands. Someone needed to remind him that I was twenty-five years old and I made my own damn decisions. If he didn't want me there, fine. That didn't mean I wasn't going to show up anyway.

But I had wanted to surprise Payton, and based on the way she was watching me, I was pretty sure I'd succeeded.

"Why the fuck are—" Conrad's question was cut off when my sister ran over to me, throwing her arms around my neck. I merely smirked back at Conrad over Aaliyah's shoulder. His frown deepened.

"Sebastian! You made it!" Aaliyah squealed loud enough to rouse the dead, but then her voice lowered, and she added, "Thank God."

I smiled, my eyes still locked with Conrad's.

When Aaliyah released me, I moved to Payton, taking her carry-on bag from her shoulder and hefting it onto mine before taking her hand and pulling her to me. I planted a quick kiss to her lips and then took a step back and watched her.

Her eyes were wide, her mouth hanging open just slightly, and she looked so damn cute I wanted to pick her up and carry her off into the sunset like some sort of knight in shining fucking armor. Like I said, crazy shit was going through my head these days.

I ignored my thoughts, figuring it would be a little too uncivilized.

"You ready?" I asked Payton, ignoring the glare from my father.

"Where do you think you're going?" Conrad asked, his voice much lower than before.

"I'll make sure she's at work when she needs to be there," I promised him. "Don't worry about her. She's safe with me."

The look I shot him dared him to argue with me. I was tired of his petty bullshit. Like I had vowed the other night, no one was going to keep her from me. Certainly not Conrad.

"Payton," Conrad called, and I watched as she turned to him.

"Daddy," Aaliyah interrupted, coming to stand in front of Conrad, her slender fingers resting gently on his arm. "Don't do this, please."

"Aaliyah, stay out of this," Lauren insisted, her tone as icy as her gaze.

My sister took instruction about as well as I did. "Mother…"

"You stay with her, Aaliyah," Conrad interrupted before Aaliyah could finish her sentence.

"Of course," Aaliyah said in that sweet voice that she used when she told them what they wanted to hear. "She has your itinerary. We'll make sure she gets where she needs to be."

That was my sister for you.

"Not 'we,' Aaliyah," Conrad scolded, his gaze flipping to me before returning to her. "You."

"Yes, Daddy."

With my arm around Payton, I turned, smirking at my father as I did. As I'd said before, I lived to piss off the old man. But honestly, this wasn't about him. The only reason I'd come to Vegas after he'd informed me that I wasn't needed or wanted was so that I could be with Payton. Five days away from her was just a little more than I could bear, and I wasn't going to risk the chaos returning, especially not when she'd managed to calm me so thoroughly.

Leif joined us just as I was leading Payton away from Conrad. His smile widened when he turned his attention to Aaliyah, reaching for her bag and hefting it onto his brawny shoulder. I wanted to slap the smirk off his face. I knew the main reason he had come with me was so that he could spend some time with my sister. The guy was infatuated with her. As much as I wanted to stand between them, I knew that it wasn't my place to make decisions for her. And since I was dealing with that firsthand thanks to Conrad's interference, I decided that during my time in Vegas, I was going to let them figure it out for themselves.

Then, when we were back home, I'd pound him into the ground if he hurt her.

"I can't believe you came," Payton whispered, looking up at me as we maneuvered through the hordes of passengers coming and going in the terminal.

I leaned over and kissed the top of her head as we walked. "Angel, nothing would've kept me away from you. Nothing."

Sebastian

FORTY-FIVE MINUTES LATER, THE four of us were walking into Aria. I had surprised Aaliyah with a hotel change, but my sister didn't seem to mind at all. Considering my father was staying at Caesar's Palace, the hotel we'd all previously been booked at, I wasn't about to stay there even though I could have snagged a villa that would've blown Payton's mind.

But this was right up our alley, a hotel that catered more to our age anyway. And we wouldn't run the risk of encountering Conrad or Lauren.

Once we were inside, we made our way to the check-in desk. Leif raided the food area while I stepped up to the counter, encountering the woman who would be helping me. She didn't look at all happy to see me, and her eyes immediately went to my lip ring, then to my eyebrow. Never once did she meet my gaze.

Aaliyah apparently found the process amusing and insisted that Payton remain there to watch.

This happened to me a lot. And, just as Aaliyah did, I often found it comical. Today I was a little antsy, not wanting to spend time fucking with the red-tape bullshit, preferring instead to be with Payton. But this was one of those things that had to be done. Therefore, I might as well enjoy myself.

Apparently, in order to be significantly wealthy, you must have a certain look about you. Or so it seemed based on the reaction I frequently received. In my opinion, I looked rather normal. Aside from the piercings and the tattoos, there wasn't anything about me that stood out. I didn't have an entourage; therefore, they didn't figure me to be a celebrity — which I certainly was not.

"Mister..." The lady glanced at the computer screen and then back to me.

"Trovato," I said, tolerating her rudeness for the moment.

"Could you spell that?"

Okay, so she was clearly going to push me to my limits, but I indulged her and spelled out my name. Very, very slowly. That earned me a sneer.

"Yes." She glanced down her nose at me and then back to the screen. "I show you've booked one of the sky villas."

I nodded.

She glanced over at Payton and Aaliyah before looking back at me. She leaned closer and lowered her voice, "Are you aware how much the room is going to be?"

"Hmmm," I pretended to ponder the question, leaning in and lowering my voice. "Did I *ask* how much it was going to be?"

"N-No, s-sir," the young woman stuttered, pulling back as though I'd slapped her. I had never in my life hit a woman, nor would I, but I could honestly say that had she been a man, she'd have been on the ground at that point.

"Then I'm not sure why you brought it up," I added a little less harshly, keeping my eyes trained on her.

The woman adjusted her clothing and then took a deep breath. "Then I'll just need your license and credit card."

Snatching my wallet from my back pocket, I flipped it open and pulled out my license and the lone credit card I kept on me at all times. I dropped them onto the counter and leisurely slid them toward her, never breaking eye contact.

As with most places I went, it wasn't until I dropped the infamous black card that I usually got eyed speculatively. The woman didn't disappoint.

That didn't stop her from comparing the license to the card, glancing at me and then to the picture on the card and back several times.

I, personally, found it entertaining.

So did Aaliyah.

Tired of playing the game because it left Payton standing there waiting, I leaned in and said, "Would you like me to get my personal banker on the phone? His name's Greg. I'll be happy to let you talk to him."

"No, sir," she said urgently, typing the information into the computer.

From that point on, the less-than-pleasant woman checked us in, and there was already someone waiting with our bags by the time I was handed the key cards. A few minutes later, we were stepping into the luxurious sky villa. The gentleman who brought our bags took them to the respective rooms where I instructed, and then, while I paid the tip, Aaliyah began dragging Payton around.

Leif, of course, was trying to play it cool. As cool as he was capable of anyway.

"You're a fancy bastard, you know that, man?" Leif stated when he came out of the guest room on the first floor. I had purposely put him there since there were two bedrooms upstairs. It was going to be my last-ditch effort to keep him as far from my sister as possible, and I could only hope that it worked.

"Shut the fuck up," I said as I made my way to the windows that overlooked the strip.

Although the hotel didn't sit directly on Las Vegas Blvd, we still had an awesome view and the best part, Conrad had no idea what hotel we were in.

Closing my eyes, I vowed that I wouldn't think about him for the rest of the trip. At least not more than I had to. As Aaliyah had told him, we would ensure that Payton got to where she needed to be when she needed to be there, but what I hadn't bothered to tell him was that I wasn't going to be far. He seemed to forget that as far as the show went, I fully intended to make an appearance as I did every year. After all, I knew a hell of a lot more than he did. I was just waiting for him to realize it.

I was probably going to be waiting a long damn time.

"So what're we gonna do first?" Aaliyah asked when she came traipsing down the stairs with Payton in tow.

"First, we need to figure out Payton's schedule," I informed them. I was going to keep my promise, but only because of Payton.

Snagging her purse from the table, Payton took it over to the leather couch and plopped down, pulling a stack of folded papers out and causing the rest of us to laugh. She looked up, wide-eyed. "What are y'all laughing at?"

"They make these things called smart phones," Leif informed her, trying to keep a straight face. "They've got all sorts of things on it, including a calendar. You don't have to kill a forest anymore."

Payton blushed, flattening the papers out on her lap and looking away.

When I passed Leif, I punched him in the arm. Hard. Unable to resist, I went to her, dropping just as dramatically onto the couch as she had, and pulled her against me, inhaling her sweet, sexy scent. From the moment I'd seen her in the airport, I'd wanted to strip her naked and bury myself inside her. But I'd refrained and knew I would probably have to a little longer, so touching her would have to be enough.

"Do you want me to beat his ass for talking shit?" I asked, also trying to keep from laughing.

Payton looked up at Leif, then over to me. She was clearly better at acting because she appeared to be considering my offer. "Let me think about that for a while," she said with a wry grin, her gaze darting back to Leif.

Smart guy, he took one step back and thrust his hands into his pockets.

"So, what's the plan?" I asked.

I'd been to enough of these trade shows to know when my father would be needed. Trovato, Inc. had representatives at the show who would manage everything when it came to the booth. Conrad likely wouldn't attend unless he was on a panel or conducting a seminar. And even those would be few and far between. But I knew he would be there sometime, which meant he would want Payton there.

Now, we just needed to get that out of the way so we could have a little fun.

Chapter Fourteen

Payton

Tuesday
After SEMA show

IF I'D HAD ANY DOUBTS before that Mr. Trovato was out to punish Sebastian, my mind was indeed set straight now. In turn, it also appeared that he was using me in order to accomplish his goal.

So far, the SEMA show wasn't all that bad. Rather interesting, actually. Between the cars, the exhibits, the people, and the excitement, it had been hard to remember that I was working. Especially when Sebastian was remaining close to my side. But Conrad had been dead set on ensuring I knew exactly why I was there. He had been disturbingly anal with his requests, and I had spent most of my time fetching things for him. At one point, he'd even sent me back to his hotel room in order to get a particular pen that he wanted to use. A pen. Like a writing utensil. Yes, that was what I considered disturbingly anal.

Something wasn't right, but it wasn't like I could say anything. After all, I was his assistant, and he was paying me to assist.

So, I'd spent the last few hours on my feet, following him around. If I wasn't getting him coffee, I was going in search of a specific booth to find a specific person so that I could set up a lunch or dinner while Mr. Trovato was there. Then I was on the phone, trying to make reservations or I was getting him water, or a particular pen that he didn't even bother to use.

What Conrad didn't realize was that I didn't mind. Not one bit. But only because Sebastian had insisted on being there with me. The entire time. So when I got Mr. Trovato coffee, Sebastian got me coffee. When I went in search of a person, I got to watch as people recognized and conversed with Sebastian as though he were some sort of mechanical super genius.

It was one of the most interesting days of my life, and it was now only six o'clock.

Sebastian and I had returned to the hotel alone. Leif was somewhere downstairs at the casino, and Aaliyah had spent the afternoon with her mother at a spa. We were all supposed to meet back at the hotel room by seven so we could go to dinner and then spend some time in the casino.

"Do I have time to shower?" I asked Sebastian when we made our way up the stairs to the bedroom he had claimed for us.

"Depends," he said, moving up behind me and sweeping my hair over my shoulder. The feel of his lips on my neck made my knees weak and my heart race. He must have realized the effect he had on me, because he wrapped his arms around my waist and pulled me into him. I could feel the evidence of his arousal against my lower back, and I was tempted to say to hell with dinner.

"On?" I asked, breathless, as he continued to brush his mouth over the sensitive skin of my neck.

"If you want me to join you or not."

The idea of getting in that huge glass shower with Sebastian was almost too good to pass up. But I knew that Leif and Aaliyah would be back soon, and if we had any intention of getting food and enjoying a little of the Vegas nightlife, we would have to avoid getting naked together.

"Okay, how about this," I said as I turned around to face him, sliding my hands up the hard planes of his chest and then wrapping my arms around his neck. "What if I change, and later, when we get back, we can spend some time in the giant tub. Alone."

Sebastian walked me backward until my back was against the wall and his muscular thigh pressed between my legs. Yeah, he was purposely making me crazy.

"I think that sounds like a plan," he whispered before crushing his mouth to mine, tangling his hand in my hair. Delicious bolts of pleasure darted from my scalp down to my core when he pulled my head back.

Yeah, if he kept doing that, dinner was going to be the last thing on my mind.

***

"So he really didn't tell you who he was when you came to the house?" Aaliyah asked, her smile wide, showing her perfectly straight, white teeth.

"He said he was a mechanic," I explained, pushing my plate away and reaching for my water.

Leif chuckled, staring back and forth between Sebastian and me.

"In my defense," Sebastian began, squeezing my knee beneath the table, "she assumed I was a mechanic."

"He made me believe no one was home to get the phone," I retorted quickly, grinning. In retrospect, it was a rather amusing story. And I liked the fact that it gave us an interesting first-time introduction story.

"So that's why you were all gaga over her at the party," Aaliyah said, her eyes glittering brightly as she laughed.

"Sebastian? Gaga? Damn I wish I had been there to see that," Leif added.

"If I recall correctly, you" — Sebastian pointed at Aaliyah — "went on and on about how cute Payton and Aaron were together."

Aaliyah's laugh had heads turning. "That's right. I remember that, too."

I smiled, remembering that Aaron had explicitly introduced himself to Aaliyah as my gay best friend who had been coerced into attending.

"And then you just happened to show up at the same restaurant?" Aaliyah asked, sipping her wine, clearly amused by the entire situation.

"Sports bar," Sebastian corrected, leaning back in his chair and reaching for my hand beneath the table, linking his fingers with mine.

The fact that he insisted on always touching me did strange things to my insides. If he wasn't holding my hand, he was touching my lower back or wrapping his arm around my shoulder. I found that I craved the feel of his rough skin against mine.

"Very interesting," Aaliyah said, placing her glass back on the table.

The waiter returned to place the check on the table, but Sebastian merely handed him his credit card without looking at the bill, and the guy sauntered off quickly.

"How's school going?" Leif asked Aaliyah, his expression changing from fun to serious all of a sudden.

I would admit that I didn't know Leif all that well, but even I could see the intense interest he had in Sebastian's sister. It was fascinating. The usual laid-back guy was replaced with someone who looked … nervous.

Leif was a good-looking guy with his messy dark hair and dark eyes. He was probably the same height as Sebastian, but he was bigger, bulkier compared to Sebastian's lean frame. Leif's hair was a bit too long, but he often hid it beneath a ball cap. Not tonight, though. Tonight he looked nice, wearing a pair of jeans and a button-up shirt, similar to what Sebastian was wearing.

"Boring," Aaliyah answered Leif, her blue eyes locking with Leif's brown eyes.

Oh, yeah, there was some powerful chemistry there. On both parts.

I cast a glance at Sebastian. He was pretending not to see the interest between his sister and his best friend. I squeezed his thigh, offering a little support. He didn't appear to be interfering, and after having to deal with Conrad all day, I was happy to see that. It was a pain in the ass to deal with someone who wanted to interfere. Sebastian, as amazing as I thought he was, wouldn't be any different if he thought he could be the one to keep those two apart.

"What are you majoring in?" I asked Aaliyah, trying to spur the conversation.

"Pharmaceutical science," Aaliyah said easily.

"Wow," I said, breathing out quickly. "That's great."

"It comes naturally for me," Aaliyah added, her gaze drifting back to Leif.

"What do you do?" I asked Leif when no one else said anything.

"I'm a shop foreman," he informed me.

"What type of shop?"

"Body shop."

"Small world. My dad owns a body shop."

"Yeah? In Austin?"

"Yes. Been in business now for twenty-eight years."

"Times are tough," Leif said, his full attention sliding my way. "With the big companies invading Austin's market, we're losing traction fast. Half the time I get up in the morning not knowing whether or not I'll have a job by the end of the day."

I knew just what he was talking about because I'd heard my parents arguing about it. Some of the larger conglomerates were coming into Austin and buying up all of the mom-and-pop shops, taking them over and cutting jobs. Since my mother had mentioned that the shop wasn't doing great financially, I knew my father was dealing with the same issues Leif was. I hadn't thought much of it, but I made a mental note to check in with my parents when I got back to Austin. At least then maybe they wouldn't be so worried that I'd gone off to Las Vegas without much notice.

"How's your mom?" Aaliyah asked Leif.

"Good. She's … uh…" Leif glanced at Sebastian and then back to Aaliyah. "She's moving in with her boyfriend. Well, technically, I guess he's moving in with her."

"The cop?" Aaliyah asked.

"Detective. Yeah."

"It's about time," Aaliyah said, reaching for her wineglass again.

Leif chuckled. "I guess so. They've been dating for a couple of years," he explained, looking at me again. "His name's Tom. Nice guy. My mother finally agreed to marry him."

"That's great," I said, hoping that was really the case.

I was a little distracted by the way Aaliyah was hanging on to Leif's every word. She clearly knew a lot about him, which meant that either she and Leif talked, or she and Sebastian did. From what I could tell, Aaliyah was fond of her brother, but I didn't get the vibe that they talked a lot. Why that was, I didn't know.

"Which is why Leif's moving into my place for a while. He's been staying with his mother so she didn't have to be alone. Now that she won't be, she's kicking him to the curb," Sebastian said, grinning.

"She is not." Leif laughed. "I'm twenty-five years old. I think it's time I moved out anyway."

I watched Aaliyah's reaction to that news, and I saw the gleam in her bright blue eyes. I think she liked the idea of Leif moving closer to where she was. Now, whether or not Conrad and her mother would approve, that would probably be an entirely different story.

"Hey, you still plannin' to do the race on Saturday?" Leif asked Sebastian directly, completely changing the subject.

My head snapped toward him, my eyes studying his face. A race.

He gently squeezed my hand beneath the table as he answered Leif with an affirmative nod. "I said I'd be there."

There was a hint of anger in his tone, and I noticed the storm clouds brewing in his brilliant gold gaze. I didn't know whether or not there was a story there, but when Leif didn't push the issue, I decided not to as well. I'd talk to Sebastian about it later.

The waiter returned with the leather folder containing the bill, and Sebastian quickly scribbled his name and retrieved his credit card.

"So, what's the plan for tonight?" Aaliyah asked, finishing off her wine.

"I say we head out to the casino, drop some money in the machine, and see if we can get lucky," Leif replied.

"I'm already lucky," Sebastian mumbled, his hand squeezing mine again beneath the table.

The man had the ability to make me swoon. I wasn't sure how someone could be so sweet and so intense at the same time, but Sebastian walked a very fine line. He treated me like I was a princess, all while he seemed to be battling the storm clouds that continued to brew in his gaze.

"Then what are we waiting for?" Leif asked, pushing his chair back and then standing behind Aaliyah, helping her to her feet.

Sebastian did the same for me and I blushed. I wasn't used to this sort of treatment.

As we started to walk out of the restaurant, Sebastian leaned over and whispered against my ear, "Just note that when we're done, I'm going to spend the rest of the night buried so deep inside you that you forget your own name."

And just like that, my body ignited into a fireball. I was surprised I managed to keep upright after that erotic promise.

"All right. On to the casino," Leif announced.

Casino?

What casino?

Sebastian

IT WAS A GOOD THING that my addictive personality didn't spill over into everything I did. For the last two hours, I'd remained at Payton's side, sitting at a slot machine and watching as she hit buttons and racked up the dollars. First timer's luck, I guess. But whatever it was, the woman looked good doing it.

Leif and Aaliyah had disappeared soon after dinner — together — and I forced them to the back of my mind. Leif was a good guy. He might be a man whore, but he was always safe, and I knew he would treat my sister with respect. He knew if he didn't, I'd beat his ass to a pulp, but that was beside the point.

Payton yawned, and I grinned, glancing down at my watch. "It's three o'clock. What do you say we head up to the room?"

"Three o'clock? In the morning?" she asked, her eyes wide.

"Yep."

"But all these people are still out." She gestured toward the people milling about inside the casino, most of them playing table games not too far away from where we sat.

"Sin City never sleeps," I told her, turning her in her chair to face me more fully.

"Conrad's gonna kill me tomorrow."

"Technically that's today, and I'd prefer we don't talk about him."

"Sorry," she said with a sweet grin. When she leaned forward, pressing her lips to mine, I had to refrain from pulling her onto my lap. I'd been sporting an aching hard-on for the last few hours, and whenever she touched me, I had to fight back the urge to sneak her into a dark corner and devour her whole.

Considering this was Vegas and every corner, dark or otherwise, had a camera, I didn't think that was a wise idea. After all, we had a great room upstairs just waiting for us.

"I'm ready when you are," she finally said.

I hit the *change* button on the machine and grabbed the ticket when it printed. We made our way to a machine that cashed out the tickets, and I handed her the money that it spit out.

"That's *your* money," she said, refusing to take it, her hands wrapped tightly around my bicep.

I snagged a twenty-dollar bill from the pile, which was what she'd started with, and held the remaining out for her to take. "This is mine," I said, holding up the bill between two fingers. "The rest is yours. You won it fair and square."

Payton's eyes narrowed as she stared down at the money in my hand. She'd done well, raking in roughly five hundred in just a few hours. Granted, this was Vegas and you could easily lose twice that much in half the time, so it wasn't something I usually did when I visited.

Reaching for Payton's hand, I twined my fingers with hers and led her to the elevator that would take us to our room.

As soon as we were in the room, I listened to make sure that no one else had come back already. When I was met with silence, I shut the door and pulled Payton to me. "How about that bath?"

"Sounds like heaven."

More so than she knew.

Surprising her, I slid my hands down her ass, gripping her thighs and lifting her, forcing her to wrap her legs around my waist. With my arms bracing her, I headed for the stairs that would take us to our second-floor bedroom.

"You're gonna hurt your back." She giggled, her arms wrapped tightly around my neck.

"I'm young, I'll deal."

Once we were in our room, I closed and locked the door before sliding her down my body until her feet touched the floor. The sexy black dress she'd put on was what I attacked first, trying to rein in my hunger for her as I lowered the zipper and allowed the strapless number to slide to the floor.

"Have I mentioned how much I love that dress?" I asked.

"You might've said something a time or two," she whispered softly, smiling over her shoulder at me.

"You look incredible in it. But you look even better out of it."

In the soft light of the bedroom, I could see the pink that infused her cheeks. Again, I felt invincible. Payton's reactions were so damn sweet, so innocent. She wasn't like other women I'd been with, always trying to prove how hot she was. No, Payton was the opposite, and truth be told, she was far sexier than any woman I'd ever met.

It was difficult not to pick her up and toss her on the bed as she stood before me in a pair of red satin panties and a matching strapless bra. When she moved closer, I was forced to lift my gaze in order to look at her face, letting my eyes graze her mouth briefly.

She made quick work of unhooking the buttons on my shirt. I helped her by releasing the cuffs and then letting the white cotton slide down my arms and fall to the floor. I wanted her hands on my bare skin, and I wasn't disappointed. Her soft, cool fingers slid over my chest and then up to cup my face.

"I'm so glad you're here," she whispered, her expression serious. "I thought I was going to have to spend five days away from you."

"I wasn't going to miss it," I told her.

I didn't want to tell her that being away from her for the last two nights had been difficult enough. I didn't want to push her too hard, but I wasn't sure how long I would be able to go without letting her know how I felt about her. I'd never felt this way about a woman, never wanted a woman to stay the night and certainly never for more than one night. Lust was a far cry from what I felt for Payton, and before her, that was the extent of any emotion that a woman had stirred in me.

But with Payton, I felt an overwhelming need to keep her close, listen to her laugh, make her smile, and make sure that no one hurt her. Spending even a few minutes apart was excruciating and not just because the chaos returned with a vengeance when she wasn't with me. The truth was, I loved her. I had fallen hard and fast, and the descent hadn't stopped yet. I was still falling for her, every second of every day.

"Come on," I said, leaning down and pressing my lips to hers. "Let's get naked and wet."

Payton giggled and her cheeks turned a brighter shade of red, which I found extremely sexy.

A few minutes later, we were in the bathtub, the only light coming from the lamp in the bedroom and the glow of the buildings outside the floor-to-ceiling windows.

"This is…" Payton's words trailed off as I slid my hands down her chest, cupping her breasts and kneading them gently while I pressed my lips to her ear.

"It's what?" I breathed against her neck.

"Beautiful," she said, her tone raspy and so damn sexy my cock throbbed with anticipation.

Neither of us said anything for long minutes while I continued to caress her slowly, sliding my hands down her stomach, teasing her beneath the water briefly before returning my hands to her breasts. When I tweaked her nipples gently, her breath hitched.

"You like that?" I asked, my throat dry.

"Yes," she moaned, pushing back against me while thrusting her breasts into my hands.

I pinched her nipples more firmly, teasing her more insistently.

"Sebastian."

The way she said my name sent chills down my spine. "Say my name again," I instructed.

"Sebastian." Her voice lowered, her hands gripping my thighs more firmly as she began to squirm against my hands. "I need more."

Sliding one hand down beneath the water again, I teased her clit, stroking softly. I didn't want to rush, although my dick had other ideas. But I wasn't going to waste this moment. I continued to tease her, slipping my finger inside her until she was moaning loudly, my name on her lips like a beacon calling me home.

"Oh, God, Sebastian … I'm gonna…"

"Come for me, Angel," I whispered against her ear, thrusting my finger inside her while I pinched her nipple between my thumb and forefinger.

Her strangled cry, along with her short nails digging into my thighs, had my body throbbing. The way her body gripped my finger, her climax tightening every muscle, I was surprised I didn't detonate right then and there.

When she came down from her release, I allowed the silence to surround us while we sat there in the warm water, her body relaxing into mine. I continued to slide my hands up and down her smooth, wet skin while we stared out into the night sky, the lights of the Vegas strip providing an incredible backdrop for what was turning out to be the most incredible evening.

When the water began to cool, I helped her out of the tub, wrapped a towel around her, and then dried myself off quickly. Dropping my towel to the floor, I swept Payton off her feet, carrying her to the bed and lowering her gently.

My intentions had been good. I was going to go slow, savor her for hours, but the next thing I knew, Payton was pulling me on top of her. One of her arms snaked around my neck, her mouth meeting mine while her other hand slid between our bodies. She found my erection hard and rigid between us, and her soft fingers wrapping around me had me trying to catch my breath.

When she aligned our bodies, guiding me inside her, I pulled my lips from hers and stared into her eyes as I sank into her. As I slid deeper, her eyes closed, her breaths becoming labored as she pressed her hips up to meet mine.

"Open your eyes," I instructed. "Look at me, Angel."

Payton's eyes slowly slid open, our gazes meeting, holding as I pumped my hips gently, burying myself deep and then retreating slowly.

"I could do this forever, you know," I said with a wry grin.

"Me, too." She was breathless, her fingernails digging into my back.

I needed her. More than I needed anything else. More than oxygen and water, more than racing, more than...

"Sebastian," she said, her eyes still locked with mine.

"Oh, God, you feel so damn good," I growled, thrusting into her more forcefully, pushing us both closer and closer to the edge. "Payton."

The noise in my head that I'd dealt with for so long was quieter than it had ever been, and I knew without a doubt that she was the reason. She was meant for me, the only thing in the world that could possibly keep me from shattering into a million pieces. And here she was, her lips seeking mine as I drove into her deeper, harder, faster. Her legs wrapped around my hips, pulling me to her, and I couldn't hold back. Our sweat-slick bodies slid together, our breaths mingling as I continued to drive into her, burying myself as deep as possible, just as I'd promised. I wanted her to think of me and only me.

"Payton," I breathed against her mouth. "Angel, you fucking unhinge me. Come for me, baby. Come *with* me."

She cried out, but I captured the sound with my mouth as we both flew over the edge, my body consumed by her. I didn't want to let her go. Not now, not ever. My release seemed to go on forever, and as I fought for air, I pulled back and stared down into her beautiful face, the next words out of my mouth surprising us both. "You own me." I took a deep breath and added, "I love you."

Chapter Sixteen

Payton

MY HEART SKIPPED A BEAT.

Maybe two.

Hell, it might've stopped beating altogether when Sebastian whispered those three words. The three words I had never heard from a man's mouth. Not like this.

My heart expanded in my chest, and a smile quickly followed. "I love you," I whispered back, the words coming so naturally. I didn't have to think about it. I'd already known that I had fallen for Sebastian, far sooner than I ever thought I would.

Sebastian cupped my face with his hand as he watched me. I couldn't tell what he was thinking, but for the first time, there weren't any storm clouds gathered in his beautiful gaze. He seemed to be at peace, and I didn't know if that was because of what I'd said or just the overwhelming feelings that seemed to be coursing between us.

"Hold that thought," he whispered, smiling before he slipped out of the bed and padded naked to the bathroom. I stared after him, peeking at his incredibly fine back side, admiring the angel wings across his back.

Ironic how he called me angel, yet he seemed to have been sent here for me. I still had a hard time wrapping my mind around all that had happened in the last couple of weeks. Between the dreams that had started, all starring a man I would soon meet, and then to stumble upon him at my boss's house, my dreams literally coming to life... Sometimes I wondered if it was too good to be true.

Sebastian returned, a washcloth in his hand. My body was so sated I could hardly move. And when he used the warm cloth to clean between my sore thighs, I fought the blush that crept up my neck. He disappeared once more and returned a minute later, sliding into bed beside me, pulling the covers up over us both before spooning behind me.

Neither of us said anything for long minutes, the only sound coming from the ceiling fan spinning up high on the ceiling.

"Is there meaning behind the angel wings?" I asked, placing my arm over his where he was wrapped around me.

"Yeah," he whispered softly, his breath blowing my hair.

I giggled. "Are you going to tell me what it is?"

"If you ask nicely," he replied, his arms tightening around me.

"Please?"

"I got the wings as a way to keep myself aware of which direction I needed to go. Without my mother here…"

I squeezed his hand. "Tell me."

"When my mother died, I had no one. One day she was there, then she was gone. My best friend in the entire world stolen from me. From the minute the police showed up at the apartment, my life changed in every way that mattered.

"After making sure that I knew there were no other options, that he wasn't choosing me but rather was being saddled with me, Conrad took me in. He didn't treat me like his son. Hell, I was lucky that he at least treated me like the hired help. And my new instant family couldn't have cared less who I was or why I was there. I remember Aaliyah back then. She wasn't nice to me at first, but I couldn't blame her. It took a few years before she finally came to accept me.

"I started acting out immediately, fighting with anyone and everyone. I stopped trying in school, came home whenever I wanted. I don't think anyone really noticed. I had no one to make sure I was doing what I should, no one to tell me that they loved me or that they'd miss me when I was gone." Sebastian paused. I heard him swallow hard before continuing. "When I turned eighteen, I went straight to the tattoo shop, gave them my design. I remember the guy thought it was cool but wanted to enhance it. I didn't let him modify it because the design had come to me in a dream. A dream I had of my mother.

"She came back. Just the one time. She came back, and she told me that I needed to pull it together. I was making a mess of my life before I even knew the impact it would have. I had contemplated dropping out of high school at sixteen because it just didn't matter. But in that dream, my mother told me that I was making a mistake. It was then that I decided I needed something to keep me moving in the right direction. Something to remind me of the path I should be on, because no one was pointing me there. Sometimes the right path isn't as obvious as it should be, no matter who you are. It's even less apparent when you're fourteen years old and your best friend dies, the only person who ever told me they loved me."

I couldn't hold back the sob that ripped through my chest at Sebastian's words. Every word he spoke was laced with emotion, and I knew it was hard for him to talk about his mother, but I wanted to hear. I wanted to know him. To know everything about him. I was grateful when Sebastian held me tighter but continued to talk.

"Even though I may not see the wings, I know they're there. And when it seems that I'm going too far from where I should be, I think of her. She's behind me, pushing me forward. I know where she is, and I'm bound and determined that one day I *will* see her again." Sebastian's voice hitched and it broke my heart. I couldn't stop the tears from rolling down my cheeks and landing on the pillow.

The idea of Sebastian spending most of his life without someone to tell him that they loved him, without someone to show him each and every day just how important he was made the tears fall faster. I could hardly swallow past the lump in my throat.

"Don't cry for me, Payton," Sebastian whispered in my ear, pulling me against him.

I tried not to, but I couldn't stop myself. The sobs came harder, my body shuddering as I replayed his statement over and over in my head. Several minutes passed before I managed to collect myself enough to speak. I turned my head to try and look at him over my shoulder. "I love you, Sebastian." He pressed his lips to my cheek, kissing away one of my tears. "And I'm going to make sure I tell you so every single day."

We lay in silence for a while. I listened to him breathe, and I thought he had fallen asleep, so I was giving in to my exhaustion but trying to hang on for a few more minutes because I just wanted to be there with him.

Just as my eyes were drifting closed, Sebastian spoke. "You didn't seem surprised when I told you that Conrad was my father."

I forced them open, turning in his arms so that I could rest my head against his chest. I wanted to touch him, because when I did, there was a connection there that felt surreal. One that gave me the feeling — real or perceived, I wasn't sure — that nothing could go wrong in the world as long as he was with me.

"Too many coincidences," I told him softly. "You were at his house, then at the party. It just seemed logical to me."

"Logical," Sebastian huffed.

I tapped his chest lightly. "You know what I mean." I sighed, snuggling closer to him. The silence returned for several long seconds before I said, "Do you think this is happening too fast?"

I felt his body tense, his arm tightening around me. "No, I don't."

His tone was firm, leaving no room for argument, so I didn't say anything more. I let the silence drift over me, relishing the warmth of Sebastian's body against mine, the steady beat of his heart against my ear. As for my thoughts on whether or not we were moving too fast, I agreed with Sebastian. I didn't think it was too fast, either. In fact, when I was with him, time seemed to stand still; therefore, the actual measurement was nearly impossible.

I loved this man.

I don't know how much time passed, but I was slowly drifting off to sleep when I heard Sebastian whisper, "I love you, Angel. More than anyone. I swear I'll never let my demons come between us."

Unraveling

Chapter Seventeen

Payton

Wednesday

THE FOLLOWING MORNING, I WOKE to the sound of music. A little disoriented, I forced my eyes open and looked around the room. The sun was shining through the floor-to-ceiling windows, warming my face. The music started again, and I realized it was my cell phone. I fumbled out of bed, gripping the sheet to my naked body, and found my purse on the floor by the door, where I'd left it when we'd come in last night. Or rather that morning.

What I thought was a phone call was actually the alarm that I'd set. I glanced at the clock on my phone, and panic set in. I was supposed to meet Conrad at his hotel that morning for a business breakfast — his words, not mine. He'd informed me of my required attendance the day before, just as I was leaving the show for the evening. I hadn't mentioned it to Sebastian, because Conrad had explicitly informed me that Sebastian was not invited and that if I valued my job, I wouldn't share that information with him.

And yes, that statement had struck me as odd, but Conrad was my boss, so I'd merely agreed with him. What else could I do?

"Shit," I grumbled, tossing the phone onto the bed and rushing into the bathroom.

It hadn't dawned on me until then that Sebastian wasn't anywhere in sight. I'd woken up alone, and he wasn't in the bathroom, either. Rather than try to find him and waste time I didn't have, I hopped in the shower and hurried through getting ready.

By the time I was dressed, my makeup done, and my hair dried, I still hadn't seen Sebastian, which worried me. I needed to be at the restaurant in less than twenty minutes, which meant I was going to have to figure out the best way to get there if no one was around to get me there. Damn it. I knew I should have thought this through all the way. Not telling Sebastian meant that I had to find my own transportation. Granted, I was an adult. I knew that I could hail a cab downstairs, but this was Las Vegas, and truth was, being alone out there just made me nervous.

Resigning myself to getting a cab at the main entrance to the casino, I grabbed my purse, dropped my cell phone inside, and then opened the bedroom door.

I was met with silence.

Crap.

From where I stood, I could see that Aaliyah's bedroom door was open and the bed wasn't made. I took the stairs as fast as I dared, proud of myself for not taking a header to the first floor. Once downstairs, I headed for the door, still not seeing a soul. I glanced back at the guest bedroom, and that door was open as well, the bed in there made.

Where the hell was everyone?

I didn't have time to waste trying to figure it out, though. I was going to be late, and Conrad was already in rare form — I didn't see any reason to piss him off more. I stopped at the check-in desk where we'd come in, and a nice woman there informed me that she would have a limo take me to Conrad's hotel. I double-timed it to the main doors and stepped outside to the sound of horns blaring and people talking.

"Ms. Fowler?" a gentleman standing beside a waiting limo called my name, and I hurried toward him, snagging a couple of dollars from my purse and shoving them toward him before darting inside the car.

Directions weren't necessary; apparently the desk lady had taken care of that for me. A few minutes later, after a hair-raising trip a few miles down the strip, the limo was pulling into Caesar's Palace. Once parked, the driver swiftly exited the vehicle to help me out. I handed him more money, offered a quick thank you, and then practically ran inside.

By the time I arrived at the restaurant I had agreed to meet Conrad and his wife at, I was sweating and out of breath. Who knew that power walking through a hotel would be the equivalent of running ten miles?

I gave my name to the hostess, and she promptly led me toward the back. I swallowed back my nerves as I approached the table, straightening my skirt and drying my now sweaty palms. Conrad and his wife had their backs to me, and on the opposite side was a young man I hadn't seen before. He certainly wasn't one of the people who Conrad had insisted I seek out and offer a dinner invitation to.

The guy looked up at me and smiled, causing Conrad to glance over his shoulder.

"There she is," Conrad greeted me kindly. Much kinder than I expected, considering I was at least ten minutes late.

"I'm so sorry I'm late," I said quickly, trying not to sound so out of breath.

"No need to apologize. I'd like you to meet Trevor. Trevor, this is my assistant, Payton Fowler. Payton, Trevor is Lauren's nephew."

"Nice to meet you, Payton."

I accepted Trevor's hand, shaking it gently. He was looking at me oddly, and I wondered whether or not I had something on my face. When he pulled out my chair, praying that I didn't have a stray streak of lip gloss, I subtly slid my hand over my mouth. I figured anything was possible given how rattled I was.

"Good morning, Payton," Lauren said icily, her blue gaze pinning me in place.

I had learned since meeting her the day before that she had two settings: lukewarm and icy. Neither of them made me feel comfortable. It looked as though she'd doubled up on the ice this morning. "Good morning," I replied, not wanting to be rude.

"We were just about to order," Conrad told me.

I felt incredibly awkward sitting at the table with them. First of all, it was strange to be having breakfast with my boss, who happened to also be my boyfriend's father. Secondly, the guy sitting next to me was much closer to my age than Conrad's, and I was curious as to why, exactly, he was there. Sure, being related to Lauren made sense, but not in regard to why I would have been invited to breakfast to meet him.

After perusing the menu for a moment, I made a selection, and after the waiter came and took our order, I sat patiently, trying to figure out just what I was supposed to be doing at this meeting.

"Conrad's told me so much about you," Trevor said, dragging my attention from rearranging my napkin on my lap. His voice was deep and smooth, his eyes the same icy blue as Lauren's. He seemed nice enough, clean cut, well dressed, but there was something that bothered me about him. Something I couldn't put my finger on.

I had no idea what to say to his comment, so I smiled.

"Trevor is in the process of moving to Austin," Conrad told me, and my eyes widened as I looked back at him.

"He's been having a little trouble," Lauren added, glancing over at Trevor, "but we've taken care of all that now. I think it'll be good for him to start over."

"Do you live here?" I asked Trevor, still trying to figure out why he was in Vegas.

"No. Conrad called me up and invited me. I'm considering a..." Trevor's eyes traveled over to Conrad and then back to me before he continued. "A career change."

When he didn't elaborate, I blurted out the first thing that came to mind. "What is it that you do?"

"I'm a mechanic."

Warning bells sounded in my head, and I wasn't sure why. Something wasn't right. Why would Lauren's nephew be having breakfast with us in Vegas if he didn't live there? More specifically, why was I having breakfast with them? Clearly, I was the odd man out. Hoping there was a logical reason, I waited patiently for someone to enlighten me.

I was obviously going to wait all day, because Lauren, Trevor, and Conrad began talking. They weren't talking business, which made me even more uncomfortable, but I tried my best to hide my distress.

My cell phone chimed from my purse, and I glanced around, wondering if it would be incredibly rude to answer while I was sitting at the table. After all, the three of them seemed to be ignoring me. Figuring it wouldn't help the situation, I kindly asked to be excused, pretending to need to go to the restroom. Instead, I slipped out of the restaurant and onto the casino floor, grabbing my phone out of my purse.

Where are you?

The text came from Sebastian.

Breakfast with your father.

What the fuck?

I hesitated before responding, but I was still creeped out by the whole thing, so I figured telling Sebastian couldn't hurt. At least then he'd know where I was if I needed him.

He insisted that I meet him, and he told me not to tell you.

What restaurant?

I quickly typed the name of the restaurant and then informed Sebastian I would see him back at the hotel in an hour. When I didn't receive a response, I tossed my phone back in my purse and returned to the table. The food had been brought out, and the three occupants seemed to be waiting for me. I sighed before making my way over and sliding into my seat, pretending that I wasn't unnerved by the whole situation.

I didn't think I was doing a very good job. But I really didn't care.

Sebastian

I WAS ON THE VERGE of losing my damned mind.

Leif was just lucky that I was more concerned about Payton than the fact that he had dragged my sister to a strip club, gotten rip-roaring drunk, and then opted to spend the night in a casino in downtown Las Vegas versus coming back to the room. How the fuck they'd ended up downtown was beyond me, but the two of them weren't talking, so it wasn't likely that I was going to find out from either of them.

Whatever had happened between them had left them both pissed off at one another, refusing to talk. In fact, I had been forced out of bed at five-thirty because Aaliyah had refused to get into the car with Leif to come back to the hotel. I'd had to get a cab to take me to the Golden Nugget and wait while I went in and practically forced her out to the car.

At the last fucking minute, Leif had refused to go with us, and I'd been close to ripping his nose off his fucking face because I was so pissed. He was acting like a fucking child, and I didn't have time to play games with these idiots.

Then, to make matters worse, when I'd gotten back to the hotel, Payton had been gone. I wasn't the type of guy to usually freak out, but I had. It was pathetic. So much so that I hadn't even thought about texting her to find out where she was until Aaliyah had told me to.

When Payton had informed me that she was with my father at his hotel having breakfast, I'd damn near torn the hotel room to shreds in a fit of rage that caught me by surprise.

Payton was alone with Conrad and Lauren.

Why, I had no fucking clue. But I knew I had to get her away from them. She wasn't safe with either of them.

Now, as I walked through the huge casino, looking for the restaurant she had mentioned, I was seething. I knew something was up. I should've known my father would do something underhanded, but honestly, I hadn't expected this. If he had actually taken her aside and instructed her to meet him without my knowing, then there were plenty of reasons for me to be worried.

He clearly didn't want me there.

Well, guess where I was?

Fuck that old bastard.

When I reached the restaurant, I ignored the hostess who tried to stop me as I entered, waving her off as I stepped into the dining area. I stopped long enough to glance around, and that was when I noticed Payton sitting at a table in the back. She was studying her coffee cup, looking like she'd rather be anywhere but there.

I took a deep breath and tried to calm down. I was just planning to politely interrupt their breakfast to see if she was ready to go.

That had been the plan.

Until I saw Trevor Yates sitting beside her.

Much too close for my peace of mind.

I approached the table as quietly as I could, unable to keep my hands from balling into fists at my side.

"What the fuck is going on?" I asked as soon as I got their attention.

Okay, so much for trying to politely interrupt. My voice was louder than I intended, and it would appear I had caught the attention of most of the people sitting around them as well.

Fucking awesome.

Payton's eyes flared, and her mouth dropped open as she looked up at me.

Yeah, I probably sounded like a raging lunatic, but she had no fucking clue just what type of crazy bastard she was sitting next to at the moment. Nor did she have any idea that the man sitting across from her was likely the devil himself.

"Conrad, I thought we agreed he wouldn't be here," Lauren said softly, her hand gripping my father's arm tightly. "Your assistant should be more than capable of handling her job without him babysitting her."

Lauren's condescending tone did nothing for my mood.

"Capable?" I asked, glaring at her. "She's quite capable, I agree. But" — I shot a look at Trevor — "when you introduce her to pieces of shit like him, I have to wonder just what your angle is."

"Sebastian, shut your mouth," Lauren snapped, her icy stare boring into me.

"Excuse me, *ma'am*," I said, tacking the last part on because I knew how much she hated that. "I didn't realize they allowed trash in this place. Had I known, I would've kept a better eye on my girlfriend."

"Girlfriend?" Conrad shot to his feet, his gaze darting back and forth between me and Payton.

Oh, come on. He really didn't know? I seriously doubted that.

I slid my gaze over to Payton.

Shit.

The look on her face reflected her embarrassment, and I knew without a doubt that I was acting like a jackass, but I couldn't help it. If she knew what I knew, she would have stayed far away from every single person at that table.

"Please tell me you haven't allowed him to brainwash you," Lauren said softly, speaking directly to Payton. "He's…" Lauren glanced down at the table, but she didn't finish her sentence.

Payton's hand came up over her mouth as though she was shocked by my stepmother's words. I wasn't. She'd said plenty worse than that before.

"I should've warned you, Payton," Conrad told her.

I was tempted to punch him in the face.

"Warned me about what?" Payton asked, her eyes moving back and forth between Conrad and Lauren. Although it was clear she was upset with me for barging in like that, I could tell she was pissed at Conrad and Lauren as well. I could deal with her anger. What I wouldn't be able to deal with was her believing these manipulative assholes.

"Conrad's son… He's" — Lauren lowered her voice and continued — "unstable."

Unstable? Seriously? That was all she had?

"Damn right I'm unstable," I ground out through clenched teeth. "But at least I'm not a…" I bit my tongue before the words slipped out. This wasn't the place to get into it. Not with a restaurant full of people who were now focused on us. "Are you ready to go?" I asked Payton, keeping a tight grip on my temper.

"If I'd known he would act like this, I would've warned you just how messed up he really is," Lauren added. "He's always been the jealous type. And he doesn't like Trevor very much."

Very much was an understatement. I despised the lying, scheming, disgusting bastard. But I didn't say as much. It wouldn't have helped the situation.

Payton got to her feet, glaring at Conrad and then turning her murderous scowl on me.

Yeah, I'd gone and fucked up royally. I knew it. I deserved her wrath.

"If you'll excuse me," Payton said softly.

I reached for her arm, but she sidestepped me, looking at me as though I'd lost my mind.

"This isn't over," I warned my stepmother before I turned to follow Payton.

I managed to take two steps, but I was pulled up short when Conrad grabbed my arm. "That's where you're wrong. This *is* over. It's been over for a long time, Sebastian."

I jerked away from him, but I managed to keep my mouth shut. Barely.

By the time I caught up with Payton, she was stepping outside in front of the hotel. She asked the valet to get her a cab, but I waved him off.

"Payton." When I reached for her again, she spun around to face me, her eyes wild, her chin trembling.

"How dare you?" she hissed, tears forming in her eyes. "How dare you embarrass me like that? Did you forget that I work for that man? He signs my paycheck. If he tells me to join him for breakfast, that is what I'm paid to do. I was handling the situation just fine."

"You don't have a fucking clue what was going on there," I growled, keeping my tone low.

"No, you're the one who doesn't have a clue, Sebastian," she retorted.

"Come on, I'll take you back to the hotel."

"Don't touch me," she snapped when I tried to take her hand. "Get the hell away from me, Sebastian."

I swallowed hard, staring at her. I knew what she was thinking. In retrospect, I could have handled that much better than I had. Then again, I could have handled it much worse. She just didn't know me well enough to see how much I'd just held back.

"I'm going to the show. I'll wait for Conrad to arrive. And I'll see you at the hotel tonight. Until then" — she paused, taking a deep breath — "I don't want to see you."

"Payton." She knocked the wind out of me with that statement, but I did my best not to let my pain show. If she only knew. If she had any idea what type of people she was dealing with.

Working for Conrad was one thing. She was surrounded by other people at the office. People who would notice if something were awry. But to be alone with him in a place where people thought he was a god because of his money... If she only knew, she would understand why, from now on, I would make it my mission in life to ensure he didn't get near her again.

He would not interfere. I would not lose her, too.

I watched as Payton turned and walked away, getting into a cab that was waiting at the curb.

Thrusting my hands through my hair, I tried to control the rage that had my insides vibrating. The chaos was back. The noise louder than ever. And as I glanced back at the hotel where my father was, I was tempted to go back inside and do what I should have done a long time ago.

But I didn't.

For whatever reason, I managed to rein myself in, stepping back from the edge.

It wasn't fucking easy.

Unraveling

Chapter Nineteen

Payton

HOW I MADE IT THROUGH the day, I had no idea. After the debacle at breakfast with Sebastian showing up and acting like a lunatic, I'd been hard-pressed to find a hole to crawl into.

Unfortunately, dealing with Mr. Trovato all day had been the equivalent of handing a three-year-old a box of crayons and convincing him not to draw on the wall. No matter how many times I told him that I didn't want to talk about Sebastian and that I was fine, he tried to find a way to bring him up anyway.

Luckily, Mr. Trovato had been scheduled to give a seminar, which gave me a little over an hour of free time. After ensuring he had his notes and water, I had ventured off on my own. I was happy to find that Lauren hadn't attended the show, and when I mentioned that to Conrad, he informed me that she wouldn't be present for the remaining two days, either. If anything positive could be said about the whole thing, it was that I didn't have to deal with her.

I'd had more than my fill of her that morning, thank you very much.

The woman scared me. Between her icy stare and her apparent dislike of Sebastian, I honestly didn't care if I ever saw her again.

After Conrad's seminar was over, we visited the Trovato, Inc. booth, and now he was sitting in on a panel of people talking about performance engines. Since I knew I had at least an hour to wait, I slipped into the hallway to call Chloe. I needed to talk to her.

"Hey, hooker. How's it going in Vegas?" Chloe's cheerful greeting instantly put a smile on my face.

"It's goin'," I replied, lowering myself to a padded bench against the wall and setting my purse down in front of me.

"Uh-oh. What's the matter?"

She knew me all too well.

Figuring she was going to get it out of me eventually, I blurted out what had happened that morning.

"Your first fight as a couple. How cute," Chloe replied sweetly after I had spilled my guts.

"Seriously? That's what you took away from all that?"

"What did you want me to say?"

"Oh, I don't know. How about telling me that I did the right thing? Or that I wasn't wrong to storm out on him."

Chloe's lack of response made my stomach hurt.

"Breathe, Payton."

Breathe? I wasn't sure that was possible. I suddenly had the vision that I would go back to the hotel to find Sebastian not there. All day, even though I was incredibly pissed at him, I'd longed to see his face, to feel his arms around me. I wanted him to assure me that everything was going to be fine. That what had happened that morning was stupid.

"Payton, you really need to talk to him about his father," Chloe said, pulling me back to the moment.

"I don't know what to ask him," I admitted truthfully. "I mean, seriously. I don't know how to deal with that sort of family drama."

"Oh, that's right. Sometimes I forget that you grew up in a bubble full of roses and dandelions."

I snorted, picturing myself in a bubble filled with flowers. "That's not what I meant, and you know it."

"Something's not right between those two, Payton. Based on what you've told me, that's not just family drama. Sebastian's intense, I'll give you that. There's something dark about him, but I can't imagine he'd pull a stunt like that without a good reason."

That was exactly what I'd been thinking that morning when I'd climbed into a cab and made my way back to the MGM Grand for the convention. "You should've seen him, Chloe. He was so pissed."

"Because you went to breakfast without him?"

"No. That wasn't it. He was angry because I was there with Conrad. And the look he gave Lauren's nephew, I'm surprised the guy didn't go up in smoke."

"Why was he there, anyway?" Chloe asked.

"Who? Trevor?"

"Yeah."

"Hell if I know. I never figured that part out. Trevor mentioned that he was considering a career change and that was why Conrad had invited him to breakfast."

"In Vegas?" Chloe's exasperation mirrored my own.

"I know, right? He doesn't live here."

"So why's he there?"

"No idea. But he gave me the creeps, to tell you the truth."

"Maybe Sebastian was right to interrupt."

"Chloe, I was having breakfast with my boss. I get that Conrad is his father, but that wasn't a casual conversation."

"Or it wasn't supposed to be," Chloe added. "It sure sounds casual to me."

She was right. It was surprisingly casual, especially considering I'd never had to attend anything like that with Conrad before.

"Maybe Trevor just showed up out of the blue. And Lauren invited him."

"I don't think so." Based on the way they'd spoken, I seriously doubted that was just a chance encounter.

I heard a muffled conversation in the background and realized that Chloe was talking to someone. She uncovered the phone and I heard her say, "I'll be right with you. One sec. Hey, Payton. I have to go. My next appointment's here."

"Okay."

"Call me later, okay? I want to make sure you're all right."

"I will," I promised and disconnected the call, staring down at my phone.

Checking the time, I realized I still had a good half hour before Conrad was out of his meeting, so I decided to call Aaron. Talking to Chloe had eased my mind, but she hadn't given me any suggestions on what I should do next, and I was still out of sorts.

I dialed Aaron's number and hit talk, glancing down the wide hallway while I waited for him to answer.

"What's up, buttercup?" he greeted, his tone as cheerful as Chloe's had been. "How's Sin City?"

"I wish I was home," I told him.

"Oh, hell. What's wrong, doll?"

Again, I launched right into my story from that morning. Telling Aaron about Conrad insisting I attend breakfast and that Sebastian wasn't supposed to know. Then about being introduced to Trevor, Lauren's creepy nephew. Aaron didn't speak until I had run through the whole thing, ending my story with me getting in a cab and leaving Sebastian behind on the sidewalk.

"Did you ask Sebastian why he did that?"

"No," I answered. "When would I have had time to do that?"

"Oh, I don't know. You've got time to call me, don't you?"

Good point.

"I haven't talked to him. I needed time to cool off."

"Listen to me, Payton. I'm gonna tell you something you don't want to hear."

I grumbled into the phone and Aaron laughed.

"Seriously. You like this guy, right?"

"No, Aaron," I said, taking a deep breath. "I love him."

Aaron was silent for a moment, and I knew what he was thinking. I'd never loved a man before. Even my college boyfriend had just been a guy I was dating. He had been my first and only sexual partner, but I'd still never loved him. I had liked him a lot, but my heart had never been fully invested.

"Well, then. That makes what I have to say all the more important."

"Spit it out, would ya?" I said, exasperated.

"Doll, if this guy means something to you, and clearly he does, you need to get his side of the story. I get that you were embarrassed, but that honestly doesn't sound like something Sebastian would do just for the hell of it."

Aaron was right. Sebastian didn't seem like the kind of guy who tried to draw attention to himself. That came naturally, but in the time that I'd known him, he hadn't once tried to be the center of attention.

"And Payton … you're an adult now. Adults have conversations. They talk things out. You might think you know him, but I guarantee you don't know everything."

"Trust me, that's the last thing I think. He's got secrets. I know that."

"Then find out what they are. Find out how you can help him. That's part of being in love. It's not all about the good times and the incredible sex."

I snorted, my face burning although Aaron couldn't see me. "I never said anything about sex."

"Honey, I've known you long enough. I know a satisfied look when I see one."

"Shut up," I insisted, giggling and letting my hair drape over my face to hide my flaming cheeks.

"Seriously, doll," Aaron said, all amusement gone. "Talk to him. The guy's a ticking time bomb, and from what it sounds like, you're the only one who can cut the wires before it's too late."

I sighed. That wasn't exactly what I wanted to hear, but I understood what Aaron was telling me. I did need to talk to Sebastian. I needed to know what I was really dealing with. We weren't going to be able to move forward until we got that part figured out.

"Thanks, Aaron. I needed that."

"I know you did. Call me later and tell me how it went. Oh, and doll?"

"Yeah?"

"Have a little fun while you're there."

"I'll try."

With that, I hung up the phone and looked up to see people piling out of the conference room. Apparently, the session was over. I grabbed my purse and jumped to my feet, going toward the fray rather than away from it. When I found Conrad, he was talking to someone so I stood back so as not to interrupt.

He glanced around and must've noticed me because he held up one finger to the guy, a signal for him to hold on before he came over to me. "Why don't you go back to the hotel early today? Maybe you and Aaliyah can go out and see the sights."

I was confused as to why Mr. Trovato was brushing me off, but I wasn't about to argue. If he didn't need me anymore, I was certainly content to get out of there. "Yes, sir."

Without so much as a good-bye — not that I had really expected one — Conrad returned to the man, and they went in the opposite direction, picking up their conversation as they walked.

I was grateful that Conrad had let me off the hook for the rest of the day, although I wasn't sure why he had made such a huge turnaround. Just yesterday, he'd been an ogre, and today he was actually being almost nice. The logical answer would be that he knew I was embarrassed about what had happened at breakfast. But for some reason, I didn't think that was the answer, either.

As I walked toward the main entrance where I'd come in, I considered that. I figured Conrad's strange attitude shift had to do with the fact that Sebastian wasn't hanging around. As happy as I was that Conrad wasn't treating me like a lackey, it pissed me off that he treated Sebastian like shit. And worse, that he seemed happier when Sebastian wasn't around.

What kind of father treated his own son like that?

"Payton."

I turned at the sound of my name to see Sebastian leaning against a wall just outside the hotel. The moment I saw him, I stopped walking.

He looked ... so damn sexy.

Apparently a couple of other women thought so, too, because they were standing a few feet away, talking and smiling in his direction. Sebastian seemed oblivious, and that made my heart do a slow somersault in my chest. To think that those women wanted him, and he was mine made some of my confusion over what had happened that morning dissipate.

I was pretty sure that Sebastian was the sexiest man on the entire planet. And standing there so casually, he looked ... hot.

How that was possible when he also looked like he hadn't slept in two days, I wasn't sure. The black sweater he donned, even though it wasn't tight, showed off his incredible physique and offset his golden eyes, making them glow. The distressed jeans showcased his muscular thighs, and the heavy black boots on his feet gave him a dangerous edge. There was still that intensity about him. His hands were thrust in his pockets, his mouth a firm, thin line, and he seemed uncertain as to whether he should approach me.

The moment our eyes met, I felt the tension drain from him. The muscles in his shoulders and neck were still rigid, but there was a second of relief that registered on his ruggedly handsome face.

"Please ride with me," he said, his voice gruff, his tone pleading as he moved closer to where I had stopped. He seemed hesitant, and I instantly remembered the argument from that morning. And then I remembered what Aaron had told me. My best friend was right. We were adults, and the only way we would get through this was if we talked it out. Running wasn't the right answer, and staying away from him was an impossibility, no matter how upset I was.

So, when Sebastian reached for my hand, his callused fingers wrapping around mine, I knew that there was no way I could even pretend to resist him, so I nodded my head.

And followed him to the car.

Chapter Twenty

Sebastian

FOR THE FIRST TIME SINCE Payton had walked away from me that morning, I felt a sense of peace overcome me. The noise in my head had settled to a dull roar. It wouldn't be completely quiet until she and I had a chance to talk, but for now, this was considerably better than the hell I had endured all day.

After she'd gotten into a cab that morning, I had gotten in another and followed her. In fact, that was what I'd done the entire day. For every minute she'd spent inside the hotel at the SEMA show, I had been right there with her. Today, I'd managed to stay out of sight on purpose. I wasn't there to stalk her. I was there to protect her. I doubt she would've understood that, but my conscience wouldn't allow me to leave her alone with Conrad. Not even for a minute.

And the instant she'd stepped outside, her eyes meeting mine, I had finally released the breath I'd been holding the entire day.

The limo ride to the hotel was silent, and we made our way up to our hotel room without speaking. But holding her hand was enough for me. Touching her was a comfort that I'd never known before.

But the silence ended the instant we stepped inside the hotel room.

"Shut up, Leif! Just shut the hell up!" Aaliyah screamed from the top of the stairs.

I followed her gaze to see Leif standing at the bottom looking both angry and dejected. Apparently, the two of them hadn't worked out their issues.

"What's going on?" Payton whispered to me, squeezing my hand tightly.

"Lover's quarrel," I muttered.

"Fuck you, Sebastian," Aaliyah squealed. "He is not my lover. I wouldn't touch him with a ten-foot pole!"

Okay, then. I should've been happy about my sister's declaration, but honestly, my head hurt, and I just wanted to spend a little time alone with Payton. I had intended to order room service and lock ourselves in the hotel room for the night, hoping for a chance to talk to Payton about my outburst that morning, but it didn't look like my night was going to go according to plan.

"What happened?" Payton asked, her voice louder. She obviously wasn't talking to me. If she was, I certainly didn't have an answer for her.

"*He* happened!" Aaliyah yelled, stabbing the air in Leif's direction before stomping to her room and slamming the door.

Leif thrust his hand through his hair and turned to face me and Payton. "I'm sorry, man."

"What did you do?" Payton clearly wasn't giving up on her questions, so I resigned myself to getting these two to talk things out.

Leif dropped onto the couch and let his head fall back on the cushion, staring up at the twenty-foot-tall ceiling. "I'm a dumbass."

"Obviously."

Payton elbowed me for my comment and then released my hand. I couldn't say I was happy about that, but I followed her anyway. She took a seat on the sofa next to Leif, watching him intently.

"Y'all stayed out all night last night, didn't you?"

"Yeah," Leif replied. "It started out as a good night."

"And then..." Payton obviously wanted him to fill in the blank.

"And then we went to a strip club."

"Oh." Payton's wide eyes made me smile, but I remained behind her so she couldn't see. Strip clubs didn't do it for me, but Leif had been known to drag me to one a time or ten. Even without Leif's explanation, I could pretty well guess what had happened.

"We both had a little too much to drink," Leif admitted. "One of the strippers kept bugging me, so I paid for a lap dance. Don't ask me why." Leif glanced over at me.

I could tell he was pained by whatever had happened, but part of me figured he deserved it, so I said, "Because you're a dumbass. You said so yourself."

"Yeah, thanks." Leif clearly didn't find my statement amusing.

Seriously, the guy had taken my twenty-one-year-old sister to a strip club in Vegas. Couldn't say that was a great selection for a first date, but what did I know.

"I'm gonna go check on her," Payton said, looking back at me over her shoulder.

I nodded, knowing that I wouldn't be able to stop her.

When I heard Aaliyah invite her into her room, I turned to Leif. "You're a fucking idiot, you know that?"

"Yep. First rate. I got that."

"Why'd you take her there?" I asked, curious.

"It was *her* idea," Leif retorted, his tone defensive. "I suggested that we go check out the casinos downtown. We got down there, had a few drinks, and all of a sudden, she wanted to go to a strip club. I'm serious, man. It really was her idea. Said she wanted to do something she'd never done before."

"And you're the idiot who took her?"

"Yeah." Leif sighed. "She was fine until the lap dance. When it was over, she stormed out. I followed her, made her get in a cab back to the hotel. She refused to come back here, so we went to the Golden Nugget."

"And then what?" I asked. "You argued about a stripper?"

Leif's gaze met mine, and I saw something I'd never seen before. Pain.

"What happened?" I questioned again, needing the details.

"She'll kill me if I tell you," Leif answered.

"I'll kill you if you don't," I ground out, keeping my voice low.

"Damn it," Leif exclaimed, thrusting his hands through his already messy hair. He leaned forward and put his elbows on his knees, head hanging low. "I kissed her."

"Please, God, tell me that a kiss didn't lead to this bullshit."

"No, it was what came after."

I was ready to punch him in the mouth. Ready to launch my fist right at him if he told me he'd tried to sleep with my sister.

But Leif surprised the shit out of me with his next statement.

"Aaliyah told me she was a virgin," Leif began quietly. "Said she had always wanted me. That she wanted me to be her first. She offered no strings attached." Leif looked over at me, his eyes sad. "When I told her I wanted strings, that I couldn't see us ever hooking up unless we were dating, she got pissed. I think she took it as a rejection."

I didn't know what to do with that information. I suddenly found myself not quite so angry, but I had no idea why. I knew Leif had liked Aaliyah for a long time. And I knew she liked him. That was apparent.

But Leif wanted a relationship with my sister? That was … interesting.

"Did you apologize?" I asked him.

"A million times. She won't listen to me. And when she does, she ends up screaming at the top of her lungs."

Definitely sounded like something Aaliyah would do.

She had the spoiled-little-rich-girl thing down pat. On top of that, she had a volatile temper like I did. But unlike me, she wasn't able to channel her anger. I had mastered that art a long time ago. Mainly because if I hadn't, I would've ended up in jail for killing someone by the time I was twenty.

Payton appeared at the top of the stairs, her gaze meeting mine. When she headed toward our bedroom, I stood, turning back to Leif. "You need to talk to her. And if she won't listen, you're gonna have to do something to get her attention."

Leif nodded, but he didn't say anything. I waited a moment but then headed upstairs, finding Payton in the bedroom with the door open.

"Can we go get something to eat?" she asked as soon as I stepped into the room, her voice soft. "I'm starving."

"Of course." Reaching for her hands, I slid my thumbs over her knuckles as I watched her.

The thought of kissing her had plagued my mind most of the day, but I hadn't intended to do so until I had a chance to explain myself. Fortunately for me, Payton took that decision away from me when she stepped closer, her hands squeezing mine before she released them and cupped my jaw, pulling me down to her.

Her lips were soft against mine, her hands cool against my face. "I love you," she whispered, and I swear to God, I nearly cried.

I hadn't cried once since the day my mother had died. Not one single time. But right then and there, with Payton whispering the sweetest words I would ever hear, the only words I *needed* to hear, I was tempted to cry like a fucking baby. I'd spent the day unraveling, scared that I'd fucked up beyond repair, but yet, she told me that she loved me.

"I love you, too," I whispered back, my voice rough with emotion. "I'm sorry about this morning."

Payton's finger covered my lips, stopping me from continuing. "Let's go get some food. Give those two a few minutes to work things out, and then we can come back and talk."

I nodded. I'd go anywhere she wanted me to. Just as long as I could have her with me, I didn't care where that was, either. I think I proved that when we made it to the food court and my beautiful girlfriend decided she wanted McDonald's for dinner.

So, while we shared French fries and ate Big Macs, I listened to Payton tell me what her day had entailed after she'd left me at the hotel. Although I'd been witness to it because I had stayed close, I still loved to listen to her talk. She could probably read me the dictionary and I'd hang on every single word. When she was finished, she went on to tell me about her conversation with Aaliyah.

Only then did I say more than two words. "So, my sister's pissed because Leif doesn't like her?"

"That's her version," Payton advised.

"But he does like her," I told her, confused.

"I know that. And you know that, but she clearly doesn't know that."

"How could she not? The guy's a slobbering idiot when she's around."

"I think that's part of it. When she tries to talk to him, I think he's too nervous to open up to her."

That was surprising as hell. Considering when I was around Leif, he never shut the hell up.

"Aaliyah said they went to a strip club," Payton told me, her eyes roaming my face as though she expected a certain reaction from me.

"That's what Leif said."

"She said it was her idea," Payton added.

"He told me that, too. He also told me that he turned her down when she wanted to sleep with him. According to him, he wants a relationship before that happens."

"Wow. She kinda left that part out," Payton said softly, her gaze remaining glued to the table.

I noticed that Payton was no longer eating, choosing rather to stir a French fry around on the tray before tossing it down and grabbing a napkin to wipe her hands. I leaned back in my chair and studied her. There was something on her mind, and I knew it had nothing to do with the argument between Aaliyah and Leif. I was expecting her to mention what had happened that morning, and I was fully prepared to defend myself, but what came out of her mouth shocked the shit out of me.

"Aaliyah told me that you're moving."

Well, hell.

That definitely wasn't what I'd expected her to say. Shit, I hadn't expected Leif to say anything to anyone, but I should've seen it coming. A close second behind Toby, Leif couldn't keep his mouth shut, either.

Before I could respond, Payton said, "I think that's really what started their argument last night. Aaliyah's really upset."

"Damn it," I muttered, leaning forward and resting my forearms on the table and clasping my hands together in front of me. When I'd told Leif that I needed him to hold off on moving in until I finalized the sale on my new house, I hadn't considered the fact that he would blab to my sister. I had wanted to be the one to tell her. I knew she wasn't going to be happy with me, but I knew that if I remained that close to my father for much longer, the shit was really going to hit the fan.

Unfortunately, I hadn't considered the repercussions of telling Leif before I talked to Aaliyah.

"Is it true? Are you moving?"

"Are you finished?" I know it sounded like I was avoiding her question, but honestly, I just wanted to find someplace else to have the conversation.

Payton nodded.

"You want some coffee?" I asked, nodding my head toward the coffee shop behind her.

"Sure," she answered.

I grabbed the tray of food and carried it to the trash can, dumping the contents before taking her hand and heading to the coffee shop. I ordered two large coffees, and after Payton doctored hers to her liking with cream and sugar, I snagged her hand again and led her through the casino and out the front doors.

The sun was setting, and the temperature was comfortable, so I opted to sit on a stone wall. After hoisting myself up, I pulled Payton back against me so she stood between my legs. I was at the perfect height to rest my chin on the top of her head, so I placed my coffee down beside me so I could wrap my arms around her.

"I bought a house," I began. "I've been debating on taking the leap for a while. I guess you could say that recent events have inspired me to move forward."

"Me?" she asked, a measure of surprise in her tone.

"Yeah." I knew it was the perfect opportunity to tell her what I'd nearly blurted out a few days ago, but I couldn't bring myself to do it. Not there. Not in a city she was unfamiliar with. I didn't want her to freak out and run away, so I came up with something on the fly. "Living at the guesthouse has its perks, but it's time for me to get out of there. I need somewhere that I don't have to worry about Conrad barging in. He owns the place, and as long as I live there, he's got me under his thumb."

Payton nodded as though she understood, her hand resting over the top of mine. "Where are you moving to?"

"North," I told her.

"North of where you are now? Or north of Austin?" she asked.

"Both," I answered, chuckling. "But definitely north of Austin."

Payton turned her head to look up at me. "Closer to me?"

I studied her for a moment, wondering what I should say. Or rather, how she would respond to it. "Yeah. Closer to you."

She surprised me when she smiled and nodded her head. I wasn't sure if that was because she liked the idea of me being closer or if it was because she thought I'd gone crazy.

But I guess a smile was a smile. And since she wasn't running far and fast, I had to consider that a win.

For now.

Chapter Twenty-One

Payton

SEBASTIAN AND I STOOD OUTSIDE the hotel talking, mostly about his new house, until the sun sank behind the mountains and the air cooled considerably. When I began to shiver, we came back inside the casino, but we bypassed all of the games and headed up to the room. We walked in to find Leif and Aaliyah sitting on the couch watching television.

Aaliyah looked content, although her eyes were puffy, proof that she'd been crying. But she certainly looked more at ease than she had earlier. She had changed into yoga pants and a T-shirt, her blond hair pulled up in a ponytail, her youthful face scrubbed free of makeup. There was an empty tray on the table in front of them, which I assumed had contained their dinner at some point.

"No more yelling?" Sebastian asked when he closed and locked the door behind us.

"Not at the moment," Aaliyah answered, her eyes moving to Sebastian. I instantly recognized the concern on her pretty face and knew she was probably wanting to talk to her brother. After all, Leif had dropped a huge bomb on her that really hadn't been his place to divulge. Then again, maybe he hadn't realized that she didn't already know.

"I'm gonna go take a bath," I whispered to Sebastian, hoping he would take the hint. His eyes raked over my face before meeting mine again, as though he were trying to understand what I was telling him. When I noticed his brows furrowing, as though he expected the worst, I leaned in and pressed my lips to his gently. "When you're done talking to your sister, maybe you can join me."

He nodded, a small smile curling the very corners of his lips, and I made my way to the stairs without looking back.

Once inside the bedroom, I closed the door and sat on the edge of the bed. I was exhausted. After last night, staying up so late, and then having to rush out of bed that morning only to traipse around the huge trade show, I was ready to just pass out.

Figuring I had a few minutes before Sebastian arrived, I kicked off my shoes and pulled back the blankets on the bed. If I just closed my eyes for a few minutes, that was all I needed, and then when Sebastian returned, we'd get in the bath together.

"Morning." Sebastian's deep voice greeted me as soon as my eyes opened. I instantly closed them, trying to block out the blinding light that was filling the room.

"Did I seriously sleep all night?" I asked, my voice raspy from sleep. I curled into Sebastian, placing my hand on his flat stomach as he pulled the blanket up over my shoulder.

"That you did. You're quite the party animal in Vegas," he told me, kissing the top of my head.

"I was only supposed to close my eyes. I was waiting for you to join me before I got in the bath," I explained.

"You were out cold when I came up here. I couldn't bear to wake you."

"Thank you for letting me sleep." As I lay snuggled in his arms, I forced my eyes open slowly, acclimating to the bright morning sun. "How'd it go with Aaliyah?"

"Better than I thought it would," he said, wrapping his arm more tightly around me. "She understands. She was just pissed that I hadn't told her."

"I don't blame her." I was a little hurt that he hadn't told me and that I'd had to hear it from Aaliyah. But we had only been together for a short time, so I didn't let it bother me.

"Want to get some breakfast before you have to go to the show?" Sebastian asked after several moments of silence.

"I need to shower first," I told him, not wanting to get out of bed. I was too warm, too comfortable being with him, and I didn't want the day to intrude on that moment. If I had a say in the matter, I'd stay in bed with him all day and say to hell with the show.

But then I'd probably lose my job, which would only start a domino effect of shitty things to happen. So, instead of wasting away the day in the comfort of Sebastian's arms, I pushed up onto my arm and looked at him. "Want to join me?"

The sexy, crooked grin that he gifted me with made my body come alive instantly. I knew that look. It was a look that said I was about to be in over my head.

Two minutes later, Sebastian proved to me just how true that statement was. The water had barely warmed before he was backing me into the huge glass enclosure that took up half of the bathroom. Before the door even closed behind him, his hands were on me, roaming, searching, teasing. When his mouth joined the mix, I had to bite my lip to keep from crying out. His lips started their journey on mine, then moved slowly down my neck, then to my breasts, where he tormented me with delicious lashes of his tongue against my nipples. And just when I thought I couldn't handle any more, he stood, pressing me against the wall.

"I need to be inside you," he murmured against my lips.

I nodded, desperate for him to do just that.

Twining his fingers with mine, Sebastian lifted my hands above my head, holding me there. While the warm water cascaded over us both, he slid inside me slowly. I moaned, my head thumping against the tile as I let the sensations overwhelm me.

"So tight," Sebastian groaned, his hips pressing into mine as he filled me completely.

As he thrust deep inside me, his teeth nibbling my neck, I closed my eyes, savoring the moment. I loved being with him, loved to feel him touching me, kissing me. The sexy words he said only launched me higher. I wasn't sure I would ever get enough of him. The way he moved, the way he thrust into me. He was so powerful yet controlled. As though he was holding back, not wanting to hurt me. For a brief moment, I wondered what it would be like if he ever unleashed the beast and took me with all the intensity I knew was built up inside him.

I doubted I would survive it.

"Angel," Sebastian growled as he moved up to my lips, his tongue thrusting into my mouth as he drove himself deeper. The need for oxygen made it difficult to kiss him, and when he pulled back, he said, "I need you to come for me, Angel."

I was close. So close, but I didn't want it to end, didn't want him to stop. But when he clasped my wrists with one hand and lowered his other between our bodies to tease my clit, I couldn't hold back.

He quickened his pace, and I lifted my leg, placing my foot on the small ledge, offering him easier access. He pounded into me, his hand gripping my wrists tightly, his thumb grazing my clit, his mouth sealed to mine as he kissed me with a ferocity I hadn't known before.

"Come for me, Angel," he demanded, his tone harsh, his control clearly slipping.

"Oh, God, Sebastian. It feels so good."

"Come for me," he pleaded, his thumb pressing against my clit, and then suddenly there were tiny colorful lights flashing behind my closed eyelids as my body shattered. Sebastian groaned, his mouth moving back down to my neck as he continued to thrust into me. "Payton. Angel." A deep growl erupted from his chest, and he stilled as he climaxed, his body pulsing deep inside me.

Twenty minutes later, after Sebastian thoroughly washed my hair and my body, then I returned the favor, we climbed out of the shower. While I put on my makeup, he dressed and went downstairs, leaving me to my thoughts.

Standing in front of the bathroom mirror, I brushed the long strands of my damp hair, allowing the hot air to slowly dry it, remembering the incident from yesterday morning. Then I remembered my conversation with Aaron. I knew that Sebastian and I needed to talk. Last night, I'd thought he was going to open up to me when we were outside, but he hadn't. But I had to wonder whether our avoidance of the conversation was more my fault or his. Or if both of us were just sidestepping the issue. Considering Sebastian was moving out of the house he lived in on his father's property and into one of his own, I knew that things were about to come to a head between them. I couldn't help but wonder what that meant for me.

Would my involvement with Sebastian cost me my job?

Did I really care?

Or would my job cost me Sebastian?

Those were things I'd never imagined I would have to worry about, but now that was all I could think about.

I loved Sebastian. That wasn't just my hormones talking, either. I loved everything about him from his quick, easy smile, his sexy laugh, to that deep-rooted vulnerability that most people never saw. I especially loved his intensity, although it scared me a little. Aaron was right, Sebastian was a ticking time bomb, and he was set to go off at any moment.

So the bigger question was ... how did I stop that from happening? And if I couldn't, how did I pick up the pieces in the aftermath?

Chapter Twenty-Two

Payton

Saturday morning

"OH, MY GOD! I'M SO glad you're home!" Chloe squealed when I walked through the front door of my apartment on Saturday morning.

Luckily I managed to brace myself before she threw her arms around my neck and squeezed me tightly or I would've landed flat on my ass. Sebastian was right behind me, carrying my luggage despite my previous argument that I could manage on my own. When he joined us inside, he offered a lopsided grin before continuing on to my bedroom, returning empty-handed and leaning against the wall.

The last two days had been relatively uneventful — thank God. I'd worked with Conrad during the day, and Sebastian had insisted on staying close. On Thursday evening, we'd gone to dinner with Aaliyah and Leif again, and I was glad to see they were back on speaking terms. The one thing I did notice was that Leif was keeping his distance. I think that whatever had happened between them had hurt Leif, but I don't know what exactly that was. Neither of them were very forthcoming with all the details from their night out. I could tell that the two of them hadn't told us the complete story, but I didn't press them on the issue, either.

Then after I'd spent most of the day at the SEMA show on Friday, the four of us had ended up going to a night club last night, where we'd danced and drunk until the early-morning hours. It was then that Sebastian had informed me that he had changed my flight so we could go home together. I was surprised to find out that Aaliyah had gone back on the same flight with her parents and Leif had gone with us.

I had initially been relieved that he'd taken the initiative to keep me with him, but then it hit me just what he'd done. It was a possessive move, one that I really needed to think about more. I was a grown woman; it would've made sense for him to ask me first, but he hadn't. Having endured more than my fair share of arguments for one trip, I had opted to keep my opinion to myself until I had time to process it more.

We were all fairly quiet for most of the flight, and I had opted to sleep for the majority of the three hours it had taken for us to get back to Austin.

At the airport, Leif had gone his separate way while Sebastian had driven me home in his Camaro, which he had parked at the airport. Now that I was standing in my apartment, I suddenly wished that our trip had lasted a little longer, because I didn't want Sebastian to leave. But I could tell by the way that he was watching me that he was about to do just that.

Shaking off the needy thoughts, I tried to focus on Chloe, who was grinning at us both.

"Did y'all have fun?" Chloe asked, stepping back and looking at the two of us with a curious smirk on her lips. "Y'all didn't go and get married while you were there, did you?"

I choked, my face heating at least several thousand degrees. Married? Good grief. The woman lived to torment me.

"Not yet," Sebastian stated seriously, and I spun around to face him only to be met with a sexy grin. "I need to get home. I've got something to take care of today."

I nodded, accepting the fact that our trip was officially over even though I didn't want it to be. Sure, I was happy to not have to go in to work for a couple of days but spending time with Sebastian had become second nature while we had been away. So much so that I feared having to spend the night alone in my bed.

Yep, the neediness was out in full force, and truthfully, it was beginning to piss me off.

"I want to take you to dinner tonight," Chloe insisted. "You can tell me all about the trip."

I glanced back at my friend, forcing a smile. I knew what she was doing. She was going to make sure I didn't sit at home tonight and pine after this man.

And I loved her for it, because if it weren't for her offer, I would probably close myself off in my bedroom and relive every minute of the trip until I made myself absolutely crazy.

"Sounds like a plan," I said with forced enthusiasm.

"Walk me out?" Sebastian asked, pushing off the wall and taking my hand.

I nodded and followed him down the stairs. We stopped beside his car, and he leaned against the door, turning to face me. I was having a hard time looking at him because I didn't want him to see the disappointment on my face.

Sebastian tipped my chin up with his fingers, forcing me to look him in the eye. "I'm glad I got to spend the last few days with you."

For some reason, that statement felt an awful lot like a good-bye, and I was suddenly scared that he was saying something more. "Me, too," I whispered, barely able to get the words out.

"I'm gonna be busy for a few days, but I want to see you, Payton."

I nodded my head, unsure what I was supposed to say. It was probably pretty apparent that I was missing him already.

"If you don't hear from me for a couple of days, please don't worry."

Okay, so now I was really worried. How could he seriously tell me that and expect me to do the opposite? "Why…" I couldn't get the question out, so I swallowed around the lump in my throat and tried again. "Why wouldn't I hear from you?"

"I've got something to take care of."

My mind drifted to everything I knew about Sebastian and everything I'd heard, but I couldn't come up with any reason that he would practically fall off the face of the earth for a couple of days. Maybe this was his way of dumping me. Had things really gone that badly? I tried to recall the last few days, but the memories evaded me. Maybe he thought that after a couple of days I would forget all about him.

I swallowed hard, pissed at myself for being so damn insecure. I wasn't the clingy type, never had been, yet here I was trying to come up with every worst-case scenario I could. And that made me mad.

"No worries," I told him, hoping I sounded more confident than I felt. "You've got things to do and so do I."

"Payton," Sebastian drew out my name slowly, his arms banding around me and pulling me to him. He pressed his mouth to my ear. "You're not getting rid of me, Angel. Not that easily."

I didn't want to get rid of him, but I didn't tell him that. Once I turned into the desperate, insecure girlfriend, we were both going to regret it. So, I simply hugged him back, pressing my forehead to his chest. "I'll be here, Sebastian."

He pulled back, but only far enough so that he could press his mouth to mine. He tasted of mint and sexy male. For whatever reason, probably because my mind was already considering this our final good-bye, I kissed him, wrapping my arms around his neck and devouring him. If this was going to be my last kiss, I was damn sure going to make it worth my while.

By the time we pulled back, we were both panting for air. I avoided his gaze but wrapped my arms around him tightly just because I didn't want to let him go.

"I'll call you tonight," he told me, but I got the impression he was saying what he thought I wanted to hear. After all, he had just informed me that I might not hear from him for a couple of days.

But I didn't call him on it. I couldn't. Hell, I could barely swallow, so I knew the words weren't coming easily.

By the time I closed my bedroom door, sealing myself in my room so that I could have a few minutes to myself, I was gasping for air.

Something was wrong. Really, really wrong. I could feel it.

And whatever it was, Sebastian didn't want me to know.

Sebastian

IF ANYONE EVER MISTOOK ME for some sort of fucking martyr, they didn't know me all that well. What I'd just done wasn't because I thought leaving Payton was what was best for her. In fact, if that were the case, then by God, I would do wrong by her for the rest of our lives because this … this was just temporary.

Although, I could tell by the look in her eye that she thought I wasn't coming back.

She was so very wrong.

Driving away from Payton was harder than it looked, and it damn sure hadn't been what I wanted to do, but it was something that had to be done. For now. I hadn't lied to her when I told her I had something to do.

Last night, after we'd come back to the hotel room, after I'd stripped Payton and made love to her for a solid hour, I had lain awake for hours, my thoughts refusing to slow long enough for me to sleep until just before dawn. Then when I finally had succumbed to sleep, I'd been plagued by that damn dream again — the one where the race ended with my Camaro engulfed in flames.

That — the race — was the real reason I had walked away from Payton. The woman calmed me to the point of distraction, and if I had any plans of walking away from the race in one piece, I needed the chaos to return.

Considering I'd dreamed about Payton and she had practically materialized right there in my world, I was getting a little paranoid about the dream. Dying in a fiery blast wasn't something that I had on my agenda these days. A couple of weeks ago … well, maybe I hadn't cared all that much then. But I certainly did now.

I wasn't leaving Payton.

And as much as I wanted to spend every waking moment with her, I knew that I needed to get my head on straight. When I'd barged into that restaurant and lost it, I'd taken a turn that I hadn't expected. Keeping my suspicions to myself was one thing. Until I had hard-core proof of what I feared, I knew that any accusations against my father would likely end up with me in a mental institution.

The bastard was a powerful man. More powerful than I usually gave him credit for.

So, after leaving Payton at her apartment, I drove toward the highway, pulling off in the gas station to make a couple of phone calls. The first one was to my realtor buddy, Jim. I asked him to meet me at the new house so I could take care of a couple of things. He informed me that everything was good to go and they'd scheduled an inspection for next week. Provided everything came back good, I was hoping to be moving in less than a month.

The next call I made was to Toby, telling him to meet me at my house in an hour. I had already asked Leif to stop by before we'd gone our separate ways at the airport. I wanted to talk to them both before the race. My chat with Toby was quick, and once he agreed to meet, I pulled out of the parking lot and headed north on the interstate.

Less than ten minutes later, I was pulling through the automatic gate that surrounded the house that I was in the process of buying. While I waited for Jim to arrive, I climbed out of the car and walked around the perimeter of the house. It was empty, had been for a few months, which had worked in my favor.

After checking things out, mostly to pass the time, I sat on the front steps, staring out at the acres of land that surrounded the property. That was what I was most excited about, I think. The idea of building a track and a shop of my own and starting the next phase of my life was getting to me. It was high time I did something that didn't include being underneath Conrad Trovato's thumb all the damn time.

Getting away from him was imperative, but more important, I had to figure out what to do about the other thing. The secret that I'd buried for so long. The suspicion I had that was transforming into fear.

I didn't scare easily, but ever since I'd met Payton, ever since she'd become the most important thing to me, I knew that I had a hell of a lot to lose. And I couldn't risk it.

"Hey, Sebastian." Jim's optimistic voice pulled me from my thoughts, and I got to my feet, reaching out and shaking his hand.

Jim let me in the house, and I spent a good twenty minutes looking things over, trying to figure out just what I needed. Moving out of Conrad's house, I would have nothing. Nothing more than my personal effects, which meant I had to make some big purchases.

I was ready.

"Hey, Jim," I called, my voice echoing in the empty house.

If I said the house was modest, I'd be lying. It wasn't as ostentatious as my father's, but it was impressive. Six-thousand square feet with an additional twenty-five-hundred-square-foot indoor pool wasn't something to balk at. But in my defense, the house was a steal. And the fact that it sat on over two hundred acres, surrounded by nothing but farmland, only made it all the more desirable, in my opinion.

"What's up?" Jim asked as he met me in the entryway.

"I need some measurements. Can you get the appraisal expedited? Or find someone who can get them to me ASAP?"

"I'll see what I can do."

I slapped Jim on the back. "Thanks. Oh, and let's get this done in two weeks. Not a minute longer."

I walked out of the house with Jim staring at me as though I'd lost my mind. Maybe I had. But after spending the last few days with Payton, I knew it was time to do what needed to be done.

And when that moment came, all hell was going to break loose.

I needed somewhere to go by that time, and this was going to be it.

Half an hour later, I was pulling through the gates at my father's estate. I continued past the main house, wondering when would be a good time to inform Conrad that I was done.

And by done, I wasn't just talking about moving out and living on my own.

I was fucking done.

Done with him period.

Considering I really was the reason Trovato, Inc. had been continuing to grow over the last few years, I didn't expect my father to take the news lightly. Although he'd threatened to replace me numerous times, even he knew that wasn't a smart move.

Now he wasn't going to have a choice.

But the bigger issue was trying to figure out how to get Payton away from him before he retaliated against me, which I was certain he would do.

Granted, just because I quit working for him didn't necessarily mean that she would have to. But then again, she didn't know my secret. And I needed to be prepared for the worst once I finally told her.

There had been more than one opportunity to talk to her while we'd been in Vegas, but I had chickened out. That was all there was to it. I didn't know how to tell her. Didn't know how she was going to react. And I damn sure didn't want her trying to get away from me in a city that she wasn't familiar with. In a place she didn't have anyone who would be there to take care of her if it came down to it.

So, I'd held back. Again.

Just like I was holding back now.

I made my way to the guesthouse, pulling into the garage. I wasn't surprised to see Toby's car parked in the driveway, nor was I shocked to see him sitting on the couch in my garage when I pulled in.

He stood and greeted me, a wide grin plastered on his face.

"It's about fucking time," Toby said, coming toward me when I climbed out of the car.

"Did you miss me, you fucking pansy?" I asked, smiling as I said it.

"Fuck no," he retorted. A lie if I'd ever heard one. "I hadn't even realized you were gone."

"Liar." I popped the trunk to retrieve my luggage, pulling out the bag and setting it on the floor.

"How's Payton?" Toby asked, following me as I headed into the house.

"Good."

"Y'all have a good time?"

"Yeah." I wasn't going to go into the fight we'd had just yet. It was bad enough that Leif knew all the gory details because he'd been at the hotel when Aaliyah had mentioned it the next day.

"Have you told your old man that you're movin' out?" Toby asked as he made a beeline for the refrigerator, pulling out two bottles of water and tossing one to me after I shrugged out of my jacket and threw it over the chair.

"Not yet." It was inevitable, but I knew my father. He was on the verge of cutting me off. Or at least he was on the verge of believing that was even a possibility. He didn't give me enough credit, though. I'd long ago taken the necessary precautions to ensure he couldn't hurt me. At least not financially.

When you blackmailed someone into handing over a significant amount of money in order to keep silent, you did what was necessary to ensure the bastard couldn't start backtracking. And I'd done that the second I'd turned eighteen.

While my father believed he was still in control of my money, I knew better. I mean, seriously, I wasn't a fucking idiot. Sure, there was a little money left in the account he knew about, but the majority of it had been moved long ago. For the last seven years, I'd allowed him to believe that I was shitty at managing my money, choosing to blow it on stupid shit, but that had never been the case. Had he looked hard enough, he would've noticed, but Conrad didn't expect much from me.

"Hey, we still on for tonight?" Toby asked, hopping up onto the counter and staring at me.

"Yep." I knew he was talking about the race. Toby was the guy I depended on to get me into the races. Due to his money situation, he rarely went in when so much was at stake, but he was always right there with me. "You didn't say anything to Chloe, did you?"

"Nope. I'm not a complete dumbass."

"Really?" I asked, pretending to be shocked by the news.

"Fuck off. And I didn't do it for you, asshole. I don't want her anywhere around that shit."

"Can't blame you there," I told him, twisting off the cap on the water bottle and tossing it into the trash can as I leaned against the counter.

A street race was significantly different than a race on private property like we'd done last weekend. There was always the risk of getting caught, which so far hadn't happened. But as the races became more popular, there were considerably more folks who came out to watch, and with crowds like what we'd seen the last few times, it was definitely getting risky.

"Leif wants in," Toby told me, his expression serious.

"Why?" I asked. If history repeated itself, Leif wasn't going to win, which meant he'd be out two grand. Although I'd give it back to him if he asked, I knew he wouldn't.

"It's not always about the money," Toby told me.

"Well, no shit." For me, it wasn't ever about the money. It was about the rush I got from driving. It was about quieting the noise in my head. Until Payton, it had been the only thing that worked.

"Does Payton know?"

I shook my head, downing the rest of my water and tossing the bottle into the recycle bin. "Nope. And I don't plan to tell her, either."

"She's gonna be pissed."

I doubted it. I wasn't one for lying, by omission or otherwise, but in this instance, I didn't want Payton to know. And what she didn't know wouldn't hurt her.

If only that were true with all my secrets.

Payton

Saturday night

"HE DID *WHAT*?" CHLOE'S VOICE was loud, causing several heads to turn and look at us.

I leaned forward and told her to keep it down, knowing it wouldn't do much good.

Aaron was sitting beside Chloe, staring at me as though I'd lost my mind.

"Why would he do that?" Chloe asked, her loud whisper not doing anything to quiet her down.

"I don't know," I admitted. "I guess he really likes her."

I had just finished telling them the story about the incident between Aaliyah and Leif. Apparently, what happened in Vegas really didn't stay in Vegas. Not when I was the one who had to put up with Chloe's constant pestering. I'd finally given in and told her the story. It was that or rehash the fight I'd had with Sebastian, something that Chloe was incredibly curious about.

Although I'd told her everything on the phone, she had insisted that I retell the story just to make sure I hadn't left out any details. When I'd refused, the conversation had moved on to Leif. And before I knew it, I was airing all their dirty laundry.

"Don't you dare say anything to Toby," I warned Chloe.

She smirked, sipping her water. "I'll try."

"So what ever happened with that guy Trevor?" Aaron asked.

Obviously he didn't have a problem remembering the details like Chloe had.

"Did you see him again?" Aaron asked, cocking an eyebrow as he waited for me to answer.

I knew I wasn't going to get out of it. Aaron was just as pushy as Chloe when he wanted to be. "Nope. Not once."

"Do you find that weird at all?" Chloe asked.

Well, of course I did, but I didn't get to answer because Aaron spoke up.

"It sounds like your boss was trying to set you up."

"With *Trevor*?" I asked, stunned. "Why would he do that?"

"To keep you away from Sebastian, maybe," he retorted.

"Like that would ever happen. That dude was seriously creepy," I told him. "But you know, he did mention that he was considering a career change. If he meant that he would be working for Conrad, why wouldn't he be at the trade show?"

"Maybe that was a lie," Chloe said, picking at her noodles with her fork.

"Why would he lie?" I asked.

"Maybe it was a set-up. Maybe they were hoping you'd tell Sebastian." My eyebrows rose as I waited for her to elaborate. I wasn't understanding what she was trying to tell me.

"You said the guy was a mechanic. It's possible that Conrad wanted you to tell Sebastian so he thought he was being replaced."

"Well, that's just stupid," I blurted.

Aaron laughed. "No one said the guy was right in his head. I mean, seriously, he keeps his own kid a secret."

"That's just weird," Chloe added. "Why would he do that?"

"I don't think he wanted people to know that he got an underage girl pregnant," I told them truthfully, taking a sip of my raspberry tea.

"Yeah, well, that's super creepy," Chloe stated, shivering.

I knew what she was feeling. It was disgusting to think that Conrad had been with a teenage girl. More so that he had gotten her pregnant and then turned his back on her.

Knowing that they would continue to grill me about Sebastian if I let them, I decided to change the subject. "So what did you and Toby do while I was gone?"

"Not much," Chloe answered, her smile once again brightening her face.

"Not much, my ass," Aaron inserted. "The guy practically lives at our apartment."

"Shut up. You're just jealous."

"Maybe," Aaron admitted truthfully, laughing.

"Are you gonna see Garrett again?" I asked, watching him closely.

"It's a possibility."

"How much of a possibility?" When Aaron didn't share details, I knew he was hiding something.

"He's coming into town next weekend."

"Have you talked to him?" Chloe asked, turning her head to look at Aaron.

"Every night."

Wow. A lot had happened in the few days I'd been gone. It appeared that Toby and Chloe were officially a couple and possibly on the verge of living together, and it looked like Aaron might've found someone to help him move on from Mark.

I was happy for them both, but even sharing that with them didn't help ease the unsettling feeling I'd had since Sebastian had driven away from me that morning.

"Where's Toby tonight?" I asked Chloe. I was being nosey, more for my own benefit than anything else.

"He didn't say," she admitted. "I told him I was taking you to dinner and that we were gonna veg on the couch and watch cheesy chick flicks all night. He said he'd talk to me tomorrow."

"Aren't they doing that street race tonight?" Aaron asked, pushing his plate away and reaching for his water glass.

I dropped my fork, the metal clattering against the glass plate. "Oh, shit."

Chloe's eyes widened as she realized the same thing I had.

Sebastian was racing tonight. That was why he'd left me that morning. That was what he'd had to do.

Son of a bitch.

"What time is it at?" Aaron asked, as though he weren't the one who had just told us what we had obviously forgotten.

Chloe snagged her cell phone from her purse and stabbed the screen several times. She was watching me as she put the phone to her ear. "Where are you?" she said by way of greeting a few seconds later.

I wanted to hear what was being said on the other end of the phone, but with the noise in the restaurant, I couldn't make out even a hint of the conversation.

"Toby Brindle," Chloe said through gritted teeth, "don't you *dare* lie to me."

There was another pause while Chloe listened to him speak.

"Shit. Okay."

Another pause and I was hanging on by my fingernails.

283

Thankfully, the waitress showed up and handed me the check. I slapped my credit card down and turned my attention back to Chloe.

"Oh, bullshit, Toby. Don't you even think about it. If you don't tell me where you're at, don't expect to see me naked ever again."

I laughed — I couldn't help myself. If that wasn't a threat, I didn't know what was.

Chloe was studying my face as she listened, her eyes widening slightly. I was holding my breath, anxious for her to tell me what he said.

"We're on our way." Chloe disconnected the call and stared back at me. "You might wanna tell that waitress to hurry the hell up. We've got twenty minutes before the race starts."

Aaron whistled through his fingers, waving his hand and getting the waitress's attention. I was too worried to be embarrassed. But it worked. The waitress arrived, took the credit card, and five minutes later, we were piling into Aaron's Honda while Chloe rattled off the directions.

Aaron was one of those cautious drivers who always obeyed the speed limit, never forgot to use his blinker, and even slowed down to a near crawl before he made a turn. I was feeling sorry for him now although I was more on Chloe's side than his at the moment. She was yelling at him, telling him to go faster, when to change lanes, where to turn. She was the absolute worst backseat driver. What made it worse was that she was riding shotgun. I was hanging on for dear life in the backseat while Aaron alternated between random acceleration and jerky turns. Chloe was clearly turning him into a basket case.

When we arrived at our destination, I looked around, trying to figure out just what was going on. If this was the place, then it was abandoned. Maybe that was part of the plan, what with an illegal street race and all, but when I say abandoned, I mean there wasn't a single soul anywhere. Not another car, not a single person walking down the street.

"Do you think he gave you the wrong place?" Aaron asked, his hands white-knuckling the steering wheel.

"He better not have," Chloe snapped, digging her phone out of her purse.

Before she got the chance to dial, I heard the rumble of an engine and turned to look out the back window, noticing there were at least fifteen sets of headlights coming toward us.

Toby's '69 Camaro pulled up alongside Aaron's car, stopping suddenly before Toby jumped out. He flung open Chloe's door and squatted down in front of her. He looked pissed.

"I really don't want you here," he told her firmly.

"Well, screw you," she argued. "I have every right to be here."

And just like that, Toby seemed to calm down. He reached up and cupped Chloe's face while Aaron and I stared at them.

"Seriously, baby. This is too dangerous. If the cops show up, I don't want to have to worry about you."

Okay, so their lovey-dovey stuff might've been sweet, but I really didn't care to sit by and watch it. Throwing open my door, I stepped out, the glare of headlights shining on me.

"Payton, get back in the car," Toby demanded, standing up straight and stepping in front of me.

"Where's Sebastian?" I asked, furious that Sebastian hadn't told me about the race. Well, technically I'd known about it, but he had deliberately left off that detail when he'd told me he had things to do.

"He's on his way," Toby replied. "He's gonna freak when he finds you here."

"Why?"

"Because he doesn't want you to get in trouble. Or worse, hurt."

I glared at Toby, not liking his answer. Mainly because it made sense. "I want to see him."

"Payton," Toby said softly, touching my arm. "Think about this for a minute. Do you really think he'll be able to concentrate if he knows you're here?"

Damn it. Why did Toby have to be so freaking logical?

Before I could argue, a big guy with a shaved head and a tattoo on his scalp walked up to Toby. "We gonna do this shit tonight, Brindle?"

"Yeah," Toby growled. "In a fucking minute."

The big guy's beady eyes narrowed on Toby, and I instinctively took a step back, closer to the car. "You might wanna send the children home to their mommies. Wouldn't want 'em to get hurt."

"Shut the fuck up, Rebel."

Rebel? Seriously?

"Honey, if you'd like to ride along, I'll be more than happy to let you climb aboard." The guy was talking to me, grabbing his crotch as he spoke.

"Fuck you," I snapped, both angry and disgusted.

I was watching the big guy named Rebel, and the next thing I knew, he was stumbling after Toby slammed into him, shoving him hard. "Stay the fuck away from them, Rebel. You hear me?"

Now, I had only known Toby for a little while. And usually, he was a sweet, laid-back charmer who was always smiling, usually making some sort of witty comment. I could not for the life of me place that guy with the guy I saw now.

"You wanna piece of me, asshole?" Rebel yelled at Toby, moving toward him and slamming his chest into Toby's.

I thought Toby was going to hit him, but he didn't. Instead, he simply said two words, and it was as though the night swallowed everyone. "She's Sebastian's."

It was eerily silent, aside from the hum of car engines, until Aaron yelled at me from inside the car. "Get in the car, Payton."

I took one step back and bumped into the car door.

"Now get in your fucking car, Rebel. He'll be here in a minute. Hey, Joey! Get 'em on the starting line." After Toby was finished yelling his instructions, he turned to face me. "Payton, I'm serious. You need to get out of here. At the least, please don't let Sebastian see you."

I nodded. It wasn't like I could argue with him. He'd just nearly beaten up a guy for the way he'd talked to me. I was a little freaked out and a lot scared, so I crawled into the car and closed the door gently, still watching Toby as he walked over to Chloe.

He leaned into the car, twisting so he could see Aaron. "If you wanna watch the race, go back there. They'll be coming around that turn." Toby pointed behind us. "But don't you fucking dare let Sebastian see her." Then Toby kissed Chloe quickly and whispered something into her ear. She didn't say anything, just nodded her head. Then Toby took a step back and closed the door.

Aaron put the car in gear and drove toward a row of buildings that made up the main street of the small downtown area. I had no idea what town we were in, but I knew it wasn't Austin. There was no way they'd be able to race on Austin roads and not get caught. But maybe, in this little nowhere town, they wouldn't get caught.

"What did he say?" Aaron asked Chloe.

She peered over her shoulder at me and then back to Aaron. "He said he has a bad feeling about this. And he wants me to keep my cell phone on me."

My heart sank right then and there. I twisted in my seat to stare out the back window, watching the headlights move as everyone got into place. I didn't see Sebastian's Camaro yet, but I knew he'd be there.

Which was what worried me the most.

Chapter Twenty-Five

Sebastian

AFTER LEIF CALLED AND TOLD me he had something he needed to take care of and he'd see me at the race, Toby had decided to head out, too. I handed over my cash for the race, and for a brief instant, I considered telling him about my dream. At the last second, I opted to keep it to myself. I figured he would try to talk me out of the race, and I couldn't back out, even if I wanted to.

When the house was quiet, I decided to spend a couple of hours working out, trying to get my focus. I blared the music, beat the heavy bag until I was drenched in sweat and my fists hurt. And when I had damn near exhausted myself, I took a shower.

The only good thing about the afternoon was that somehow I'd managed to get my head on straight. That was the reason I was behind the wheel of the Ferrari and my Camaro was sitting in the garage with my keys in the seat. I had backed it out once but immediately pulled it back in. I just couldn't let go of the dream, and since it was always my Camaro that I was in when the thing exploded, I figured I might be able to avoid the inevitable if I left the damn thing at home.

It was dark when I left the house. I took the toll road because I knew it would have the least amount of traffic and I could hit speeds in excess of one-twenty, which I did almost the entire way. But once I exited the highway, I dialed it down a notch as I made my way through the small town that had clearly closed up early on a Saturday night.

I found Toby standing outside with a handful of others. They were all placing bets and ribbing one another about who was going to win. I tuned them out, making my way over to Toby. "Have you heard from Leif?"

"He's on his way," Toby said quickly, turning to take money from some other guy.

I spun in a circle, looking at the crowd that had gathered. If we didn't get this show on the road, some backwoods deputy was going to likely come upon us soon. I turned back to Toby. "Let's get a move on. I've got shit to do."

Toby nodded. "You heard the man."

With that, I made my way to my car, slid inside, and grasped the steering wheel with both hands, inhaling deep and slowly exhaling. I waited for the others to take their places on the line. There were only three cars that pulled forward; the others scattered in all directions. And I waited before pulling up on the far right.

Toby stopped at each of the cars, chatting with the drivers, probably getting their money as well. I turned up the radio, refusing to get lost in my own thoughts. Just a little while longer and then I'd be home free. I had even decided that once the race was over, I was going to stop at Payton's. I needed to see her. Screw giving her a few days. I wasn't going to last that long without seeing her beautiful smile.

I nodded my head when Toby passed by my car, his fist pounding once on the roof before he moved on. The engines were beginning to rev, and I glanced down the line, noticing that there were still only three.

Some chick I didn't know, dressed in a halter top and jeans although it was cold as shit, came strutting out in front of the cars, waving what looked like a scarf.

I waited, the car in neutral, one foot on the break, the other tapping the gas. I kept my eyes trained on the girl, waiting for her to give the go-ahead. I was beginning the countdown in my head when I saw another set of headlights brighten the street in front of us. I glanced down to see a black car at the end, pulling into the line. Before I could try and get a better look at the driver, the girl in front of us waved her hand up slowly and then slapped the air when her arm came down.

And the race was on.

Although I wasn't used to racing the Ferrari, the damn thing had some serious power, and I used every bit of driving skill I had, pulling out in front and staying there. Accelerating down the straights, double-clutching around the turns, weaving in and out, keeping the others behind me. I glanced in my rearview a couple of times, trying to keep up with the location of the other drivers while still keeping my eye on what was in front of me. I noticed the black car gaining, sliding in front of the yellow Mustang, easing beside the electric-blue Charger, so I did a few evasive maneuvers. It wasn't until a particularly sharp turn that I got a better look at the black car.

My car.

My fucking Camaro.

And Leif was at the wheel.

Shit.

Fuck.

Damn.

My heart skipped a beat as I peered out in front of me, noticing our location. The route had been mapped out ahead, and we were closing in on the finish, only a couple more turns to go. I swallowed hard, my eyes flipping back and forth between the night in front of me and the car in my mirror.

Fucking shit.

It took everything in me to keep my thoughts on the finish line, but as we got closer, that became harder and harder. One more turn and then it would be straight the rest of the way. The corner was sharper than I'd anticipated, but I managed to keep the car under control, kicking up the RPMs and downshifting through the turn.

I had just made it through when I looked in the mirror to see the others coming around the same turn and then it happened…

My world went into slow motion when the electric-blue Charger clipped the back end of my Camaro, sending Leif into a spin and then…

"Fuck! No!"

Oh, God. No.

No. No. No.

My worst nightmare had just come true, but worse than seeing my car go up in flames was watching my best fucking friend in my Camaro rolling multiple times before coming to an abrupt stop on its roof.

I slammed my foot on the brake, turned the wheel, and damn near collided with the fucking Charger coming head on. Fuck the race. I had to get to Leif.

I could see the Camaro, upside down on the side of the road, flames licking from under the hood. I was pretty sure my heart stopped beating. Everything else I did from that moment forward just happened; I don't recall making any conscious decisions.

I just did.

I just moved.

And somehow, I just breathed.

"Leif!" I screamed his name at the top of my lungs after launching myself from my car, running full out to where he was.

I could see him. His face was a bloody mess, his head cocked to the side, his arm twisted at an odd angle, and he was dangling upside down, the seat belt holding him in place. I could smell gasoline, knew it was leaking.

The flames were what scared me.

"Fuck! Leif, wake up, man!"

I had to get him out. The nitrous was going to ignite.

"Leif! Wake the fuck up!"

I managed to wrench the door open a little, cramming myself between the door and the body of the car, using all of my strength to force it open. When I managed to get my shoulders through, I reached around Leif, trying to find the seat belt buckle. I fumbled a few times, unable to get it unlatched.

"'Bastian," Leif murmured, his usually booming voice so damn weak.

"I'm here, man. Gonna get you out."

I carried on an unintelligible conversation for the next few seconds, until finally I managed to free the fucking seat belt. Not moving Leif wasn't an option. I only prayed that I wasn't doing more damage, but as the flames grew, I knew that nothing was going to matter if I didn't get him away from the fucking car.

I heard the squeal of brakes and then Toby's voice.

The next thing I knew, we had pulled Leif free of the car, dragging him back toward the street.

"It's gonna blow," Toby yelled as we continued backward, trying to put as much distance between us and the car as we could.

There was a roar, and then the world exploded around us, knocking me off my feet. I flew through the air, hit the pavement hard, slamming my shoulder, and then my head met the concrete. I was momentarily stunned, but I managed to make my brain work, rolling over onto my back. Forcing my eyes open, I could see Leif lying a few feet from me, Toby crawling back toward us.

The sirens in the distance were getting louder.

"Wake up, Leif! Hey, Sebastian? You okay?" Toby's voice sounded strange to me, like I was in a tunnel.

"I'm good," I replied, unsure if he could hear me.

My head was pounding, there was blood running down into my eye, and my shoulder throbbed like a motherfucker. I must've hit my head, but I didn't remember it. Fighting the blackness that teased the edges of my vision, I crawled over to Leif and Toby. Just those few feet took everything out of me.

I could hear people moving around us, more cars, more doors slamming.

My body gave out beside Leif, but I managed to stay conscious, watching Toby's face as he checked Leif out. It was bad. I knew that much. The sirens were loud now, the noise making my head throb.

"Sebastian! Sebastian!"

I knew that voice.

My angel.

Payton.

I tried to look around, but I could hardly move my head. It felt like someone was stabbing me in the face with an ice pick.

"Sebastian! Oh, God. Oh, my God."

When Payton appeared in front of me, I nearly broke. I reached for her, and then she was in my arms, tentatively touching me, brushing my hair aside, looking at my face.

"The ambulance is on the way," she informed me.

I shook my head. "Leif." I didn't need an ambulance. Leif did. He was the one who was hurt. I would be fine. I just needed to close my eyes for a little while.

"Is he okay?" Payton asked, and I opened my eyes enough to see that she was talking to Toby.

"Leif," I muttered again.

"He's right here," she told me, glancing past me and then back down at my face. "Hang on, Sebastian. Please hang on."

"Angel," I whispered, squeezing her hand, "I love you."

Unraveling

She whispered that she loved me, too, and then the world went black.

Chaos

The Unhinged Trilogy, book 3

Secrets...

The secrets are still there, plaguing me, disrupting my everyday life, only now... the unthinkable has happened.

Lies...

Payton insists that it is time that I deal with the lies that seem to make up my entire existence, the ones that have produced the chaos in my head. I don't know if she realizes it, but if it weren't for her being by my side, I don't know how I would survive.

Greed...

Everything is unfolding right before my eyes, the truth is being revealed and there are people who don't want us to be together, but as I have vowed before, no one will keep her from me.

Payton is my anchor in the waves that are crashing through my life and I will do anything to keep her safe.

My name is Sebastian Trovato, and this is the conclusion of my story.

Chaos

Chapter One

Payton

Saturday night
At the hospital

NEVER IN MY LIFE HAD I been as scared as I was when I found Sebastian lying beside the exploding car on the side of the road just a couple of hours ago. Not even when I was seven and I fell out of the tree in my parents' backyard and broke two bones in my right leg. And I'd been terrified that day, but only because no one had been there to see it happen. No one had been there to help me.

But this... This disturbing chain of events was far more frightening than anything I'd ever experienced.

I had been sitting in Aaron's car with Chloe and Aaron, just as Toby had instructed the three of us to do. We saw the cars take off from the line — there were five in total when the sleek black sports car joined them at the last second. I had a good view of tail lights for about ten seconds, at most, but then they disappeared behind buildings. At that point, between wringing my hands in my lap and grinding my teeth together, I was considering asking Aaron to just take me home. I didn't understand the point of watching a race that I couldn't actually see.

Then things got weird. Minutes passed, people were standing around the finish line, jumping up and down, squealing and laughing, and I figured the race must've been close to being over. I watched, my eyes trained on the street where Toby said the racers would end up. And then there he was... Sebastian's white Ferrari barreled around the corner. I thought for a moment that he had lost control of the car, but he corrected. The car lurched forward and was coming right toward us, leading the charge.

The next thing I knew, he was spinning around while a blue Charger zoomed past him, rapidly approaching the finish line. My heart lodged in my throat, and I could hardly swallow around the lump. I had no idea what Sebastian was doing, why he was going the other way when he'd just been yards from finishing first.

But then I saw it.

Fire.

There was a car upside down, farther down the street. I couldn't make out much due to the distance between us and the accident, but I could tell that there were glowing orange flames licking up around the body of the car, and Sebastian was now heading toward it, not driving away. I knew it was bad, even though I hadn't seen it happen. I had a strange feeling in the pit of my stomach. A cold chill started in my chest and radiated outward, ending in my numb fingertips.

It didn't help when Toby's big form darted across the road, diving into his car and tearing out of there as if the cops were chasing him. Two of the five cars had made it to the finish line, one was upside down, Sebastian's was now sitting in the middle of the road not far from the wreck, and another had pulled off to the side close to Sebastian's.

"Go!" I yelled to Aaron. "Go down there!"

"We have to stay here, Payton," Aaron said softly, his eyes wide as he watched the same horrific scene I was watching.

"Get me down there," I yelled at him. "If you don't do it, I'm getting out." I reached for the door handle, fully intending to carry through with my threat. Sebastian was down there, and it wouldn't take me long to get to him if I ran full out. No one was going to keep me away from him.

Not Aaron. Not Toby.

No one.

"Okay. Calm down, doll," Aaron said in a soothing tone, but I could hear the fear in his voice. He was just as freaked out as I was.

Thankfully, Aaron figured out how to get his car to move, pulling forward and making a U-turn in the street. Before we were turned around and heading in the opposite direction, toward the wreck, the world exploded.

A fireball erupted in the sky and then there was screaming. I knew it was me, but I couldn't stop the obnoxious screeching sound coming from my throat. Chloe was crying, and Aaron was driving toward the flames licking into the inky night sky.

Chaos

At that point, I was on autopilot. Aaron hadn't even stopped the car before I threw the door open and jumped out, nearly landing on my knees when I stumbled. I could see them. Toby, Leif, and Sebastian. Toby was crawling on his hands and knees, Sebastian was trying to drag himself across the asphalt, but that wasn't the worst of it... Leif... Oh, God. Leif wasn't moving.

My heart felt as though it had been ripped from my chest. I started yelling Sebastian's name as I ran to him.

Then I started praying.

Now, two and a half hours later, I was pacing the waiting area in the stupid emergency room. Despite my frequent requests and the one tantrum I had thrown, they still wouldn't let me back to see Sebastian, and worse, no one would tell me what was going on.

Aaron had had the good sense to call Garrett about Leif, relaying the details of the accident as we knew them. Garrett in turn had called their mother, Tammy. She'd arrived shortly after we had, her boyfriend — the detective — with her. Then two other guys, who I'd only recently learned were Leif's other brothers, showed up, going straight back through the double doors that led to the rooms where Leif and Sebastian were being taken care of.

"Chloe, I need to know what's going on," I pleaded, tears streaming down my face. I could no longer hold them back. I was growing desperate, my worry overwhelming every other emotion. I turned to look at her when I stopped my incessant walking back and forth, crisscrossing the room full of strangers.

"Did you call Conrad?" she asked as she came over to stand directly in front of me, her hands gripping my shoulders, as though she might be able to keep me in one piece.

At this point, I wondered whether I was going to shatter into a million tiny fragments, so maybe it was necessary for her to grip my arms tightly. Hell, I didn't know. I was numb, from the roots of my hair to the tips of my toes.

"Yeah," I answered, and I was sure Chloe could sense the disappointment in my tone.

I had called Conrad as soon as I got to the hospital, but I'd gotten his voice mail. Not wanting to leave a disturbing message for fear it would send him into a panic, I had hung up and called Lauren, praying she would answer her phone. Luckily, I had put her number in my contacts before the trip to Las Vegas, in the event I might have needed her for something. I never imagined it would have been this. "He didn't answer, so I called his wife."

"And?" Chloe asked.

"I told her what happened and where he is." I remembered the conversation, the way I had spewed the details, probably sounding like an emotional lunatic. Lauren hadn't seemed all that concerned, but I had been hoping I was only imagining her indifference. Considering that had been over an hour ago and neither Conrad nor Lauren had shown up, I had to assume the worst. They weren't coming.

Truthfully, I didn't give a shit whether they showed up or not. I just needed to get back to see Sebastian, and they would've been my only hope. I probably should've called Aaliyah, but I didn't want her to worry until we knew more about Leif. Even my selfish need to see Sebastian hadn't overwhelmed my need to protect Sebastian's sister from this horror for a little while longer.

I watched Toby as he ambled up to the window where patients were to check in. He spoke to a nurse, but I saw her shake her head before closing the window again.

I looked at him expectantly, needing something. Anything.

"Nothin'. Sorry. I tried."

"I have to go back there," I told him. I was ready to storm the building, taking out whoever I needed to just to find Sebastian, to get some sort of assurance that he was okay.

Toby was scanning the room, his focus settling on a set of double doors where I'd seen a few people go during the time I'd been waiting. He peeked back at me, his brow arching as though he was asking a silent question. But before he could tell me his plan, I heard someone yelling, the voice familiar.

Sebastian.

"Bull-fucking-shit I am," Sebastian growled from the other side of the closed doors, his voice echoing off the tiled floors of the busy waiting room as it grew closer to where we were standing.

Yep, he sounded about as frustrated as I felt.

Chaos

The doors flew open and... Holy shit. There he was. My breath lodged in my chest as my eyes consumed him from head to toe, taking stock of his injuries along the way. He had a white gauze bandage on his forehead, his gray T-shirt was covered in blood, his arms were scraped and scratched, and a couple of nasty-looking bruises marred his cheek. But he was in one piece.

"Payton." When he called my name, it hardly registered.

"Go to him," Chloe instructed, giving me a gentle nudge from behind.

That was all I needed before I was moving toward him, my legs feeling like they were made of noodles, definitely unstable as I closed the gap between us. My relief was palpable, and as soon as I was close enough to touch him, my legs gave out. Strong arms came around me, keeping me from dissolving into a puddle on the floor. Sebastian's face was inches from mine.

"It's all right, Angel," he whispered as he lowered me to a chair that was suddenly behind my knees, likely Aaron's doing.

I touched Sebastian's face tentatively with my fingertips, examining the scratches and bruises that marred his beautiful skin.

"I'm fine," he told me, but I wasn't sure I believed him.

"How's Leif?" Toby asked, and that was when I realized Toby was standing beside us, Chloe tucked up under his arm, her hand resting on his broad chest. His shirt also had blood on it, I noticed. Aaron was standing beside them both, watching the four of us with a quiet curiosity.

"Don't know," Sebastian replied, his gaze darting up to meet Toby's. "Nurses wouldn't tell me shit."

I pressed my forehead against Sebastian's chest, ignoring the blood that spotted his shirt and the smell of gasoline that emanated from him. He was alive and in one piece, save for a few dings and abrasions, and I felt as though my world had finally righted itself after having tipped on its axis for the last couple of hours.

The warm strength of Sebastian's touch cradled the back of my head as he held me, and I fought the urge to cry. I didn't know what was spurring the tears, but I felt like every emotion I possessed was wrapped in a flimsy bubble, threatening to burst at any moment. It was overwhelming. Both the relief that Sebastian was okay and the fear because we still hadn't heard anything about Leif.

As I gripped his shirt in both of my fists, I took deep breaths. I was going to hold it together. Sebastian wasn't critically injured, and although we didn't have news on Leif, I was going to take that as a good sign. And most important, I was going to ignore the violent rage that was boiling in my veins for the simple fact that Conrad wasn't there to check on Sebastian.

I think, quite possibly, the last part was what bothered me most, and I wasn't sure what I was going to do about it at this point.

But for now, my prayers were for Leif only.

Chaos

Chapter Two

Sebastian

I WAS SHAKING, ALTHOUGH NOT nearly as violently as I had been a few short minutes ago when the bitchy fucking nurse had refused to allow Payton back to see me. Someone should probably warn the high and mighty ones that when a patient said he was gonna get up and walk out, he meant it. And that was exactly what I did when she told me for the umpteenth time that only family members were allowed back.

As far as I was concerned, Payton was my family.

But they had quickly learned just what I was capable of when I'd ripped the IV from my arm and the patches that had been stuck to my chest. I'd yanked on my clothes and then glared at the disbelieving nurse as I'd walked right out of that tiny ten-by-ten room that, for the last hour, had felt more like a prison than a hospital.

Now that I had Payton in my arms, my anger was subsiding. I knew I had to get some information on Leif before I'd be able to relax completely. As it was, the tension in the waiting room was increasing with every passing second. I could tell that Toby was hanging on by a very thin thread, and when he snapped, no one was going to want to be in his path.

"Can you try to get ahold of Garth?" I asked, directing my question at Aaron.

"Already did. He hasn't answered me since he got here."

If Garrett wasn't answering, that meant one of two things: either they had to turn their cell phones off while they were back there, or he was pissed. I couldn't necessarily blame him if he was mad, but that didn't stop me from wanting to know what the fuck was going on. Leif was as much a brother to me as he was to Garrett, and it irked me that no one was bothering to share any information.

"What's Tammy's boyfriend's name?" I asked Toby, cupping the back of Payton's head as she leaned her forehead against my chest. I slid my palm down her silky hair, over her back before repeating the movement again and again. I couldn't stop touching her. For the last hour, since I'd been wheeled into the emergency room, fading in and out of consciousness, I had thought of nothing else except her. The fear that had been etched on her beautiful face just before the world faded to black was the last thing I remembered. I knew she had been scared. Hell, I'd been scared there for a while.

"Derrick," Toby said quickly. "What're you thinkin'?"

"You okay?" I asked Payton, leaning down and whispering the words against her ear and then pressing my lips to her head.

She nodded, still not lifting her head from my chest. Her hands were gripping my T-shirt as though if she held me to her, things wouldn't be quite so bad. I honestly wished that were the case.

Focusing on Toby once again, I said, "I think we need to get him out here. Maybe if we use that angle, we can get some information."

"I can do it," Chloe offered. "I'll go over to the nurse at the window and tell her there's a detective back there and I have some information about the wreck."

My eyes darted back to Toby, and when he nodded, I gave Chloe the go-ahead. She stood up straight, adjusted her shirt, and marched over to the nurse sitting behind the glass pane. I watched from the corner of my eye, trying not to look too interested in what was going on. I hoped that this didn't backfire. The last thing we needed were local cops showing up to take a statement.

Speaking of… "Have the cops showed up?"

Toby nodded. "I had to give a statement at the scene. Told them I'd been driving by when I saw the car flip. Haven't talked to any since we've been here, though. There were a couple of uniforms wandering around a little while ago, but they went back."

Chloe glanced back over her shoulder. "Do y'all remember his last name? I forgot what he said it was."

I shook my head, as did Toby and Aaron, giving a little plausibility to Chloe's lie. The nurse talked to Chloe for a little while longer but then closed the glass again. Chloe turned toward them, offering a small smile as she hung her head down.

"When he gets out here, let me talk to him," Toby insisted.

I didn't argue with him. I wasn't in any mood to talk to anyone, especially if this guy wasn't willing to share any information. As it was, I was ready to stomp back through those doors and peer in every room until I found Leif, or at least his family members.

Twenty minutes passed, and I was beginning to give up hope when the double doors opened and out walked Garrett. He looked as though he'd aged ten years since the last time I'd seen him. Both Payton and I got to our feet immediately, following Aaron, Toby, and Chloe as they led the way. Garrett nodded his head toward the exit doors, signaling for us to follow him outside.

"How's he doin', man?" I asked as soon as we were standing beneath the awning that covered the driveway where the ambulances pulled up to deliver patients.

The lights were on, casting a glow that carried just a couple of feet out from the covered area. From what I could tell, we were alone, except for a woman walking an elderly lady out into the parking lot, slowly disappearing into the darkness.

"He's fucked up," Garrett stated directly, his dark eyes darting back and forth over all of the faces staring back at him, anxiously awaiting some sort of news.

"But he's gonna be all right, right?" Chloe asked, hope ringing in her voice as she clung to Toby's arm.

"He's fucked up," Garrett repeated roughly.

Payton placed her hand on Garrett's arm, giving him a gentle squeeze. The guy looked as if he was about to lose his shit. I knew how he felt.

Finally, after taking a deep breath and blinking a few times, Garrett exhaled. "He's got three fractured ribs. Those'll heal on their own, according to the doc, just cracks, no risk of complications from them. Two or three months at the most, if we can keep him from overdoing it."

I sighed, finally able to breathe for the first time in hours.

"That's not all, Sebastian."

I waited for Garrett to continue, my fingernails digging into the palms of my hands. A sense of impending doom washed over me, and I clenched my teeth together as I waited.

"They said something about blood in the thoracic cavity. Hemothorax or some shit. They're putting in a chest tube to drain the blood. If it doesn't stop, they're gonna have to open him up to try to stop the bleeding."

"Shit," I barked, thrusting my hands through my hair and turning around. I couldn't stop the angry tears that flooded my eyes. I wasn't sure who I was mad at. Myself for the race, Leif for showing up in my fucking car, or Rebel for causing the damn accident. Or maybe all three of us.

Payton immediately made her way to my side, sliding her arms around me. Leaning forward, I buried my face in her neck, wrapping my arms around her tightly. "How the fuck did this happen?" I asked, mumbling against her skin.

A strong hand landed on my shoulder, and I released Payton, turning to face Garrett. "Man, I know it's bad, but seriously. If he'd been in his Mustang... Holy fuck, Sebastian," Garrett said with a strangled sob, "he'd be dead right now. The roll cage in your Camaro pretty much saved his life."

I glanced over at Toby. "Why the fuck was he in my car?" It wasn't the first time Leif had borrowed one of my cars, but he only did so when there was something wrong with his. And never had he raced a vehicle that wasn't his own.

"No idea," Toby retorted quickly. "Last I heard, he just told me he wanted in. I didn't even know he was going to be there until he drove up."

"How'd you get here so fast, anyway?" I asked Garrett, realizing he'd been on the road just a few hours ago when Aaron had called him.

"We were just an hour outside of Austin when Aaron called." Garrett glanced over at Aaron briefly. "We were taking a couple of days off."

"Will you go back?" I asked.

"Not right away, no. I need to be here with my mom and Leif."

"How long will he be in the hospital?" Payton asked, holding my arm with both hands. She shuddered, and that was when I realized she was shivering. It was cold as shit outside, but I hadn't even noticed. My blood was pumping too hard and too fast for me to feel much of anything.

"Right now they don't know. Once they do the chest tube, they'll attempt to drain the blood. If that works, then great. If not, and they have to do surgery, it could be a while. I'm not leaving until he's home."

I nodded, understanding Garrett's need to stay with his brother.

"Has anyone contacted Aaliyah?" Garrett asked, meeting my eyes.

I informed Garrett that I hadn't had a chance to call anyone, and Payton and Toby confirmed with a headshake that they hadn't called my sister, either.

"I'll call her," I told him.

"Good. He was calling her name at one point. They've got him sedated now, though."

"Will we be allowed to go back and see him?" Toby asked.

Garrett nodded. "I'll let you know when they get him to a room. If he's in ICU, we'll be limited to when we can see him and to how many can go back at a time."

I met Toby's eyes over Payton's head. I had a question for him. One that I knew better than to ask with Garrett there. As it was, I wasn't sure how I was going to handle it if the answer wasn't what I wanted to hear.

"I need to get back there," Garrett said, turning his attention to me.

I walked over and hugged him, slapping his back a couple of times. "Thanks, Garth. Keep me updated. We'll be close, but I've got something I need to take care of. And as always, if you need anything, holler."

Stepping back, I met Garrett's dark gaze. He knew I was up to something. Hell, they all probably did. But at that moment, the only thing that mattered to me was that Leif got up out of that bed and walked out of the hospital. I didn't care if it was one day or thirty. I just needed him to be whole.

Payton and Chloe hugged Garrett, and Toby slapped him on the back. What surprised me the most was when Garrett asked Aaron if he could talk to him, both men going back into the hospital together.

"What're you thinkin'?" Toby asked sternly, pulling my attention to him. He knew me better than anyone else. Well, anyone else except maybe Leif.

"We've got something to take care of." Whether Toby knew what I was thinking or not, he merely nodded in agreement. I reached for Payton, pulling her flush against my chest. "I've gotta leave for a little while."

Payton's eyes reflected her concern, but she didn't argue. "We'll be here."

"You sure?" I asked. "You can go home and get some sleep. Come back in the morning."

"I won't be able to sleep," she admitted.

I knew exactly how she felt.

Kissing Payton softly on the lips, I cupped her face and drew back enough to look in her eyes. "Call my sister. Tell her what's going on." She nodded, and I kissed her again. "I'll be back in a couple of hours."

"Be careful."

I didn't tell her that probably wasn't going to happen. After all, she had enough to worry about.

Chapter Three

Sebastian

AN HOUR LATER, LONG AFTER it was probably appropriate to just show up on someone's doorstep unannounced, I pulled into the driveway of a dilapidated old house that hadn't seen its glory days since the early sixties at least. From the dim light of a yellow street lamp, I could see that the wood siding was peeling and rotted. The roof appeared as though it was barely holding up. The front windows were cracked and looked like they let more air in than they kept inside the house.

"Man, you've gotta keep your cool," Toby warned when I put the Ferrari in park. Toby had tried to convince me to let him drive. His Camaro would've been notably less conspicuous, but I knew that riding in the passenger seat would've left me with even more pent-up energy than I currently had.

However, it wasn't lost on me how out of place my car looked in front of this house, especially in this particular neighborhood, but at the moment, I really didn't give a shit. "I can't make you any promises," I told Toby honestly, opening the door and climbing out.

"I knew I shouldn't've told you where he lives," Toby mumbled as we walked up the cracked sidewalk path to the front door.

The lone light fixture on the house put off a golden glow that lit our trail to the rickety front porch and the screen door that was hanging awkwardly, one of the hinges clearly broken. With care, so as not to have the thing come off in my hands, I pulled it open. The accompanying squeak was loud enough to notify the neighbors that their neighbor had a visitor.

Again, I didn't care.

I rapped my knuckles on the door. It was just after eleven, and I figured visitors weren't welcome at this time of night, but I couldn't let this go.

"This better fuckin' be good," the gruff, angry voice sounded from the other side of the wood door just before it opened.

As soon as Rebel had the door open wide, I rushed him, shoving him back hard enough to send his big ass stumbling. He managed to right himself before landing flat on his ass.

"What the fuck, man?" Rebel shouted.

"Good to see you're in one piece," I snarled, still stalking him. I heard the sound of the front door being closed behind us, which meant Toby had come inside.

"Shit," Rebel groaned. "What's your fuckin' problem?"

Rebel came toward me, chest puffed up like he was king of the world and hadn't been knocked nearly off his big-ass fucking feet by a guy considerably smaller than he was. Not that I was small, but even at six foot two, I was no match for Rebel's six-foot-six-inch frame. The dude was built like a fucking hundred-year-old oak tree. The sweat coating his bald head glistened in the dim light of the living room, and he smelled like cigarettes and sex, not an appealing combination, but it beat the stench emanating from the house.

"Holy fuck, man. It smells like shit in here," Toby stated.

"Fuck off, Toby. No one invited you into my house."

"Yeah, well, we didn't figure an invitation was necessary," I informed Rebel. "Especially since my best fucking friend is laid up in a hospital right now."

I was up in Rebel's face, trying to refrain from punching him in the fucking mouth, when a short, dark-haired woman stepped out of the dark hallway, wrapped in a sheet, her eyes wide.

"Go back to the bedroom, Darla," Rebel ordered.

I glared at her, and she trotted off down the hall. I only hoped she wasn't one of those feisty chicks who went looking for some sort of weapon to defend her dick of a boyfriend.

"So that's how it works? You nearly kill my best friend and you're at home getting your dick sucked while we're waiting to see if he's gonna live or die?"

Rebel didn't reply, his eyes narrowing on my face. "You got a point here? I did my job. I finished the race. No rules, remember?"

"Common decency says you check on the guy whose car you sent rolling. *That's* the way it works," I informed him bitterly.

"He's alive, man, what the fuck do you want from me?" Rebel snapped, and the noise in my head built to a crescendo, blinding me with a rage I hadn't felt in quite some time.

The next thing I knew, I was whaling on Rebel, kneeling over him, pounding my fists into his face while Toby tried to pull me off. I could hear the girl screaming and Rebel groaning, but I couldn't stop. The fucker didn't give two shits whether Leif lived or fucking died. My best fucking friend. I pounded on Rebel, not caring what kind of damage I did. I lost track of time, beating Rebel until my knuckles were bloody and my head was throbbing.

Toby yanked me to my feet, spinning me around and getting right up in my face. "We're done here," he snarled. "Let's go."

I nodded, the red haze still clouding my vision. I glanced around Toby to where Rebel was lying on the ground. He was spitting blood onto the dingy carpet, his beady eyes focusing on me once again.

I opened the door and turned back to see Toby standing over Rebel. "Your winnings," Toby bit out, tossing an envelope onto Rebel's chest. "If I ever fucking see your ugly face again, the beating you just got will feel like a day at the beach. You feel me?"

In all the time I'd known Toby, rarely had I ever seen him quite as pissed as he was right then. I felt the guy's pain, understood his rage. As it turned out, Toby just had significantly more restraint than I did.

Not that I was apologizing.

It was closing in on three o'clock in the morning when I managed to convince Payton to let me take her back to my place. After handling things at Rebel's, Toby and I had returned to the hospital for a couple of hours, but as the minutes continued to tick by, I knew we would have to go at some point. Considering it was late — or early, depending on how you looked at it — I figured a little sleep might do us all some good. My house was the closest to the hospital where Leif was staying, so everyone agreed to crash there for a few hours before heading back north after the sun came up. When I pulled into my driveway, I noticed Leif's Mustang sitting there, and it took a moment for my brain to register what I was seeing.

Pulling into the garage, I parked the Ferrari and helped Payton out. By the time I was wandering over to the Mustang, Toby's Camaro was pulling up behind it, Aaron's Honda, with Garrett riding shotgun, behind him.

"Why'd he take the Camaro?" Toby asked as soon as he got out of his car, joining me as I studied the fire-engine-red sports car.

"No idea," I said, not seeing anything wrong with the car. "That's the first question I want him to answer."

Taking Payton's hand, I led her into the house, motioning Toby and the rest of the crew following close behind us toward the guest bedrooms. "Two rooms. One couch. We'll see y'all in the morning."

I didn't stop walking, pulling Payton along with me. I was exhausted. Between the two hours we'd lost when we'd come back from Vegas that morning and the rest of the events from the day, I wasn't sure how Payton was still standing. I wanted to put her to bed, and we'd worry about the rest of the shit in the morning.

"I need to shower," Payton said after I closed my bedroom door, sealing us off from the rest of the world for a little while.

I nodded toward the attached bathroom as I lowered myself onto the bed, resting my head in my hands.

Payton came to stand in front of me, my forehead pressing against her stomach, careful not to hit the bandage covering the gash I'd received earlier. She placed her hands gently on the top of my head, her fingers linking into my hair. It was the safest I'd felt since early that morning before I'd dropped her off at her apartment. Having her there with me... I wasn't sure I was going to be able to be away from her anymore.

As fast as our relationship seemed to be moving, it made sense to me. It felt right. I could breathe through the pain that had taken up residence inside of me. She made my existence bearable. I loved her. I needed her.

However, now wasn't the time to drop that little emotional bomb on her. She'd been through enough that day already.

"I love you, Sebastian." Payton's whispered words had me looking up. Wrapping my arms around her waist, my palms flattening against her back, I pulled her even closer, pressing my face to her stomach, breathing her in.

I sat there like that for a couple of minutes, completely content just to be with her. My thoughts continued to drift to Leif, who was laid up in a hospital bed, clinging to life while his family waited patiently for more information. The few minutes I'd been allowed to go back and see him hadn't been enough. His mother had hugged me, assuring me everything would be all right. All the while, I had wondered how she could be so strong. How Leif could be so strong.

At least he had family to help him through.

Payton's hands slid from my head, down over my shoulders and then my arms. She pulled them from around her waist, linking her fingers with mine. "Shower with me," she whispered.

I nodded. No matter how exhausted I was, there was no way I could tell her no.

She led me to the bathroom, and while she turned on the water, I grabbed towels from the closet, placing them within reach of the shower. While she undressed, I looked at myself in the mirror. I still had the bandage on my forehead, so I peeled it back, revealing the jagged cut beneath. They hadn't stitched it up, probably because I wasn't all that cooperative, but they had used some sort of tape to keep the gash closed. The other scratches and bruises that marred my face were minimal, especially compared to the damage that Leif had endured.

When Payton was in the shower, I pulled off my clothes and tossed them on the floor with hers before opening the glass door and joining her. She maneuvered around me so that I faced the wall beneath the shower spray. While I pressed my hands against the tiled wall, my forehead resting on my knuckles, I fought the tears that still threatened. They were a mixture of anger and pain, desperation and total relief. The only thing that made it manageable was when Payton proceeded to wash my hair and then my body. I could hardly move, every muscle beginning to ache, my head throbbing from the intimate contact I'd had with the concrete earlier. But still I stood there, motionless, savoring the feel of her smooth hands on my skin.

When she was finished with me, she reached for a towel and urged me out from under the spray. While I dried off, Payton washed up, joining me outside of the shower a few minutes later, wrapping herself in the other towel.

After pulling on a pair of shorts, I grabbed a T-shirt from my closet and helped her pull it on over her head. I left her alone after that, offering her a few minutes of privacy.

My legs finally gave out on me, and I dropped onto the bed, reclining on my pillow and staring at the ceiling.

Of all the shit that was going on in my life, I just couldn't believe that this had happened.

And worse ... I didn't know what it meant for the days to come.

Payton

FOR THE LAST COUPLE OF hours, I think I'd been walking around in a daze. My body was tired, my mind equally so. The events of the day had taken their toll on me. By the time I climbed into bed with Sebastian, I could hardly keep my eyes open, but even when I tried to close them, my brain wouldn't stop processing everything that had happened.

It seemed as though the day would never end. From the limited amount of sleep I'd gotten last night to the flight back from Vegas that morning, dinner with Chloe and Aaron, the race, the accident, the hospital… It all seemed to morph together into one giant nightmare, and I was ready for it to be over. If it wasn't for the fact that I had some things on my mind, things I needed to tell Sebastian, I would've just closed my eyes and forced my brain to cease for a little while.

But there were a couple of things I needed to share with him. Important things that he needed to know before we woke up to a new day. What I had on my mind wasn't easy to share, but I knew I had no choice.

After curling up to Sebastian, my head on his chest, I listened to his steady heartbeat for a couple of silent minutes before I garnered the nerve to talk. When the words came, I think they surprised me as much as they did Sebastian. "I tried calling Conrad today," I admitted softly. Part of me was hoping he was asleep and he wouldn't hear the words.

I didn't get that lucky.

"Tried?"

"Yeah," I explained. "He didn't answer, and I didn't want to tell him about the accident on his voice mail, so I didn't leave a message. I called Lauren."

I felt Sebastian's head turn. He was trying to look at my face, but I didn't move. I didn't want to look him in the eye, for fear he would see my anger and frustration. Not at him. At them. The people who were supposed to be his parents, his family. The ones who had blatantly turned their backs on him when he'd needed them.

"What did she say?" he asked, his tone even, belying the tension that I could feel in his body.

"She pretty much said okay." That wasn't far from the truth.

"Okay? What did you tell her?"

"I explained about the wreck, informed her we were at the hospital and that I didn't know how you were. I told her you were unconscious when the ambulance came and that Leif was in bad shape."

I heard Sebastian's deep exhale, his chest rising and falling beneath my head.

"Doesn't surprise me," he stated, his tone harsh yet apathetic.

I understood his pain. I wanted to give that woman a piece of my mind. One of them, either Conrad or Lauren, preferably both, should've been there for Sebastian. But they hadn't been.

"I also tried to call Aaliyah, but she didn't answer."

"Really?" Sebastian asked, this time moving enough to look at me. I peered up at him, meeting his gaze in the dim glow filtering into the room from the light I'd left on in the bathroom.

"No. I told her I needed her to call me. She hasn't yet."

Sebastian's body tensed, but he lowered his head back to the pillow, and I adjusted my position, placing my arm over his chest and holding him.

"There're some things you need to know, Payton," Sebastian said, his voice soft, soothing.

"About your family?" I asked, having already gathered that there were issues within the family structure. I mean, I knew that Sebastian and his father didn't get along, but this… His family didn't even care enough to come to the hospital to check on him.

That went far beyond normal disagreements.

"Remember back when I told you that Conrad was my father?" he asked me.

Rather than answer, I nodded, my head still resting against his chest.

Sebastian placed his hand on the back of my head and began stroking my hair. It was still wet from the shower, and the warmth from his fingers felt good against my scalp.

"There's more to the story."

"I figured as much," I told him.

"Before I tell you this, I need you to make me a promise."

I lifted my head and looked into Sebastian's golden eyes. He was dead serious. Whatever he was about to tell me wasn't going to be like the stories he'd told me about his mother, or the pain of being thrust into the unknown, forced to live with a man who didn't want to act as a father.

"I promise," I whispered, knowing I would keep that promise, even though I feared it at the same time.

Sebastian took my chin between his thumb and forefinger, holding my head still so he could look at me. I wasn't sure what he was hoping to see in my eyes, but he must've found it, because he released my chin and cupped the back of my head, urging me back down to his chest.

Silence encompassed us once again, but it only lasted a few heartbeats.

"I don't think my mother's death was an accident," he said, his tone a strange mixture of sadness and anger.

I sucked in a breath, holding it. I was trying to process his words. They'd been spoken so matter-of-factly, so easily, as though he'd given this some serious thought. I wasn't sure what I was supposed to do with that information. Thankfully, he didn't give me time to think too much before he continued.

"Like I told you, I was fourteen years old when she died. I was old enough to hear things and understand what was going on, and I knew that the weeks preceding her death had been particularly difficult for my mother. She'd already told me that she was considering reaching out to Conrad, trying to get money from him to help. We were going to be evicted from the apartment — it had gotten that bad.

"My mother seemed to be more upset than usual. I'd seen a couple of notices on the door, informing her that she had days to produce the back rent and bring the account current or they would be locking the doors. When I asked my mother about it, she wouldn't go into detail, telling me that it was nothing to worry about.

"As I usually did, I went about my business, going to school, stirring up shit, working a few hours here and there to make some cash, but I still worried. One night before my mother went to her second job, I asked her about child support. She told me all the gory details about Conrad and how he hadn't wanted anything to do with us. I'd been livid, but I told her that he owed us that money. She shouldn't've had to go it alone, but she did. All those years, she busted her ass to raise me. Alone."

Sebastian's heart rate had sped up; the steady thump beneath my ear had become a rapid beat. He was breathing harder and faster, but I didn't know how to comfort him, so I didn't move, letting him continue.

"She told me she was going to reach out to him, see if he would help in some way. For the days that followed, I asked her whether she'd contacted him. She would brush me off, but she did tell me she had tried. She would never admit to talking to him, but I think she did."

Sebastian took a deep breath, exhaled slowly. "Payton, I can't prove it yet, but if it is the last thing I do, I will. I can't keep going on like this. I can't keep going through every single day not knowing the truth."

"What truth?" I asked, scared to hear the answer.

There was silence for a minute, maybe two, before Sebastian finally spoke. And before the words came out, I knew that his next words were going to change the rest of our lives.

"I think my father killed my mother."

The next thing I knew, Sebastian was over me, his warmth penetrating every inch of my skin. Without hesitation, he pushed the T-shirt I was wearing up and over my head, leaving me completely naked beneath him. His shorts disappeared just as quickly, and then he was kissing me, slowly at first. I had so many questions running through my mind, begging to be released, but I knew the time for talking had ended.

He was causing a distraction, and I couldn't necessarily blame him. This was deep, too deep to discuss when we were existing on adrenaline and very little sleep.

His hands wandered over my skin, his fingers pinching my nipples until I was moaning his name, begging him for more. The entire time, his face was pressed against my neck, my hand cupping the back of his head. And when he thrust into me, I was ready. My body had ignited from his touch, but there was something more there. Something considerably deeper than any other time we'd been together.

Sebastian's hips surged forward, my legs wrapping around him, taking him deeper. As deep as possible. He continued the steady, unhurried pace, driving me closer and closer to the edge. But I knew he wasn't with me. He was using sex to bury the pain, hiding from me. I didn't want that.

"Sebastian," I whispered, twining my fingers into the longer hair at the top of his head and pulling him back. He gave in, lifting his head, and that was when I saw his eyes. They were wild with both fear and rage, and I knew it had to do with the thoughts warring inside of him. But I didn't want that rage there between us.

I used all of my strength, finally managing to force him over to his back. I didn't waste any time resuming my position over him, sliding down on him, taking his body into mine as I moaned, the feeling so exquisite I nearly forgot the reason I was doing this.

"Look at me, Sebastian," I demanded.

Sebastian's golden gaze locked with mine as I leaned forward, rocking on him as he impaled me, his hands gripping my hips firmly.

"Don't leave me, Sebastian. Stay right here with me," I insisted.

"Payton," he whispered, tears forming in his eyes. "Angel."

"I'm here," I told him, leaning into his touch when he cupped the side of my face in his hand. "I'll always be here."

"Tell me you love me, Payton."

I watched him, continuing to ride him slowly, not wanting the connection to be broken. There might've been pain, but I wanted it to be forced out — at least for the moment — by pleasure. The pleasure that only we could bring one another.

"I love you, Sebastian," I whispered.

His hips began to thrust upward, and the intense sensation accosted me, sending shards of pleasure ricocheting through my insides.

"Sebastian." I breathed his name out as my body tensed.

"Look at me, Angel," he commanded. "Look at me when you come."

I forced my eyes open, locking them with his, and what I saw reflected there combined with the sensations he was building within me were too much.

"I love you, Angel," he whispered hoarsely, his hand cupping the back of my head as he stilled beneath me. I felt him pulse inside me as my orgasm crested.

And when I rested on his chest, trying to catch my breath, I knew that the journey we were about to venture on was going to be a long one. Possibly painful at times. But I vowed right then and there that I would be there, however he needed me. Sebastian Trovato was the man I loved, the man I would spend the rest of my life with.

But as I accepted this, I prayed that Sebastian could find closure from whatever had happened all those years ago, and above all else, I prayed that whatever demons he might be fighting — real or not — could be conquered.

Chapter Five

Sebastian

Two weeks later
Friday afternoon

I CUT OUT EARLY, UNABLE to keep up the pretenses of working for Conrad and not hating every fucking second of it. I'd spent the last two weeks going through the motions, doing the best I could, because I was more worried about Leif than I was about stirring shit up at the moment.

But today was the day.

My house was ready for me to move in; the furniture I'd ordered had been delivered yesterday and overseen by Toby because I'd had other shit I'd needed to take care of and couldn't get over there. I was trying to do everything I could to keep Conrad off my back. So far it had worked, but tonight, when I started moving my stuff out of the guesthouse, my guess was that Conrad was going to get wind of what was going on. I needed to get it all in one trip, because I had a feeling he was going to lock up the estate and refuse to let me back in.

I got that. I did.

Over the course of two weeks, most of the scratches and bruises on my face had healed, but never once had Conrad asked about them. Not one fucking time. Using the rift that had been formed from the Vegas debacle as an excuse, I had avoided having dinner with them. Aaliyah had tried to talk to me, but I had brushed her off. I was cautious of her at the moment. She hadn't returned Payton's phone call, and she seemed completely oblivious to the accident, but I couldn't be certain. Part of me wondered whether Lauren had managed to turn her against me, and until I knew how to handle the situation, I was keeping her on the outside, as well.

So, with my family keeping their distance, I figured there was no time like the present to get my shit and get out.

It wasn't that I was running because of recent events. I wasn't bailing because Conrad hadn't even asked about Leif once in the last two weeks. Payton and I had come to an agreement the night I'd spilled my guts to her. We were going to keep the information to ourselves. She was going to continue to work for Conrad, and together we would see what we could find out. Although I was tempted to ask her to quit her job, she had brought up a good point. As long as she was at Trovato, Inc., there was a better chance of her getting information that might help us solve the mystery of my mother's death.

But that didn't mean I had to pretend to be okay with him. I wasn't. Not by a long shot.

So, I had designated today as moving day.

Payton and Chloe had agreed to go to the store when Payton got off work. They wanted to pick up groceries and deliver them to the new house. They were going to spend time putting things away as we brought them over, as well. She told me to consider it a moving in party.

Whatever she wanted to call it, I didn't care. Just as long as she was there.

The house was finally mine. I had signed the papers late yesterday, after Jim had worked miracles to make that happen, but it was all done and over. I had spent less than an hour scribbling my name on one line after another while Jim sat by my side. When we were finished, he'd clapped me on the back and congratulated me. I'd bolted straight to Payton's after that, telling her what I'd done.

Yeah, I had kept it a secret up to that point, not wanting to jinx it. After breaking the news, I had explained that until I had signed on the dotted line, it wasn't official. She had been a little surprised, but overall, when she'd thrown her arms around my neck and hugged me tightly, I'd known I'd done the right thing.

Truth was, I'd been keeping my eye on that house for a few months now. I'd known, even before Payton had walked into my life, that things were deteriorating between my father and me, and the secret I was holding on to had become too much for me to deal with. It was time for me to move out, to live my own life without him breathing down my neck every second of every day.

But packing my shit was probably going to be the easiest part of the entire process. I still had to inform my father that I was leaving, but I was planning to hold off until another day. I wanted to be out first. However, informing him that I was done was high on my priority list.

And by done, I wasn't just talking about moving out and living on my own.

I was fucking done.

Done with him period.

Considering I really was the reason Trovato, Inc. had continued to grow over the last few years, I didn't expect my father to take the news lightly. Although he'd threatened to replace me numerous times, even he knew that wasn't possible.

But now he wasn't going to have a choice.

And eventually, I had to get Payton away from him, too.

It took me less than five minutes to drive from the garage at my father's house, where I worked, to the guesthouse, where I'd lived since I was eighteen years old. I realized as I approached the place that I wasn't going to miss it. I'd never had a sentimental attachment to anyone or anything here. The closest thing I had to family was my sister, Aaliyah, and I even wondered how sturdy that bond was from time to time. Her mother had some serious pull with Aaliyah, which was why I hadn't told her any additional details about my plans to move out. Leif had already told her, but as of yet, Aaliyah and I hadn't discussed it. She was upset, and it wouldn't be any better once I did finally talk to her, but there were plenty of other things she was going to be upset about.

Namely the fact that Leif had been laid up in a hospital bed for the last two weeks and no one had told her. After Payton had informed me that she'd tried to call Aaliyah but hadn't reached her, I'd told her not to say anything. Not yet.

I wanted to see whether or not Lauren actually revealed the details Payton had relayed to her that day. Not surprisingly, she hadn't said a word. Not to Conrad and not to Aaliyah. Or if she had, neither of them were giving away that they knew.

Whenever I chose to inform Conrad that I had moved out and that I no longer planned to work for Trovato, Inc., I would let him know just what had happened and how his bitch of a wife had kept those details to herself. I didn't like the woman. Never had. And as time went by, she continued to give me more and more reason to despise her.

No love lost there, though. I knew she felt the same about me.

I was a threat to her.

As I pulled into my driveway, a new thought drifted into my head. What if my father wasn't responsible...? What if...?

Holy shit.

I shook the thought away. I had other things to do at the moment and wondering whether my stepmother could've stooped so low as to eliminate anyone she saw as a threat to her... Yeah, I couldn't think about that now. The rage would consume me, and I would be useless.

I wasn't surprised to see Toby's car parked in the driveway, nor was I shocked to see him sitting on the couch in my garage when I pulled in. I was glad he was there. I needed someone to keep me focused, and Toby could easily do that. He somehow managed to keep me smiling most of the time — I happened to think he did it on purpose, but I'd never mentioned that to him.

He stood and greeted me when I pushed open the door to the truck, a wide grin plastered on his face.

"It's about fucking time," Toby said, coming toward me when I climbed out of the car.

"Did you miss me, you fucking pussy?" I asked, smiling as I said it.

"Fuck no," he retorted, a lie if I'd ever heard one. "I could've come over to the house if I wanted to see your ugly mug."

"Yep, I knew it. You missed me."

Toby rolled his eyes, then nodded his head toward the empty space in the garage, the spot where my Camaro used to sit. I closed the truck door and came to stand beside him. "You plannin' to replace it?"

"Yeah," I told him honestly. "Eventually."

"Good." That was all he said before slapping me on the back, sending me stumbling forward a step.

"The furniture was delivered yesterday, right?" I asked as I righted myself and glared at him over my shoulder.

"Yep," Toby confirmed. "All your new shit's been set up."

Thank God.

"Payton and Chloe should be there in a bit," I told him. "They're getting groceries."

"I hope you didn't give them your credit card," Toby said, laughing.

"I did." I smiled. I'd told Payton to buy whatever she thought we might need. Yes, I had inserted the word "we" into that sentence, and she hadn't balked at it, either. I had informed her that damn near everything in the guesthouse belonged to my father, so if it wasn't in the house now, I probably didn't own it. She informed me she would stop by first, check it out, and then run to the store.

Pushing open the garage door to the house, I left it open so Toby could follow me. "Did the pools get taken care of?"

"Yep. Guy came early yesterday when I was waiting for the furniture guys. He set everything up. You're good to go, man." Toby followed me into the house, still talking. "You tell Conrad yet?"

"Nope," I answered, heading straight for my bedroom.

"Plannin' to do that soon?"

"Maybe," I offered. "But not today."

"What can I do?" Toby asked as he followed me up the stairs.

"Load the truck up with the shit in the workout room, would ya?"

"Might've been nice for you to mention that when I was downstairs," he grumbled as he turned back toward the stairs.

"Lazy ass," I retorted, laughing.

Toby stopped with his hand on the top rail, grinning. "Hey, we still on for tomorrow?"

"Yep." I knew he was talking about Leif. Toby and I had both gone to visit Leif every day since he'd been moved to a regular room. They had put him in ICU for two days, and even then, we'd managed to get in to see him. Once I'd found out about the closing date on the house, I had brought the subject up with Leif, trying to get a feel for whether or not he still wanted to move in. He'd assured me he did, and I had even stayed when he'd talked to his mother.

Tammy hadn't been all that happy about the news, but she wasn't against it either. I told her that she was welcome at the house anytime she wanted to stop by and check on him. Leif had delivered one of his *I-am-gonna-hurt-you* glares, but in the end, he and his mother had hugged, and he was set to move in when he was released tomorrow.

"Now get to work. We've got places to be."

Toby saluted me before he jogged down the stairs. I opened my bedroom door and gave it one last once-over. Almost everything in there was mine, so this was going to take a while.

Two hours later, I was finished packing up my bedroom and the bathroom, and Toby had finished with the workout room. Pretty fucking sad that at twenty-five years old, it only took me that long to pack up everything I owned. Even worse was the house still looked the same as it had before I'd started.

Then again, the majority of my possessions were in the garage. The truck was full, both inside and out, and Toby had even filled the trunk of his car.

"Aaron and Garth are on the way. Garth said Sean and Dale are behind them."

"Good deal. I'll have Garth take the Ferrari," I told Toby. Since I no longer had the Camaro, I didn't need another body to take that car, so it would work out. "Did Sean and Dale by chance bring their trucks?"

"Yup," Toby said as he made his way to the toolboxes and began loading up the tools that were strewn across the floor and the cabinets. "I told 'em we've got tools."

As though they'd been summoned straight out of my thoughts, Aaron's girlie little Honda pulled into the driveway behind Toby's Camaro, and the rumble of diesel engines sounded from farther down the driveway. Garrett climbed out of the passenger seat of Aaron's car, grinning. Who the hell knew what he was smiling about, but Aaron's goofy smile matched, so I figured the two of them were figuring things out between them.

I did not need to know the details.

Sean backed his big-ass Ford into the garage bay where my Camaro previously had sat and hopped out of the truck. The cowboy hat sitting on top of his head made me laugh, but Sean was used to me giving him shit about being a redneck. I thought Toby was a country boy, but Sean made him look like a wannabe.

"What's up, man? You finally blowin' this joint?" Sean asked, clapping me on the back as he made his way over.

"Yep. Figured it was about time."

"Leif told me all about it, man. Glad you're gettin' out."

"How's he doin'?" I asked, referring to Leif.

"Good. We stopped by on the way over here. He's ready to get out of there, and he's makin' sure the nurses know it."

"What's up, little man?" Dale asked as he sauntered over, a smug smirk plastered on his face.

"Not much, old man," I retorted. Dale was the oldest of the four Connelly brothers. He was thirty-four, and Sean came in second at thirty-one. Their mother had spaced out their births pretty well, and I always told them it was because she'd been scared shitless of making another one. Dale was the one who picked on me most, just like he did Leif. Although we were roughly the same height and weight, he still liked to refer to me as little. I'd always taken it in stride.

Chaos

"Well, we better hop to it if we wanna get this done today," Sean stated, making his way over to Toby, greeting him by pulling him into a headlock. That was a sight to see, because Toby wasn't a little guy. Not by a long shot.

Everyone got to work, loading the boxes we brought from the house and packing up the tools in Sean's and Dale's trucks. Close to two hours later, we had everything strapped in, and from the looks of the six vehicles, I had a lot more shit than I'd thought I had.

Now it was time to get it the hell out of there.

Chapter Six

Payton

WHEN SEBASTIAN HAD GIVEN ME the key to his new house, I hadn't been sure what to think. He had blown me away when he'd announced that he'd bought a house. Of all the things I'd been expecting him to tell me when he'd showed up at my apartment yesterday, that wasn't it. Not that I wasn't happy for him. I honestly believed that getting his own place, away from Conrad, would allow them to put some much-needed distance between them. At least until Sebastian could come to terms with his suspicions.

But a key. For me.

At first, I'd thought he was just handing it over so that I could stop by after I picked up some groceries, something we had briefly discussed moments before he handed over the key. That wasn't his intention, he'd informed me. The key was for me. Anytime I wanted to come over, I had a way to get in.

I wouldn't admit this out loud, but receiving that key was better than jewelry. It held a significance that nothing else could compare to.

Especially after we'd had to spend so much time apart. For the better part of the last two weeks, the real world had intruded, and we'd found it more difficult to conjure up enough hours in the day to see each other. During the day, I went to work. In the evening, if I managed to sneak out of work early enough, Chloe and I would go visit Leif in the hospital, then return to the apartment and have a quick dinner before calling it a night. Toby had come over and stayed with Chloe a few times, and Sebastian had come over twice. Sebastian and I had quickly learned that I did not get nearly enough sleep when he was around, so we had agreed, at least for the time being, that we would spend weeknights at our own places.

But now… Now Sebastian was moving into his house, which was less than ten miles from my apartment, and the possibilities seemed nearly endless. I would get to see him whenever I wanted, and I could honestly say that I was not at all disappointed with that. If we saw each other more, I figured the temptation to stay up all night would eventually dissipate and we'd manage to sleep so that we could both work with all brain cells firing.

Then again, I wasn't sure I'd ever get enough of Sebastian. When I wasn't with him, I wanted to be. When I was with him, I didn't want to be anywhere else.

Chloe pulled the car into a space close to the front door of the superstore where we'd decided to go to pick up the things that Sebastian would need. Aside from food and kitchen gadgets, I figured he needed all sorts of stuff, and I wanted to make sure I bought things that he would like. Since I was using his credit card to fund the purchase, I also didn't want to go overboard, although he had informed me that money was no object. I tended to disagree.

In my world, money was an object. A big one. And I was going to show Sebastian just what it was like to live in my world. He might have a ginormous house and more land than a small town, but he could still get good deals.

"Come on. Let's do this," Chloe said before pushing open her door and hopping from the car.

The second I'd mentioned shopping, she had been practically skipping around like a kid. Unlike me, Chloe lived to shop, and in her defense, she was even more adept at finding bargains than I was, so I figured we would make a good team.

I grabbed a shopping cart when we walked through the automatic doors, and I was surprised to see that Chloe grabbed one as well. My eyes dropped to the basket in front of her before meeting hers once again.

"What? Did you really think it would all fit in one? You'll be lucky if we don't need another one."

I laughed, but there was no humor in it. Her words had me picturing just how many dollar signs we were going to be looking at before this was over.

The two of us started on the side of the store sectioned off with household goods. By the time we made it to the food, two hours had passed and one cart was overflowing. There were small kitchen appliances and gadgets, a few pots and pans, towels, sheets, pillows, rugs. I had even started a list of items that we figured we could find better deals on — not to mention nicer quality — online.

"Food time!" Chloe squealed, leading the charge with her empty shopping cart.

Shopping for food took us less time, but we still spent an hour going up and down every aisle until we had filled Chloe's cart and somehow managed to squeeze a few more items into mine.

"Have you told your mom that you're moving in with Sebastian?" Chloe asked as we pushed our carts down the cereal aisle.

I jerked my head around to look at her. "What are you talking about? I'm not moving in with him."

Chloe smiled. "You say that now."

"No, I say that always," I retorted.

"Come on, Payton. He clearly wants you to move in with him."

"He didn't say that," I told her, trying to recall our conversation about his new house. Never once had he mentioned me moving in.

"I think you should probably introduce him to your folks," Chloe said, passing me as I stood rooted to the floor.

She was right, I really should introduce him to my parents. I'd given that a lot of thought recently. Other than talking to my mother on the phone almost every day since I'd returned from Vegas, something we had always done, I hadn't gone to their house. Maybe because I feared my mother would be able to tell just how happy I was. I doubted she would figure that my new job had put the glow on my face or the spring in my step, and I really wanted to avoid an interrogation. She had just gotten over being mad at me for springing the Vegas trip on her without any notice. Regardless, Chloe was right. If I intended for this relationship to keep moving forward, I needed to introduce Sebastian to my mother and father.

As I pushed the cart down the aisle, I wondered just how they would react to him. I'd never brought a boy home to meet them. I made a mental note to text my mother to see about Sunday dinner. The thought made butterflies sprout in my stomach.

When we reached the checkout lanes at the front, I was dreading how much the purchase was going to be, and thankfully that had scattered all thoughts of Sebastian meeting my parents. There were more important things to worry about at the moment. Mainly, figuring out how I wasn't going to max out Sebastian's credit card with just one purchase.

"Don't think about it. Everything we bought was a necessity. And trust me, after looking at Sebastian's furniture, I don't think he's gonna care."

I tended to side with Chloe on that part. I had been a little overwhelmed when I'd walked into Sebastian's house to find it full of furniture. I hadn't had time to go on a tour, but the rooms I could see did have new furniture. The living room, dining room, breakfast nook, they all sported brand new pieces that looked expensive, and I figured the rest of the house probably looked the same. The one thing I noted about the things I did see was that Sebastian's furniture looked like it would be lived on, not used as decoration the way Conrad's house had been. While those few rooms hadn't been empty, I realized that he had purchased the basics, which meant eventually he would have to do some decorating. I figured he wasn't all that worried about that just yet, which was why I had only picked out a few things that would add a little color to the place.

The woman who checked us out was friendly and efficient, talking to us the entire time she rang up the items. And when I swiped the credit card and signed my name, I refused to look at the total. Chloe whispered in my ear that it wasn't nearly as bad as I thought, but I still couldn't bring myself to look.

We were loading the stuff into the trunk and the backseat of Chloe's car when she announced the final total.

"Why did you do that?" I exclaimed, recoiling when she revealed the dollar amount.

"What? I think the fact that you kept it under fifteen hundred was pretty remarkable."

I was pretty sure I was going to have a heart attack right there in the parking lot of the superstore where I had just spent one thousand, three hundred, forty-seven dollars and twenty-three cents.

"Holy shit," I mumbled, forcing the last bag into the backseat and closing the door before it spilled out onto the concrete.

"If you think about it, you really did well," Chloe assured me.

"I've never spent that much money in my life," I told her.

"Well, I get the feeling that Sebastian doesn't consider that a lot."

We'd see about that.

We arrived at Sebastian's to find cars and trucks parked all along the driveway, a couple backed into the four-car garage. Because we had so much to carry in, I told Chloe to pull into the garage, since that would be the closest to the kitchen. She eased into one of the empty bays and shut off the engine. Before I could get my seat belt unbuckled, Sebastian was at my door, pulling it open and smiling down at me.

"Hey, Angel," he whispered as he stood back, allowing me to get out. "Sorry, I'm sweaty," he said, cupping my face briefly and then pressing his lips to mine. His lip ring was cool as it pressed against my lower lip. "Do you need help with this?"

I glanced into the backseat before meeting his eyes again. "I'm so sorry. I spent over a thousand dollars. I don't know how it was that much, but—"

Sebastian pressed his mouth to mine again, effectively cutting off my rant. "It's good, Angel. I trust you."

Yeah, well, I wasn't sure I did. But now wasn't the time to argue. I could see that the trucks in the garage were still full of Sebastian's things, which meant the guys were unpacking. I figured I'd done enough damage, no need to get in the way of progress, too.

"We can get this stuff," I told him, forcing a smile I didn't feel.

"Seriously, Payton," Sebastian said, wrapping his arms around me and pulling me to him. "It's all good." He was right, he was sweaty. His navy-blue T-shirt was plastered to his chest, and his hair was wet, but it didn't bother me at all. In fact, I found I liked sweaty Sebastian. He was kind of hot.

"We're almost done with the cars out front, so we've just got this stuff left." He motioned to the two trucks in the garage. The beds were full of tools and a few boxes.

I nodded. "We'll help when we're done putting this stuff away," I told him, pecking him on the lips once more.

"Okay. And later, after all these people go home," Sebastian said, leaning down until his mouth pressed against my ear, "I'll give you a tour. We've got a few rooms to christen."

Heat infused me, bubbling in my veins and rushing up to my face.

He stepped back and smiled, his thumb sliding over my cheek. "Have I mentioned that I love it when you blush?"

"Hush," I told him and turned around to see Chloe watching us intently. Crap.

Without saying another word, I opened the back door of the car, careful to keep the items from pouring out onto the garage floor. As I set my mind on getting the car emptied and the groceries put away, I did my best not to think about the wicked promise Sebastian had made.

That wasn't nearly as easy as it looked.

Chapter Seven

Sebastian

I HAVE TO SAY THAT moving wasn't high on my list of things I enjoyed doing. Without the help of my friends, I doubt it would've been as easy as it was, either. But now that all my shit was inside my house, I realized I had a long way to go before I actually got settled in. The boxes had made it to the appropriate rooms, but that was about it.

It was late, and Sean and Dale had taken off, leaving Toby, Chloe, Aaron, and Garrett there with Payton and me. Everyone was still working, unpacking boxes and cleaning, but I was ready to call it a night. Not to sleep, but I figured everyone needed a break.

"How about pizza?" I asked as I joined the others in the kitchen, where Payton and Chloe were putting away the last of the things they'd bought at the store earlier. Once the girls had put away the food, Payton had insisted on helping to get the vehicles unloaded, which meant her purchases were still sitting in bags on the kitchen counter.

"I'm game," Toby announced.

"You're always game if it has to do with food," Chloe teased him.

Payton turned around and smiled. It never ceased to amaze me that she could steal my breath with just one look. I could actually imagine walking into that kitchen to see her beautiful face every single day for the rest of my life.

"I'll order," Payton offered. "If y'all will tell me what you want."

"You still have my credit card, right?" I asked, making my way over to her and putting my hands on her hips.

"Oh, crap. Yes. Let me get it."

When Payton tried to turn away, I held her in place and waited until she met my gaze again. "I wasn't asking for it back. Use it to pay for the pizza."

"No way," she insisted, shaking her head. "I'll pay. I've already spent too much of your money today." The last part she said in a whisper, but I was pretty sure everyone else in the room heard her, based on the chuckles from Chloe and Toby.

"That was stuff you bought for me, Payton." I leaned down and pressed my lips to her ear. "Let it go."

When I stood back up, meeting her eyes, I could see the concern was still there. I thought it was cute that she worried about how much money she'd spent today. I'd been with women who wouldn't have thought twice about spending every penny I had, and Payton was concerned about spending a thousand dollars although she'd probably bought out half the store. Some women wouldn't bat an eyelash at spending that amount on a fucking purse.

"What does everyone want?" I asked, looking at the other faces in the room, who were trying to pretend they weren't paying any attention to us.

Everyone rattled off their selection, and I took Payton's hand and led her into the foyer so I could get my cell phone. With her hand still in mine, I made my way to the stairs and dropped down onto one of the steps, pulling her until she sat in front of me, directly between my legs. I wrapped my arms around her, fumbling with my cell phone in front of her face. She leaned back and rested her head against my chest. It took a few minutes to figure out what pizza delivery place came out there, but finally I located their information and dialed the number. After I rattled off the order, I told the guy I'd pay cash when they delivered, and then I hung up the phone.

Unable to resist, I slid Payton's hair out of the way and pressed my lips to her neck. "Thank you for being here today."

She nodded, tilting her head slightly to give me better access to her soft, smooth skin. She smelled sweet, like vanilla, and my body hardened, thinking about sneaking her up to my bedroom and having my wicked way with her while the rest of our friends congregated in the kitchen. I knew I couldn't, but it didn't mean I wasn't thinking about it.

"Stay with me tonight?" I asked.

"Yes," she whispered, her arms looping around my lower legs, her warm hands pressing against my shins. She was sitting on the step just beneath the one I was on, cradled between my legs, and I wasn't sure that I wanted to move from that spot for the rest of the night. Every muscle in my body ached from hauling boxes for the last few hours, and if it weren't for the fact that I was starving, I probably would've thrown everyone out. Everyone except for Payton.

We were both silent for a moment; the only sound was the foursome in the kitchen laughing and joking. I rested my chin on the top of Payton's head, enjoying the brief moment I had with her alone.

"I have a question for you," Payton said a short time later, her hands sliding up and down my shins.

"What's that?" I asked.

She tilted her head back so that she could look up at me. "Would you consider meeting my parents?"

I smiled. I couldn't help myself. Before I'd met Payton, that sort of question would've thrown me for a loop. And the answer would've been an easy no, but for her, I found I'd do damn near anything, including meeting her parents.

"Is that what you want?"

"Yeah," she said, lowering her head once more. "They're gonna love you, Sebastian."

I wasn't so sure about that, but if I intended to spend the rest of my life with this woman, which I did, then I was going to have to face her parents at some point. "Then yes, I'd love to meet them."

"Okay," she said simply, making my grin widen.

I loved her. That was all there was to it.

"I heard Sean and Dale say they'd be back tomorrow," Payton said.

"Yeah. They're moving Leif's stuff in."

"Which room is he taking?" she asked. I liked that she asked that question. It meant she was thinking about us.

"He'll take one of the rooms downstairs," I answered, pointing toward the section of the house in front of us.

"How many rooms are down here?" she inquired.

"You haven't looked around yet?" I asked.

She shook her head.

"Well, we'll have to rectify that in a little while. How about we eat, then I'll show you around. And maybe after that, you can join me in the shower."

"Sounds like a good plan."

As it turned out, it was the best plan.

The pizza was delivered within thirty minutes and devoured in half that time. Chloe insisted on helping to clean up the mess before she and Toby left for the night. According to her, they were going back to her apartment. I noticed Aaron's frown when she announced the news, and I offered to let him stay in the guest room downstairs if he wanted. Surprisingly he declined my offer, but I later learned that he and Garrett had planned to go out for a couple of hours.

Chaos

Technically, since tonight would be the only night Payton and I had the house all to ourselves before Leif officially moved in, I was grateful that Aaron had passed. I wanted to spend the evening with Payton. Alone.

Payton walked everyone out while I locked up the rest of the house, making sure the garage doors were closed and the cars pulled in. We met up in the kitchen not long after, and just like earlier, I couldn't resist the urge to touch her. Pulling her into my arms, I pressed my lips to her forehead.

I hadn't thought about it much, but it seemed that the chaos in my head had died down considerably in the last couple of days. Maybe it was because of the move, knowing that I was taking the first step toward getting out from under Conrad's thumb, or maybe it was because I knew I'd get to spend more time with the woman I loved. Either way, I realized that a significant amount of tension had been released, and I wasn't as worked up as I usually was.

It was nice. It was also something I was beginning to get used to.

"Are you gonna give me the guided tour?"

"You really didn't look around?" I asked her, finding it hard to believe that she hadn't.

"I was waiting for you to show it to me."

"Okay, then. What're we waiting for?" I took her hand, linking her fingers with mine as I led her through the downstairs rooms. The place was still relatively empty, although I had managed to purchase furniture for every room. It was still missing something, but I wasn't too worried about it at the moment.

I showed Payton the two bedrooms on the main floor. They were in a wing all their own, both equipped with oversized private bathrooms. She looked around, seemingly studying the bones of the house, because there really wasn't much else to look at. Unlike the guesthouse I'd been staying in, there weren't any decorations on the counters, no plants sitting in corners, no art on the walls. Nothing that really personalized the space yet.

I was hoping Payton would help me with that.

"Living room," I said unnecessarily as we trekked back through the room that the house was pretty much centered around. "And you've seen the kitchen."

"That I have," she said.

With her in tow, I made my way to a doorway beneath the stairs. Pushing open the French doors, I stepped back and allowed her to enter. "This is my office."

"Your office?" she asked, giving me a questioning look.

"Yep. I figured I'd need one." I didn't elaborate as to why. I still had to figure out how I wanted to tell her what my plans were. As it was, I'd sprung the new house on her. I wasn't sure she'd be able to handle the newsflash that I was planning to quit working for my father and start my own business. I'd save that for another day.

"It's nice," she said, sliding her hand along the mahogany desk that sat in the center of the room. Aside from that, a file cabinet, matching credenza and bookcase, and an executive chair, there wasn't anything else in the room. No pens, no paper. Not even a computer.

Yet.

When she had looked her fill, I led her back through the living room, then the kitchen, and down a hallway off the kitchen, stopping to point out the laundry room. "Just making sure you get the whole experience," I told her when I backed her against the dryer, pressing my hips to hers before claiming her lips. When her arms came around my neck, I was hard-pressed to stop. I could imagine boosting her up onto the washing machine and fucking her until she was screaming my name.

But I withheld the urge. That could come later.

When we were both breathless, I pulled back and took her hand again. We ventured back down the hall and through two sets of doors, the last of which were made of glass. I pushed the door open and allowed Payton to walk inside before I followed.

"Holy crap." Payton looked at me once, then around the twenty-five-hundred-square-foot room that held an indoor pool and Jacuzzi. The outer walls and ceiling were constructed of tinted glass, and one wall held sliding windows that could be opened entirely to let the outside in. "That's a swimming pool."

I chuckled. "That it is."

"Inside," she stated, as though I hadn't noticed.

I laughed. "Yes, ma'am."

"You have two pools?"

"I do," I confirmed, smiling.

"I can see why you bought the house."

"You think it was for this?" I asked.

"It wasn't?"

"I didn't say that. I'm quite partial to this room. Especially if it means I can get you naked in that pool sometime in the near future."

"Is it heated?"

"If I said yes?"

"Then I'd say what are you waiting for?"

Holy shit, the woman was going to drive me completely insane. Because I just couldn't resist the temptation, I backed her against the glass doors, this time sliding my thigh between her legs as I resumed my position at her mouth.

When her hands reached for my T-shirt, I realized she wasn't joking. And quite frankly, I was too horny to deny her. We'd spent the last week away from each other because Payton insisted she needed to get more sleep in order to function at work. Which meant Sunday night through Thursday night were off limits for me to stay with her.

But now that it was Friday, I had a whole week to make up for.

Chapter Eight

Sebastian

SELF-CONTROL WAS SOMETHING I HAD a hard time maintaining when I was around Payton. She stripped me bare with just a look, and I found it difficult to restrain my hunger for her. Even after all these weeks, being with her was a test of my willpower, had been since the first time I'd seen her in the driveway of my father's house.

"Payton," I growled as I led her toward the pool.

Somehow, we had managed to lose our clothes, tossing them every which way while I continued to feed on her mouth, my hands caressing every inch of her. I backed down the steps into the water, pulling her with me until I was chest deep. At that point, I drew her closer, forcing her legs to wrap around my waist as I eased deeper into the water before backing her against the pool wall.

"I'm not sure I can be easy, Payton," I warned her, aligning my erection with her entrance, barely stemming the urge to slam into her, to feel the tight fit of her around my dick.

Payton scraped her nails down my back, jerking me to her, effectively lodging the head of my cock in her tight entrance. "Oh, fuck," I groaned.

"Not easy," she said breathlessly, her mouth sliding over my neck, her teeth nipping, sending electric shards of pleasure through my nerve endings.

Holding her hips, allowing the water to carry most of her weight, I managed to bury myself deep inside her, our bodies pressed together from hip to chest. We were close, so very close. But still, it wasn't enough, never enough. I didn't pull out, just merely rocked my hips forward, driving myself into her before slowly pulling back, never enough to pull out. I continued the slow, gyrating movement until she was moaning, her fingernails digging into my back. I never wanted to stop. This was the perfect moment, right here, alone with Payton. As much time as I planned to spend in that pool, I knew that there would never be a moment that would measure up to this.

"Sebastian, I need..." Payton lifted her head, closing her eyes and looking skyward as she tried to increase the friction between our bodies. "I need more. Oh, yes."

It'd been far too long since I'd been inside the heaven of Payton's body, and quite frankly, I wasn't sure how I was managing to hold myself together this long. She felt too damn good. The velvet grip of her body hugging my dick, the way her nails scored the skin of my shoulders, the look of sheer ecstasy on her beautiful face... I never wanted it to end.

But I could feel my release building, that ever-intensifying electric charge that started at the base of my spine and was climbing higher and higher until I knew I couldn't contain it any longer.

I powered my hips against Payton's, battling the opposing force of the water, keeping our bodies locked together to minimize the resistance. "I need you to come for me, Payton."

Payton moaned. "Harder."

I gave her what she wanted, and just when I thought I wouldn't be able to hold back, her body tensed, gripping me, ripping my orgasm from me. I growled, the animalistic sound reverberating through the open pool area.

Several minutes passed, but I didn't release Payton from my arms. I pulled out of her but didn't move away, content to hold her right there.

"I'd say that was a hell of a way to christen the pool," Payton whispered into my ear a short time later.

I smiled against her neck. "You think so?"

"Yep."

"Well, we've got plenty more rooms to go," I informed her.

Payton's soft chuckle filled me with the tranquility I'd come to crave when she was around me.

After using the pool for its intended purpose — swimming, albeit naked — for another half hour, Payton and I finally made our way back into the main part of the house. I hadn't unpacked my things, but most of the bathroom boxes had made their way to my bathroom. She got in the shower while I rummaged through one after another, trying to find shampoo and other necessities. After handing those off to her, I gave her a few minutes while I went in search of the clothes boxes, which I found downstairs in the living room. How the hell they'd ended up there, I had no idea.

I offered her a T-shirt and a towel before trading places with her. I showered off the chlorine and then joined her in the bedroom. She must've found the boxes with the linens, because the bed was made, complete with pillows.

Considering the time, we opted to call it a night, and for the first time in months, my brain shut off completely, and I managed to sleep without dreaming. It might not sound like much, but for me, it was something I'd definitely needed.

***

I woke alone in my bed the following morning. It took me several seconds to realize where I was, but after searching the room, trying to identify my surroundings, I fell back on my pillow and exhaled. Home. Payton wasn't in bed, but I could hear music coming from somewhere else in the house, so I assumed she was roaming around somewhere.

I pulled on a pair of jeans and made my way downstairs. She was in the kitchen, standing at the stove, glaring at the pan in front of her.

"Morning," I said, both greeting her and announcing my presence.

She turned to look at me, her eyebrows scrunched as though she was deep in thought.

"Something wrong?" I asked.

"Do you know how to make pancakes?" she asked.

I smiled.

"I do. Why? Is Toby coming over?"

Payton looked confused at first, but then her face softened and her shoulders relaxed. "Something like that."

I still gave Toby a hard time about the first breakfast we'd had at Payton's apartment. Turned out that Chloe's Saturday morning ritual involved making pancakes, something Toby didn't particularly care for. Although he'd forced them down until I'd called him on it. It still amused me the lengths the guy would go to for Chloe.

All of the ingredients were sitting on the counter, and the pan was on the stove, but that was about as far as Payton had gotten. I found it endearing that she was trying to cook breakfast for me, although it was clear she didn't have a clue how to make that happen.

"Want my help?" I offered.

She nodded, her smile widening.

I backed her against the opposite counter, kissing her good morning as I lifted her up to sit on the granite top.

"I'm not sure how I'll be able to cook from here," she informed me, cupping my face when I released her mouth.

"You can supervise," I told her, taking her in from head to toe. She was still wearing my T-shirt and nothing else. It was the sexiest thing I'd ever seen.

"I think I can manage that," she replied when my eyes returned to hers.

Cooking in my own kitchen with Payton sitting close by was another one of those moments that took me by surprise. It was so natural it almost felt as though we'd been doing it all of our lives. I found that was the case with a lot of what we did. Being with her just felt right. She made me whole, made me forget for a little while that I wasn't, made it almost possible to believe my life hadn't been ripped to shreds so many years ago.

Without my smile slipping, I managed to make the pancakes and deliver them to the table before waiting for Payton to join me. She went to the refrigerator and pulled out two glasses of orange juice that she had clearly placed in there earlier.

We ate while we discussed the plans for the day, what boxes we would work on unpacking, when Leif's brothers would arrive with his things, when Leif would arrive. It was all normal Saturday morning stuff, but even I could sense that we were avoiding the deeper conversation. For the last two weeks, Payton had given me space, not questioning me in regard to the revelation I'd made about my father, but I knew she wasn't going to be able to last much longer before her curiosity won out.

Although I didn't want the topic to bring down the mood, I realized now was the perfect time to pick it back up.

"How'd it go at work this week?" I asked, not sure how to start.

Payton looked up from her plate, meeting my gaze. The humor that'd been reflected in her eyes just a few moments ago disappeared far too quickly for my peace of mind. She didn't answer right away, choosing to move the rest of her pancake around in the syrup on her plate.

"Trevor started working there this week."

I sat up straight, dropping my fork onto my plate, the metal against glass making a loud clatter. "What?"

Payton nodded, as though confirming that I'd heard her correctly. "Conrad brought him up to his office on Wednesday."

"Why didn't you say something before now?" I asked.

"What was I going to say, Sebastian? I knew that you would be upset and ... well, I don't particularly want to be the one to piss you off."

She had a good point. I thrust both hands through my hair and held my head, staring at the wall across from me. After taking a deep breath, I lowered my arms to the table. "Did he say anything to you?"

"Who? Trevor? Or Conrad?"

I lifted an eyebrow, my only response.

Payton sighed. "After he met with Conrad, Trevor came out of your father's office and tried to talk to me. I pretended to be on the phone. Unfortunately, he waited, and I couldn't pretend for long. He told me that he looked forward to working with me. I asked him what he'd be doing because I doubted I would see him much, and he told me he was going to take over some of the upcoming projects."

"The prototype," I mumbled. "Conrad brought Trevor in to replace me." Why that made me smile, I had no idea, but I could see Payton's confusion, so I explained. "It looks like my father was either expecting me to leave or he was going to send me packing. Either way, it all falls in line with my plans."

"What does that mean?" she asked, gently laying her fork on her plate and turning toward me.

"It means that things are working themselves out," I told her. The conversation had already derailed from my original intent, and I didn't want to keep it going in the opposite direction.

Payton looked around the kitchen briefly before meeting my eyes once more. "Is that what this is? You're making a clean break?"

"Something like that," I admitted softly. "Look, Payton," I began, wanting to explain to her just why I felt the need to get away from him. Before I could get the rest of the words out, she stood. I thought for a moment that she was going to walk away from me, refusing to hear what I had to say. She surprised me when she came to stand in front of me.

I turned sideways in my chair, and she lowered herself to my knee, cupping my face in her hands. "You don't have to explain to me why you're doing this. I get it. I might not understand everything, but I get this."

"You're not mad?" I asked, surprised.

"No. I'm a little relieved, actually. I hate how Conrad treats you. It bothers me more than I can let on. I can't say that, over the course of the last two weeks, I haven't considered walking out on my job and never coming back."

"That's always an option," I said quickly.

Payton squeezed my face gently. "No, it's not. Not until we get some answers. And we *are* going to get some answers."

Relieved that she wasn't pissed and that she understood my reasoning, I cupped her face in my hands, sliding my thumbs over her cheeks before pulling her closer to me. I pressed my lips to hers gently, then more insistently.

I wanted to tell her so many things, starting with the fact that I wanted to spend the rest of my life with her, but I knew now wasn't the time. There were too many things going on, too many answers I still needed before I could ever expect anyone to want to spend their life with me and the chaos that my life entailed. But after this conversation, I had no doubt that if ever there was a woman who could handle me, Payton was that woman.

And I had every intention of making sure she knew just how much she meant to me. For the rest of my life.

Chapter Nine

Payton

WHEN I TOLD SEBASTIAN ABOUT Trevor, I had been nervous about how he would respond. That was the main reason I hadn't told him the day that it'd happened. His initial reaction hadn't been far off the mark of my expectations. He was pissed. I knew he was. I couldn't say that I had been excited to see Trevor standing in front of my desk that day, either. The guy gave me the creeps, and I wasn't quite sure why that was.

At first, I thought maybe I was judging him based on what Sebastian had told me about his mother. Yes, admittedly, I was grasping at every possible answer to what Sebastian suspected. Had Conrad had something to do with Sebastian's mother's death? Or possibly Lauren? What if Lauren had paid Trevor to do the dirty work? The last thought had given me pause, so I had done a little digging.

So maybe I'd been watching too many crime shows on television, but my brain had linked all of the possibilities together until I had convinced myself that was the only answer. Then again, I wasn't particularly fond of Trevor, so it was possible I was coming up with anything to explain the strange reaction I had to him.

Sure, as I had rummaged through the electronic files on my computer, I'd known that I could probably lose my job if Conrad found out that I'd done some digging into personnel files, but I'd been so consumed by the possibility I hadn't thought about the consequences until after I'd pulled up the employee file for Trevor Lowell Webster.

What I'd found didn't tell me a lot. As it turned out, most of his application had been left blank, but I was able to get his birth date. Not that I was relieved in the least. Trevor was older than I'd thought. After meeting him in Vegas, I had been under the impression he was closer to my age. That wasn't the case. He was thirty-two years old — seven years older than Sebastian — which would've made him twenty-one at the time of Sebastian's mother's death.

The guy had creeped me out from the get-go, but now... Now I would pretty much do anything to avoid being anywhere near him. What I hadn't bothered to tell Sebastian was that since that first day that I'd seen Trevor in Conrad's office, he had waited for me to get off work. Every day. Although I refused his offer, he insisted on walking me to my car. Every freaking day.

I knew that was information Sebastian would want to have, but I feared what he would do if he found out that Trevor had taken to stalking me. There was so much going on right now, with the accident, Sebastian moving, and now Leif coming home, I really didn't want to put Sebastian back on edge. We would figure this out, I knew we would. And in the meantime, whenever Trevor was around, I would be extremely cautious.

"I was thinking we could have dinner with my parents on Monday night," I told Sebastian now, still sitting on his lap.

"Monday works," he said, a smile tipping the very corners of his mouth.

"I tried for tomorrow, but they've got something to take care of."

"I'm not arguing, Payton," Sebastian said firmly. "I'm looking forward to meeting them. The day doesn't matter to me."

I don't know why I felt compelled to explain myself. I guess I was just nervous about the entire thing. What would they think of Sebastian? What would Sebastian think of them? Like I said, I'd never done this before. Cupping his face, I decided to tell him as much. When I finished the statement, his eyes widened, and the small smile that had formed when I changed the subject only grew wider.

"Never?" he asked. "You've never brought a guy home to meet your parents?"

"Not unless Aaron counts. He was my prom date."

Sebastian's smile lit up his eyes, and I liked that he was happy about the news.

"Well, if I have anything to say about it, I'll be the only guy you ever bring home to meet your parents."

I liked the sound of that more than I could admit. And just to make sure he didn't see the tears that formed in my eyes, I pressed my lips to his. And I didn't release him until I managed to get them under control. By then, something else was completely out of control.

But that feeling I'd grown accustomed to.

The morning flew by faster than I'd anticipated, but mainly because Sebastian had insisted that we go shopping while we waited for the others to arrive to deliver Leif's stuff. *We* being him and me. He gave me an excuse that he needed to pick up a few things that I had forgotten at the store yesterday. As it turned out, that excuse had been bogus.

I should've figured that out in the beginning, though, because I had spent over one thousand freaking dollars. I still couldn't believe it'd cost that much, but I had stopped apologizing for it after Sebastian had scolded me the night before. Although I'd conceded, I knew deep down that I'd never let that happen again, no matter if he said it was okay or not.

As it turned out, I hadn't forgotten anything that *he* needed yesterday. What he wanted to pick up was for me. A toothbrush, shampoo, conditioner, body wash ... all of the necessary essentials for me to stay over at his house without the need to bring anything. He even attempted to buy me clothes, but I drew the line there, informing him that if he was serious, I would bring over a couple of pairs of my own clothes to leave there. I didn't need anything new. However, since I didn't keep spare toothbrushes or other bathroom items at my apartment, I allowed him to buy them for me. It seemed to make him happy. Why, I wasn't sure. I didn't question it.

The fact that Sebastian wanted me to feel at home at his place warmed my heart in ways I never expected. Not that it didn't feel a little overwhelming, but not any more than the feelings I had developed for him. For the last week, while I lay in bed at night alone, I would think about those particular feelings, trying to dissect them, understand what they were composed of. Did I really love Sebastian? Or was I trying to save him? And if the latter was in fact true, what was I trying to save him from? A legitimate evil? Or himself?

Unfortunately, I could only come up with questions, no answers. I was afraid to talk to Aaron or Chloe about my feelings for fear that they would warn me away from Sebastian. Regardless of what my emotions were comprised of, I still loved Sebastian. That was a fact.

And I considered myself strong enough to make the right decisions. I'd never been the type of girl to lean on a man or to try to find a sense of my own worth from the kindness bestowed upon me by the opposite sex. I didn't need that to make me feel good about myself.

It all boiled down to the fact that I had never been in love before. And what I felt for Sebastian was far stronger than anything I had ever expected to feel for anyone.

Now, as I sat on the couch in Sebastian's living room, watching people move about — Sean, Dale, and Sebastian unloading the trucks that contained Leif's personal belongings, Chloe and Aaron making dinner after the guys had grumbled that they were going to be starving after the move, and Toby and Garrett getting Leif situated in the recliner in front of the television — I realized I was exactly where I wanted to be. In a weird way, Sebastian's new place felt like home to me.

Then again, that could've very well been because Sebastian was there. I'd noticed that I felt at home no matter where we were, as long as we were together.

Pushing up off the couch, I approached Leif when Garrett and Toby finally gave him a breather. They'd been fussing over him from the minute they'd brought him in the house, asking him if he needed something to eat or drink, did he want to watch television, was he warm enough? They'd supplied an endless barrage of questions, and I could see the relief on Leif's face now that they were walking away.

"How are you doing?" I asked softly, glancing over at the two men as they made their way to the kitchen.

"Kinda feel like someone's getting ready to change my diaper or some shit."

I smiled at Leif. "That bad, huh?"

Leif leaned toward me and lowered his voice. "Would you do me a favor?"

I squatted down beside his chair, stabilizing myself by holding on to the arm. "What's that?" I asked, just as quietly.

"Could you maybe drop a few hints that my legs aren't broken, I've got full use of my arms, and, if all else fails, my mouth still works, so I could always ask for something if I need it?"

"I can do that," I told Leif, loving that his sense of humor was still intact. "Give it a day or two. They'll be giving you shit for not helping out around here. Then they'll bitch about having to move all your furniture without your help."

Leif laughed, holding his ribs as he did. "Don't make me laugh. It still hurts."

"Sorry," I said, grinning. "But if it's any consolation, we really are glad you're home."

"Me, too. If I never see the inside of a hospital again, it'll be too soon."

I stared at Leif for a moment. There'd been one thing on my mind for the last couple of weeks, but I had never managed to force out the question. Now that Leif was home and hopefully the horrors of the crash had abated somewhat, I found myself needing to ask.

"Can I ask you something?"

"As long as it doesn't involve you getting me something, then sure," Leif said, his dark eyes locking with mine.

"Why did you take Sebastian's car that night? For the race?"

Leif didn't answer me right away, his attention turning to the raised voices in the hallway. When he turned back to me, he looked as though he was choked by emotion. "I'd been having issues with my brakes for a while. I needed to get 'em replaced but hadn't done it. I wanted in the race but didn't figure the car would handle well, so when I stopped by to talk to Sebastian, I noticed he'd left the Camaro. So I took it."

Leif sat motionless for a moment, but then he continued.

"If I'd driven my Mustang, I'd be dead right now. The doctors told me that the roll cage saved my life."

Payton remembered that Garrett had mentioned the same thing.

Leif looked right at me. "Did Sebastian tell you that he had a dream that the Camaro exploded during a race?"

I narrowed my eyes on him. "No, he didn't."

"Yeah," Leif said, exhaling slowly. "Turns out that was why he didn't take the Camaro. He thought he'd avoid disaster if he didn't drive it. Apparently he'd had the dream more than once."

Holy crap.

Sebastian hadn't shared that little bit of information with me, but now that I thought about it, it explained why Sebastian had been trying to assume the blame for Leif's accident.

But it was just that … an accident. It was unfortunate, but Sebastian was no more to blame than Leif was.

"I don't even know what to say to that," I told Leif.

"Nothing to say. I'm alive and breathing. That's all that matters."

That was true. Having Leif home was all that mattered. I snagged the remote from the coffee table and handed it to Leif. "If you do need anything, just yell. I'll make sure someone comes running."

Leif nodded, looking down at the remote briefly. When his eyes slid back to mine, I saw a question reflected there.

Pushing him to open up wasn't going to do any good. I'd learned that from Sebastian, so I just sat there, willing my legs not to go to sleep beneath me.

"Have you ... uh..." Leif glanced over at the kitchen before returning his attention to me. "Has anyone talked to Aaliyah?" Leif's eyes bored into me as though he was trying to figure out whether my answer would be a lie or not.

I had no reason to lie to him. "I tried calling her right after the accident. I left her a message to call me, but I didn't tell her what it was about." It was my turn to glance back to see if anyone was listening. When I noticed no one else was in the room, I lowered my voice and said, "I don't think she ever got that message, Leif."

His dark eyebrow lifted slightly. I didn't break the eye contact, willing him to think about what I'd just said. His eyes darted back to the remote briefly but then back to my face. A subtle nod was all I got in response.

I knew that Sebastian hadn't told Toby or Leif his suspicions about his father, but he would eventually have to. Especially if there was any chance that we were going to figure out just what had happened to Sebastian's mother. If Conrad was somehow responsible — I still shuddered at the thought — then we were going to need all the help we could get. And being that Leif's mother's boyfriend just happened to be a detective, I fully intended to encourage Sebastian to open up to his best friends soon.

Patting Leif's hand, I pushed to my feet and forced a smile. "If you need anything, just let me know."

"Thanks, Payton."

Heading to the kitchen, I glanced back at Leif once more. I knew Sebastian and I had agreed to leave Aaliyah out of this for the time being, but I truly believed it was time for her to know. She was probably going to be pissed, because despite what might've happened between them in Vegas, I knew without a doubt that Aaliyah cared about Leif.

The question was, who was trying to keep Aaliyah away from him?

And why?

Chapter Ten

Payton

MONDAY MORNING CAME WAY TOO quickly. When I'd walked into the office at five o'clock in the morning, I had even tried to recall what had happened to make the weekend go by so fast. At that time, my brain had been little more than a foggy jumble of thoughts, so I'd given up, realizing it wasn't worth the effort until after I'd had coffee.

Now, as I sat at my desk, realizing it was a little before seven, waiting ever so patiently for Conrad to arrive, my sleep-filled brain became less of a mess. Every event since Friday night at the grocery store rushed back to me, leaving me feeling incredibly content. It didn't even matter that Conrad was an hour late and I could've slept in if he'd just given me some sort of notice.

The past weekend could easily be categorized under the heading *Best Weekend Ever*. Helping Sebastian move into his new house, spending almost every minute with him... It had felt so incredibly normal. Mundane even. And last night when I'd gone back to my apartment, I had missed being with him. Sebastian and I had spent an entire weekend together, and it had felt almost as though we were playing house. Only we weren't playing. That was real life. During the brief times there hadn't been someone else lurking about the house, when we hadn't been making love, we'd been in the pool or the hot tub. Granted, we'd made love there, too, so that wasn't a very accurate statement.

On Sunday, we had lounged around on the couch, watching the Bourne movies with Leif, ordering out for food rather than cooking. The three of us had shared breakfast and lunch, pretty much vegging out most of the morning. Then Sebastian had surprised me when he'd made me follow him to his bedroom. Instead of getting naked and sweaty like I'd originally thought we would, he found some cheesy chick flick on TV, and we'd cuddled in his bed and watched it while eating popcorn. Like I said, very mundane.

And perfect.

Chaos

Before I was ready, the day had been ending and I'd known I had to go home. Sebastian had seemed reluctant to let me go, but after I'd reminded him what time I had to be at work, he'd given up trying to convince me to stay.

When I'd gotten back to my apartment, Aaron had been there watching television. Alone. I'd interrupted him long enough to ask where Garrett was. He told me he'd gone home, and the statement had been followed by a wide grin. Seemed that the two of them were hitting it off, spending quite a bit of time together since Garrett had been home for the last two weeks. In the beginning, I had been a little relieved that Leif's brother was on tour and would be away for a few weeks, but now, after seeing Aaron so happy, I kind of wished Garrett could stay home a little longer. Admittedly, I just hoped Aaron was fully over Mark. That debacle was still fresh, and Aaron was the type of guy who would jump into something new too quickly and then eventually feel guilty. He was one of those men who would try to come up with a way to sabotage his own relationship.

If something was going to happen between Aaron and Garrett that was going to result in a lasting relationship, they needed to take things slow.

Then again, who was I to predict how anyone's love life would turn out? It wasn't like I had a lot of experience in that arena. This thing I had with Sebastian was just as new, just as fresh, and there were moments I felt like I was in over my head.

But I loved him.

Around eight o'clock, when Chloe hadn't come home, I'd sent her a text only to learn that she was going to stay at Toby's. We'd shot messages back and forth for a little while, but then I'd let her go so she could spend time with her man.

It seemed we were all easing our way into relationships, and since I didn't have a single regret about being with Sebastian, I knew I couldn't pass off my fears to my friends, so I vowed to be happy for them. They were adults; they knew how to take care of themselves. Not to mention, every waking moment when I wasn't with Sebastian, I was thinking about him, which meant I had little time to worry about anyone else.

I was jolted from my thoughts when Conrad came up the stairs from the main floor. I glanced up from my computer screen to see him. He shot a look my direction, and I could tell that something was different. Something was wrong. I could feel it in the air that crackled around him.

"Hold my calls, Payton," he ordered as he stormed across the reception area and into his office. He slammed the door before I had a chance to say anything.

As was my routine, I pushed to my feet, keeping a cautious eye on his door while I made his coffee. Since the day I'd started this job, I had always waited ten minutes and then rapped on his door to bring him his coffee, but today, I didn't think that was a good idea. Although, based on the brief glimpse I'd seen of him, he could use a cup. Or two.

I weighed my options as I sat at my desk, the coffee sitting in the carafe behind me. Should I email him and ask if he wanted me to bring it in? Did I just wait until he opened his door?

Shit.

Unfortunately, I didn't have to wait long for my answer, because Conrad's door flew open and he stuck his head out. "Do we have a problem, Payton? Is there any reason you're sitting there and not doing your job? Do I need to find someone else who can do something as simple as bring me coffee?"

I felt like he'd slapped me across the face. Hard.

I'd never been talked to like that. Not only was he yelling at me, he was scowling.

I was affronted and angry, but none of that was apparent when the tears formed in my eyes. That's what happened when I got mad — I cried. I took a deep breath and jumped to my feet, moving to the coffeepot as fast as my feet would take me while saying, "No, sir" in as steady a voice as I could muster.

When I turned back around, Conrad wasn't standing in his doorway, but he hadn't closed the door behind him. I swallowed hard and tried to regain some of my composure before forcing my feet to carry me to his office.

I set the coffee mug in the same place I usually put it and then turned to walk out.

"Hold on, Payton."

I stopped but didn't turn around to face him. "Yes, sir?"

"Why don't I have my itinerary for tomorrow's trip on my desk?"

This time I did turn around to look at him. Was he serious?

Apparently he was, because he was still grimacing, his forehead wrinkled and his ears red. Was he mad? At me?

Oh, crap. Maybe this was about Sebastian moving out of the guesthouse. It was possible he had found out even though Sebastian had informed me that he hadn't told him personally. Yet.

But would he really be that upset? At me? So much so that he would yell at me first thing?

"I'll get it, sir," I mumbled and then pointed my feet toward the door. I hadn't made it far when he called me back again.

"Shut the door and have a seat, Payton."

My first thought: Could I make it down the stairs and out the front door before Conrad could catch me?

My second thought: Had I bothered to update my resume after I'd started working for Trovato, Inc.?

My third thought: No, I couldn't get out fast enough, and no, I hadn't bothered to update anything. Now I was going to have to endure Conrad's wrath and pray he didn't fire me, because if he did, I was going to have to update my resume pretty damn quickly.

I forced my feet to move forward, secretly peeking outside his office, hoping someone might be out there.

Maybe I could create a distraction.

Closing the door, I realized that probably wasn't a viable option.

After the door clicked shut, I took a deep breath and moved across the room, gracefully lowering myself into the chair facing Conrad's desk, opposite him. When I looked up, Conrad was staring at me sternly, his forearms resting on his desk, his hands clasped together in front of him.

"I need to ask you a question, Payton."

I nodded. My voice had buried itself deep inside of me, refusing to come out until it knew it was safe, leaving me with no other option.

"I assume you were aware that Sebastian moved out of my house."

I still couldn't find my voice, so I couldn't say anything. Since technically Conrad's words were phrased as a statement and not a question, I figured I was safe.

For a minute.

"Were you aware of this?"

Okay, there was the question.

I nodded.

As expected, Conrad didn't appear too thrilled with my lack of verbal response. I cleared my throat and replied with a slightly off-key yes.

"And were you aware that he was going to quit his job this morning?"

Now, that I did *not* know, and I was pretty sure my expression announced my surprise.

Conrad leaned back in his chair, resting his hands on his lap as he studied me. "Payton, I realize that you and Sebastian have established some sort of a relationship."

I didn't reply, assuming he didn't need an answer.

"I know you probably don't want to hear this, but—"

Suddenly my voice returned, and I managed to stop Conrad before he continued. "Sir, with all due respect, I'm not so sure this is an appropriate conversation to be having."

Conrad seemed to ponder that for a moment, but he continued, clearly believing that he knew best. "I'm not sure what's going on between you and Sebastian, but I need to warn you that—"

I stood abruptly. "Sir, I'm not comfortable with this." That wasn't what I really wanted to tell him, but I figured informing my boss that I didn't want to hear him say anything negative about Sebastian was probably not going to get me any points, either. "Now, if you don't mind, I need to get back to work."

I made it as far as the door before Conrad spoke again.

"You can believe what you want, Payton. And you can ignore all of us who are trying to warn you, but Sebastian isn't stable."

I pivoted on my heel and glared at Conrad. "I would appreciate if you would keep your opinions to yourself."

With that, I pulled open the door, ready to return to my desk, but I came face-to-face with Trevor, who was standing just outside the door. He appeared surprised at first, but that was followed by an unnerving grin. I squeezed between him and the door and returned to my desk. I was tempted to grab my purse and leave, but my lunch break wasn't for another couple of hours.

Which meant I had no other choice but to suck it up for now.

Chapter Eleven

Payton

LUCKY FOR ME, IT APPEARED that Conrad was expecting Trevor, because by the time I returned to my desk, Conrad's door was closed and Trevor was on the opposite side. I stared at my cell phone lying on my desk, wondering whether I should call Sebastian, or at the very least send him a text.

I chose to do neither.

No matter how hard I tried, I couldn't come up with something to tell him. I didn't want to send Sebastian into a rage, and as much as I disagreed with Conrad about Sebastian being unstable, I couldn't deny the fact that he did have a temper. And right now, with Sebastian's thoughts dwelling on the idea of his father having something to do with his mother's death, it wasn't going to do any good.

Maybe by the time I got home that evening, I could come up with a logical way to explain to him what had happened without sending him spiraling out of control. Although, no matter how I worded it, he wasn't going to take kindly to Conrad confronting me about him.

But we both knew that this was the reason I was still there. If it were up to me, I would've quit the day after Sebastian had informed me of his suspicions. Sure, I believed in the whole *everyone is innocent until proven guilty* stuff, but things just weren't adding up for me. And by being there at Trovato, Inc., I had an in when we needed it. I was hoping that I would be able to dig up the information that would be necessary to prove Sebastian's theories one way or the other. He needed closure, and though I prayed that Conrad was not responsible for Sebastian's mother's death, I had to admit that I was already just as suspicious.

My desk phone rang, and I glanced down at the flashing light. I didn't want to answer it, but that was part of my job description, so I took a deep breath and willed my hands to stop shaking as I reached for the handset. "Conrad Trovato's office, how may I help you?" I answered, my tone reflecting some of the anxiety that still raced through my bloodstream.

"Payton."

I stilled. I'd been answering Conrad's phone long enough to recognize many voices, and the one on the other end of the line was not one I was hoping to hear from. Ever.

"Yes, Mrs. Trovato?" I replied, clenching my teeth together.

"Is Conrad in?"

"Yes, ma'am. But he's in a meeting. I can have him return your call as soon as he's finished."

"Thank you, Payton."

The iciness was even present in Lauren's phone voice. Truth be told, the woman freaked me out. I wasn't sure what it was about her, but I detected something malicious in her gaze.

I was just about to hang up when she spoke again. "One more thing, Payton."

"Yes, ma'am?" I asked hesitantly.

"I heard about Sebastian quitting. I'd like you to relay a message to him for me."

I didn't respond, because I couldn't agree to that. It all depended on what she had to say.

"I'd like you to tell him that he has now severed all ties with this family, and I would greatly appreciate if he would keep it that way. His volatile behavior has no business in my family."

I sucked in a breath, my heart pounding against my ribs.

My family.

That was the one word I had noted above all others.

"Are you there, Payton?" Lauren asked.

"I am," I assured her, trying to regulate my breathing.

"Can you give him that message?"

I swallowed hard, glancing up at the closed door to Conrad's office. I turned slightly in my chair, hoping to muffle my voice enough so that no one else would hear me. "Mrs. Trovato, I'm sorry to say this, but your request is not in my job description."

"Payton, *dear*," Lauren's tone hardened even more, "if you plan to have a job, you'll do as I ask. Understood?"

I sat back up straight in my chair and stared out at the empty waiting area in front of me. "No, ma'am. I don't think I do."

I hung up the phone without waiting for her to say another word.

Chaos

Putting a nail in my employment coffin early on a Monday morning probably wasn't the best way to start the week, but at that moment, I really didn't give a shit. First, Conrad had confronted me, and then Lauren had threatened me. I knew I should've just told her what she wanted to hear, but I hadn't been lying when I said I wouldn't relay her message to Sebastian.

That coldhearted bitch had another thing coming if she thought I would do her dirty work.

Did I think she was capable of getting me fired? Absolutely.

Did I think she was capable of trying to break me and Sebastian up? Absolutely.

Did I think I was going to let her get away with either? Absolutely not.

In fact, Lauren Trovato had just given me the incentive that I needed to figure out this whole mystery of Sebastian's mother's death. Since I knew Sebastian and I weren't capable of doing that alone, I accepted the fact that it was time we banded together.

I grabbed my cell phone and pulled up Sebastian's contact info. I sent him a short text.

Are we still on for dinner at my parents'?

I didn't have to wait long for a response.

Of course.

Good. I was thinking that I might stay the night tomorrow night.

After typing the message and hitting send, I waited patiently.

You're welcome to spend the night every night.

Although my heart expanded in my chest, I replied, remembering the original reason for my text.

Do you think we can have dinner at your place tomorrow night?

Sebastian replied almost immediately. *Absolutely. Should I have dinner ready when you arrive?*

I replied right back. *Depends.*

On?

Whether or not you can cook a meal for seven.

Seven?

Yes, seven.

What's going on, Payton?

I waited a beat before I sent the last message. But as soon as I did, I felt a little better.

It's time we talk. To everyone.

Sebastian's response didn't come back as quickly as I would've liked, but ten minutes later, I received a confirmation from him. A simple okay was all I got. Through that one word, I could practically feel Sebastian's tension. But he knew as well as I did that we had a much better chance of figuring this out if we asked our friends for help. And the people who would be there tomorrow night cared about him. There was no doubt in my mind that they would support him.

But tonight, I got to look forward to introducing him to my parents. I tried to ignore the knot that formed in my stomach.

I found Sebastian sitting in his truck in the parking lot of my apartment complex when I got home from work earlier than usual. I had informed Conrad that I needed to leave work early after Trevor had left his office, and though I don't think Conrad had been too impressed with my candidness, after our run-in that morning, I didn't much care.

As it was, I'd spent the better part of the day trying to find a good way to tell Sebastian what had happened. Since I never came up with anything, I decided to focus all of my attention on dinner with my parents. I had even texted my mother, giving her a few more details about the guy I was bringing. She, of course, had called me right away.

Yes, I'd surprised her with the news, but there hadn't been an ounce of disappointment in her tone. She'd been curious as to who he was, how we'd met, how long I'd known him, and most important, why I hadn't mentioned him until now. I managed to answer all of her questions, except for the last one. I didn't want to tell her that I was a little hesitant to introduce them only because I didn't want to scare Sebastian off.

Then the moment had arrived. Based on the way he held my hand and talked all the way to my parents' house, I don't think he was at all intimidated. I was more than a little relieved.

Sebastian parked his truck on the street and came around to help me out. I'd been paying attention to him so much that I hadn't realized my father was standing on the porch, watching us intently. Luckily, I didn't try to jump Sebastian or vice versa, because that would've been a little embarrassing.

We walked up to the porch, hand in hand. I was just about to make the introductions when my father spoke up first.

"Hal Fowler," he said as he thrust his hand in Sebastian's direction.

"Nice to meet you, sir. Sebastian Trovato."

My father immediately looked at me, his eyebrows scrunching together. I smiled, a little embarrassed.

"Nice truck," Hal said, looking over my head at Sebastian's cherry-red '65 Chevrolet parked at the curb in front of my parents' house.

"Thank you, sir."

"You restore it yourself?"

"Yes, sir."

Realizing that I wasn't part of the male bonding conversation going on, I released Sebastian's hand and excused myself. "I'm going to tell my mother we're here."

Sebastian nodded, making his way up onto the porch to stand beside my father. I was a little hesitant to leave them alone, but they seemed to be hitting it off fairly well.

So far.

I knew my father was going to have questions about Sebastian. Especially about the fact that his last name was Trovato. Back when I had questioned my father on whether or not Conrad had a son, he'd made reference to a rumor that had once been around. I guess he was about to realize that the rumor was true.

Or he would think Sebastian was Conrad's nephew.

"Mom?" I called as I made my way to the back of the house toward the kitchen.

"In here," she called back.

I found her in the kitchen, wearing an apron just as I'd expected, her hair pulled up on top of her head. She'd been working when I'd talked to her earlier, which she did out of their house, so the jeans and sweatshirt she wore now were probably the same outfit she'd been wearing all day.

"Where is he?" she asked, looking past me when I stepped into the kitchen.

"On the front porch with Dad. They're admiring his truck."

"What does he drive?" my mother asked as she drained the pot of spaghetti noodles into the sink.

I explained what he drove, and she replied that their conversation could very well take a while knowing my father.

While I waited anxiously for Sebastian to come inside and meet my mother, I set the table, repeatedly glancing down the hall as though he might materialize at any moment.

A good five minutes passed before my father and Sebastian joined us in the kitchen. My father did the honors of introducing Sebastian to my mother, and I stood back watching the whole thing with a grin. I was pretty sure that in the first ten minutes, my father had grown quite fond of Sebastian.

"Dinner's ready," my mother informed them.

I watched her watching Sebastian.

I wasn't sure what I had expected, but I had to admit that the whole thing wasn't nearly as nerve-wracking as I'd anticipated. Sebastian joined me at the dining room table, pulling out my chair for me and waiting for my mother to take her seat before he lowered himself into the spot beside me. Food was passed around, and plates were filled before my mother started in with the questions. I was surprised she lasted that long.

"So, Sebastian, how'd you and Payton meet?" my mother asked.

I shot her a glance that said, "Really?" She merely replied with a tilt of her eyebrow. The sort of look that said, "I'm your mother; I can ask any question I want."

Sebastian glanced over at me and smiled. "She came to my father's estate to pick up his cell phone. She thought I was the mechanic."

Okay, so maybe I hadn't told my mother in those exact words.

"Is that right?"

"Yes, ma'am. Then I ran into her at a sports bar a few days later. I convinced her to let me take her out for ice cream."

My face heated and I focused on twirling my spaghetti around my fork. The way Sebastian spoke of how we'd met with such confidence did strange things to me. It cemented every feeling I'd ever had for him.

"You said your father's estate," Hal said. "Conrad Trovato is your father?"

I glanced over at Sebastian, watching as he met my father's gaze. "He is."

I was surprised my dad didn't interrogate him more on that fact, considering we both knew that it hadn't been public knowledge. "What is it that you do?"

"Mostly work on cars," Sebastian answered easily, then took a bite of food as though this was the most normal meal he'd ever had. "I work for my father, but I'm responsible mostly for the performance engines. Testing them, tweaking them. That sort of thing."

My father nodded as he forked spaghetti into his mouth.

"My father owns a body shop," I told Sebastian.

He smiled. "You told me."

Okay, maybe I had, but I felt odd sitting there not talking.

"I have a couple of friends who work in the body shop industry. One's a painter, the other a foreman."

My father and Sebastian launched into a boring discussion about the body shop, mostly technical. I ate, doing my best not to interrupt. At one point, my mother leaned over and nudged my elbow. "I like him."

Yep, the tears nearly came. I had no idea why that one sentiment could make me feel quite like I'd just won the lottery, but it had. I glanced back at Sebastian, trying to see him through my parents' eyes. He was confident when he spoke, constantly smiling and laughing at my father's comments. He looked as though he was as comfortable with my parents as Aaron was when he joined us for dinner.

"I do, too, Mom," I whispered just as softly. "So much."

Sebastian

FOR WHATEVER REASON, THE IDEA of meeting Payton's parents hadn't bothered me. Not when she'd asked me and not when we'd arrived at their house. Maybe I should've been nervous, but the more I thought about it, the more I knew it was a necessary step. Truth was, I'd never met a girl's parents.

I liked her father immediately. Although he'd greeted me on the porch with an intimidating glare, we had hit it off right away. We had a lot of things in common, besides the fact that we both loved his daughter.

Dinner had been fantastic, worlds different than any family dinner I'd ever had at my house. Unlike in the Trovato household, there were no condescending remarks, no irritated glares in my direction. After Hal had asked me about what I did for a living, we'd started in about body shops, and I learned that Hal had actually started his body shop more than twenty years ago. His business was steady, and he loved the work more than he loved the money, which I guess was a great reason to follow that career path.

Payton had seemed a little confused during the conversation, and my guess was she hadn't expected it to go quite so well. I wasn't sure why that was, because her parents were great.

After dinner, Payton and I did the dishes, sending Susan and Hal into the living room, where we joined them a little while later. The highlight of the evening was when Susan broke out Payton's baby book, giving me an inside glimpse into Payton's early years.

"Are you serious right now?" Payton squealed, trying to snatch the book out of her mother's hands.

"Quit that," Susan said sternly, grinning. "I've been waiting for twenty-three years to be able to do this."

"Twenty-three years, huh?" Payton retorted. "Since the day I was born, you've been eager to embarrass me in front of my boyfriend?"

I watched Payton, fascinated. The fact that she referred to me as her boyfriend had me wanting to high-five someone. Yes, the little things were what got me most.

"Yes, I have," Susan stated.

I glanced at Hal, who was laughing at the two women as they fought over the book. I finally managed to get my hands on it, but only after I moved over onto the sofa next to Susan. Payton offered me a glare, but I answered it with a smile.

We skimmed through baby photos, starting with the ones of Payton in the hospital the day she was born. She was a cute, chubby baby. There were more of her as she got bigger, some of her crawling, then when she took her first steps. In all of them, Payton was usually smiling at the camera. Susan continued to flip the pages until we got to Payton's first years in grade school.

I laughed, placing my hand on a picture, stopping Susan from turning the page. "Interesting outfit."

"Oh, you don't know the half of it," Hal interjected. "I cringed every time her mother took her clothes shopping."

Payton blushed. She had been a cute kid, but nothing compared to the beautiful woman who sat by watching with an amused smirk as I talked to her mother about her daughter's choice in outfits. For a brief moment, I actually envisioned this moment in a different setting. It would be Payton and me showing off pictures of our daughter when she brought her boyfriend over to meet us.

I slid my eyes up to meet Payton's, and I knew, one day, we would be doing this exact same thing.

"Well, we really oughta get going," Payton told her mother a few minutes later. "I've got to be at work by five in the morning."

"I'm so glad you came," Susan said, standing as Payton and I did. "It was great to meet you. And now that Payton has kindly introduced us, we'll expect y'all over for dinner more often."

"I'd be honored," I told Susan.

After hugging her mother and father, Payton came to stand beside me. I thanked them both for dinner and told them how great it was to meet them. They walked us out onto the porch, waiting until we pulled away from the house, waving good-bye one last time.

"I can't believe my mother did that," Payton said with a huff.

"What?" I asked, knowing exactly what she was referring to.

"Showing you my baby pictures."

"It wasn't the baby pictures I found most interesting," I told her.

"Shut up. There wasn't anything wrong with the clothes that I wore when I was a kid," she said defensively.

"No, I guess not. At least not if you were looking for a career that involved dancing around a pole."

Payton laughed, slapping my arm. "My favorite movie as a kid was Coyote Ugly."

"Why am I not surprised?" I stated, chuckling. I could totally picture a young Payton dancing as if she were going to be the center of attention one day. It was significantly different from the woman I knew, but still, I could definitely see her as a rambunctious, cheerful kid.

"Are we still on for tomorrow night?" Payton asked as we entered the highway that would take us back to her apartment.

"Yep," I told her. I'd been thinking about her suggestion to invite our friends over for dinner for the better part of the day. I wasn't sure how I felt about exposing my suspicions to everyone, but for now, I was going along with it. My curiosity as to why she had suggested we do this now had me nearly questioning her, but I decided that could wait until tomorrow. We only had a few more minutes before we made it back to her apartment, and I didn't want to get into a conversation that couldn't be finished.

"I told Aaron and Chloe about it," Payton said. "They'll be there. And Aaron asked if Garrett could come. Of course I told him yes."

I nodded. "Good. I'll probably order out if that's okay."

Payton took my hand, moving closer to me on the bench seat. "My mom really likes you," she told me.

"The feeling's mutual," I said. "Your parents are great. Thanks for inviting me."

Payton laid her head on my shoulder, neither of us saying anything for the few minutes it took us to get back to her apartment.

After parking the truck in an empty space, I walked her to her door. When we got inside, I noticed no one else was there. Taking advantage of the solitude, I flipped the deadbolt on the door and led Payton to her bedroom. I engaged the lock in there, too. When I turned to face her, there was a brilliant smile on her face.

"Are you thinking what I'm thinking?" I asked her, stalking her across the room.

"Depends. Are you thinking about being naked right now?" she asked, her voice soft.

"I'm thinking about *you* being naked, yes," I told her.

"I like that idea, too."

Without hesitation, I slid Payton's jacket off her arms, placing it on the chair before removing my own. Then I moved in closer, lifting her shirt while I kept my eyes trained on her face.

After ridding her of her bra, I cupped her breasts in both hands, squeezing gently until she was moaning softly. "Have I mentioned how beautiful you are?"

She didn't answer, but I hadn't expected her to. Leaning down, I sucked one perfect pink tip into my mouth, loving the way she gripped the back of my head, holding me to her. Alternating to her other breast, I laved the puckered tip with my tongue before lowering myself to my knees and unhooking the button on her jeans.

Payton toed off her boots, and I proceeded to pull her jeans and panties down her legs, leaving them in a puddle on the floor.

"Sit on the bed," I instructed, not getting up from my knees.

I looked up to see she was studying me intently. She knew what I was after without me having to tell her. It only took one step before she was sitting on the bed. I pressed one hand against her chest, urging her to lie back while I forced her legs wider by inserting myself between them.

"Sebastian." The soft, sexy way she said my name only encouraged me.

I pressed a kiss to her most intimate spot, sliding my tongue over her and then dipping inside, until she was gripping my hair tightly. I didn't let up until her body tensed, her climax causing her to cry out. While she relaxed on her bed, I disrobed, crawling over her and finding her mouth with mine.

It didn't take much before I was sliding inside her warmth, grinding my hips against hers over and over. I linked my fingers with hers and held them on each side of her head while I continued to penetrate her slowly. Ever so slowly.

Making love to Payton was truly the best feeling in the world. The feeling of being inside her, our bodies one, never ceased to surprise me with its intensity.

"I love you, Angel," I whispered, my eyes locked with hers.

"I love you, too," she replied, her eyes closing briefly as I increased my pace, thrusting forward hard before withdrawing.

"You feel so good, Payton." I kept my voice barely above a whisper, my eyes never leaving her face as I drove into her. "So good, Angel. This is the only place I want to be."

Her fingers squeezed mine, and the urge to claim her overtook my desire to keep things slow and sensual. The next thing I knew, I had flipped her over onto her stomach, only going slow until I was once again lodged inside her. With my chest against her back, I linked our hands, driving into her harder and faster until there wasn't enough air in the room to fill my lungs. The need to come growing stronger by the second.

I didn't relent until Payton cried out, mumbling my name as her body gripped me, milking my release from me.

Somehow I managed to keep from crushing her by rolling to my back. She turned to her side, facing me, a wondrous grin on her face. "I think you should stay the night tonight."

My eyebrow arched in question. We'd had this conversation not too long ago. "Are you sure? The last thing I want to do is keep you up all night."

"I'm exhausted," she whispered. "I just don't want to go to sleep without you."

I knew just what she was feeling. Pulling her closer, I managed to draw the blankets up over us both before pressing a kiss to the top of her head. I was already getting used to this. So much so, it was difficult to sleep when she wasn't with me, but I hadn't bothered to tell her that.

The reassurance that she was feeling the same thing had my brain tossing around so many ideas.

I knew we were in for some rocky moments as we began to unearth what had really happened to my mother, but there was no doubt in my mind that Payton and I would make it through this. Stronger than before.

And with that last fleeting thought, I closed my eyes, giving in to sleep with Payton in my arms.

Chaos

Chapter Thirteen

Payton

Tuesday night

I WENT TO SEBASTIAN'S RIGHT after work. Fearing that Trevor would try to walk me to my car again, I actually snuck out early. With Conrad on a business trip in California, I figured what he didn't know wouldn't hurt him. And if it did, I just couldn't find it in me to care.

When I arrived, I found the front door unlocked, so I let myself in. Leif was still in the recliner in the living room as I passed by him, making my way to the kitchen. I found it was empty, so I returned to stand beside him. "Where's Sebastian?"

"Workout room," he said, motioning his hand without ever looking away from the television.

Great.

After dropping my purse on the kitchen table and assuring myself that this was a good idea for the hundredth time today, I made my way past the laundry room, then out to the pool area and to the workout room on the opposite end. The door was closed, but I could hear the music blaring. It was a wonder Sebastian still had eardrums for as loud as he always blasted his music.

I didn't bother knocking; he wouldn't have heard me anyway. When I stepped inside, he saw me immediately. He looked much as he had the last time I'd found him working out. He was coated in perspiration, hugging the heavy bag, his back muscles flexing and the angel wings moving with every deep inhale and long exhale.

The man was beautiful. Sleek, corded muscle covered by smooth, tan skin. I would never tire of looking at him.

He gifted me with a smile, but even I could tell it was forced.

"I didn't expect you so early," he told me.

"I wanted to talk to you before everyone arrived."

Sebastian nodded, peeling the tape from his hands. Aside from the first time he'd acknowledged me being there, he wasn't making eye contact, and I knew he was upset. He had seemed just as concerned that morning when I'd reminded him that we were going to get together tonight to talk to everyone. Apparently, his mood hadn't changed with the passing hours. I knew he probably didn't understand why I had made the suggestion, but Sebastian had to realize that this was the only way we could figure this out.

As it was, we hadn't made any strides on our own, but mostly because I had no idea what we were supposed to be looking for. We needed someone who knew what they were doing. Someone like Leif's mother's boyfriend. The detective.

Granted, we could've just asked to talk to him directly, but after the phone call I had received that afternoon, I was more hell-bent on clearing the air once and for all. As much as it pained me to do so, I had to reveal to Sebastian just why I was making this request.

Leaning against the wall, I kept my eyes on him as I spoke. "Something happened yesterday."

His head lifted and his eyes pinned me in place. There was concern reflected in his golden gaze, but he didn't say anything. "Yesterday?"

"Yeah. I didn't want to ruin dinner with my parents, so I didn't tell you last night."

I had debated on how I would tell him about the incident with Conrad, mulling over it in my head for the last several hours. At one point, I had opted not to tell him anything, but I knew I had to. Sebastian had lived with too many secrets his entire life. The last thing I wanted to do was keep something from him.

"Your father confronted me yesterday morning," I said, keeping my voice even. "Before you get upset, hear me out."

I noticed his hands were balled into fists at his sides and his eyes had narrowed on my face.

"He asked me if I knew you had moved. I told him yes. Then he asked me if I knew you'd quit your job." I cocked an eyebrow. Sebastian hadn't informed me that was happening, and I could tell he realized that. "I told him no."

"I'm sorry, I—"

I held up my hand. "You have nothing to apologize for. And that's not the point, anyway."

Sebastian dropped his head and paced in front of me before stopping just a few feet away. When he was paying attention to me once again, I continued. "I told your father that I was uncomfortable with the conversation. What I do in my personal life is none of his business. And what you do in your personal life does not affect my job."

Sebastian nodded, apparently understanding.

"I walked out of the meeting with your father without letting him finish. I didn't want to hear what he had to say."

"Shit."

I stepped forward and put my hand on his arm. He was hot to the touch, his skin slick from his sweat. Oddly, I found that incredibly sexy.

"Trevor was there when I left Conrad's office. He spent a couple of hours behind the closed door with Conrad. I don't know what they talked about. I don't care. But there is something else I need to tell you."

Sebastian was the one to lift an eyebrow in question this time. I couldn't look at him when I told him the next part. I had informed Lauren that I would not relay her message, but as I'd thought more about it throughout the day, my fear had gotten the best of me. Especially after she'd called me again.

There was something about her. She terrified me.

"Lauren called. Yesterday *and* today."

That got Sebastian's attention, and he moved closer to me, lifting my chin and forcing me to look in his eyes.

"What did she say, Payton?"

His eyes raked over my face, and I knew he was trying to figure out if I would lie to him or possibly omit some of the facts. I wasn't going to do that. I had no reason to.

"When she called yesterday, she said—" I swallowed hard, blinking rapidly to hold back the oncoming tears. I was pissed and the tears were proof. "She said that now that you have severed ties with her family, she wants you to keep it that way. She said your volatile behavior has no place there. In *her* family."

"*Her* family?" he asked.

I nodded.

"And what did you tell her?"

"I told her I wouldn't relay the message and I hung up on her."

"Fuck."

Yep, in one word, Sebastian had pretty well summed it all up.

"She called again today. I knew as soon as I heard her voice why she had called. She wasn't looking for your father, because he's in California for two days."

"Shit."

"She told me that Conrad had told her about what had happened. She wanted to check in with me, make sure I was okay. I told her I was fine. She asked if I had told you what she'd said. I told her no. She told me that if I wanted to come to work tomorrow, I had to tell you."

A minute passed. Long, painful seconds ticked by while Sebastian simply stared at me. I wanted to know what was going through his head, but I was scared to ask.

Finally he spoke. "And that's why you wanted to talk?"

I nodded again. Putting my hands on his biceps, I met his gaze head on. "Sebastian, we need to figure this out. If you have concerns that your father might've somehow played a part in your mother's death, we have to find proof. Someone needs to be brought to justice. Our friends can help us."

"How do you figure?" he asked, releasing my chin and turning away from me. My hands slipped from his arm as he did.

"Leif's mom's boyfriend is a detective," I told him firmly. "We might be able to leverage that. Get him to check into the reports of the accident."

"Okay. That's a compelling argument for bringing Leif in. But what about the others? Why do we have to tell them?" Sebastian stared at me from across the room.

"If we start digging, Lauren and Conrad are going to figure it out. Especially if there is something they're trying to hide. We're gonna need all the eyes we can get to watch our backs. I know this sounds crazy, Sebastian, but I want to figure this out as much as you do."

"Why?" Sebastian barked. He didn't move closer, but his eyes were locked on mine. "Why do you want to be part of it?"

"Because I love you, Sebastian," I said simply, my voice soft. "I love you."

I don't think that was what he'd expected me to say, and whether it was the words or my honesty or just the heat of the moment, something had Sebastian stalking me until my back was against the wall. His mouth landed on mine. Hard.

Throwing my arms around his neck, I held him to me, meeting the firm thrust of his tongue in my mouth. When his rock-hard thigh pressed between my legs, I moaned into his mouth. This was the Sebastian I knew. The one who lurked beneath the cool exterior. He was on emotional overload, and when he released some of the pent-up energy, he had the ability to overwhelm me in the best possible way. Without words, he conveyed to me exactly what he was feeling.

He unhooked the button on my jeans and slipped his hand down into my panties, his fingers sliding through my slick folds. I writhed against him, unable to fight the sensations that soon swamped me. I had to break the kiss because I needed air.

"That's it, Payton. I want you to come on my fingers."

Well, he was going to get his wish if... "Oh, God, Sebastian." The words were barely heard, drowned out by the moan that accompanied them as he curled his fingers and thrust two inside me.

Right there, against the wall in Sebastian's workout room, his eyes locked with mine, his fingers driving me to absolute, perfect madness, I shattered.

And just like always, he was right there to hold me together.

When I said I loved him, it truly didn't do justice for the feelings I had inside.

Sebastian Trovato was my everything.

Sebastian

I DON'T KNOW WHAT OVERCAME me or why I did what I did, but the chaos had come back with a vengeance, even though Payton was right there with me. I think it was the conversation, the blind rage that I felt when she informed me that my father and his wife had confronted her. I had needed to console her, needed to release the tension that had ratcheted up inside me. The next thing I knew, I was driving my fingers inside her, making her come with the sweetest moan I'd ever heard.

"I didn't hurt you, did I?" I asked, stepping back and allowing her to fix her clothes.

"No," she told me. "That was actually kind of…"

"What?"

"Kind of fantastic," Payton whispered, smiling.

God, she was so damn beautiful when she smiled.

For the better part of the afternoon, the noise in my head had intensified. Louder than it had been in a while. I knew it was likely due to the conversation I'd had with my father early yesterday morning, the same conversation that had probably spurred him to confront Payton. When I hadn't showed up for work at his house yesterday morning, Lauren must've called him. In turn, he'd called me.

"Why aren't you at work?" Conrad questioned as soon as I answered my cell phone.

"Good morning to you, too," I snarled, switching the phone to my other ear.

"Sebastian—"

Rather than listen to him rant, I interjected. "Look, I'm sure you've known this was coming for a while now. I know that you brought Trevor on board, and I'm sure he can be your puppet better than I can. So, if it's all the same to you, I'm done."

"Done?" Conrad questioned.

"Yes, done. I'm sure you haven't noticed because I don't think you give a shit what I do, but I've moved out, and now I think it's time that I move on."

"What are you saying?"

"I quit. That's what I'm saying."

I was pretty sure I could've handled the confrontation with Conrad better. I should've sat down with him face-to-face to have the conversation rather than wait for him to call me when I didn't bother showing up for work, but I just couldn't find it in me to keep working for him. After I'd informed him that I quit, Conrad had told me I would regret it, that he would make sure I didn't walk away with a single penny.

I'd informed him that it was too late. He couldn't touch my money, and now that I'd moved out of his house, he couldn't touch me, either.

Unfortunately, I hadn't considered the fact that he might confront Payton. Now that I knew just what lengths they would both go to in order to screw with my life, I knew Payton was right. It was time we figured this out.

"Have you called your sister?" Payton asked me, drawing my thoughts back to the present.

"No."

"Do you think we should?"

I didn't know the answer to that question. Hell, I didn't know the answer to a million questions running through my head.

"We need to tell her about Leif. I think she's gonna want to know."

I agreed with her there. But I also knew she was going to be pissed when she found out I'd kept it from her. Although I had managed to brush her off on many things, Aaliyah wasn't going to forgive me for what I'd done. Keeping the accident from her, not confirming that I was moving, and not bothering to tell her that I was quitting my job... Those were relatively big deals. She had every right to be angry. However, for whatever reason, Lauren was trying to keep Aaliyah away from me, and as much as I wanted to have my sister in my life, I wasn't sure now was the right time.

"Sebastian," Payton said softly. I slid my eyes up to meet hers. "I think we need to tell her about Leif. We won't say anything about the other stuff yet. But I don't want her to think we were keeping it from her."

She was already going to think that, but I didn't say as much. Payton would realize it soon enough.

"Okay. I'll call her tonight. After everyone leaves."

"Fair enough."

I glanced down at myself. I needed a shower before everyone arrived. I also needed a few minutes alone. "Why don't you hang out with Leif while I shower? Dinner'll be delivered soon."

Payton nodded, a frown causing her forehead to wrinkle. I moved to her and pressed my lips to hers, hoping to reassure her. I didn't bother to mention that I needed that reassurance as much as she did.

After all, in less than an hour, my friends were about to find out my deepest, darkest secret. Either they'd be on my side or they'd think I was crazy.

I wasn't sure that I was happy about either option.

When I returned to the kitchen after I'd showered and changed, I found Payton and Chloe setting the table in the dining room. The one in the breakfast nook wasn't big enough to hold seven people apparently. Having remembered a conversation I'd had with Payton early on, I had ordered Chinese food for dinner, knowing it was one of her favorites. I hadn't known what to order, so I'd just gotten a little of everything.

Leif refused my help when I offered to assist him to the dining room table. He was still walking slowly, but I could tell he was feeling better. I'd never had fractured ribs, but I couldn't imagine they'd be all that comfortable to live with while they were healing.

I refused to sit at the head of the table, thinking it seemed a little ridiculous. Toby, however, had jumped at the opportunity, referring to himself as king of the castle. In turn, I made sure the "king" couldn't reach the food.

"So, I hear you got to meet the parents," Chloe said, looking right at me. She was trying to create a distraction, but I caught on to her game, pushing the food farther away from Toby.

He grunted and then stood, making his way down to the other end and grabbing one of the containers.

"I did," I told her, grabbing a set of chopsticks as Toby took his seat. Of course, I tossed his chopsticks down to the other end of the table. He glared at me, but I noticed the smirk he was trying hard to hide.

"Hold on," Chloe shouted, passing Toby's chopsticks back down when Leif handed them to her. "Don't eat yet."

We all stared back at her, waiting for her to tell us why we couldn't have dinner since, you know, we were supposed to be having dinner.

"We've got to open the fortune cookies first."

"First?" Leif asked.

"Yes, first," she declared. "That's the only way it works."

"You do know you're supposed to open them after, right?" Leif asked.

"Says who?"

Leif didn't respond, but he did catch the fortune cookie that Chloe tossed his way. Once they were all passed out and opened, I set mine down on the table upside down.

"What does it say?" Chloe asked curiously.

"That's none of your business," I told her with a grin.

"Mine says…" Toby stared at the piece of paper before looking up at Chloe. "It says: lucky you. Get out your party clothes."

"What the hell kind of fortune is that?" Garrett laughed gruffly. "Mine says: old friends make best friends."

"That's not really a fortune," I told him. "In fact, it's not really anything."

"My turn." Chloe interrupted the round of laughter. "Mine says: magnanimity will bring you universal respect."

No one said anything; we all just stared at Chloe.

"What the hell does that mean?" Leif asked, his face reflecting the same confusion everyone else's did.

Aaron spoke up. "Mine says" — he cleared his throat as he stared at the paper — "Dinner will be cold if you don't eat now."

Payton laughed, tossing her fortune toward Chloe before digging into the food. I noticed she kept her eye on me throughout the meal. Chloe, of course, questioned me about dinner with Payton's parents. I relayed the events, skipping over a few of the details, but I did mention the baby book.

"Don't you love her outfits?" Aaron asked, laughing. "It's a good thing she developed some fashion sense as she grew up."

"I'm not sure that's the case," Payton admitted, chuckling as they teased her. "If it weren't for Chloe, there's no telling what I might be wearing these days."

"What about y'all?" I asked Chloe and Toby. "Have you met each other's parents yet?"

Chloe shook her head and her eyes fell to her plate. "Not yet."

"How come?" Payton questioned.

"Hasn't come up," Chloe answered quickly, never lifting her eyes from her plate.

"Do you want to meet my parents?" Toby asked, sounding seriously shocked by the notion.

"I'd thought about it," she said, looking at him while the rest of us stared at her.

"Well, why didn't you say so?" he asked. That was one thing about Toby, he didn't necessarily take hints very well. It was much easier to be blunt with him. I figured Chloe would learn that over time.

"I thought you'd bring it up."

"I hadn't even thought about it."

"Obviously," I mentioned. "But Chloe, seriously, be careful what you wish for."

Toby's mother was great, as was Toby's stepfather, who had been a part of Toby's life since he was eight. I just wanted to give her a hard time.

I glanced down at the other end of the table to see Leif eating quietly, his gaze traveling over the rest of the table.

"You hanging in there?" I asked him.

"Yep."

I met Payton's eyes briefly. I wondered what his deal was, but I didn't ask. When she shook her head ever so slightly, I knew it was best that I didn't.

"How's school, Aaron?" Chloe asked, taking some of the heat off Leif.

"I'm ready for break."

"That's right, Christmas break is coming up," Payton stated. "What're your plans this year?"

"No idea," Aaron said. "Not sure if Mom and Dad are gonna have dinner at their house or not."

"I need to ask my mom what she's planning to do," Payton told him. "But whatever I do, I hope you'll be there with me."

I realized she was talking to me.

Christmas with Payton. I couldn't think of anything better.

Thanksgiving had gone by in a blur of events. Payton hadn't mentioned it and neither had I. My father hadn't done anything special for dinner that night, or if he had, they hadn't invited me. From what I could tell, if I wasn't spending Christmas with Payton, I'd probably be spending it at home alone. Possibly with Leif or Toby and their parents.

"Wherever you are, I'll be," I reassured Payton, touching her knee beneath the table.

"Y'all are sickeningly cute, you know that?" Chloe asked, grinning from ear to ear.

"It's no different than having to watch you make goo-goo eyes at Toby all the time," Payton retorted.

"I do *not* make goo-goo eyes at him," Chloe said defensively, glancing over at Toby and, yes, making what Payton referred to as goo-goo eyes.

After that comment, and Chloe's ensuing embarrassment, the laughter died down somewhat, and we finished our meal. When Payton offered coffee, everyone's attention turned to me. Why, I had no idea.

"Is something wrong?" Chloe asked, watching Payton retreat to the kitchen while Aaron helped her carry the empty cartons and plates.

"Depends on how you look at it," I lied. Yes, there was something wrong. And it didn't matter how the story was spun, it was still very, very wrong.

But I needed to wait until Payton returned. She was like my backbone, my rock in all of this, and I couldn't imagine sharing this news with anyone without her at my side.

Unable to sit still with so many eyes on me, I pushed my chair back and grabbed the last of the food cartons and plates from the table. I found Payton in the kitchen, pulling coffee mugs out of the cabinet. She tossed me a small smile over her shoulder while Aaron took the cups she'd retrieved and carried them into the dining room.

We waited, just the two of us alone, for the coffee to finish brewing while the others talked in hushed tones not far from where we stood.

"Are you ready to do this?" Payton asked, putting her hand on my arm.

"No," I told her truthfully. "But I wasn't ready to tell you when I did, either."

"They're gonna have your back on this, Sebastian. Trust me."

I sure as hell hoped she was right. Because if not, I might just be looking at an extended vacation at the mental health facility.

Payton

I HOPED THAT NO ONE could see how incredibly nervous I was. For the last hour, while we'd shared dinner with our friends, I had gone over the topic we'd be discussing more than once in my head. Hell, I'd gone over it more than ten times, and no matter how many times I laid it out in front of me, it still made me hesitant to tell anyone.

Not because I didn't think they'd believe Sebastian. If anything, I think Toby and Leif were going to have a couple of aha moments. After all, they'd been friends with Sebastian since he'd moved into Conrad Trovato's world. They might not know every gory detail of his life, but I had a feeling they knew more than they ever let on.

That didn't mean I thought they'd ever suspect Conrad or Lauren of doing something so heinous. And again, these were still just suspicions, but I knew we had to get to the bottom of them. Quickly.

Up to this point, neither Sebastian nor I had done anything with the information, and Lauren seemed to be escalating. Whatever she had against Sebastian, she was using this current situation to push him farther away.

Sebastian retrieved the coffeepot when it finished brewing, carrying it into the dining room where the others were still sitting around the table. I took my seat, and he handed the coffeepot off to Chloe, who did the honors of pouring for those who wanted some.

"Are you going to enlighten us, bro?" Leif asked, his gaze locked tightly with Sebastian's as he spoke.

I remembered the conversation regarding Aaliyah that he and I'd had the day he'd come home. I had mentioned that I didn't think she had ever received my message for her to call me. At that time, I think Leif's curiosity had been piqued. He seemed just as genuinely interested in what was going on now as he had been that day.

"If I'm gonna do this, I need to start from the beginning," Sebastian said, taking my hand and holding it between both of his on top of the table. I moved a little closer, making sure he knew I was there.

"Sure thing," Toby said, clearly realizing this was serious. His gaze darted back and forth across everyone at the table before landing on Sebastian.

"Leif has known me since I was fourteen and moved in with Conrad. For the first fourteen years of my life, I didn't know who my father was. My mother knew, but when I was born, after he'd tried to convince her to have an abortion early on, he told her that he didn't want to have anything to do with me or her. It probably had a lot to do with the fact that my mother was seventeen when she got pregnant with me and Conrad was twenty-six and married. Trovato, Inc. hadn't gotten too far off the ground at the time, but he was working on it. I doubt that spreading the word of him having an illegitimate kid with an underage girl would've been good for business, so he tried to pay my mother off.

"Her emotions got the best of her, and she refused him, insisting that she go it alone, which she did until the day she died. We didn't have any other family besides my mother's sister, who didn't visit often, but she did make an attempt to keep in touch. She had her own issues, and after I went to live with Conrad, I never heard from her again. My grandparents didn't want to have anything to do with my mother from the moment she told them she was pregnant, claiming she was an embarrassment. Even with the odds stacked against us, my mother and I managed somehow.

"It wasn't until a short time before my mother died that I realized how bad things had gotten. We were about to be evicted from our apartment. My mother hadn't paid rent in months, and the landlord was tired of giving her chances. She told me she was thinking about contacting Conrad about child support."

A collective gasp sounded at the table, and I knew that Chloe, Toby, and Leif had put two and two together the same way I had.

"Did she ask him for money?" Chloe asked, moving closer to Toby while she watched Sebastian intently.

"I had pestered her about it for days, but she never confirmed whether she did or not, but I think she did."

"Why do you think that?" Leif asked, his tone sympathetic and not at all combative.

"My mother was very proud. She worked two jobs just to take care of me. She didn't want anything for herself, never splurged. The only thing she worried about was having a roof over our heads and food on the table. For the most part, we had both, but things were getting harder for her. I knew that the last thing she wanted to do was to contact Conrad. And if she had thought there was any other way, she wouldn't have.

"But I don't know if that ever happened. She died before I ever found out."

"How did she die?" Aaron asked, resting his forearms on the table and staring at Sebastian.

"She was killed in a hit-and-run accident. The other driver was never located."

I noticed that Toby and Leif traded glances, but neither of them said anything.

Squeezing Sebastian's hand gently, I encouraged him to continue.

"Maybe it's because I need closure, I don't know, but something has always nagged at me regarding her death. I've been suspicious since the day the cops showed up at our apartment to tell me she was dead. Even more so when Conrad swooped in and took me in. From day one, we've had a volatile relationship. I was broken when he found me, and he never tried to put me back together," Sebastian said, glancing down at the table.

My heart broke for him again. I was pretty sure I'd never get comfortable with this story.

Sebastian took a deep breath and then continued. "Conrad married his first wife when he was twenty-three. They divorced when he was twenty-seven. I suspect it was because he couldn't keep it in his pants. Then he married his second wife when he was twenty-eight, less than eight months after his divorce was final. They divorced when Conrad was thirty. I don't know for sure, but I have a feeling it had a lot to do with Lauren."

"Aaliyah's mother," Leif said. It wasn't a question.

"Yeah. Lauren has worked for Conrad since the very beginning. She started out as his assistant, and she's been in his life through every marriage and every divorce. When I first moved in with them, I was curious, so I looked it up. Conrad married Lauren when she was four months pregnant with Aaliyah. It's safe to say that Lauren and I have never gotten along.

"When I first moved in with them, she looked past me whenever I came into a room. I think she despised the fact that I'd come into their lives. No more than I despised her for being there, I assure you. It wasn't long before I knew the ins and outs of my father's business. I learned early on, and Toby and Leif can vouch for me, that I was good with cars. My father realized it, too.

"But I was so pissed, so fucking angry." Sebastian's voice rose an octave. "I didn't want to have anything to do with him. Then one day after I'd been sent home for fighting, I heard the two of them talking. Lauren didn't want me there. She tried to convince Conrad that I was a bad influence on Aaliyah, which, now that I think about it, I probably was."

Sebastian's smile was sad. Again, I squeezed his hand.

"Surprisingly, he didn't have a talk with me like I thought he would. In fact, almost a year and a half went by before he made any effort to talk to me more than at the dinner table. By then, my anger and rage had been simmering for so long I didn't know how to function without them. So when he decided to do me a favor and offer me a job, I decided to do him one better."

All eyes were on Sebastian, including mine.

"I blackmailed my father."

I gasped. Sebastian had failed to mention that part to me.

"I extorted money from him and a piece of Trovato, Inc. In return, I would keep his secret. I had a DNA test that proved he was my father, and I told him the press would have a field day if they found out. After all, I was about to be sixteen, and he'd kept me a secret all those years."

"No one knew he had a son?" Aaron asked incredulously.

Toby was the one to chime in. "They all kept it under wraps. Including Sebastian."

"Seriously?" Chloe questioned.

"Sebastian was one of those guys who didn't let anyone get close," Leif explained. "If it hadn't been for the fact I wasn't gonna spend my days worrying if he was going to go off on me, I wouldn't be here today. The first time he tried to fight me, I put him in his place. He could've easily kicked my ass, I knew that much. But I didn't give him a chance."

Sebastian smiled at Leif. "I still remember it. He probably saved me from myself."

"Did either of you have interaction with Lauren or Conrad?" I asked Toby and Leif directly.

"Very little," Leif admitted. "Let's just put it this way … she's never been the friendly type."

"Did you spend much time at Sebastian's?" I asked them.

"Probably more time than he spent at either of our houses. Although Lauren and Conrad were usually home, the place was big enough that we never had to see them."

"So you blackmailed him for money," Chloe stated, steering the conversation back to the original topic.

"A lot of money," Sebastian admitted, motioning his hand around the room as though referencing the house. "If I never wanted to work again, I wouldn't be hurting."

"In return, you told him you'd keep his secret? I find it hard to believe it was that big of a deal for him." Chloe glanced over at me briefly before turning her attention back to Sebastian.

"I don't think he really gave a shit," Sebastian said. "But Lauren didn't want the secret to get out. She was finally Mrs. Conrad Trovato after all those years of sticking by his side waiting for him to come around. They had Aaliyah, and Lauren was all about the attention. For herself. I think she was the one to convince him to give in to my demands."

"A fifteen-year-old kid blackmailed Conrad Trovato," Garrett muttered, the first thing he'd said since Sebastian had started talking. "Now I've seen it all."

"You ain't seen nothin' yet," Sebastian said, his tone turning dark.

"What does that mean?" Chloe asked, her eyebrows raised in question.

I turned my head to look at Sebastian, knowing that he wasn't having an easy time explaining all of this.

"I've spent the last eleven years living under Conrad's thumb. Although I got what I wanted out of the deal, he still held the reins. We've fought every day for years, and it hasn't gotten any easier. My relationship with Lauren is nonexistent mainly because we despise one another. The only person I could consider family, aside from Toby and Leif, is Aaliyah. We don't have the best relationship, but that's because of the fighting. She tries to steer clear of it, and I can't necessarily blame her. But throughout all of this, I've also lived with something else. A suspicion that I can't seem to shake."

Chaos

"About your father?" Chloe questioned, leaning closer to Toby.

I think she knew something big was coming. Based on the way Leif's eyes had widened, I think he had already figured it out. I was surprised he hadn't spoken up, but maybe he was like I had been, waiting for Sebastian to reveal it.

"Yeah," Sebastian said, nodding as he looked directly at Chloe, then his gaze drifted to Leif and lastly to Toby. "I've spent more than a decade wondering just why my mother died that night. The more I think about it, the more coincidental it seems. I truly believe she had reached out to Conrad for money. But he never had to pay up or worry about his secret getting out because she died. In a hit-and-run car accident with no witnesses."

"Oh, my God," Chloe said, her voice small. "You think…?"

"That my father killed my mother. Yeah. That's exactly what I think."

Sebastian

THE SILENCE THAT FOLLOWED MY final statement made my stomach churn. I kept my eyes on Toby and Leif, flipping from one to the other, waiting for someone to say something.

"Do you think that maybe it wasn't Conrad?" Chloe asked.

I was surprised by how engaged she'd been through the entire conversation. She was the only one who seemed to be peppering me with questions.

"Do you think it might've been Lauren?" Toby asked before I could answer Chloe.

I met Toby's dark, stormy gaze. He was dead serious. And in that moment, I couldn't have loved him more. He had always been like a brother to me, and the relief of knowing he wasn't questioning my sanity was almost too much to bear.

"I'm with Toby," Leif added. "As much as I dislike your ol' man, I'm leaning toward thinking Lauren had something to do with it."

"Seriously," Toby added. "What would Conrad have to gain by offing her? But Lauren…"

"Exactly," Chloe added. "Lauren had everything to gain. If your mother did ask Conrad for money, then Lauren probably knew about it. If Lauren thought your mother was desperate enough to go public, then Lauren would have to endure that black cloud over her perfect life."

"I'm not sure that's enough of a motive to kill someone," Aaron stated. "Not that I don't see where everyone's coming from, but what if she'd gotten caught? Then it would've all come crashing down around her anyway."

"But no one was caught," Leif tacked on.

"That's why we're here," Payton spoke up. "Obviously Sebastian needs closure, and we're his family," she said, speaking to everyone at the table. "But he's not just bringing this up now to stir up shit."

I thought she was incredibly cute when she cursed; I had no idea why. I smiled, grasping her hand between both of mine, where I'd had it for the last half hour.

"Did something happen?" Toby asked.

"When we were in Vegas," Payton began, "Conrad insisted that I meet him and Lauren for breakfast. Without Sebastian. Lauren's nephew, Trevor, was there. I only recently learned that Conrad was hiring him. It looks like he's being put in Sebastian's place."

"What does that mean? Like replacing you? Conrad's gonna fire you?" Toby asked me directly.

I glanced around at the others, realizing I hadn't yet told them that I'd quit. "He can't fire me," I replied, "I already quit."

The table was silent for a moment, everyone looking at me as though I might have more to say. I didn't. That was the gist of it. I quit. End of story.

"What do we know about this guy?" Leif asked, breaking the silence, his face stern.

"We know that he's been brought up on charges of aggravated sexual assault," I announced.

Payton's head turned toward me so fast I was surprised her neck didn't hurt.

"Are you serious?" she asked.

"Yeah."

"I wonder if that was what Lauren was referring to when she said he'd been in some trouble, but they'd gotten that taken care of."

"Money does buy a lot," Chloe offered.

"Anyway," Payton continued, turning her attention back to the others. "Monday morning, when I was at work, Conrad confronted me about Sebastian moving out and quitting his job. He tried, for the second time, mind you, to convince me that Sebastian was unstable."

"Right," Toby snorted. "Sebastian's the unstable one."

"I told him I was uncomfortable with the conversation and eventually walked out on him. But Lauren called and..." Payton's sentence trailed off as she looked down at the table. "Lauren threatened me. Told me that if I wanted to keep my job, I needed to tell Sebastian that he wasn't welcome back in her family now that he had officially severed ties."

"What a bitch!" Chloe exclaimed, causing Aaron and Garrett to laugh.

"You could say that. She called me again today. Told me that I didn't need to bother coming to work tomorrow if I didn't tell him."

"Fuck them!" Chloe shouted. "You don't need that shit."

"But I do," Payton clarified. "Working for Conrad is the only way we might be able to find out some things. I don't know how and I don't know what yet, but we've kinda run out of other options."

"Derrick might be able to help us," Leif stated, referring to his mother's boyfriend. "He's a detective with the Austin PD. I can talk to him if you want."

"I think I should be the one to talk to him," I told him. As much as I appreciated the help, I knew I had to be the one to face this head on.

"We can talk to him together," Leif inserted.

"I wanna be there," Toby said.

"Me, too," Chloe added.

"This is some serious shit," Aaron muttered.

"Yeah, it is," I told him. "And I completely understand if you don't want to help."

"Oh, I didn't say that," Aaron said more confidently. "I wanna bring the crazy bitch down just as much as the next guy. I'm just not sure how I can help."

"I'm sure we'll come up with something," Toby said.

"What about Aaliyah?" Leif asked, drawing all eyes to him.

"What about her?" I asked.

"I take it she doesn't know any of this."

"No, she doesn't," Payton clarified. "The night of the wreck, I tried calling Conrad. When he didn't answer, I called Lauren and told her what happened. She listened to me, but she never showed up."

"Conrad hasn't mentioned anything to me about the wreck," I added. "Not once. My guess is she didn't relay the message."

When I was finished, Payton continued, "I also called Aaliyah that night and told her to call me. She never has."

"I haven't talked to her much," I told them. "I saw her a few times, but I was trying to keep her out of this as much as I could. Knowing that Lauren didn't tell my father or my sister that I'd been in a car accident made me wary."

"Rightfully so," Garrett mumbled.

"I think she needs to know," Payton tacked on. "I think she's gonna be pissed that we kept this from her."

I met Leif's gaze from the other end of the table. "Yeah, she's not gonna be too happy with me. Especially when she finds out what happened to you."

Leif's eyes lowered to the table, and I think he was relieved to know that Aaliyah wasn't avoiding him. She just didn't know what was going on. Not that I was looking forward to dealing with my little sister's wrath, but I agreed with Payton. She needed to know. At least some of it. After all, she was the one who had access to their house.

"Well, I think we need a plan," Chloe said, looking at me directly.

A chorus of "I agree" sounded at the table, and for the first time all day, my lungs actually filled with air. I'd been holding my breath, not sure what they would say or do when I shared my story with them, but it looked like Payton had been right.

Now we just had to figure out what we were going to do and how we were going to do it.

It was late by the time Payton and I crawled into bed. I was surprised when Payton had taken a break to call Conrad, leaving him a message on his work voice mail that she wouldn't be in the office tomorrow. She told him she wasn't feeling well.

When I looked at her, she merely shrugged her shoulders.

I got it. I really did.

After Garrett, Aaron, Toby, and Chloe had left, I had spent a solid half hour talking to Leif while Payton had taken a shower. My best friend wasn't all that happy with me, but he told me he understood why I'd never said anything. He also made a call, talking to his mother for a few minutes before asking her for Derrick's phone number. He came up with some lame excuse, but she eventually gave it to him. Leif told me that he'd make the call first thing in the morning.

Now, as I lay in bed with Payton in my arms, I couldn't go to sleep. She had crawled beneath the blankets, clad in one of my T-shirts, and not five minutes after she'd laid her head on my chest, I heard her breaths even out. I was exhausted, but I couldn't get my brain to shut off.

I had so many things to do, and not everything revolved around this shit with my father and his wife.

I had a business to get off the ground. I'd made a point to call a few of the people I'd worked with closely at Trovato, Inc., mainly a couple of suppliers and one account rep who I'd spent time talking to whenever I had a new prototype in the works. All three of them had been keenly interested in my new business venture.

Conrad wasn't going to be too happy with the news, but his reaction didn't bother me in the least. I knew what I was doing when it came to the direction I wanted to go for my new business. Or at least I hoped I did.

However, I had no fucking clue what I was supposed to do in regard to figuring out my mother's death. I wasn't a cop or any sort of investigator, so I didn't have the slightest idea where to begin. While telling my friends, who also weren't cops, mind you, had taken some of the weight off my shoulders, I couldn't see how it was going to help.

But my secret was out. The only thing I could do was put one foot in front of the other the same way I'd done for the last eleven years. See what tomorrow would bring and deal with it then.

For now, I just wanted to be content with what I had.

Payton.

So, as I forced my eyes closed, I thought about Christmas, which was just a couple of weeks away. I already knew exactly what I was getting Payton, and I hoped, with Chloe's help, I could have it ready by then.

Chapter Seventeen

Sebastian

Ten days later
Friday

CHRISTMAS WAS LESS THAN A week away, and for the last several days, I'd been so busy, half the time I didn't know what day it was. I'd spent some time with Derrick, Leif's mother's boyfriend, giving him the gory details of my suspicions. Just as I'd thought, he hadn't seemed too positive that he could help. According to him, digging into a decade-old case based on a hunch or suspicion was probably going to raise more questions than answers.

I'd resorted to taking Payton to work and picking her up because Trevor was becoming a nuisance, and truthfully, I didn't trust the asshole as far as I could throw him. When Payton had informed me that Trevor insisted on walking her to her car every day, I'd put a stop to that shit instantly. In an attempt to not interfere with Payton's job, I had waited outside for her one evening, and when Trevor had come waltzing out the door alongside her, I'd told him exactly how things were going to work. Today Aaron had offered to pick her up, but he was in on my plan, so I was okay with that.

What I really wanted to do was confront Conrad and ask him what the fuck he was thinking, but we weren't really on speaking terms.

As for my house, it seemed as though there was one stranger or another traipsing through it every single day. Between the alarm system, satellite, Internet, pool equipment, and yard stuff, it was a never-ending trail of one person after another interrupting my day. But that had ceased for the last few days, everything seemingly in its place. Finally.

Leif had gone back to work last week, still taking it easy but pushing to get back to his fighting form. He and I had started working out in the evenings together, and hopefully in a couple of months, he would be up for running with me as well. For now, he still had to go slow. Toby had even graced us with his presence a few times, insisting that he was there to provide comedic relief. The guy was crazy, but I appreciated the effort. Surprisingly, neither of them were treating me with kid gloves, which I appreciated more than they knew.

We were planning another get-together tomorrow night for dinner at my house. This time Aaliyah was coming. I had put off talking to her until now, not quite sure what I was supposed to say. But I knew it had to be done.

However, tonight was just going to be Payton and me. I'd decided to take her back out to the track so we could be alone for a little while. I had no desire to race, not sure I ever would again after what had happened to Leif, but the track was somewhere I'd gone to clear my head before, and now seemed like a good time to revisit it.

I'd decided to make it an official date because Payton and I hadn't been on one in a while. She'd seemed excited about that. After informing her that it would be casual, I'd told her I would pick her up at seven. She'd assured me that she'd be home, and now, as I was pulling into her apartment complex, I saw her car parked in her usual space.

It was cold outside, but not unbearably so. December in Texas was generally iffy as far as weather went. The temps could vary drastically, ranging from below freezing to upwards of seventy degrees. We hadn't seen any seventy-degree days in at least a week, which mean winter was now upon us. No snow for us, though; at most, we'd get some sleet in the coming days, but tonight was clear, the breeze minimal. However, I did come prepared.

Walking up to Payton's second-floor apartment, I was surprised to find I was a little nervous. Although she'd spent a few nights at my place, she'd spent several in her own bed. I was hoping to put a stop to that soon. If she was on board with the idea, that was. Asking Payton to move in with me was a big step, and some might think we were rushing things, but I didn't. Not to mention, I didn't really give a shit what other people thought, anyway.

I rapped my knuckles on the front door and waited. I wasn't surprised to see Toby's smiling face when the door opened. Nor was I shocked when he shut the damn thing in my face, either. I merely turned the knob and let myself in. He was giving back as good as he got.

"Hey," Chloe greeted from where she stood in the kitchen.

"Hey. You making pancakes for your man tonight?"

"Oh, shut it." She laughed. I still loved to give her shit about it.

"I'm sure there're other things he doesn't like that he hasn't told you about yet."

"Whatever, bro. I've told her everything."

"Right," I replied, glancing at Payton's closed bedroom door. "She in there?"

"Yep. She'll be out in a sec. She said to tell you to wait for her."

I'd wait a lifetime for her, but I didn't say that to Chloe or Toby. Instead, I flopped on the couch beside Toby. "How's work?" I asked him, trying to make small talk.

"Same ol' shit, different day," he answered, not taking his eyes off the TV.

"Did the buyout go through?" I asked, referring to the fact that the independently owned shop he'd been working at for the last few years had just been bought out by one of the big boys who had bled their business down to Austin from Dallas.

"It'll be complete next week."

"You still gonna have a job?"

"Not sure," he said glumly.

"Well, I've got a proposition for you. Maybe we can get together on Sunday to talk?"

Toby peered over at me, a little bit of interest sparkling in his eyes. "Yeah. What time?"

"Doesn't matter to me. Just don't wake my ass up at the butt crack of dawn."

Toby nodded, then turned his attention back to the television.

Payton's bedroom door opened and she stepped out. She was wearing jeans and a long-sleeved T-shirt, with her jacket flung over her arm. As far as I was concerned, it didn't matter if she was wearing jeans or a formal gown, the woman was stunning.

I instantly stood.

"Hi," she greeted shyly. It still amazed me that she seemed bashful at times around me. We'd been together long enough that I would've thought we'd be past that point. Nonetheless, it was nice. Then again, everything about her was nice.

"You ready?" I asked.

"Yep," she said and then turned to Chloe. "I'm staying at Sebastian's for the weekend."

"Gotcha," Chloe replied, chopping something on the counter. "We'll see y'all tomorrow night, right?" Her eyes slid up to meet mine briefly.

"Yep. We're still on for tomorrow."

Payton came to stand beside me, and I helped her put her coat on, smiling down at her while I did. When she was buttoned up, I took her hand and led her to the door.

"Hey, Chloe?" I called as I pulled the door open.

"Yeah?"

"Did Toby mention that he doesn't like salad?"

I ushered Payton out onto the landing and closed the door to Chloe's disbelieving rant.

"Is he serious? You don't like salad? Why didn't you tell me that?" Her high-pitched squeal was the last thing I heard as I shut the door, again smiling down at Payton.

"Is that true? He doesn't like salad?"

"No, he likes salad fine. I just figured I'd give him a hard time. He'll have to work overtime to convince her otherwise, though."

Payton giggled as I led her down the stairs and into my truck.

After she climbed inside, I shut her door and walked around to the driver's side. A few seconds later, we were pulling out of the apartment complex.

"Where're we going?" she asked, reaching forward and fumbling with the heater controls.

"I thought we'd have dinner first. You hungry?"

"Starving," she admitted. Once she was content with the blast of the heater, she put her hand on my leg. I glanced down at her fingers, instantly thinking about her Christmas present.

Forcing my gaze back to the road, I made the short drive to the Italian restaurant that she loved. It wasn't one of those fancy chain restaurants, and I'd been surprised the first time she had convinced me to take her there. I'd been meaning to take her back, but as usual, so many things had happened, we hadn't been able to go on a date in a while.

But here we were. I parked in the semi-full lot close to the door. She climbed out the driver's side door behind me, and we headed into the restaurant hand in hand.

I was shocked as shit when we were greeted by name, but Payton didn't seem at all surprised, so I went with it. Apparently, when it came to small, family-owned restaurants, they remembered their patrons, even if they'd only come in once before. Kind of nice, actually. We were seated immediately, and dinner, as it always was when I was with Payton, was fabulous.

A couple of hours later, after making it through the gates of the track and locking them behind us, I pulled the truck off into the grass. I climbed out, then helped Payton out behind me. Before rolling down the window and turning up the radio, I reached behind the seat, grabbing two blankets that I'd stashed there before I left the house.

"You keep blankets in your truck?" Payton asked suspiciously as she waited for me to take her hand. I led her a few feet from the truck and then spread one of the blankets on the thick grass.

"I do." It wasn't a total lie. After all, I did have two blankets in the truck. But she didn't have to know that I'd stored them there for just this particular instance. I'd known before I'd picked her up where I wanted to take her, and as far as I was concerned, it was always good to be prepared.

Payton lowered herself to the blanket while I unfolded the other one. She reclined on her elbows as she stared up at the sky, the stars bright overhead without the harshness of city lights to hinder their glow. Her jean-clad legs were out in front of her, ankles crossed. I joined her, lying on my side and propping myself on my elbow so that I could look at her.

"What's so special about this place?" Payton asked, but the question wasn't condescending. She sounded as though she honestly wanted to know. "I mean, I get why you came here before. You needed to get away, needed the release you get when you race, but really. Why here?"

"I started coming here when I was sixteen. The minute I got my license, I knew what I wanted to do."

Payton glanced over at me, her eyebrow sliding up. She was encouraging me to talk, I knew. She'd gotten rather good at that over the past couple of months. "Race?"

I nodded. "Racing's like a drug. The faster I go, the calmer I feel."

"Do you prefer racing for money?"

I hesitated for a moment, thinking about the last race. The one that had ended with Leif's life hanging in the balance. "If you asked me that a couple of months ago, I probably would've said yes," I told her, meeting her gaze. "I've raced for money too many times to count. But honestly, for me, it was never about the money."

"Do you want to race again?" I could tell she was thinking back to that night.

"I'm not sure. Right now, no. I don't know if that'll always be the case, though."

"Because of what happened with Leif?"

I studied her face in the dark, the glimmer of the moonlight on her hair, the whiteness of her teeth glowing in the dark. "Yeah," I replied.

"What about this?" she asked, nodding her head toward the track. "It seems more controlled."

"It is. That doesn't mean there aren't wrecks. But there aren't so many variables, I guess."

"Is it still there? The need to clear your head?"

I didn't pull my eyes from hers as I said, "Not so much anymore, no. And that doesn't have anything to do with what happened." I paused, swallowing. "Since I met you, it's been easier to deal with."

"What has?"

"The chaos. The noise in my head." I glanced out at the darkness in front of us. "I'd gotten so used to it, but then I met you, and I found out what it was like without the constant chaos. Before you, I used racing and working out to quiet it. I don't need them as much anymore."

Payton stared back at me, but she didn't say anything. She seemed to be scrutinizing me. And then she smiled, wide and bright.

I chuckled. "What're you smiling at?"

"You."

"Why?" I didn't mind her smiling, it was actually one of my favorite things, but I could tell she was thinking.

"Is it bad that I want you to kiss me right now?" she whispered, her smile slowly fading, although I could still see remnants of her happiness at the corners of her eyes.

"No, definitely not a bad thing," I whispered back, easing closer to her as I cupped her face with one hand. Turning her head slightly, I glanced down at her mouth, swiping my thumb over her bottom lip, then met her gaze once again. Unable to resist, I leaned in and pressed my lips to hers. She was so soft and so warm. When she relaxed onto the blanket, her arms wreathing my neck, I gave in to her.

Chaos

Her mouth was sweet, her tongue teasing mine gently. But I knew I couldn't restrain myself for long. I wanted this woman with a desperation I'd never known before. It didn't seem to matter how many hours or days or weeks passed, I didn't think I'd ever get enough of her. I looked forward to a lifetime with this woman. From the beginning, I hadn't been looking for a one-night stand with Payton. I'd known the very first time I'd laid eyes on her that I wanted much, much longer than that.

Easing even closer, I slid my hand behind her neck, cradling her head as I slipped my tongue deeper into her mouth. When she kissed me back as though she was craving me as much as I was her, I nearly lost what remaining good sense I had left.

Before I knew it, Payton was practically under me, her hands traveling beneath my jacket, then beneath my T-shirt. The gentle scrape of her fingernails against my skin had my hips thrusting forward, my erection rubbing against her.

Oh, hell. This woman was going to be the death of me.

The air was cool against my overheated skin when she lifted my shirt, but not enough to reduce the heat that was boiling inside me.

The song changed, although I wasn't paying much attention. In fact, it wasn't until Payton drew back, looking up at me, that I noticed anything other than the feel of her lush body beneath mine.

"You listen to country music?" she asked, grinning.

I lifted my head to try and make out the song. A new one by Florida Georgia Line was playing. "I listen to everything," I told her.

"Good." Her approval made my chest swell.

But then she pulled me back down to her, our lips crushing together, our tongues dueling. Within minutes, I thought my head was going to explode. I knew if I didn't stop now, I'd end up making love to her outside, beneath the stars. And as awesome as that sounded, it wasn't the way I intended the night to go. I wanted to ravish her all night and wake with her in my arms in the morning. That wasn't possible out here, so I lingered for a little longer before I pulled back.

We were both breathing hard.

"I could do this all night," I told her.

"Me, too," Payton whispered.

It took a few minutes for me to get my body under control, but I managed. When I felt a little more level-headed, not quite so keyed up, I sat up, resting my forearms on my knees, and stared at the track.

"Are you gonna drive again?" Payton asked, seemingly reading my mind.

"I don't know, Payton. I really don't know."

"Well, I think you will one day. Maybe not for a while, but it'll come back to you. And when it does, I'll be right here beside you, ready to cheer you on," Payton said, her tone encouraging.

I hoped she was right. Not because I needed the adrenaline rush that came with racing. But it was something I loved. I had plans to build my own track, but not just to use for personal use. The more I'd thought about it, the more I wanted to do something to give back.

"I bought that house mostly for the land," I told Payton. "I'd love to have a track of my own one day. A track and a shop."

"A body shop?" she asked.

I peered at her over my shoulder. "Yeah. Something like that. I was thinking about talking to Toby and Leif. See if they might want to go into business together."

"Partners?"

"Something like that. We've always loved cars, and we've got the means between the three of us to do more than just open a body shop, but I like the idea of having something stable."

"And the track? What do you plan to do with that?"

"I was thinking about…" I turned my head away from her, staring out into the darkness again. "It might sound crazy, but I was thinking about opening it up to kids who are like I was. Give them something to look forward to. A little encouragement, possibly a skill that they can use in the future."

I felt Payton move, her hands circling my bicep. "I think that's a brilliant idea." She rested her head against my shoulder. "It's perfect, Sebastian."

I rested my cheek against the top of her head. "I want you to help me, Payton."

"Help you how?" she asked, her voice soft.

"I want you to be part of it. I want you to help me build it. All of it."

The silence drifted on the night breeze for only a moment before she said the words that I needed to hear. "I'll be right there with you. Every step of the way."

Chapter Eighteen

Payton

Saturday afternoon

I SPENT THE MORNING CLEANING Sebastian's house while he slept. I knew he wasn't sleeping much these days, and I'd awoken with the sun, anxiety nipping at me. Today we were going to talk to Aaliyah, and I was probably more nervous than Sebastian was. I hadn't talked to her since Vegas, and as far as I knew, she didn't have a clue as to what had transpired over the last few weeks. I didn't know her well enough to be able to predict how she was going to take all of the news.

Telling her about Leif was going to be easy compared to what Sebastian had to tell her. We still didn't have any information, no leads for Sebastian's mother's case, but Leif had left a note on the kitchen counter last night letting us know that Derrick wanted to stop by today. When, he hadn't said, so I figured I would get the house cleaned up, although there really wasn't much that needed to be done.

I was tempted to go for a swim, anything to help take my mind off the myriad thoughts racing through my head. I was thinking about today and the conversations to be had, but I continued to drift back to the discussion I'd had with Sebastian last night. He wanted to build a race track and a body shop right there on his property. The location for both was almost perfect, and I really was excited about the idea. More so about Sebastian, though.

I was so proud of him. He'd overcome so much in such a short time, and though we didn't have all the answers, he was moving forward and in a direction I wouldn't have expected. The idea of using the track for kids who were going through what Sebastian had once been through was admirable. Sebastian was going to take all that he'd learned in life and use it to help others.

Every day, just when I thought it wasn't possible to love him more than I already did, he proved me wrong.

Leif sauntered into the kitchen while I was cleaning the sink.

"Mornin'," he greeted, his voice rough from sleep.

"Hey."

"Are you ... cleaning?" he asked, pinning me with a bewildered stare.

"I am," I confirmed with a smile. "Why? Were you hoping to do the honors?"

Leif laughed, scratching the stubble along his jaw as he opened the cabinet and pulled out the coffee.

"Already made," I told him, nodding toward the full coffeepot.

"Have I mentioned how much I love you?" he mumbled, still half asleep.

"She's mine, so don't get too attached," Sebastian said, wandering up behind me and wrapping his arms around my waist. "Good morning."

"Good morning," I told him, turning my head to the side so I could meet his lips for a kiss.

"You know, I'll hire someone to do that."

"No, you won't," I told him sternly. "We are all quite capable of keeping this place clean. No need to spend the money."

Sebastian chuckled and headed for the coffeepot, retrieving the last of the mugs I had set on the counter. Once his cup was full, he turned and leaned against the counter. While I ran the water in the sink, I stole a sideways glance at him. He had on a pair of jeans and nothing else, and he looked even more delicious that morning than I'd ever seen him. Maybe it was the bed head or the stubble that lined his jaw. Then again, it could've just been the muscles that flexed in his arms when he lifted the cup to his mouth, or the way his abs contracted as he crossed one ankle over the other.

Not wanting to get caught ogling him, I returned my focus to the sink, using the sprayer and then wringing out the sponge.

"What time's Derrick coming?" Sebastian asked Leif.

"He didn't say. Just texted me and said he had something to talk to you about."

I glanced over my shoulder at Leif.

"Is it news?" Sebastian asked. "Or more of the same shit?"

"Don't know."

These two amused me to no end. They were both half asleep, sipping coffee, and trying to hold a conversation.

"What time is Aaliyah coming over?" I asked.

"Don't know. Why?" Sebastian said.

"I was thinking I could go back to my apartment for a little while today."

Sebastian lifted an eyebrow but didn't say anything.

"I just thought y'all might want a little privacy. That's all."

Sebastian reached out and grabbed my pinky finger with his. "I'd like you to be here."

I nodded. If he wanted me there, then I'd be there. I just didn't want to intrude if they needed to have a private conversation.

"I want you here when Derrick shows up, too."

"Okay," I told him. I really didn't have anything else to do, aside from going to the grocery store.

"I'm gonna go for a swim. Then I'll shower," Sebastian said, pouring the rest of his coffee in the sink and rinsing the cup before depositing it in the dishwasher. He gave me a quick peck on the cheek before he disappeared down the hall to the pool.

Leif backed up until he could see down the hall, obviously watching Sebastian leave. When he returned, he moved close and lowered his voice.

"What do I need to get?" he asked.

"I've pretty well got it covered," I told him, pulling open a drawer and retrieving the note pad I'd placed in there earlier. I flipped the page until I came to the list. "My parents are bringing a ham and sweet potato casserole. Chloe and Toby agreed to bring desserts. Aaron and Garrett are taking care of the bread. Your mom and Derrick are gonna bring mashed potatoes and a couple of other side dishes. Sean and Dale volunteered to bring drinks. Oh, and Toby's parents are bringing napkins and stuff."

"Did you get the turkey yet?" he asked, his eyes darting back to the hallway where Sebastian had disappeared.

"Not yet. I was gonna do that today, but I'm not sure I can. If not, I'll send Chloe."

"So we're still on, though?"

I nodded, my gaze traveling to the empty hallway as well.

It wasn't easy pulling off a surprise Christmas dinner. Especially not when so many people were coming. I'd come up with the idea one night when Chloe and I had been sitting at the apartment, trying to figure out just what we were going to do for Christmas. She'd mentioned Sebastian, and that was when I'd decided to put together a surprise Christmas dinner for him. When I'd revealed my plans to Leif and Toby, they'd thought it was a brilliant idea. According to them, Sebastian wasn't planning to do anything for Christmas, the same way he hadn't done anything for Thanksgiving.

Now, we were just tasked with pulling it all together without him knowing.

"I'll need your help with the turkey, though. You can ask anyone, I'm the world's worst cook."

Leif laughed. "I'll help however you need me."

"Good. Then I think we're set."

Leif went to the sink and rinsed his cup, also placing it in the dishwasher before he headed toward the door that led to his wing of the house. He stopped, placing his hand on the doorjamb before turning back and looking at me. "You're the best thing that's ever happened to him, Payton."

I stared at him for a second and then gave him a watery smile. "I think it's the other way around, but thank you."

A brief nod was all I got from Leif before he disappeared from the room, leaving me standing there by myself. And though I was alone in the kitchen, I didn't feel alone. Not anymore.

***

"Wait. Repeat that," Sebastian insisted, stopping Derrick mid-sentence.

We'd been sitting in the living room for the last fifteen minutes, listening to the detective go over a new lead he'd gotten. How he'd managed to dig that deep, I still didn't know. I was baffled by the amount of information he had this time versus the last time he'd paid Sebastian a visit.

"I did some digging into Conrad and Lauren's credit cards," Derrick repeated as Sebastian had requested. "And it wasn't easy, let me say that up front. Considering how old this case is, it's hard to find records. Most places don't have to keep them after seven years, but I lucked out. Sort of."

"What were you looking for?" Leif asked. He looked as tense as I felt.

"There was obviously a car accident, and since we know someone hit Sebastian's mother, based on the accident report, it means there was another vehicle damaged. Without much to go on, I looked into the vehicles that Conrad and Lauren owned at the time. Nothing came up on them. So, then I decided to dig a little deeper. If I'd had the case at the time, I would've looked into local body shops, tried to see if any of them did work on a vehicle that had damage coinciding with the damage to Sebastian's mother's car. Unfortunately, that wasn't an option.

"However, I did pull Lauren and Conrad's credit report and found that Lauren had applied for a credit card shortly after your mother's accident," Derrick told Sebastian. "I figured what the hell. I called the credit card company and asked if they had any records that dated back to that time. Hoping maybe their accounting department was behind on tossing out old files."

I was sitting on the edge of my seat, my fingers linked with Sebastian's.

"They didn't have anything that far back, but they did have some records for months following that. Turned out, Lauren's credit card had been used at a body shop here in town. However, it was six months after the accident. I know it was a long time ago, but do you ever recall Lauren being in an accident?"

All eyes slid to Sebastian. "Not that I remember, no."

I had to wonder whether Sebastian would've remembered something that had happened so long ago. Hell, I had a hard enough time remembering things that had happened last year, much less more than a decade ago, especially when I was a kid.

"What body shop?" Leif asked.

Derrick glanced down at the pad of paper he was holding in his hand. "Fowler Body and Frame."

My stomach lurched. Was Derrick serious?

"Oh, God." I jumped to my feet and bolted to the nearest bathroom, slamming the door behind me and dropping to my knees in front of the toilet, my lunch returning with a vengeance.

And when I'd puked until my stomach was empty, I started crying.

Chapter Nineteen

Sebastian

WHEN PAYTON RAN FROM THE room, I got to my feet, ready to go after her, but Leif stopped me, holding up his hand. "Give her a minute."

Derrick's attention was flipping back and forth between me and the hallway where Payton had fled. "What's going on?"

I glanced down the hallway, refusing to sit until I knew that Payton was okay. But I could at least answer Derrick's question. "Fowler Body and Frame... That's her father's body shop."

"Holy shit," Leif muttered, watching me.

"I'll be right back."

When I reached the bathroom door, I tapped on it with the tips of my fingers. Payton didn't answer, so I tried the knob. My heart wrenched when I saw her sitting on the floor, her knees pulled into her chest. She had a washcloth in her hands, and her face was streaked from the tears streaming down her face.

"Angel," I whispered, lowering myself to the floor beside her.

"Oh, my God, Sebastian. I'm so, so sorry."

I gripped her chin and forced her to look at me. I knew my confusion was etched across my forehead. "What are you talking about?"

"My father's shop. They probably fixed the car that was used to kill your mother."

"Payton," I said firmly when more tears escaped her eyes. "Stop it."

Her eyes opened wide and a sob wracked her body.

"This isn't your fault, if that's what you're thinking. Or your father's."

"But—"

I cupped the back of her head and pulled her face against my chest, holding her as she tried to collect herself. I could understand her shock. It seemed surreal the coincidence, but aside from Lauren using her credit card at Payton's father's body shop, there was nothing else that tied the two together. We still didn't know what Lauren had fixed at the time. I could admit that I was reaching, desperate for answers, but I had to remind myself that this could all very well be a dead end.

"Do you think Derrick talked to my father?" Payton asked, her voice raspy from her tears.

"No," I assured her. "I think your father would've called you if someone came in there mentioning my name." As a matter of fact, I would bet money on that. Hal would've called Payton instantly if he thought for a second that there might be something awry, and having a detective show up asking questions about something that had happened more than ten years ago would've been a red flag.

I ran my hand down her hair, waiting until she calmed down.

"Feeling better?" I asked when her body stopped trembling.

Payton nodded against my chest.

"Ready to go back out there?"

Another nod. I got to my feet and helped her to stand.

"Can you give me a minute?" she asked when she was on her feet.

"Yeah. I'll be out there if you need me."

"Okay."

I left Payton in the bathroom and returned to find Derrick and Leif talking quietly.

"She okay?" Leif and Derrick asked at the exact same time.

"She's fine. She'll be back in a minute." I lowered myself to the couch once again and focused on Derrick. "I take it you haven't contacted the body shop. Considering Hal would recognize my name, he would've called Payton. This was obviously the first she'd heard of it."

"That was my next step. It's a long shot that they might have records from that far back, but the good thing is that most of it would've been paper records rather than electronic. If we're lucky, they stored that paperwork somewhere and forget about it."

I nodded, hoping he was right. Before I could say anything, Payton returned to the room. She took a seat at my side once again, but she didn't meet my gaze.

"Do you think it would be better for me to go to my father?" she asked Derrick directly, her voice much stronger than it had been a few minutes ago.

"Do you think it's a possibility that he'll have the records from that long ago?" Derrick questioned.

"More than likely," she told him. "My father doesn't throw anything out. Ever."

I knew my relief could be heard in the breath I took, but again, Payton didn't look at me.

"If you think you can look through the records, that'll help me. I can go talk to him, but he could very easily tell me that he doesn't want anyone rummaging through his old files."

"If he has it, I can get it," Payton assured Derrick.

My phone beeped, signaling a text. I grabbed it from the arm of the couch and looked at the message. Glancing over at Leif, I gave him a subtle nod. Aaliyah was on her way.

"All right," Derrick said, getting to his feet. "I'm gonna get out of your hair for now." He looked at Payton as we all stood. "If you find out anything, please let me know. And if you can get your hands on the files, I need everything you can find. Pictures, estimates, credit card receipts."

"Okay."

"I'll walk you out," Leif told Derrick.

I watched as the two men headed toward the front door and then outside. When Payton and I were alone, I pulled her against me, pressing my lips to her forehead. "I love you, Angel."

"I love you, too," she whispered.

I tipped her chin up so our eyes met. "Despite what you think, this is actually good news. Lauren could've used any body shop in town to have a car worked on. The fact that it happens to be your father's shop is nothing short of a miracle. If he does have the paperwork, then we're that much closer to figuring this out."

Payton swallowed. "You're right. I know you are. It just feels so... I don't know. It just doesn't sit well with me to know that my father could've very well repaired the car that was used to kill your mother."

"We don't know that he did, Payton. We have no idea what Lauren took to him. But hopefully, we'll find out soon enough."

Payton's arms tightened around me, and I leaned down, pressing my lips to hers. I'd known this would be emotional for me, having to relive what had happened to my mother all over again, but I'd never imagined that it would take a turn like this. It gave me an entirely new outlook on the whole six degrees of separation thing.

"Aaliyah's on her way over," I told Payton when she pulled back from me.

"Do you mind if I go upstairs for a little while?" she asked softly.

"Not at all."

The front door opened and Leif walked inside. Behind him was Aaliyah, her eyes wide as she looked around my house for the first time.

"I'm gonna say hi to her and then go upstairs," Payton told me before making her way over to my sister.

The two women greeted one another and spoke softly before Payton headed up the stairs. I smiled at her and she smiled back, but it was forced. As much as I was worried about her, I had other pressing things on my mind. Things that I needed to get out in the open.

And this time, they involved Aaliyah.

My sister approached me slowly. She wasn't smiling. In fact, her face was void of all expression as she looked around slowly.

"Nice place," she said, her voice just as cold as her eyes.

She was pissed, but I had known she would be.

"Thanks."

Aaliyah's crystal blue eyes locked on mine as she said, "Why'd you ask me to come over, Sebastian? After all these weeks? You haven't wanted to have anything to do with me, and all of a sudden here I am."

"We need to talk," I told her, gesturing toward the couch.

In that prissy way I was more used to from Lauren than from Aaliyah, my sister lowered herself to a cushion, placing her purse at her feet. "Then talk."

Leif, who had disappeared briefly, returned to the room, nodding at me to take a seat in the recliner. I smirked at him but traded places so he could sit beside Aaliyah.

Aaliyah's gaze darted back and forth between the two of us before stopping on me. "What do you need to say, Sebastian? I've got things to do."

"Cut the crap, Aaliyah," I said smartly. "I know you're pissed and you've got every right to be. I moved out without telling you directly. As far as I'm concerned, that's the least of my concerns at the moment. What we have to say to you is probably going to have you hating me more than ever."

Aaliyah's gaze lowered to the floor. "I don't hate you, Sebastian. I'm just… I don't know. I'm hurt. We all went to Vegas, and I know shit happened, but I didn't think you'd turn your back on me because of it. Leif and I fought, but I didn't think that would affect our relationship."

"What the hell are you talking about?" I asked, not giving her time to answer me. "Is that what you thought? Shit. Aaliyah, that's not what happened." I hadn't thought about the fact my sister would've believed I could turn my back on her because she'd had an argument with my best friend. Hindsight being twenty-twenty and all, I could totally see how she would jump to that conclusion. "I'm sorry, Aaliyah. Really sorry. But that's not what happened."

"Then what did happen?" she asked, her eyes sliding over to Leif briefly.

Not giving Leif a chance to explain, I jumped right in. "The same day we came back from Vegas, I had a race scheduled. Then the unthinkable happened that night. There was an accident."

Aaliyah's eyes widened, and I noticed she looked me over as though she was trying to find signs of damage. "I wasn't hurt, Aaliyah." That wasn't entirely true, but my injuries had been far less serious than what Leif had endured. "Leif was, though."

Her head snapped over, and I watched as she studied Leif. "What happened?"

"Some asshole clipped the car and it flipped. Sebastian and Toby managed to get me out before the car went up in a fireball."

"Oh, my God."

"Aaliyah," I said sharply, wanting her to turn her attention back to me. "That night, when Leif and I were in the hospital, Payton tried to call you. She tried to call Conrad first, but he didn't answer, so she didn't leave a message."

"I didn't get a message, either, Sebastian," Aaliyah snapped.

"I know. Payton called your mother and told her what happened."

"She actually spoke to my mother?" Aaliyah asked incredulously.

"Yeah. Payton explained what had happened, and Lauren said okay. No one showed up at the hospital to see how I was doing."

I could tell Aaliyah was processing the information, and it wasn't long before her eyes widened and her mouth fell open. "My mother knew what happened and she didn't tell anyone?"

I didn't answer her directly, just continued with the story. "Leif was in the hospital for two weeks. When he got out, he moved in here."

Aaliyah's attention was once again on Leif.

"Are you okay?"

"I am now," he said, a note of indifference in his tone. I could tell he was happy to see her, but I could also sense that Leif didn't want her to know that.

"But, Aaliyah, Payton did leave a message on your voice mail. She didn't tell you what happened, but she did ask that you call her."

"I'm serious, Sebastian, I didn't get a message," she said defensively.

"And I believe you. However, I believe that's because your mother didn't want you to get that message."

Aaliyah stared at me in disbelief for a moment before she huffed. "You can't be serious, Sebastian. Are you telling me that my own mother wouldn't want me to know that my brother was hurt?"

"That's exactly what I'm telling you."

"There's no way that's true."

"Oh, it's true," Leif stated, leaning back against the cushions, propping his arm on the armrest.

"Why didn't someone try to call me again?" Aaliyah asked.

"Because by then we didn't want to pull you into it. I knew that Lauren had kept you from getting that message. And she never told Conrad about the wreck. I was still living there for two weeks after it happened, Aaliyah. He never brought it up. Hell, he didn't even ask about the scratches or bruises."

"Is that why you stopped coming to dinner?"

"That and other reasons," I told her honestly.

I got to my feet and started to pace the floor, trying to figure out how I wanted to tell my sister the rest of the story.

It wasn't going to be easy, I knew that much.

Sebastian

BEFORE I COULD COME UP with a rational way to tell my sister that I thought her parents were murderers and not sound like I needed to be put in a straitjacket and locked in a padded cell, Leif spoke up.

"Just tell her what's going on. And *you*," Leif said to Aaliyah directly, "I want you to sit right there until he's finished. Don't get up and try to leave just because you don't like what he has to say. When he's done, you can choose to believe him or not. Until then, keep your pretty little ass right there on the couch. Understand?"

I half expected Aaliyah to get defensive and tell Leif just what she thought of his commands, but she didn't. She nodded her head and then looked up at me.

So what did I do? Leif had just given me the perfect entry for the hardest conversation I'd ever planned to have, and instead of blurting out all of the facts as I knew them, I panicked. And now I was pacing the floor of my living room, likely wearing a hole in the hardwood, contemplating what would happen if I ran out the door.

I knew I couldn't. My sister would think I was a nutcase. Then again, maybe she already thought that. At this point, I was pretty sure that diagnosis wasn't too far off the mark, but I really didn't want Aaliyah to think I'd lost my damn mind.

Worse, she was just watching me from where she sat on my couch, waiting patiently for me to get to the point.

Perhaps because Lauren was Aaliyah's mother, announcing my suspicions about my father and stepmother was far more difficult now than it had been when I'd shared my revelation with Payton. Although I'd thought Payton would bolt for the door, I pretty well knew that Aaliyah would.

And unlike Payton, I hadn't kept any secrets from Aaliyah as far as Conrad was concerned. With Payton, she hadn't even realized that Conrad was my father at first. Aaliyah already knew, so I couldn't use that to ease into the harder parts.

"Sebastian," Leif called out, pulling me back to the present.

I lifted an eyebrow in response.

"Get on with it, bro."

Right. Get on with it. I wanted to see him try to tell his sister that he believed their father was a killer.

I'm pretty sure Conrad's the man responsible for killing my mother.

Those were the words. Now if I could just get my voice to attach to them, we'd be in business.

My body went from eighty to zero in a matter of seconds, my heart stealing all the blood from my body, including my brain. This was a hell of a lot harder than it looked.

Meeting Aaliyah's hard gaze, I decided to go for it.

Dropping to the recliner, I rested my elbows on my knees and lowered my head, speaking to the floor when I did finally find my voice. But I finally did. And I told Aaliyah everything I knew without looking at her once.

And the last words I spoke were, "I have reason to believe that Conrad and Lauren are responsible for killing my mother."

I expected a shriek from my sister, or maybe a verbal assault. I got neither. So I forced my head up, my eyes sliding up to meet hers from across the room. Even as she stared back at me blankly, Aaliyah still hadn't said a word. Even now, as her eyes pinned me to my chair, my heart rate double-timing it, she wasn't saying anything.

But then there was a hand on my shoulder, and I flinched. Turning my head, I saw Payton standing beside me. She was watching Aaliyah with a concerned expression on her face. When she noticed me watching her, she looked down and gave me a sad but reassuring smile.

"I called my dad," Payton said, talking to both me and the others in the room. "I'm gonna go to his shop tomorrow when they're closed. I told him I'd stop by tonight and explain what I was looking for and why."

Peering back at Aaliyah, her silence bearing down on me until it was difficult to breathe, I had no idea what I was supposed to do now. That was information that I'd never imagined having to share with her. None of it.

"Aaliyah?" I prompted my sister, needing her to say something.

"What?" she asked, sounding completely torn up on the inside. I knew just how she felt.

"Aren't you gonna say something?"

Leif moved closer to her, and when he reached for her hand, Aaliyah didn't pull away. She merely linked her fingers with my best friend's and continued to stare back at me.

"I don't even know what to say, Sebastian. When you first started the conversation, I actually envisioned myself jumping up and running out of the house screaming at you. But now…"

"Now what?" I asked when she left her sentence hanging.

Payton lowered herself to the arm of the chair and kept her hand on my shoulder. I needed to have her close, and she must've realized that.

"So you don't think I'm crazy?" I asked, aiming for a little humor but failing when the words came out stricken with fear.

"Well…" Aaliyah gave me a small smile. The one that said she was my little sister and she would always think I was crazy. "Shit. I don't know what to think. It all sounds so… I don't know. It sounds too real."

"It is real," I told her. "Granted, nothing has been proven, and I have no idea where this will lead, but Aaliyah" — I paused to swallow — "I have to figure this out. I have to know."

"I get that," she replied. "I do."

"I have a question," Leif said, his attention on Aaliyah.

I watched as my sister turned her head to look at the man sitting by her side, offering her a comforting hand.

No one said anything; we just waited for Leif to continue.

He finally did. "Why don't you sound surprised?"

"I… I…" Aaliyah stuttered, but didn't finish what she'd been about to say.

We all continued to watch her, waiting. I was literally on the edge of my seat, my hands wringing together between my knees. I had just spilled some crazy shit, and Aaliyah wasn't saying anything. Worse than that, I didn't know what was going through her head. I wanted to shake her, to force the words loose, because I knew she had something to say.

Finally, Aaliyah's back straightened. "I know my mother hates you," she said. The statement was so matter-of-fact it was almost like my sister had slapped me across the face.

Not that I didn't know that already, but honestly, it still hurt just a little.

"Hate is a pretty strong word," Payton said.

"I know," Aaliyah said sadly. "But honestly, I don't think it's necessarily Sebastian that she dislikes so much. I've heard her when she goes on a tirade. Sometimes I think she dislikes me for the simple fact that she has to share my father with me. I'm not making excuses for her, though."

"Why not?" I asked, confused. "Why wouldn't you be defending her, Aaliyah?" My voice rose with every word I spoke. If I'd been wrongly accusing someone, I'd like to think that her own daughter would come to her defense.

"I don't know," Aaliyah snapped. "I… Shit, Sebastian. I've lived with them my entire life. Do you think I'm clueless? Do you think I don't see how volatile she can be? Or how selfish she is? I'm the one who has had to deal with it firsthand. Not you."

"Not *me*?" I retorted angrily. "You don't think that I had to put up with being treated like a visitor in a house that was supposed to be my home?"

"Sebastian," Payton said, her tone soothing, as if she were trying to calm a wild animal.

I bit my tongue and stared at Payton. My eyebrow slid up into my hairline; my breath lodged in my chest as I waited. When she didn't say anything more, I took a deep breath and briefly touched her hand with mine before turning back to Aaliyah.

"Look, Aaliyah," I finally said, my hands sliding into my hair and then to the back of my neck. "I don't know what all of this means. I know you're trying to process it, and I'm a shithead for throwing it all at you at once, but I didn't know what else to do. I moved out because I had to get away. Had to get out from under Conrad's thumb. Your mother is practically celebrating now that I'm gone, but—"

"Why do you think that?" Aaliyah interrupted.

I was about to explain the conversation Payton had had with Lauren, but I didn't have to. The woman I loved more than life itself spoke up, defending me as she relayed, very calmly, the threat that Lauren had made toward her.

"She threatened to have you fired?" Aaliyah asked, her eyes wide with her surprise.

"Yes. And on top of that, I feel like I've got someone watching me while I'm at work. Every time I turn around, Trevor is there."

"Trevor?" Aaliyah asked, sparing me a brief glance. "My *cousin* Trevor?"

I nodded.

"Why is he there?" she asked. If I was reading her correctly, that was a hint of fear in her tone. It made the hair on the back of my neck stand on end.

"He works there," Payton told her simply.

"For my father?" Aaliyah's tone was bordering on hysterical now.

"What's the matter?" Leif asked. I could see he had picked up on her mood change. He moved an inch closer to her, squeezing her hand.

"Dad promised me that Trevor would never be allowed back at the house. I only assumed that meant he would never be anywhere near any of us."

The chaos seeped into my head once again, a blinding rage building in my bloodstream as I watched the fear on my sister's face. She didn't need to explain for me to know that something had happened. Something she hadn't yet told me.

"Aaliyah," Leif said softly, his fingers hooking beneath her chin to turn her to face him. "I need you to tell me what that means." His voice was dead calm.

Tears formed in Aaliyah's eyes, and I knew right then and there that Trevor wasn't going to be walking for long. And for the first time, it probably wasn't going to be me who doled out the beating he deserved.

No, if Trevor thought he should fear me, well, he was about to learn it was one thing to get me to unleash my anger. It was something else entirely for Leif to lose control.

Shit.

Chapter Twenty-One

Payton

AS I SAT ON THE arm of the recliner, feeling the tension in Sebastian's body, I knew whatever had spooked Aaliyah was going to have everlasting repercussions on him. Just the mention of Trevor had her eyes widening and fear tightening the perfect skin of her lovely face. The woman was terrified, and Sebastian had noticed.

However, for the first time since I'd met Sebastian, I knew by watching Leif that the rage that Sebastian battled every day wasn't anything compared to what was now churning inside Leif. I'd seen him irritated when everyone had wanted to treat him with kid gloves after he'd come home from the hospital, but I'd never seen him pissed.

Quite frankly, it scared me just a little.

I wondered whether we should give Aaliyah a minute for her to gather herself. I was just about to make the suggestion when she started to speak.

"When I was sixteen," Aaliyah began, and Sebastian's body tensed even more, "Trevor came to stay with us for a couple of weeks around the holidays. To be honest, he always made me nervous. I found it strange that he was supposedly family, yet he leered at me whenever I was in the room. It gave me a creepy feeling, so I found myself trying to stay away from him as much as possible. I had been doing a good job when my mother told me that I needed to spend more time with him. That was one of the few times I'd ever questioned an order from my mother. I remember that she hadn't been happy, and her answer had been that he was family and he wanted to spend time getting to know me.

"At first, I pretended to agree, but I still managed to sneak around, avoiding him at all costs. But then I'd been home from school during Christmas break, and when I tried to convince my mother to let me go out with my friends, she told me no." Aaliyah looked up, her eyes touching every face in the room briefly. "Maybe it sounds snooty, but I wasn't used to being told no. I argued with her, and my father told me to go to my room. I did, without arguing with him, too. I'd been in there for a couple of hours when Trevor knocked on my door. I didn't want to let him in, but I did. After closing the door, he came to sit on the edge of my bed. He asked me what had happened, and I told him, leaving out some of the details. That was the first time he tried to touch me."

Leif jumped up from the couch, scaring the shit out of me. He roared as he paced to the opposite side of the room and stopped as he looked out the window. Apparently, he knew, just as I did, where this conversation was going. The nausea that had hit me earlier when I'd learned that my father had worked on a vehicle that could possibly be the one that had run Sebastian's mother off the road and ultimately resulted in her death came flooding back.

Knowing Leif was in no position to console Aaliyah, I took his spot on the couch, placing my arm over her shoulder. She was shaking, her eyes downcast. "You don't have to continue," I told her.

"I do," she said softly.

Aaliyah didn't speak for a couple of minutes, but then she seemed to gather herself, and she surprised me when she took my hand in hers.

"That time, he just put his hand on my leg. I knew immediately that it wasn't a friendly, consoling touch, either. It grossed me out and I pulled away. I could tell he was irritated, but he pretended it didn't bother him. Luckily my father came to my door. I told him to come in, and he dismissed Trevor so that he could talk to me. I didn't tell him what had happened with Trevor; I just listened while he tried to tell me that family was important and I needed to make Trevor feel welcome in the house. He told me that Trevor was giving my mother a hard time about not feeling as though he was part of the family. It all sounded like a bullshit sob story, but I couldn't very well tell my father that."

Aaliyah paused, her head lifting, and she glanced across the room, where Leif was still standing, his back rigid as he stared out the back window, overlooking the vast acreage that belonged to Sebastian.

"You said that was the first time," Sebastian said, his tone lethal.

"Yeah," Aaliyah answered, looking directly at her brother. "He stayed until New Year's. My mother put on an elaborate party that year, and I was told I had to attend, so I did. I had tried to be cordial to Trevor, but I hadn't wanted to be around him, and I think he noticed. That night" — Aaliyah's voice shook — "at the party, Trevor cornered me. I'd gone down to the kitchen, hoping for a few minutes alone, and I hadn't been down there long when he walked in. He tried to talk to me briefly, telling me he was going back home in a couple of days. In an effort to get him to leave me alone, I told him that it had been good having him there. I then excused myself and told him I needed to get back to the party. I'd made it halfway down the hall when he came up to me from behind." Aaliyah's eyes filled with tears. "The next thing I knew, he had me backed against the wall, his hand roughly going beneath my dress. He tried to get—" Aaliyah's sob nearly broke my heart and I squeezed her hand. "He tried to get into my panties, but I fought him off."

"Son of a motherfucking bitch," Sebastian barked as he got to his feet, his head tilted back as he stared up at the ceiling. "Why the fuck didn't I know about this?"

Aaliyah was crying at this point, and I knew she needed to take a break. This was obviously painful for her, but she kept talking.

"One of the security guys, Anthony, came down the hall, and I yelled. Trevor backed off instantly, telling Anthony there was nothing to worry about. When we were alone again, Trevor told me that if I told my mother what had happened, she wouldn't believe me. At first, I remember thinking that was bullshit, my mother always believed me, but then I thought about how she had been treating me since Trevor had arrived. I didn't tell her."

"You said earlier that your dad promised that Trevor would never be allowed back in the house," I prompted.

"I was nineteen when Trevor … when he tried to rape me."

I looked up, immediately locating both Leif and Sebastian. They looked as though they would snap at any second, and I feared that they would. The veins in Sebastian's arms were protruding, his biceps flexing as his hands balled into fists, the muscle in his jaw ticking as he clenched his teeth together. This was bad and only getting worse.

I gave Aaliyah's hand a reassuring squeeze, and I got to my feet. Sebastian was going to lose it any second, and I figured Leif wasn't that far away. Not that I blamed either of them. I was tempted to kill Trevor with my bare hands.

"Leif," I called to the man probably lost in his own hate as he tried his best to avoid the situation.

He turned to face me slowly, his face reflecting every ounce of anger and hatred he possessed.

"Can you sit with Aaliyah for a minute? I'm going to get us something to drink."

Leif nodded, his feet carrying him back into the room, but I could tell he was somewhere far, far away in his head.

I took Sebastian's hand and tugged him, forcing him to come with me. I was surprised when he didn't even attempt to struggle.

When we were in the kitchen, I released his hand and found the cabinet where he'd put the whiskey. I grabbed four glasses and set them on the counter before turning back to him.

Leaning against the counter opposite from where he stood, I merely watched him until his eyes focused and he looked at me.

"I know this is hard," I said softly, trying to keep my voice low enough that it didn't carry into the other room, "but we really need to keep it together for Aaliyah."

"Keep it together?" he asked in a strangled voice. "Are you fucking serious?"

I moved closer, pressing my hands on his chest and forcing him back against the counter. "I'm very serious right now," I assured him in a much harder tone than I'd ever used with him before.

His eyes raked my face, his mouth a hard, thin line. I knew he was pissed, and quite possibly, he was now angry with me, too, but I really didn't care.

"Don't you see what's happening?"

"Yeah," he answered, the word clipped. "I get that Lauren let a fucking rapist into that house. And the bastard hurt my sister."

"Yes, but..." I waited until I had his full attention before I continued. "At least once during that story, did you not wonder why Lauren would've allowed that?"

"What the hell are you talking about?"

"If Trevor has something on Lauren, she wouldn't've been in a position to stop him."

"Bullshit," he growled. "I don't give a fuck what he might be holding over her head, no mother should ever allow that to happen."

"Agreed." I definitely couldn't argue with his logic, but I still didn't think Sebastian had connected the dots. "Sebastian, what if Trevor was the driver of the car? What if Lauren paid him to do her dirty work?"

Chaos

His eyes narrowed, his face an inscrutable mask. That lasted all of about three seconds.

"Son of a bitch."

Yep, now he got it. Not that it made me feel any better. The idea that Trevor would've done something so heinous to Aaliyah, his own cousin, reiterated just how sick the guy was. And it all made too much sense.

I cupped Sebastian's face and held it. "Sebastian, I don't think your father is the one who had your mother killed. I think... I think it was Lauren and if I had to guess, she used Trevor to do her dirty work."

Chapter Twenty-Two

Sebastian

A KNOT THE SIZE OF a small state formed in my stomach, and I fought the urge to throw up.

Could it be possible? Could Conrad really be innocent in all of this?

I wasn't sure why my thoughts were gravitating in that direction, but what Payton said made so much sense. More sense than I'd thought possible.

It explained so much, including why Trevor was currently working for my father. If Trevor was holding this over Lauren's head, I could understand how she might be pulling the strings harder than normal. However, if that really was true and Trevor was the one who had T-boned my mother, pushing her car off the road and ultimately resulting in her death, then he was the murderer.

Then again, Trevor was scum of the earth, and he'd already been charged with aggravated sexual assault once. The scary part was, Aaliyah wasn't the one who'd pressed charges, I knew that much. Although she should have. Which meant Lauren had intervened. Lauren definitely had more to lose than he did.

I glanced over my shoulder, looking at Aaliyah. She was still sitting on the couch. Leif had his arms wrapped firmly around her, and she was crying. It made me want to put my fist through the wall. Of all the things I'd thought Aaliyah would say after I told her that I believed Conrad had something to do with my mother's death, this certainly hadn't been on the list.

I had expected her to throw a fit or argue that I was out of my mind or even tell me to go to hell. But definitely not this. To think she'd walked around with a secret like this sitting on her shoulders all this time… It went to prove just how inward my thoughts had been for so long. Until Payton had come along, I hadn't thought about much other than my anger and my hatred for the shit life had dumped on me.

Peering down at Payton, I realized she was studying me intently, probably waiting for me to fly off the handle. Admittedly, I was pretty damn close, but thanks to her, I was holding it together.

Unclenching my hands, I wrapped my arms around her and pulled her against me, cupping the back of her head and pressing my other hand against her back. She slid her arms around my waist, her fingertips digging into my back as she held me just as tightly.

"I love you, Angel," I whispered against her hair.

She squeezed me tighter, and that was all I needed. This woman, not only did she unhinge me, she pulled me together when I felt as though I was unraveling.

For the first time, I noticed the bottle of whiskey sitting on the counter along with the four glasses.

"Were you planning to get us drunk?" I teased, feeling significantly calmer than a few minutes ago although I was still ready to pull Trevor apart, one limb at a time.

"Something like that," she said, pulling back and looking up at me. "Let's go back in there. Your sister needs you right now. Just as much as you need her."

Payton was right. On both counts.

As easy as it would be just to walk out the front door and not come back until I could think straight, it wouldn't be fair to Aaliyah. She had just shared something I'd never expected, and I owed it to her to hear her out. Even if I wanted to rip Trevor's head from his body and play Hacky Sack with the damn thing. It wasn't going to help my sister.

My sister needed me, and I couldn't very well leave things like this.

I wouldn't put it past Aaliyah to jump to conclusions and assume that she had somehow brought this on herself. I'd heard of some women doing that. And I was a firm believer that no woman — I don't give a fuck what she was wearing, what she said, how she acted — brought it on herself.

I also didn't want her to think I was going to go off half-cocked. And I was pretty damn sure I'd looked rather crazy when I'd lost my shit a little while ago.

As I looked at Payton now, the expression on her face gave very little away. I wasn't sure whether that was sympathy or pity, not that I wanted either. This was a fucked-up situation all the way around. Aaliyah had just laid some heavy stuff on us, after I'd done the same to her, and Payton was there, still holding me together.

"I should go in there and talk to her, huh?" I asked, cupping her face in my hands.

"Yes, you should," Payton said, her voice calm and gentle. "I'll go with you."

Payton pulled away from me and reached for the bottle of whiskey, handing it over to me before turning back and grabbing the glasses.

My laugh sounded a little hysterical; however, I thought the whiskey was a rather brilliant idea. Getting drunk wasn't in the plan, but something to settle the nerves definitely wouldn't hurt.

We joined Aaliyah and Leif in the living room. The first thing I noticed was the crazy look in Leif's eyes. Yeah, I certainly wasn't the only one ready to dispense my own brand of justice. I knew my best friend was going to lead the pack on this one.

Aaliyah had stopped crying, but her head was still resting on Leif's shoulder. Her eyes widened when we walked into the room.

"That for me?" she asked, forcing a smile.

"It's for all of us," Payton said kindly. "I think it's been one of those days."

Payton placed the glasses on the table and then took the bottle from my hands, pouring a small amount into each glass before pushing them to the four corners of the table.

I reached for mine at the same time Payton reached for hers. Leif and Aaliyah were a little slower to get with the program, but they eventually retrieved their own glasses.

Payton held up her glass and cleared her throat. I noticed that Leif and Aaliyah grinned, and I followed suit. She was making a toast.

"To answers," Payton said, a slight wobble to her voice. "Because we will get answers. One way or another."

"Amen," I added, looking at Leif. Payton was right about that. We would get answers. I could pretty much guaran-fucking-tee it.

After spending the better part of the afternoon talking to Aaliyah, I wasn't sure if I felt better or worse. As much as I hadn't wanted to hear the details of what Trevor had done to her, I had stuck it out, listening to her soft words, barely audible half the time over the roar of my blood in my ears. By the time she was finished rehashing that horrific day, I was ready to hunt the bastard down and show him just what I thought of him. He wouldn't have walked away from that, I assure you that much.

When all was said and done, Payton had excused herself to go call her father. She was gone for a good half hour, and it was then that I realized she had opted to call him and tell him what was going on, rather than going to visit. When she'd returned to the room, I had told her I'd be more than willing to take her to see her parents. She had refused the offer, insisting that she didn't want to leave Aaliyah.

Since the others, Toby, Chloe, Aaron, and Garrett, were supposed to join us, Payton had also handled making those calls. Tonight just wasn't a good night.

Not that Aaliyah needed a babysitter, but she didn't need an audience, either. She and Leif had actually gone for a walk nearly two hours ago. I knew they had a lot to talk about, but I still worried. Payton tried to assure me that they were fine. I knew they were, but still.

I think the problem was that I was still too keyed up from the earlier discussion.

"Why don't you show me your office," Payton said, catching me off guard when she appeared in the living room a second later.

"Huh?" I asked, confused.

"Your office. You haven't shown it to me since you got it all set up."

I watched her, trying to figure out just what her angle was, but her expression was cool.

"Yeah, okay," I told her, pushing to my feet.

I wasn't sure if there was much to see in my office, but clearly Payton was trying to distract me, and I welcomed it. A chance to get out of my own head wasn't necessarily a bad thing.

Payton waited for me to stand and didn't move until I did, falling into step behind me as we made it to the closed doors beneath the stairs. I'd had blinds installed on the French doors to give me privacy, in the event that I needed it. I hadn't used the office but maybe once since everything was set up.

After walking in, I stepped to the side, trying to see the room from her point of view. The desk was still clean, nothing on the top. The credenza against the wall held my laptop but little else. There was a pencil holder, lacking the pencils, and a framed picture of Payton. I wasn't sure she knew about that one. I'd taken it with my cell phone while she was sleeping. It was a close-up of her face, peaceful as she slept in my bed. I had other pictures of her on my phone, mostly candid shots she hadn't realized I'd taken, but there were a couple of selfies we'd taken together. I intended to add a few of those to the office when I got a chance, but things had been a little crazy lately.

Payton closed the door when she stepped inside. It wasn't until I heard the lock engage that I realized my sweet angel wasn't just looking for a tour of my office, she was seriously creating a distraction.

I held my breath, and when she took my hand, smiling up at me, I saw the gleam in her hazel eyes.

She tugged my arm until I moved, leading me around the desk and then gently urging me to stop in front of my chair. I was tempted to drop into the chair and pull her into my lap, but she clearly had other plans.

She unhooked the button on my jeans and lowered the zipper, still watching my face. When she pushed my jeans to my knees, taking my boxers with them, I nearly lost what little control I still had.

"Sit," she demanded softly, urging me into my chair.

When she dropped to her knees in front of me, I let out an involuntary groan.

There were more to follow when she wrapped her soft, cool fingers around my shaft, stroking me slowly until I was hard as steel in her palm.

"Payton." I said her name more as a warning, but she didn't seem to care.

Her eyes met mine, her smile still firmly in place. I quickly got lost in the smooth stroke of her hand up and down my dick. She was teasing me, and my body responded instantly, my cock pulsing in her hand.

Payton didn't seem to be in a hurry, and I was just getting used to the idea of a hand job when she leaned forward and pressed her lips to the head of my dick. I sucked in air and closed my eyes. My hands were on the arms of the chair, my fingernails digging into the leather as I hung on for dear life.

"Oh, damn, baby," I groaned, relishing the feel of her tongue as she laved my cock as slowly as she had been stroking it.

I squeezed my eyes shut when she wrapped her lips around me and lowered her head, taking me all the way into the sweet heaven of her mouth. I wasn't going to last, but I didn't think it really mattered.

"Payton, baby," I whispered, "if you're trying to distract me, you're doin' a damn good job."

She didn't respond, but the gentle vibration of her lips as she moaned against me nearly sent me into oblivion. Payton worked me over for a couple of minutes, and I managed to refrain from exploding, but it became more and more difficult. When she cupped my balls in her hand, I knew I couldn't take much more.

Linking my fingers into her hair, I guided her head until she was bobbing faster and faster. It wasn't long before my breath lodged in my throat and every muscle in my body tensed.

"Payton, if you don't stop, I'm gonna come in your mouth." Another warning, one I expected her to heed, but she didn't, and a second later, I exploded, my dick pulsing in her mouth as I came so hard I knew it was a damn good thing I was sitting down.

As I came back down to earth, I realized something: my sweet angel had a naughty side.

And I loved her even more, although I hadn't thought it was possible.

Chapter Twenty-Three

Payton

Sunday

SEBASTIAN INSISTED ON COMING WITH me to my father's shop. We got up early, but not due to an alarm clock or any other annoying wake-up call. I'd had a hard time sleeping although both my brain and my body had been exhausted.

After we crawled into bed the night before, Sebastian had paid me back for the little impromptu blow job I'd given him in his office. He gave back tenfold, making me scream his name on more than one occasion until my body was sated. Too bad my brain hadn't shut down enough to sleep soundly. I woke before the sun was up but didn't move, not wanting to disturb Sebastian. It wasn't long before he was awake, though. And when he suggested a quick shower, I didn't refuse him.

Our breakfast consisted of coffee and a breakfast sandwich at the first drive-thru that we came to. We arrived at my father's shop around eight. On a Sunday morning, that was unheard of. Luckily, no one would be there to question us because Fowler Body and Frame was closed on Sunday.

I still carried a key to my father's shop on my key ring because he told me I never knew when I might need it. I was grateful for his foresight, because it came in handy this morning and saved us at least an hour trip out to my parents' house and back.

When we arrived, I didn't bother giving Sebastian a tour because I knew he didn't care any more than I did. The goal was to check out the old files to see if we could find something to tie Lauren back to the accident that had killed Sebastian's mother. My father had informed me the files that dated that far back were in a storage shed at the back of the property behind the paint booth, so that was where we went.

As I opened the door and saw the rows of boxes stacked to the ceiling, some of them dusty from the length of time they'd been stored there, I knew we had our work cut out for us. I set my coffee cup on the window ledge, and we left the door open to air the place out but immediately got to work. Some of the boxes were labeled, others weren't. I went with the idea that the older boxes would be in the back, so we moved them around, placed those that we knew held more recent files on one side and others that were closer to the time frame we were looking for in another corner, unsure whether we would need to look in them but keeping them separate just in case.

Six boxes a piece and nearly two hours later, Sebastian said my name softly. I looked up to see his eyes glued to a file in front of him. I lowered the box I'd had resting on my lap and stood, stretching my aching back muscles as I moved closer to him. Leaning over his shoulder, I read the name on the top of the file: Hodges, Lauren.

"Is that her maiden name? Hodges?"

"I guess," Sebastian answered. "I was just looking at every Lauren I came to. The address on this one matches."

I lowered myself to a box beside Sebastian and placed my hand on his arm. "Did you see pictures of your mother's car from the accident report?" I asked, wondering what type of damage we would be looking for.

"Yeah. The notes mentioned there was white paint along the driver's side front and rear doors."

That meant if the car in the pictures was white, more than likely it was the one used in the accident. My heart rate tripled as I waited for Sebastian to open the folder. His finger was lodged between the papers, as though he'd already been through them, so my guess was that he already knew the answer to the unspoken question.

He opened the folder, and there in vivid color was a white SUV with significant front-end damage. That would match up to the fact that Sebastian had told me his mother had been T-boned in the accident.

I gasped, my eyes filling with tears as I looked at the pictures, knowing without a doubt that we'd found the evidence we needed to identify Lauren as, at the minimum, an accomplice in Sebastian's mother's death. And as far as I was concerned, the "accident" had just been bumped to "murder."

I hadn't realized I was crying until Sebastian put his arms around me, burying his face in my neck. He was sobbing, too. Desperately, I wrapped my arms around him, cradling the back of his head as I held him. I considered myself a fairly strong woman. I've been known to shed a tear, but never have I felt as lost and hopeless as I did right then with Sebastian's body trembling in my arms. I could only imagine how much he'd held in since the day he'd learned his mother had been killed. It'd taken more than a decade for him to get some sort of answers. And what we'd found... It was enough to break down the hardest man.

The proof was in my arms.

I wasn't even sure how much time had passed while I held Sebastian and cried for the boy who'd lost his mother, shed even more tears for the grown man who'd endured so much over the years, holding it all inside because he didn't have anyone to lean on. I hated Conrad Trovato for that. Maybe he was innocent in all of this — God, I hoped like hell he was innocent in all of this — but he still held the honorary title of shitty father because he'd shunned his own son from the day he was born.

I didn't want to go back to Trovato, Inc. tomorrow and face the man. I wasn't sure I could and still keep the secret that I now carried. I knew we had to talk to Derrick, to provide him with this evidence and see where he decided to go with this new lead. Considering he wasn't officially on this case, I didn't even know how this worked.

When Sebastian pulled back, wiping his eyes with the heels of his hands, I quietly wiped my own tears away.

"We need to get this to Derrick," he said, speaking my thoughts aloud.

"I think we need to make copies, keep the originals here in a safe place. And then I should probably tell my father," I told him.

Sebastian nodded in agreement and then got to his feet, offering me his hand. I let him pull me up, and I brushed off my jeans while Sebastian placed the folder on a box near the door.

We spent the next few minutes putting the boxes back in their rightful places, then locking the shed behind us before returning to the main building. Once inside, I took the file to the copy machine and made three sets of copies. Don't ask me why I did that, but I'd seen enough movies to know that this was the point when something would happen to destroy the evidence. Sure, maybe I was being extra paranoid, but as far as I was concerned, one could never be too careful.

I figured I had to keep my eyes open for anything, at this point. Lauren had resorted to threatening my job, which meant I wasn't the only one who was paranoid. Trevor was lurking, or so it seemed to me, and it was enough that I was nervous to have him in the building, much less popping up every time I turned around.

I finished making copies, placed the original file in a locked cabinet in my father's office, and took the three sets of copies with me. One for Derrick, one for Sebastian, and a backup copy that I would leave at my apartment. Now that I was finished, I did think it might've been overkill to have quite so many copies, but again, never hurt to be careful.

"You ready?" Sebastian asked when I met him near the front doors.

"As I'll ever be," I told him. "Should we stop by my parents' house? We can go over this with my father. I doubt he'll remember from so long ago, but at least he'll be apprised of the situation."

Sebastian nodded as he pushed open the front door. After locking the doors, we went to his truck, and for the first time that I could recall, Sebastian didn't take my hand, and he didn't open my door for me. Not that I expected it, but I knew then that he was off somewhere else in his head.

And that worried me more than anything else at the moment.

Chapter Twenty-Four

Sebastian

Monday morning

BY THE TIME I CRAWLED out of bed, I had slept maybe a solid hour all night. Without Payton in my bed, I was learning I couldn't sleep for shit. Between the absence of her soft, warm body and the millions of thoughts running through my head, I'd tossed and turned and now felt completely worthless.

My thoughts drifted back to the conversation Payton and I had had with her parents last night. Rehashing all of the details that Derrick had shared, along with the proof that we'd found, hadn't been an easy discussion. And when Hal had reacted similar to the way Payton had, blanching at the news that he'd repaired a vehicle that had been used to kill my mother, I'd had a hard time sitting there. Fortunately, Susan had made dinner, distracting us with food. It wasn't until we were leaving that Hal had taken me aside, apologizing as though it had actually been his fault. I assured him that there was no way he could've known, but I had seen in the man's eyes that he was going to shoulder the blame much the way Payton had.

That was just another reason I hadn't been able to sleep last night.

When I made it to the kitchen, I realized that Leif had already left for work, and that left me home alone. I took advantage and went to the workout room. After a solid hour of pounding away at the heavy bag, I dove into the pool and did laps to try to escape the chaos that had amped up in my head. The noise was so loud I wasn't sure if I would ever escape it. Realizing I wasn't going to get away from it, I gave up when my muscles could no longer carry me across the pool.

After a quick shower, I went to my office and pulled up my email. I was tempted to shoot off a note to my father, but I refrained. We had faxed Derrick the information we had retrieved from Payton's father's files last night, and I knew I couldn't say anything until we heard from him. I prayed it would be soon.

Although I'd waited eleven long, painful years to solve this, I felt like every minute that passed now was an eternity. And on top of that, I had to figure out when I was going to give Payton her Christmas present.

Pulling open the top drawer of my desk, I reached to the very back and found the small velvet box that I'd hidden there. With it in my hand, I leaned back in my chair and flipped it open, staring at the diamonds — four karats total — set in a platinum band. I was going to ask Payton to marry me. If it wasn't for the fact that the ring was the only Christmas present I had for her, I would've probably sprung the question on her by now. I was that eager.

Even with all the shit raining down around me, Payton still managed to put a smile on my face just by being in the same room. She was the only thing keeping me from completely unraveling.

As though she knew I was thinking about her, my cell phone rang, and I hit the talk button as soon as her name came up on the screen.

"Hey," I greeted, a smile on my face.

"Hey," she replied, sounding not nearly as happy to hear my voice as I was to hear hers.

"What's wrong?" I asked, instantly worried.

"Nothing," she answered quickly. "Well, nothing more than usual. I'm just finding it really difficult to be here right now."

"No one's giving you a hard time, are they?" I immediately thought of Lauren's threats. I was pretty sure my stepmother knew that something was up. That or she was just nervous. It made sense to me, considering what she'd done — or what I'd suspected she had done, anyway — but I wasn't sure how she would've been tipped off to what we were doing.

I think it was more due to Trevor's presence. If he had been the one driving the SUV that had hit my mother, I was pretty certain he was now using that as leverage against Lauren. For what, I didn't know.

"No, everything's fine. Conrad's not here this week."

"What about Trevor?" I asked, my concern growing.

As much as I hated my father for the lack of love he'd shown me throughout my life, right then he seemed like the only possible protection for Payton. No matter how hard I tried to tie him back to my mother's death, I couldn't. Not anymore. Based on the new information, I was beginning to think my father was completely clueless when it came to the actions of his wife, which, in my opinion, made him just as guilty.

"Why don't you come home? If he's not there, maybe take the next few days off. Christmas is on Thursday, so the office will be pretty empty this week."

"It is. The only person I've seen is Maude, but she said she was leaving early and would be out for the rest of the week. Ron's not even here."

"Ron's not there?" I asked, sitting up straight. The hair on the back of my neck stood up when I thought about Payton at the Trovato, Inc. office without a security guard on hand. Especially if… "Have you seen Trevor?"

There was a long pause, and I knew that Payton wasn't telling me something.

"Payton? Talk to me."

"Yeah, he's here. He met me when I got here this morning. He was sitting at my desk."

I got to my feet. I had a bad feeling that I couldn't seem to shake. "Payton, you need to leave."

"I can't. I've got to be here to answer the phones."

"Screw the phones, Payton. I'm serious, you need to come home."

Shit. I wasn't as close to my father's office as I would've been had I still lived there. Which meant I wouldn't be able to get to her for at least half an hour. And I really had a bad feeling about her being there alone with Trevor.

"Payton, listen to me," I told her, my voice firm. "I want you to shut everything down and walk to your car. If you don't, then I'm heading that way and I'm taking you home."

"No," she told me firmly. "It's fine. I really just wanted to call to hear your voice."

"Payton, I'm serious." As much as I wanted to acknowledge the fact that she missed me, I couldn't. I was getting antsy at this point, and it had everything to do with the fact that Payton was probably there alone with Trevor, and she didn't even realize it.

"I'll be fine. I'll probably head out early, anyway."

"No. I want you to leave right now. Do you understand me?"

"Sebastian." Payton's tone was firmer as she spoke softly. "I'm fine."

"Then I'm on my way." I was already moving through the house. I grabbed my truck keys from the bar in the kitchen, snatched my jacket off the chair by the door, and went to my truck, keeping Payton on the phone.

"Crap," she said suddenly. "The phone is ringing. I'll have to call you back."

"No," I said urgently. "Don't hang up your cell phone. I'll hang on."

"Sebastian, seriously. I'm fine. I'll call you back in a little while."

Son of a fucking bitch.

The call disconnected. I almost threw my cell phone across the garage. Instead, I gripped it tightly as I climbed into my truck. I narrowly missed the edge of the garage door when I backed out, too impatient to wait for it to open completely. I hit the button to close it but didn't bother waiting until it was all the way down before I peeled out of my driveway.

My heart was racing, trying to keep pace with my rate of speed as I hit the toll road going ninety-five. I tried Payton again, and when she didn't answer, I damn near lost my shit. I tried calling Toby, but he didn't answer, so then I tried Leif.

"Hey, man. What's up?" Leif greeted.

"Where are you?"

"The shop. Why?"

"How long would it take you to get to the Trovato office?"

"Ten minutes."

"Can you go over there? Something doesn't feel right."

I heard Leif mumble something and then another muffled voice replied before Leif returned to the phone. "I'm leaving now."

"Hurry. When you get there, go in the main doors and up the stairs. No one should be there to stop you. Once you get to Payton, call me."

"Okay, man. Something I should know?"

"Something's off. Conrad's not there; neither is Maude or Ron. Payton shouldn't be there. Conrad should've given her the week off, but he didn't. She's not answering her phone."

"I'm on my way now," Leif said, the loud rumble of his Mustang's engine sounding in the background, assuring me he was doing as he said.

I hung up the phone and put both hands on the wheel. I was pushing the truck over one hundred miles per hour, and I knew it was about to top out, but even then, I knew I wasn't going to get there before Leif.

I debated on whether or not I should call my father. I picked up my phone, put it down. I did that three times before I said fuck it. I dialed his cell and waited for him to answer.

"Sebastian," he answered gruffly.

"Where are you?" I asked, my voice coming out anxious and hurried.

"I'm at the house, why?"

"Why didn't you give Payton the week off?" I asked him. "If no one's there, what the hell is she supposed to do?"

"What are you talking about?" Conrad asked, his voice softer than before. "I sent her an email last week telling her to take the week off due to the holidays."

"What?" I exclaimed.

"I sent another to her over the weekend, wishing her a happy holiday. What the hell is going on, Sebastian?"

"Shit if I know," I growled. "She's in the office. She hasn't received any emails telling her not to be there. Where's Trevor?"

"He's at…" Conrad didn't finish his sentence, but I knew what he was thinking. After hearing Aaliyah's story, I knew there was something fucking wrong with Trevor. He shouldn't be in the picture, and Conrad knew that as much as I did.

"Go to the office now," I demanded. "Leif's on his way and so am I. I can't get Payton to answer the fucking phone."

I figured I would get a rebuttal from my father, but he surprised the shit out of me when he told me he was on his way. The phone disconnected, and I tried Payton one more time before I gave up. I was still ten minutes out, and that was only if I kept at the speed I was at. If I wasn't careful, I was going to get pulled over, and that wasn't going to help me one fucking bit.

I was depending on a radar detector, my best friend, and my father to get to my woman. And the only thing I could do was pray that none of them failed me now. Because if they did and something happened to Payton, then I knew without a doubt, my life was officially over.

Chapter Twenty-Five

Payton

AFTER I DISCONNECTED WITH SEBASTIAN, I answered the main line, but there was no one there. Not two seconds after I hung up, it rang again. Again, no one on the other end of the line.

I was just about to do as Sebastian told me and grab my stuff and go, because truthfully, I was starting to freak out, but every time I did, the phone would ring. On the fourth time with no one on the other end, I started to panic. I didn't know if I really had anything to worry about or if it was just Sebastian's tone that had me on edge, but I suddenly felt a strange sense of foreboding. I figured it was probably nothing, but I decided not to chance it.

Tossing my cell phone in my purse, I undocked my laptop and slid it into the computer bag. Just as I got to my feet, Trevor came up the stairs.

"Hey, Payton," he greeted, his tone overly cheerful.

"Hey." I tried to insert at least a modicum of pleasantness in my tone, but that was difficult considering the only thing I could think of was Aaliyah's face as she'd told the story of what this asshole had done to her. He made me want to vomit by just being in the same room.

"Going somewhere?" he asked as he moved closer to my desk.

"I was going to take off early," I explained simply. "Wanted to get some last-minute shopping done before Christmas."

"Does Conrad know you're leaving early?" Trevor's head cocked to the side as though he was expecting me to lie.

"I sent him a note." That was a lie, but Trevor didn't know that.

"I doubt he's gonna see it right away," Trevor told me. "You should probably stick around until you hear from him."

I didn't even know what to say to that. I wasn't sticking around. I didn't give a shit if Conrad fired me at this point. Being left alone with Trevor made my skin crawl, and there was no way in hell I was going to spend the rest of the day with him hovering over me.

"Are you done for the day?" I was trying to make small talk as I reached in my purse to retrieve my keys. I had a small bottle of pepper spray attached, and I figured if nothing else, I could use it to get Trevor to back off if necessary.

"Not yet," he said, his tone eerie. "I was just coming up here to see if you wanted to go to lunch."

I glanced at the clock on the wall. "It's only ten, Trevor." Not that the time mattered. It could've been high noon and I still wouldn't have accepted a lunch invitation from the rapist standing in front of me. Knowing he wasn't going to leave me alone until I got in my car and drove away, I decided to do just that. "I'm not quite hungry yet."

"Well, I think we should get lunch," Trevor said more firmly. "I'll drive."

As I walked past him, intent on ignoring him completely, Trevor took my car keys right out of my hands. I jumped back when he did, startled when his fingers made contact with my skin. "I said I wasn't hungry, Trevor." I held out my hand for him to return my keys. "I really do need to go. Sebastian's waiting for me."

Another lie.

Sort of.

"Well, I guess he'll just have to wait, now won't he?"

A chill ran down my spine at Trevor's cruel tone. I'd always suspected there was something wrong with him, but until now, he'd always been pleasant when he spoke to me. A little creepy, but nice enough.

There wasn't anything nice in his eyes. In fact, he looked menacing.

"I'm sorry, Trevor, but I ca—"

I didn't get my statement out before Trevor's hand gripped my arm painfully, and he pulled me toward the stairs. I tried to pry my arm out of his grip, but it was no use. He was incredibly strong, his fingers digging into my arm. I had two choices then. I could either follow him or we were both going to go down the stairs, and it wouldn't be on our feet. I was tempted to sacrifice myself so I could get away from him, but when he pushed me forward, making me walk in front of him, the opportunity was lost.

As I made my way down the stairs, I kept my purse and my laptop bag close while I glanced out the windows into the parking lot. That was when I noticed it was completely empty. I knew some of the mechanics parked out in the shop, but there was no one out front. Maude was gone, Ron was off, Conrad wasn't there, and no one else was wandering in the main reception area downstairs. I was alone with Trevor, and he had my car keys.

Just when we made it to the main floor, a bright red Mustang screeched to a stop in front of the doors. I immediately recognized Leif as he jumped out of the car, but Trevor obviously did, too, because he caught me off guard, yanking me backward, causing me to stumble. When I righted myself, he pulled me toward the doors that led to the shop. Without stopping, he barreled through the door and then slammed it behind me, engaging the lock.

I'd only been in the shop once. That had been the time that I'd realized it wasn't a warehouse as I'd originally thought. The only thing they stored there was cars. Most of them were the same, only different colors. One had decals on it, like something they would use at a NASCAR event, but as far as I knew, it had never moved.

"This way," Trevor growled, pulling me toward another door.

It led to a set of offices that were used by the mechanics. The other offices were in the main building, but I had noticed as Trevor led me through there that the doors had been closed and the lights were off, which meant no one else was there. What was usually a bustling building was a ghost town today.

"Why are you here today?" I asked Trevor, hoping to get him talking. Why, I didn't know. I had no idea what he was planning to do, but I knew that I needed to do something or, in a matter of seconds, I was going to be in one of those offices with him.

And that was the last place I wanted to be.

"I had something to do," he said sharply.

"I figured you'd have the week off," I told him.

"You were supposed to have the week off," he said, a smarmy grin tilting the corners of his mouth.

"What are you talking about?" I asked. No one had told me that I'd have the week off. It did seem a little strange that I would be the only one working, but truthfully, I hadn't thought much about it.

"Your boss sent you an email last week, letting you know that you could take the week off. I wanted to see you, though."

Yep, this wasn't going to be good. I only prayed that Leif would find a way into the building before I was completely at this crazy man's mercy. Or better yet, if Sebastian would just walk in... God, I couldn't believe this was happening.

"Can I ask you something?" Figuring I was in for a world of hurt as it was, I decided to go for broke.

"Sure," he told me as he went to one of the office doors and turned the knob. It didn't open.

Thank God.

While he was distracted with the door, I tried to pull away, unsure where I was going to go but knowing I had to get away from him. Trevor was faster than I was, though, grabbing my arm roughly and pulling me so that I stumbled, the laptop bag on my shoulder going sideways. It fell from my shoulder, taking my purse with it before it crashed to the floor. For the first time, I realized my cell phone was ringing from the dark abyss that was my purse.

"What's this?" Trevor asked, glancing down at the floor. He was looking at the paper that had fallen from my purse, the copies I'd made at my father's shop. "Hmm. That car looks familiar."

I wanted to slap the creepy grin off his face, but my heart was pounding painfully in my chest, my fear ratcheting up a notch. Until that moment, I hadn't really been scared, maybe because I knew Leif was out there. Someone was going to help me. I knew they were.

"Where'd you get these?" he asked, picking up the papers and flapping them in front of my face.

"Lauren had the car repaired at my father's shop. We know all about what happened," I told him, hoping that when I admitted what I knew, he'd let me go.

I should've known that wasn't how this stuff worked.

Remembering that I'd had a question for him, I waited until Trevor met my eyes again. "When did you start doing Lauren's dirty work?"

Oops.

That hadn't been a question that Trevor had been expecting. His shock registered on his face, and then next thing I knew, he was yanking me toward him, his attention back on the doors he had been trying to open.

"What are you talking about?" he asked seriously, his beady eyes raking over my face.

"I was just wondering."

Trevor stood there staring at me until the sound of one of the garage doors being raised pulled him back to the present. I turned, hoping like hell that was Leif coming inside.

"Shit," Trevor exclaimed, realizing just as I had that there was someone else there and he hadn't been able to lock them out completely.

Before I could catch a glimpse of the person responsible for raising the door, Trevor yanked my arm and pulled me to the next door. Unfortunately, that one was open. He turned the knob and shoved me. My momentum sent the door crashing into the wall. I couldn't keep my feet beneath me, and I landed on my knees on the concrete floor, a yelp escaping me as the pain ricocheted up my legs.

The door slammed behind me, and I looked up to see that Trevor had locked us in the room. There were no windows and only the one door. If someone hadn't seen us go in there, I doubted they would know that's where we were.

Feeling trapped, I did the only thing I could think to do — I screamed, and I didn't stop until Trevor backhanded me. I tasted blood, and the sudden throb of my lip told me he'd split it open. At that point, I knew I was screwed. My heart was pounding like a bass drum, and I was shaking. The fear had taken over, and I was having a hard time maintaining that calm I'd dug so deeply to produce. I knew I couldn't panic. I needed to figure out how to get myself out of this mess.

Unfortunately, I couldn't come up with a plan.

Yep, I was screwed.

Not to mention, completely and totally at this bastard's mercy.

I was just about to scream again, not caring if he hit me, because I didn't have any other options at that point. I was locked in a room with a psychopath.

"Shut up," Trevor growled as he pulled off his jacket and threw it onto a chair.

"What are you doing?" I asked, the words coming out in a rush.

I didn't need him to tell me. I knew.

The crazy man was going to do the same to me that he'd tried to do to Aaliyah.

"Since Lauren couldn't keep her promise, I decided to do things my way," he uttered.

"What are you talking about?" I wasn't sure I wanted to know, although I had asked.

"You asked me when I started doing Lauren's dirty work."

"Yeah," I answered softly, my voice trembling.

"Well, the answer is too long ago. It didn't take long for me to realize just how selfish Aunt Lauren really was. So much so that she would pretty much promise me anything just to ensure that she got her way."

Why didn't I have a recorder on me?

I knew that was a crazy thought, but at that moment, I wasn't sure how this was going to end, and I really wanted to get the information Sebastian needed to prove that his mother had been murdered. I knew, without a doubt, that this man was crazy enough to have killed her, but there was still no proof.

"Payton!"

I heard Leif yelling my name, and I sucked in a breath, hoping he would find me before Trevor lost it. Hell, I could see by the crazed look in his eyes that he was close.

"My sweet aunt promised me that I could have you, but she didn't deliver."

"*Me*?" What the hell was he talking about? "Why me?"

"Because," Trevor said, sliding his finger down my cheek. "When I saw you in Vegas, I just knew you were the one."

"The one what?" I asked stupidly.

"You didn't wonder why we'd been introduced that day? Why I was there to have breakfast with you and your boss?"

Well, of course I had, but I didn't tell Trevor as much. "I just figured it was business. Conrad wanted to let me know that you would be working for him," I lied, trying to keep my hands from shaking. I did not want Trevor to see just how scared I was.

"Oh, that was part of it. I told Lauren that it was time for me to start over. I needed a fresh start. And this was the perfect opportunity. Then she told me she had someone she wanted me to meet."

Shit.

They were both fucking crazy.

"From the moment I laid eyes on you, I knew you were perfect. I was just biding my time, waiting for Sebastian to screw up. The guy's unstable."

I laughed. I knew it sounded hysterical, but I couldn't help myself. "Why the hell does everyone keep saying that?"

"Because it's true." Trevor slid his hand down my arm and took my hand, pulling me to my feet. I was tempted to remain on the floor, not wanting to get any closer to him, but he was too strong. I rose to my feet, and he backed me up against the desk. I immediately put my hands up, trying to push him away, desperate to get away from him, but he didn't budge. In fact, he moved closer. "He's always been that way. Ever since his sweet mother died. It didn't help that Lauren hated him and her plan backfired. I doubt she thought about him having to come live with his father when his mother died, but suddenly, one day, there he was. Right on her doorstep."

"Oh, my God," I whispered, trying to swallow the bile that rose in my throat.

"That's right," Trevor said with a wicked grin. "Sebastian showed up on his daddy's doorstep, and her perfect little family wasn't perfect anymore. It worked out great for me, though. After all, I'd done her a huge favor. She owed me."

"Is that why you tried to rape Aaliyah?"

"I never tried to rape her!" Trevor screamed. "The little bitch told her father that I tried. She wanted me, I knew she did, but she wanted me on her terms."

My stomach lurched.

"Conrad wasn't quite as easy to manipulate as I thought he'd be. Especially when Lauren didn't bother to tell him what leverage I had over her. She said he wasn't going to know, either."

I swallowed hard, trying to back away as Trevor got closer to me. "Wasn't going to know what?" The words came out as a croak. I was fighting the urge to throw up, but I needed Trevor to keep talking. Because if he stopped, I feared he was going to do to me what he'd tried to do to Aaliyah.

"Payton!"

My ears perked up when I heard that voice. That wasn't Leif yelling my name that time. I was pretty sure that was...

"What the hell is he doing here?" Trevor barked.

Conrad.

"Well, I'm sorry, love, but I think the time for talking is now over."

I was just about ready to scream when Trevor's hand landed over my mouth, effectively shutting me up.

That's the moment that my fear damn near incapacitated me.

Sebastian

WHEN I PULLED INTO THE Trovato Inc. parking lot, my back tires squealed, and my heart damn near leapt out of my chest. I saw Payton's car alone in the front lot, then caught a glimpse of Leif's Mustang pulled up near the front door, but I didn't see anyone. I drove around to the back first, and that was when I found the bay door open. I pulled my truck inside the building, passing my father's Lexus, which was parked haphazardly off to the side. I slammed on the brakes, threw the truck into park, and bolted out.

The first thing I heard was Leif yelling Payton's name. When the echo of his voice stopped bouncing off the metal walls, I stood motionless, listening.

"They're here somewhere," Conrad shouted as he walked back in from the main offices. "But they aren't upstairs."

That meant they were in the shop. And since I didn't see them, there were only two options. Two sets of doors on opposite sides of the shop.

"Payton!" I yelled as I made my way to the closed doors. The first knob I turned gave easily, and I pushed it open, finding a storage area full of parts and boxes. I slipped inside, making my way down the aisles, looking in every nook and cranny. Two minutes later, I came up empty.

Back in the shop, I went to the next door, pushing it open. It was the single-person restroom—empty.

That left two doors, both offices that were used by the mechanics.

I nodded my head toward the first door when Leif and my father looked at me expectantly. They both nodded and moved in that direction.

I looked at my father, giving him the go-ahead. If anyone was going to get through to Trevor, it would be my father. That or I was going to tell Trevor that I was going to rip him to shreds.

"Trevor?" Conrad called, shouting louder than necessary.

With my ear pressed to one door and Leif's pressed to the other, we both listened. That was when I heard Payton's muffled cry.

Yeah, fuck the reasoning. I didn't give a shit if Conrad could talk Trevor down or not. I tried the knob. It didn't turn. I took one step back and then kicked the door right beside the knob with the heel of my work boot. It cracked but didn't cave. I did it two more times before it flew in, slamming against the wall behind it.

"Two seconds, Trevor," I told him. I could hardly see him through the red haze that had clouded my vision. "One…"

Trevor didn't back away. He moved behind Payton, holding his hand across her throat. From what I could tell, he didn't have a weapon, but I wasn't about to risk hurting her.

"Let her go," Conrad growled. "Right now."

I turned my head to see my father standing there.

With a fucking gun trained at my girlfriend's head.

"Dad! Goddammit!"

"Let her go right now, Trevor, or so help me God, I will shoot you. And I won't fucking miss."

"Aww, it's kinda sweet that Daddy Dearest is coming to the rescue now. Took you long enough, old man."

"Now, Trevor." Conrad's tone was harder than I'd ever heard it before, and trust me, I'd heard him as pissed off as I'd thought he could get.

Apparently he'd been holding back on me.

Somehow Trevor made himself smaller, hiding behind Payton until there wasn't a chance my father would get a clear shot of him. I met Payton's wild eyes. Trevor's hand was crushed over her mouth, and she was crying. That was the first time I realized her clothes were torn, her T-shirt ripped and tattered.

I willed Payton to understand what I was telling her. I looked at her face and then dropped my eyes to the floor quickly. I needed her to go to the floor, and I only prayed that my father didn't shoot Trevor. That was a fucking mess we didn't need.

"Dad," I called to Conrad, glancing his way briefly. "Put the gun down."

My father didn't even look at me when I spoke. His eyes were trained on Trevor, and I had the feeling he was imagining shooting him in the head. If my father had any idea what Trevor had done to Aaliyah, then I wouldn't doubt that he was running through the whole scenario of pulling that trigger and watching Trevor bleed out.

Shit.

I met Payton's panicked stare once more and signaled her to do as I asked.

In an instant, Payton's body went completely lax, her legs giving out beneath her as she crumbled to the floor, surprising Trevor. I took two steps forward and threw a right hook, then a left, both landing perfectly on each side of his face.

And just like that, it was over. Trevor's eyes rolled into the back of his head, and I reached for Payton, pulling her toward me as Trevor's limp body dropped like a ton of bricks.

"Cops are on their way," Leif announced from the doorway.

"Put the gun away, Dad," I barked. "Now."

My father looked at me, then back at Trevor, but I wasn't sure he was there with me. He was lost somewhere in his head, and I knew the feeling. I'd been there many times.

Payton cried in my arms, and I lowered myself to the floor, pulling her head against my chest. "I've got you, Angel. I've got you."

Dealing with cops was not something I looked forward to doing. Unfortunately, there was no getting out of that today. We spent two solid hours giving statements about everything that had happened since the time Payton had walked into the office that morning. I listened to Payton recall every single minute, and I was ready to pound Trevor into the pavement once again. Since he was in the back of the cop car, that wasn't going to happen, but that didn't stop me from imagining it.

My father continued to apologize to Payton profusely after the EMTs had looked her over, doctoring the cut on her lip. At one point, Conrad even hugged her, which surprised the shit out of me. She'd seemed a little freaked out, too, but I wasn't sure if that was because her boss had hugged her or because of everything that had happened.

While we'd been dealing with all the shit, Leif had called Derrick, who'd kindly come out to the scene to help sort things out.

As it turned out, Trevor had deleted the emails Conrad had sent to Payton, so she'd had no idea she had been given the entire week off. Which was exactly Trevor's plan, and it had played out beautifully. The bastard.

There was one positive outcome from the whole debacle. Apparently Trevor was scared shitless of going to jail, and since that was definitely on his agenda for a little while, he was ready to sing like a fucking canary. All of the details that Payton and I had pulled together were going to take care of Lauren as well.

Now I just had to sit my father down and talk to him. I doubted anyone was going to believe that he was completely innocent in all of this, but I still had to wonder. Based on the events of the day, he sure as shit didn't seem like he knew what was going on.

When the cops finally left with Trevor, I decided I needed to get Payton home. And by home, I meant to my place. Toby had called me back after seeing that I'd called earlier, and I had explained to him what had happened. He'd offered to have someone drop him off at the offices so he could drive Payton's car back. She was in absolutely no condition to drive. Hell, her hands were still shaking. I knew the instant Chloe and Aaron learned of the events, they were going to be all over Payton, so her day wasn't anywhere close to being over.

I was leading Payton to my truck when Conrad approached me.

"Thanks for coming up here," I told him.

"No problem." Conrad's face was drawn tight, his eyes hard.

After I helped Payton into the passenger side and closed the door behind her, I turned to face my father. "We need to talk."

He nodded.

"Today, Dad."

Conrad glanced around as though he'd just realized where he was. "All right," he said gruffly.

"Follow us to my place," I told him, not giving him an option. I was not taking Payton to his place.

"Let me check in with Lauren. She needs to know what happened."

I touched my father's arm. "No, she doesn't. Not right now."

My father's forehead wrinkled, his eyebrows downturned. "Why?"

"I'm serious. Don't call her. We need to talk first."

I knew my dad wanted to know what the hell was going on, but this wasn't the place to tell him all that had happened.

"Okay," he finally relented. "I'll follow you."

The drive back to my place wasn't as eventful as my drive to the offices earlier. First of all, I kept my speed significantly closer to the limit. Not to mention, I wasn't on the verge of having a stroke not knowing where Payton was.

She was sitting beside me, her hand on my leg. I put my arm around her while we were on the highway, but when we exited, I had to downshift, which meant I had to pull away. She didn't budge, though, her head still resting on my shoulder. She'd been quiet the entire drive back. It wasn't until I was pulling into the garage that she actually spoke.

"Are you going to tell your father what's going on?" she asked softly.

"Yeah. But you don't have to be there for that. Why don't you go upstairs and take a bath?"

"I want to be there when you tell him," she said firmly. "Can you just give me a minute to shower and change?"

"Of course."

While Payton went upstairs, I gave my father a brief tour of the house. Surprisingly, he seemed interested in my place. In fact, he seemed to have done a complete turnaround from the last major conversation we'd had. I think he realized the same thing I had. We'd been at odds for so long, but it wasn't just our conflicting behaviors that had contributed to the rift between us. There had been outside forces, namely his wife, who had been working against us.

Granted, that didn't mean all was going to be sunshine and roses from here on out. We had a long way to go before we figured out how to bridge the chasm that had developed over the years. But I was hoping that by getting things out in the open, we might actually have a chance.

When Payton came downstairs, she went right to the kitchen and made a pot of coffee. My father and I joined her, sitting at the table in the breakfast nook. He hadn't said much while I'd shown him around, but I didn't necessarily need him to. What I needed from him was a lot of answers to a million burning questions I still had.

I only hoped he was ready to talk.

After bringing the coffeepot and three mugs over to the table, Payton took the seat to my left, moving closer to me and linking her fingers with mine. I wasn't sure if that was her way of showing support or if she just needed to touch me as much as I needed to touch her. There was no doubt that, in the coming days, I would have nightmares about what had happened that morning. I knew for a fact that there was no way I wouldn't be spending the night with her. If she insisted on going back to her apartment, that was exactly where I would be. Either way, I wasn't leaving her side.

"I have a question," Payton spoke up, glancing between my father and me.

"Yes?" Conrad asked, realizing at the same time I did that her question was for him, not me.

"How did you meet Sebastian's mother?"

My father's eyes widened at the same time mine did. I hadn't been sure how I was going to ease into the conversation, but obviously Payton didn't have any issues with getting right to the point.

"I ... uh..." Conrad looked at me and then back to Payton.

"It's something he should know, don't you think?" Payton asked, her tone firm.

Conrad was silent for a moment, and then he sighed heavily. "Yeah, I guess he should."

I waited with bated breath, eager to hear how this man had made my mother fall in love with him.

"It wasn't a glamorous introduction," Conrad began, his voice low, his eyes dropping to his hands, which were wrapped tightly around the coffee cup in front of him. "I met her at the restaurant she worked in. She was the most beautiful woman I'd ever seen. I hadn't meant for things to happen between us, but we started talking. The next thing I knew, I was coming into the restaurant every week just to get a glimpse of her. Every time, we would spend a few minutes talking until, out of nowhere, I asked her for her phone number."

"You were married," I said unnecessarily.

"Yes, I was," Conrad replied. "Judy and I had been married for three years by then, and things were going downhill." He met my gaze head on. "Honestly, I hadn't meant to get involved with Rachelle, but..." Conrad's sentence trailed off.

"You fell in love with her," Payton said, completing my father's sentence.

"I loved Rachelle more than I've loved any other woman. We spent months getting to know each other, but never quite enough for me to realize just what I was doing. I had no idea, until Rachelle got pregnant, that she was underage."

"Did she lie to you?" I asked.

"Not directly, no. I never asked her age, and she never volunteered it. She looked so much older, and I assumed because she was working that she was out of school. It was a mistake I would never make again."

"What did you do when Rachelle told you she was pregnant?" Payton asked.

Conrad's face contorted, reflecting what I could only assume was the pain he felt from days long past.

"I told her she needed to get an abortion. My marriage was rocky, and I wasn't sure how it was going to end. Judy was threatening to take me for everything."

"Why would she do that?" I asked.

"Because I…" Conrad glanced out the window briefly. "Because I was having an affair."

"She knew about my mother?"

"No," Conrad said firmly, meeting my gaze again. "She knew about Lauren."

"Lauren was your assistant at the time." It wasn't a question, but Conrad responded anyway.

"She was. I'd been having an affair with her for a few months toward the end. She came on to me one night when we were away on a business trip. I'm not making excuses. I was just as much responsible for what happened that night as she was."

"Did Lauren know about Rachelle?"

"She did," Conrad confirmed. "When I was away on business, it was the only time I really had to talk to Rachelle. Lauren must've overheard one of my conversations, because she confronted me."

I waited, not willing to interrupt at this point.

"Lauren threatened me. She told me that if I didn't break things off with Rachelle and insist she get an abortion, she would go to Judy and to anyone who would listen to her."

It made more sense than it should, but I still hated Conrad for what he'd done. "So you told my mother to get an abortion and that you'd pay her off to keep quiet?"

"I did. She refused my money and insisted that she was keeping you."

"Why didn't you have anything to do with Sebastian after he was born?" Payton asked, her tone harsh.

I loved her more right then for being so defensive when it came to me. I'd never had anyone stand up for me the way she did. I gave her hand a gentle squeeze.

"Lauren held that over my head for a long time. In order to protect Rachelle and Sebastian from Lauren, I severed all contact. I told Lauren that Rachelle had an abortion and there was nothing to worry about. Judy and I divorced, and less than a year later, I was married again. I hated Lauren at that point. She was doing everything she could to blackmail me. I had stopped sleeping with her, but she loved me. Or that's what she told me, at least. I met Theresa at a conference, we hit it off, dated for about six months, and I proposed. I did it to piss Lauren off."

"You married someone because you were mad at your mistress?" Payton questioned, her eyes narrowed.

"Payton," Conrad said firmly, locking eyes with her, "I've made a million mistakes in my life. I've never pretended to be something I'm not. I'm not perfect. But, no, I never intentionally hurt anyone. To be honest, I still loved Rachelle, but at that point, I couldn't risk Lauren finding out about Sebastian. I didn't want Rachelle to be dragged into that mess."

"So you married Theresa…" I stated, wanting to get him back on topic.

"I married Theresa. That lasted less than two years. She didn't like the fact that Lauren was always around. Although Lauren was my assistant, she had inserted herself in my life at every turn. During another business trip, I ended up sleeping with Lauren. I was tired of the fighting, and I gave in. She got pregnant. On purpose."

"Holy shit." I don't know why I was surprised. The woman was as manipulative as they came.

"Exactly. She got pregnant with Aaliyah before my divorce was final. Once it was, she insisted that I marry her, or she would expose me. By that time, Trovato, Inc. was rising in the ranks quickly. I knew there was no such thing as bad publicity, but I couldn't risk it. So I married her. Five months later, Aaliyah was born."

"Sebastian was four," Payton told my father. "While Aaliyah was being born, your four-year-old son was growing up without a father. While Lauren was living off your money, blowing it on clothes and bullshit, Rachelle was working two jobs to take care of Sebastian. *Two.*"

I squeezed Payton's hand. Her voice was growing louder as she spoke, her anger reflected in the clipped words.

"I know that," Conrad bit back. "If you think I'm proud of what I did, you're wrong. I loved that woman. I wanted more than anything to be with her, to swoop in and try to be the knight in shining armor that she deserved, but it wasn't possible. Lauren would've decimated both of us."

Payton leaned forward, one hand still in mine, the other flat on the table, the tips of her fingers white as she pressed them against the wood. "She did that anyway," Payton snapped. "Your wife... Your wife killed Sebastian's mother."

Conrad's head snapped back as though she'd slapped him. His mouth was open, but no words came out. I watched him stare at Payton, confusion causing the skin on his face to draw taut. When he looked at me, I fought the urge to punch him in the face as the reality of what had happened really hit me.

My father might not have killed my mother, but his actions, his selfish fucking actions, had ultimately resulted in her death.

And if he hadn't realized it before, I think he certainly did now.

Chapter Twenty-Seven

Payton

I WAS SO ANGRY I wasn't sure how I had managed to remain in my seat for this conversation. While this should've been Sebastian's fight, I couldn't sit back and listen while Conrad told us his sob story.

After the events of the morning, I was strung tight. Having been assaulted by Trevor, I was hanging on to my sanity by the skin of my teeth. I wanted to scream and yell, but I managed to keep my voice relatively low. For the last few minutes, my anger had seeped into my words, and I couldn't hold it back.

I honestly didn't think Conrad realized that every single thing he'd done, every lie he had told, had ultimately led to Rachelle's untimely death. He was the reason Sebastian had lost his mother, although he might not have been the one to kill her.

He was still responsible.

And I hated him for that.

"Did my mother contact you about child support?" Sebastian asked, his voice low. I think I'd taken him by surprise with my fury, and I was proud of him for keeping it together. It seemed as though the tables had turned, and I was the one fighting the chaos while Sebastian's eerie calm kept us both in line.

"She … uh…" Conrad looked back and forth between us briefly. I think I'd stunned him stupid with my statement earlier, but it hadn't been a lie. Lauren was responsible. And Trevor, per his own admission, was the one who had done the dirty work. "Rachelle contacted me once. She actually left me a voice message, but she didn't tell me what she needed, just that she wanted me to call her. I had saved it, intending to call her back. I was willing to give her anything she needed if I could've just heard her voice. I waited a couple of days, and when I went to get the phone number, I found that my call log and the voice mails were gone. All of them. So, no, Rachelle never actually talked to me about child support. However, she did try to contact me."

"Did you not think it was a bit of a coincidence that his mother died after she contacted you?" I asked, which prompted Sebastian to start talking.

Conrad looked at his son, and I listened with half an ear while Sebastian went into the same story I'd heard more than once. About the accident, how his mother had been run off the road by a hit-and-run driver only to die from her injuries. He continued laying out the cold, hard facts while Conrad sat there, completely pale, his face a hard mask of confusion as he listened intently.

Unable to take any more, I grabbed the file folder that I'd retrieved from my father's office — I had stashed it on the chair beside me earlier — and then got to my feet. "I need some air," I told Sebastian, pulling my hand from his. "I'll be back." Looking at Conrad, I dropped the folder in front of him and said, "You should look at this."

Grabbing my jacket, I went out the back door and walked the enormous patio for a few minutes before lowering myself to the steps that led down to the outdoor pool — the one that Sebastian hadn't used yet — below. I sat there, letting the chilly December wind swirl around me. I was too numb to feel, and it wasn't due to the temperature. I needed to pull myself together, because Sebastian needed me to be strong for him. Although we'd solved the mystery, this was only the beginning.

Lauren was going to pay for this. She was going to go to jail for whatever charges she could be brought up on. At least I hoped that was the case. We would have to deal with that, and with Aaliyah. I didn't know if Aaliyah actually understood the magnitude of what Lauren was capable of. Or maybe she did. After all, in order to buy his silence, Lauren had practically handed her daughter over to a disgusting man who had attempted to violate her in the most horrific way possible.

Hell, I felt violated after what Trevor had done to me, and I thanked God every single second that Leif and Conrad had arrived when they had. They had offered a distraction, and though Trevor had seemed intent on doing me harm, he hadn't been focused enough. I had managed to get away from him once before Sebastian kicked in the door, but then he'd ripped my shirt, groping my breasts, squeezing them until they hurt. But then Sebastian had been there.

Chaos

The relief I had felt was overwhelming, and the only thing that had probably saved my life was the fact that Trevor hadn't had a weapon. But Conrad had. I'd seen the hatred in Conrad's eyes when he'd pointed the gun at me and Trevor. It was then that I'd realized Conrad did know what had happened to Aaliyah, and it all made even more sense, as fucked up as it was. Conrad might not have known that Lauren had plotted Rachelle's death, but he knew what she was capable of. If I had to guess, she'd been holding even more things over his head for all these years.

I don't know how much time passed while I sat shivering on the stairs, staring out at the vast amount of land that Sebastian owned. The land he would eventually turn into something good and solid, something he could be proud of. It wasn't until Sebastian's warm arm came around my shoulder that I realized he had joined me.

"Where's Conrad?" I asked, leaning my head against his neck, burying my face into his skin.

"Derrick and Leif are here. Derrick's talking to him."

I would've lifted my head to look at him, but Sebastian cradled the back of my head, holding me in place. Instead, I allowed the safety and security of his arms to envelop me. He made me whole again just with his simple touch. It was as though all the bad things just disappeared when he was with me.

Chaos. That's what I'd heard Sebastian refer to the noise in his head as. It wasn't until today that I understood just what that felt like. To have all of that noise inside, unable to get it to ease up. I'd been overwhelmed with it just now until I was in Sebastian's arms.

"I love you," I whispered to him, sliding my arms around his waist and holding him.

"I love you too, Angel," he whispered back. "So damn much."

A few minutes passed, and I finally did lift my head to look at him. "What do we do now?"

"We move forward, Payton. That's all we can do. We put one foot in front of the other."

I understood what he was saying. It made me think of the angel wings on his back and how he said his mother was always there, pushing him forward, guiding him to the right path when he veered off course.

Linking my fingers with Sebastian's, I smiled at him. "I'm ready to move forward."

"Me, too, Angel. Me, too."

Sebastian pressed his lips to mine, gently at first. His mouth was firm yet soft against mine. When he slipped his tongue between my lips, I opened for him, allowing him inside. Our tongues melded together as did our bodies. I held him close, he held me closer, and my world righted itself again.

The sound of someone clearing their throat had me pulling back from Sebastian to look up. I smiled when I saw Chloe and Aaron standing there, watching us. The worried looks on their faces seemed to dissipate slowly, probably as they realized that I was okay.

And I was okay. More so than I thought I would be.

By the time the house was empty again, I wasn't sure how I had managed to remain upright. I was exhausted, both mentally and physically. I had rehashed what had happened with Trevor to my best friends, assuring them both that I was fine until they finally believed me. Toby and Leif went out and got food, while the rest of us sat around and talked. Derrick had left, telling Conrad that he would be in touch, and Conrad had spent at least an hour ignoring his phone, which continued to ring. It was Lauren, he'd told us. Since Derrick had informed him that the police were on their way to pick her up to take her in for questioning in regard to Rachelle's death, Conrad hadn't wanted to talk to her.

We'd been informed that they wouldn't be able to charge Lauren with anything at this point; however, they could bring her in. If they were lucky, she'd break as quickly as Trevor had. If not, then Conrad would have a long road ahead of him. There was nothing to guarantee that Lauren was going to jail for what she'd done, no matter how much I wished it so.

Before Sebastian's father left, the two of them went into Sebastian's office alone to talk. There wasn't any shouting, which I took as a good sign. Conrad was far from innocent, but it was a relief to know that he wasn't directly responsible for Sebastian's mother's death. And it seemed that the turn of events had possibly brought Sebastian and Conrad closer.

As for me and Conrad, I wasn't quite sure where we stood. Before he left, he took me aside and apologized again for what had happened. I told him that it wasn't his fault and I didn't hold him responsible for it. We agreed that we would see how things went after the holidays when the office reopened. As of now, I would be returning to work, but I didn't know exactly how long that would last.

But I had asked Conrad one last thing before he left. I'd asked him to join us for Christmas dinner, informing him that it was a surprise for Sebastian so he had to keep quiet. I had choked up when tears had formed in his eyes. He'd accepted the invitation and offered to bring something. Since it was last-minute, I'd told him that wasn't necessary, but knowing Conrad, he wouldn't show up empty-handed. So I would just have to wait to see what he brought with him.

"You ready for bed?" Sebastian asked when he joined me in his bedroom. I had escaped to brush my teeth and change into one of his T-shirts.

"More than ready," I told him, crawling beneath the covers and watching him as he stood there, staring back at me.

I noticed he was hesitant as he shed his clothes and crawled into bed, still wearing his boxers.

"Are you okay?" I asked, situating myself as I always did so that my head was resting on his chest.

"Yeah, I'm just…"

I lifted my head to look into his eyes. "You're what?"

"Are you sure you're okay for me to be here?"

"What are you talking about?" I was confused, and I knew he heard it in my voice.

"After what happened with Trevor…"

Ahh. So Sebastian was worried about the psychological damage that had been done. "As long as you're here with me," I told him, "I'm perfect."

"I'm going to have nightmares about what happened, Payton," he told me, his face stony.

"I've got something that might stop that from happening," I told him, pressing my lips to his softly.

"What's that?" he asked, his body hardening beneath mine.

My eyes raked over his face. I knew he was worried, and maybe he had every right to be. But the events of that morning seemed so long ago. There wasn't a chance in hell I could ever be in the same room with Trevor again, but as far as being traumatized by the event, I wasn't.

"Remember a while back when you promised me that you wouldn't let anyone hurt me?" I asked him, pressing my fingers against his cheek.

He leaned into my hand, his eyes closing. "I remember. And I failed."

Turning his face, I waited for his eyes to open. "You didn't fail, Sebastian. You protected me. You saved me."

"Trevor got to you, Payton."

"But you were there. That's all that matters. You followed your instincts, and you made sure that nothing happened."

He didn't seem convinced by my words, so I kissed him again, this time more insistently than before. I coaxed his mouth open with mine, and when he gave in, I pulled him until I was on my back and he was hovering above me.

"I love you," I whispered. "More now than ever before." I pressed my lips to his quickly and then pulled back. "And I didn't even think that was possible."

Realizing I was going to have to take the reins, I slid my hands over his shoulders, then down his back, caressing his skin as I went. I slipped my fingers beneath the waistband of his boxers and lowered them down his hips. He got with the program, forcing them down his legs and off before ridding me of my T-shirt.

And when we were naked, Sebastian slid into my body, all the while keeping his eyes locked with mine. Words weren't necessary right then because everything he felt was reflected in his brilliant gold gaze. Love, fear, worry… The emotions swirled together, and I felt them in his kiss, in the beautiful way he buried himself inside me.

I held on to him, holding him as close as I could, feeling him to the depths of my soul.

And while he continued to send me higher until I knew I didn't stand a chance of holding back any longer, I realized there was one emotion that was missing.

The chaos. It was completely gone.

Our eyes met moments before my orgasm exploded through me, and I saw, just as I felt, Sebastian's body tighten, his release taking hold, the moment he realized that, too.

Chapter Twenty-Eight

Sebastian

Thursday (three days later)
Christmas Day

THE GRAY SKY AND FREEZING drizzle that tapped against the bedroom window suited my mood for the moment. I'd woken up that morning with Payton in my bed, and I'd been happier than I ever remembered being on Christmas. At least since my mother had passed away.

While I lay there, not wanting to move and possibly disturb Payton while she slept, I thought back to the last Christmas I'd had with my mother. My heart hurt when I realized that the memory was fuzzy.

It was true, time moved on. Those of us who were left behind did keep moving forward, even when it hurt so much that I thought it wasn't possible. Somehow, I'd made it through one day. Then another. And another until I found myself lying in bed with the woman of my dreams next to me and a whole new future set out in front of me.

That was where I had found myself when I'd tried to conjure up the image of my mother on that cold Christmas morning when I'd woken up to find the leather jacket I had been wanting beneath the ratty little Christmas tree that we'd been using for as long as I could remember.

"Open it."

"What is it?" I teased my mother, who was sitting on the edge of our dilapidated sofa, watching me with bright eyes.

"Open it, silly. I'm not gonna tell you."

"Fine," I said, pretending to be upset that she wouldn't just tell me what it was.

Grabbing the box wrapped in a thin paper dotted with Christmas trees and reindeer, I dropped to the couch beside my mother.

"You're the slowest gift opener I know," my mother told me, laughing.

What she didn't realize was that I was enjoying her excitement as much as I was looking forward to opening the gift. If it meant she would keep that smile on her face all day, I'd go even slower.

It took me a few minutes because I made sure I didn't tear the paper, being methodical in how I peeled back the tape before unfolding the paper from around the brown cardboard box. Whatever was inside was heavier than I'd expected it would be. But based on the square shape, I had no idea what it could possibly be.

My mother must've gotten tired of the anticipation, because she grabbed a butter knife that was sitting on the table and quickly sliced the tape that kept the cardboard closed. Her laughter was infectious, and I found myself chuckling as I pulled open the box and peered inside.

"Holy shit," I muttered.

"Do you like it?" my mother asked, completely ignoring the fact that I'd cursed. She usually got on me for my language, but not today.

"It's..." I looked at my mother as I pulled the black leather jacket out of the box and laid it across my lap. "Mom, this is too much."

"Oh, hush. It is not."

The jacket was the only thing I had wanted for Christmas, but I'd never told my mother that. I knew we couldn't afford it, and I had given up on the idea of even saving enough of my own money to get it. Yet somehow she'd known.

I hadn't realized that I was crying until a sob wracked my chest and Payton looked up at me, her sleepy gaze finding mine in the soft light peeking through the blinds.

"Are you okay?" she asked softly, her hand planted firmly over my heart.

"Sorry," I said, my throat tight. "I didn't mean to wake you."

"What were you thinking about?"

"My mother," I told her, pulling her closer to me and pressing my lips to the top of her head. She pulled the blankets up over us both and curled up against my side.

"Can you tell me?" she asked.

I told her about the memory of that morning, and by the time I was finished, a tear had escaped her eye, landing on my chest. She didn't say anything for a few minutes, and I thought she had possibly gone back to sleep, but then she spoke. "Do you think we could go visit her this morning?"

"My mother?" I asked stupidly.

"Yeah."

"I'd like that." It had been over a year since I'd visited my mother's grave, and I liked the idea of spending Christmas morning with her. It would give me a chance to introduce her to the woman I intended to marry.

Payton and I showered together, lingering for longer than necessary after I buried myself inside of her against the tiled shower wall. I hadn't been able to resist, and neither had she. In all honesty, it was the best Christmas present I'd ever received, being able to make love to her first thing in the morning.

Knowing most places would be closed, Payton made coffee and then we slipped out the door. I hadn't seen Leif yet, so I figured he'd slept in. Forty-five minutes later, we were pulling up to the grave site, parking on the narrow road that wound through the cemetery. There were other cars pulled off in the grass, and I figured there were plenty of families having to make their Christmas visits to their loved ones the same way I was.

What I hadn't been expecting was to find my father's Lexus parked in the grass, just a few yards from my mother's headstone. I swallowed hard and then climbed out of the truck, helping Payton out behind me. We walked hand in hand across the frozen grass that was littered with dry leaves that had yet to be raked up.

Rachelle's headstone had been cleaned off, probably by my father, and there was a bouquet of roses in the small vase that had been pulled from its hiding place in the ground.

"Hey," Conrad greeted us both.

He looked as though he'd been crying, and I think that was the first time in my life that I'd seen him cry. It made him seem more human to me, something I'd had a hard time believing him to be for the last decade.

The three of us stood there in silence for a little while, and then Payton surprised me when she introduced herself to my mother. I couldn't hold back the tears, and I didn't give a shit what it made me look like. I'd cried plenty of tears for my mother over the years, but never because I wished she could've been there to meet the love of my life face-to-face. She would've loved Payton, and Payton would've loved her. I knew that much.

Payton continued to talk to her softly, her hand squeezing mine tightly. When she was finished, she took a step back, releasing my hand. I knew it was my turn.

"Mom," I said, my voice rough with emotion. I swallowed hard, trying to get the words out. "This morning, when I woke up, I was thinking about the leather jacket you bought me for Christmas that last year we were together. I'm not sure I ever really told you how much that jacket meant to me. I've still got it, actually. One of the few things I have from back then. I just wanted to let you know that you've outdone yourself this year, though. That jacket, it meant so much to me. But the gift you gave me this year is something I promise to cherish for the rest of my life. So, thank you."

I glanced at my father, noticing he was studying me, tears in his eyes.

Payton stepped forward, linking her arm with mine and hugging my bicep. "What did she get you this year?" Payton asked softly.

"You," I said simply.

Chapter Twenty-Nine

Sebastian

AFTER AN EMOTIONAL MORNING, I didn't think anything could possibly change the course of the day for me. After visiting my mother's grave, Payton managed to convince me to take her to the track. We spent two hours out there, sitting on the track in my truck while we talked. She told me about Christmases at her house growing up, and I told her about some of the ones that I remembered. There weren't many from after my mother died, because Christmas hadn't been the same without my mother, and even though he seemed somewhat remorseful now, Conrad still hadn't been much of a father to me. Not even on holidays.

Usually I'd spent the day alone; sometimes I'd spent it with Toby's or Leif's family. Knowing that I would never have to spend another Christmas alone because I had Payton had been the upturn in my day.

But then we pulled up in front of my house right at noon. Payton had said she needed to get something so we could go to her parents' house for dinner. Upon seeing the influx of cars in my driveway, I realized it had all been a setup.

"Surprise," Payton said softly, her hand on my knee.

I stopped the truck and stared over at her.

"You did this?"

"Well, it wasn't all me."

I recognized several of the cars parked out front; others I had no idea who they belonged to. Finally, Payton urged me to pull around to the garage, so I did. When she led me inside, the overwhelming aroma of turkey flooded me, along with the chatter of at least a dozen people. Maybe more.

"What the fuck?" I mumbled under my breath as I looked around my kitchen. There was food everywhere, and Leif was sporting an apron, of all things, as he pulled a turkey from the oven.

"Merry Christmas." I turned to respond to the greeting to see Payton's parents standing side by side smiling at me. Her father shook my hand, a knowing look on his face.

I figured he was remembering the conversation we'd had last week when I'd made an impromptu visit to his house.

After I hugged Susan, Payton led me through the crowd, stopping to say hello to everyone there. It took a while, because it seemed everyone I knew *was* there. Aaron and Chloe, Leif's three brothers—Garrett, Sean, and Dale—and their mother were all in the kitchen working side by side to get the food ready. Derrick, Toby, and Toby's parents were in the living room, talking. Aaliyah was standing off to the side, watching Leif. Even Aaron's parents were there, now chatting with Susan and Hal.

"I can't believe you did this." I pulled Payton against me, pressing my lips to her forehead.

"I wanted to get you something for Christmas that no one had ever gotten you."

"Well, I'd say you succeeded."

"Come on in here and help with the food," Leif yelled, his eyes meeting mine over the heads of the others.

I laughed, releasing Payton and making my way into the kitchen. "I'm willing to help, but don't expect me to put on an apron."

"No worries, bro. I'm secure enough in my masculinity to wear this thing," Leif told me, his gaze moving past me.

I didn't have to turn around to know he was looking at my sister, who was still holding up the wall less than a foot away. I reached for her, pulling her against my side and kissing her temple. "I'm glad you're here."

"Me, too," she said softly. "I'm glad Payton invited me."

"How do we wanna do this?" Toby asked, his burly form moving through the kitchen, forcing others out of the way. "We takin' it in there or just serve yourself in here?"

"There's too much food. Just serve yourself," someone else said.

While everyone piled their plates full, I watched from the sidelines, waiting until the room had emptied somewhat. I urged Aaliyah to get food, and she did, but not until Leif motioned her toward him. Once they were out of the way, I grabbed Payton, and we made our way through the line, filling our plates before joining everyone in the dining room. The dining table didn't hold that many people, but I noticed that someone had relocated the table from the breakfast nook so that everyone had a seat.

The doorbell rang just as I was about to take my seat. I excused myself to see who it was. When I opened the door, I got another shock. My father was standing on the front steps.

"Hey, son." His words came out choked, as though the emotion he'd been riddled with that morning was still lingering.

"Hey, Dad. Come in." I stepped back out of the way so he could come in. That was when I noticed he had some people with him. A woman and a man, along with two young kids, probably around ten or eleven.

"Hi, Sebastian," the woman greeted softly.

Payton arrived to stand beside me, her arm wrapping around my waist as I stared back at the woman.

"I hope you don't mind that I invited a few people," Conrad said softly.

"The more the merrier," Payton said. "Come in, please."

I took a step back, but my eyes were still trained on the woman.

"Sebastian, I'm not sure if you remember, but this is…"

"Tina." Her name barely passed my lips.

When it was obvious I wasn't going to say anything more, Payton stepped in and introduced herself while I listened intently.

"I'm Payton. And you are?"

"Tina. I'm Sebastian's aunt. This is my husband, Randy. And our kids, Chelsea and Jeremy."

I swallowed hard. My aunt Tina was standing in my foyer, her husband and kids by her side. She looked nothing like the woman I remembered. She looked … healthy. No longer did she have dark circles beneath her eyes or sallow skin. Clearly she'd cleaned herself up over the years and even managed to start a family, although if my math was correct, she'd started a little later than most parents.

When she stepped forward, looking as hesitant as I felt, I smiled. "It's good to see you," I told her.

"Truer words have never been said," she whispered, wrapping her arms around me and squeezing me so tightly I thought my head was going to pop off my body.

"Hey, kids. I hope y'all are hungry because we've got so much food." Payton took the kids as though she'd known them all her life and led them into the kitchen, leaving me with the adults.

Tina gave me a small smile and then took her husband's hand, following them into the kitchen. And then it was just my father and me standing there, watching the others.

"You've got a good woman there," Conrad said, and I glanced over at him.

"Payton's ... amazing," I said.

"She's certainly managed to open my eyes," Conrad told me.

I looked at him, unsure what to say to that.

"It might take a while, Sebastian," he began softly, "but I'm going to make it up to you. I've been a shitty father, I won't deny that."

I watched him briefly, then glanced back at my aunt. My mother's sister. The woman who'd been plucked from my life so long ago. I hadn't heard from her once in the last eleven years, but now she was in my house, eating my food.

"It wasn't her fault," Conrad said, apparently reading my mind. "It was mine. I've spent far too many years cowering beneath my own mistakes, Sebastian. I wouldn't let her see you, although she tried so many times."

"Lauren?" I asked knowingly.

"As much as I want to put all the blame on her, I can't. I made my own decisions. I just didn't make the right ones, son."

I turned to look at my father then. And this time I really looked at him. At the man I'd hated for so long, and I realized right then that I could forgive him. It might take some time, but I could eventually forgive him.

"Thanks," I said, holding out my hand to shake his.

He ignored my hand and reached for me, pulling me into his arms and hugging me tightly. It took a moment for me to return the gesture, but I finally did.

After all, it was the first time he'd hugged me.

Ever.

Chapter Thirty

Payton

DINNER WAS AMAZING, BUT IT wasn't just the food that made it complete. Everyone we had invited had shown up with more food than we could possibly eat. On top of that, Toby and Chloe had brought over a Christmas tree that morning, and they'd decorated it while we'd been gone. I hadn't even noticed it at first until Sebastian said something to me. I'd been too engrossed in the fact that they'd all come through for Sebastian.

It was truly the best Christmas ever.

Now, as we all sat in the living room talking and drinking coffee, I watched Sebastian move around the room. He was talking to his aunt Tina, laughing at something she said. She looked as though she'd been given the gift of a lifetime, and I was so glad Conrad had thought to invite her. The kids had already bonded with Sebastian, grabbing his attention at every opportunity.

Yes, Sebastian looked happier than I'd ever seen him.

Not that I was taking credit for the smile on his face, but I was glad to have contributed to it. I listened half-heartedly to the conversations going on around me, answering when someone spoke to me, acknowledging others, but I still found myself watching him most of the time. When he looked my way and smiled, my heart swelled each and every time until I wasn't sure I could contain all the love I had for this man.

The sound of metal against glass sounded, and the room grew quiet. I looked around, finding Toby grinning as he tapped a fork against his glass, Chloe at his side.

Sebastian started my way, and I moved over so I could give him room to sit beside me, but he continued to stand, facing the room.

"Hey, sorry to interrupt," he addressed everyone in the room, laughing. "I really just wanted to say a quick thank you for coming. I'm still in shock, or maybe that's just the turkey. After all, Leif did cook it. And Chloe, for the record, Toby does like turkey."

A round of laughter escaped as Leif tried to defend himself. Aaliyah stopped him with a hand over his mouth, which only invited more laughter. Chloe laughed at Sebastian's inside joke, and Toby grinned sheepishly, pulling her against him.

"So, thank you all for coming here today. For you to spend your Christmas with me… Well, let's just say I'm humbled."

"It was our pleasure," Dale announced, slapping Sebastian on the back. "We were promised food. Who could refuse that?"

More laughter.

"I'm truly grateful to have you all here." Sebastian turned his gaze on me and smiled again, making my insides light up like the colorful, glowing bulbs on the Christmas tree. "But most of all, I'm grateful to you," Sebastian said to me directly.

I smiled, suddenly feeling my face heat from the embarrassment. I knew everyone was looking at us, which made me slightly uncomfortable.

But then Sebastian did something that caused my face to flush completely and my hands to start trembling uncontrollably.

He lowered himself to one knee in front of me, smiling as he did. When he took my hand, I knew he could feel the shudder that raced through me. Hell, I was surprised the other people sitting on the couch couldn't feel it.

"Payton," Sebastian began, "from the instant I saw you in front of my father's house, I knew… No, wait, let me take that back. From the first time I dreamed about you, long before I actually met you, I knew that you were the woman I was going to spend the rest of my life with."

"You dreamed about me?" I asked. I probably shouldn't have interrupted such an intimate moment, but that was the first time he'd ever mentioned dreaming about me.

"I did. Several times before I saw you in front of my father's house."

My heart stuttered. He had dreamed about me. And I had dreamed about him. There was no way that was a coincidence.

"I knew from that moment that you were the woman I was going to spend the rest of my life with. You've made me whole in ways I never imagined possible. You manage to keep me together when I feel like I'm falling apart, and you manage to unravel me in the best ways possible. I love you, Angel."

"I love you, too," I whispered, tears forming in my eyes.

"Payton Michelle Fowler, will you marry me?"

Chaos

I swallowed past the lump in my throat, nodding my head and trying desperately to force the word out. I finally managed, offering Sebastian a rough version of the word *yes.*

When he slipped the ring on my finger, I stared down at it in complete and total shock. It was the most beautiful ring I'd ever seen in my entire life. Granted, it was a little bigger than I had ever imagined a diamond that resided on my finger would be, but it was beautiful nonetheless.

I threw my arms around him, hugging him to me as the room erupted in whistles and applause.

There was no doubt about it — that was a Christmas that I would never forget.

Sebastian

Three years later

"SEBASTIAN?" PAYTON CALLED TO ME from somewhere in the shop.

"Over here," I answered, rolling out from underneath the car I'd spent the better part of the morning working on.

"Can you take him for a little while?" she asked, moving toward me with our little boy in her arms. The instant he saw me, his eyes lit up, and he reached out for me, nearly launching himself from his mother's grasp.

"Of course I can," I replied, getting to my feet and moving toward them, catching Devon as he flung himself in my direction. "What's up, little man?"

"He's being a little ornery this morning," Payton said, mussing Devon's dark hair as she smiled down at him.

"Car," Devon stated.

"Yep, that's a car," I told him.

"No, car," Devon demanded.

I laughed. I knew exactly what he wanted. I'd taken to driving him around the race track early in the mornings. The promise of getting to go the following day was something I used to get him to go to sleep at night. Getting him to bed was never easy, not even on a good night, but these days, the terrible twos were certainly gripping him firmly, although we still had three months until he turned two.

"Remember, my parents and Conrad are coming for dinner tonight," Payton reminded me, leaning forward and kissing me on the mouth. I wrapped my arm around her, holding her to me and refusing to release her.

"I remember," I grumbled good-naturedly, my lips pressing against hers. She flicked my lip ring with her tongue, and I smiled. "Are we gonna tell them the news this time?"

It was a regular occurrence for Conrad and Payton's parents to visit. They claimed it was to come by and check on us, but I knew it was really so they could spend time with Devon. Not that I minded. He'd certainly been spoiled by all of the love from his grandparents and having them over certainly wasn't a hardship.

"I think we probably should tell them," Payton replied. "If not, my mother's gonna figure it out soon enough."

"Why's that?" I asked, lifting Devon into the air and making him squeal.

"Because I want you to paint the room next to Devon's."

"Is that right? Is that gonna be the new nursery? What do you think about that, boy?" I asked Devon. "You wanna have a room right next to your sister?"

"We don't know if it's a girl yet," Payton said, laughing at me.

"Oh, I know it is," I assured her, still grinning up at Devon. "A sweet little girl. Sweet and beautiful, just like her momma."

"Car!" Devon announced, pointing at the car behind him.

"All right, we'll go for a ride," I told him.

"I've got a couple of errands to run today, and Aaliyah and Chloe are gonna go with me," Payton informed me.

"Okay. Do I need to do anything while you're gone?"

"Just keep an eye on him."

"Will do. We're gonna have fun, aren't we, buddy?" I asked my son. "We'll go for a ride, then maybe we'll hang out with Uncle Leif."

"Unca Feef," Devon muttered, making me laugh as he always did when he tried to pronounce words.

"Maybe Uncle Toby will come over, too," I told him.

"Unca Poby. Unca Feef."

"Yep, we're gonna be fine," I told Payton.

"Good. And while I'm out, I'm going to pick up the trophies that you ordered for the race next weekend. I got a call this morning that they're ready."

"Fantastic," I told her. It'd taken us almost two years to get everything up and running once we'd finally broken ground for the new track, but next weekend, we had the first race scheduled. Not only would we have the official race, which I would be in, along with Toby and Leif, but we also had the first race with the kids. All sixteen- and seventeen-year-olds who'd been practicing with us for the last six months would finally get a chance to show their stuff on the track. I was both nervous and excited.

It was actually going to be a pretty big deal. There were news crews, and we even had sponsors, including Trovato, Inc., which had become a huge supporter over the last few years. Although I'd gone into business with Payton, Toby, and Leif and we'd opened a body shop that was doing surprisingly well, I still consulted for my father from time to time. Since the tension between us had dissipated after Lauren and Trevor had been tried and convicted of murder, my father and I found ways to work together quite often.

I still wasn't sure how it all had come together, but I knew without a doubt it had everything to do with the incredible woman who stood beside me through every endeavor.

"I love you, Angel," I told my wife.

"Angel," Devon repeated.

"I love you, too," Payton replied. "Both of you. Now be good while I'm gone."

"Did you hear that?" I asked Devon. "Your momma wants you to be good while she's gone."

Payton laughed, a glimmer in her beautiful hazel eyes. "I was talking to you."

Of course she was.

*****

I really hope you enjoyed the Unhinged Trilogy. Payton and Sebastian came to me one day because I wanted to write a book my daughter could read, something that she would connect with.

Want to see some fun stuff related to the Unhinged series, you can find extras on my website. Or how about what's coming next? Find more at: www.NicoleEdwardsAuthor.com

If you're interested in keeping up to date on any of my series, as well as receiving updates on all that I'm working on, you can sign up for my monthly newsletter.

Want a simple, *fast* way to get updates on new releases? You can also sign up for text messaging. If you are in the U.S. simply text NICOLE to 64600 or sign up on my website. I promise not to spam your phone. This is just my way of letting you know what's happening because I know you're busy, but if you're anything like me, you always have your phone on you.

And last but certainly not least, if you want to see what's going on with me each week, sign up for my weekly Hot Sheet! It's a short, entertaining weekly update of things going on in my life and that of the team that supports me. We're a little crazy at times and this is a firsthand account of our antics.

About Nicole Edwards

New York Times and *USA Today* bestselling author Nicole Edwards lives in Austin, Texas with her husband, their three kids, and four rambunctious dogs. When she's not writing about sexy alpha males, Nicole can often be found with a book in hand or making an attempt to keep the dogs happy. You can find her hanging out on Facebook and interacting with her readers - even when she's supposed to be writing.

By Nicole Edwards

The Alluring Indulgence Series
Kaleb
Zane
Travis
Holidays with the Walker Brothers
Ethan
Braydon
Sawyer
Brendon

The Austin Arrows Series
Rush
Kaufman

The Bad Boys of Sports Series
Bad Reputation
Bad Business

The Caine Cousins Series
Hard to Hold
Hard to Handle

The Club Destiny Series
Conviction
Temptation
Addicted
Seduction
Infatuation
Captivated
Devotion
Perception
Entrusted
Adored
Distraction

The Coyote Ridge Series
Curtis
Jared

The Dead Heat Ranch Series
Boots Optional
Betting on Grace
Overnight Love

By Nicole Edwards (cont.)

The Devil's Bend Series
Chasing Dreams
Vanishing Dreams

The Devil's Playground Series
Without Regret
Without Restraint

The Office Intrigue Series
Office Intrigue
Intrigued Out of the Office
Their Rebellious Submissive

The Pier 70 Series
Reckless
Fearless
Speechless
Harmless

The Sniper 1 Security Series
Wait for Morning
Never Say Never
Tomorrow's Too Late

The Southern Boy Mafia Series
Beautifully Brutal
Beautifully Loyal

Standalone Novels
A Million Tiny Pieces
Inked on Paper

Writing as Timberlyn Scott
Unhinged
Unraveling
Chaos

Naughty Holiday Editions
2015
2016

BECAUSE NAUGHTY CAN BE OH SO NICE®

NE
LTD

www.ingramcontent.com/pod-product-compliance
Lightning Source LLC
Chambersburg PA
CBHW072016020726
47501CB00006B/1834